THE EDGE CHRONICLES

THE LAST OF THE SKY PIRATES
BOOK 1 OF THE ROOK SAGA

www.edgechronicles.co.uk

NEW SANCTAPHRAX

THE STONE GARDENS

SCREE TOWN

OLD UNDERTOWN

THE MIRE

THE DEEP WOODS

THE TWILIGHT WOODS

THE EDGELANDS

The Edge.

THE EDGE CHRONICLES

THE LAST OF THE SKY PIRATES
⊷ BOOK 1 OF THE ROOK SAGA ⊷

PAUL STEWART AND CHRIS RIDDELL

CORGI

THE DEEP WOODS SETTLEMENTS

THE FOUNDRY GLADE

THE GOBLIN NATIONS

THE EASTERN ROOST

THE SILVER PASTURES

THE
FREE GLADES

THE SLAUGHTERERS'
CAMP

THE IRONWOOD
GLADE

SOUTH
LAKE

WOODTROLL
TIMBER YARDS

THE GREAT LAKE

LAKE LANDING

WAIF GLEN

NORTH
LAKE

LULLABEE
ISLAND

NEW
UNDERTOWN

CLODDERTROG
CAVES

THE FREE GLADES

THE LAST OF THE SKY PIRATES
A CORGI BOOK 978 0 552 56969 9

First published in Great Britain by Doubleday,
an imprint of Random House Children's Publishers UK
A Random House Group Company

THE LAST OF THE SKY PIRATES
Doubleday edition published 2002
First Corgi edition published 2003
This Corgi edition published 2014
Text and illustrations copyright © Paul Stewart and Chris Riddell 2002

'The Slaughterer's Quest'
First published in Great Britain by Corgi, 2007
Text and illustrations copyright © Paul Stewart and Chris Riddell, 2007

3 5 7 9 10 8 6 4

The Random House Group Limited supports the Forest Stewardship Council® (FSC®),
the leading international forest-certification organisation. Our books carrying the FSC label
are printed on FSC®-certified paper. FSC is the only forest-certification scheme supported
by the leading environmental organisations, including Greenpeace. Our paper
procurement policy can be found at www.randomhouse.co.uk/environment

Corgi Books are published by Random House Children's Publishers UK,
61–63 Uxbridge Road, London W5 5SA

www.randomhousechildrens.co.uk
www.totallyrandombooks.co.uk
www.randomhouse.co.uk

Addresses for companies within The Random House Group Limited can be
found at: www.randomhouse.co.uk/offices.htm

THE RANDOM HOUSE GROUP Limited Reg. No. 954009

A CIP catalogue record for this book is available from the British Library.

Printed and bound in Great Britain by Clays Ltd, St Ives plc

For William, Joseph, Anna, Katy and Jack

INTRODUCTION

Far far away, jutting out into the emptiness beyond, like the figurehead of a mighty stone ship, is the Edge. A great river – the Edgewater – pours down endlessly from the overhanging rock. It was not always so. Fifty years earlier, almost to the day, the river ground to a halt.

This was no random occurrence, but rather a pre-ordained event – for the stopping of the river heralded the arrival of the Mother Storm which, once every five or six millennia, would roar in from Open Sky to seed the Edge with new life.

With the Anchor Chain severed and the floating city of Sanctaphrax lost, the Mother Storm swept on to Riverrise. There, she discharged her vast reserves of energy, rejuvenating the river and sowing her precious seeds of new life.

The Edgewater flowed once more. Riverrise

blossomed. A new Sanctaphrax rock was born. Yet all was far from well on the Edge, for a terrible pestilence was already spreading out from the Stone Gardens.

Stone-sickness, it was called. It was a name that was all too soon on everyone's lips.

It halted new growth in the Stone Gardens where, for centuries, buoyant rocks had sprouted and grown; rocks that had become the flight-rocks of league ships and sky pirate vessels, enabling them to fly. It passed from sky ship to sky ship, causing the flight-rocks of the leaguesmen and sky pirates alike to decay, lose buoyancy and plummet from the sky. It even attacked the great floating rock upon which New Sanctaphrax was being built, causing it to crumble and sink.

Some claimed that the Mother Storm had brought the terrible sickness with her from Open Sky. Some maintained that Cloud Wolf – the valiant sky pirate captain who had perished inside the Mother Storm – had somehow infected her. Others insisted, with just as much conviction, that there was no connection between the arrival of the Mother Storm and the outbreak, but that stone-sickness was a punishment on those Edge-dwellers who had refused to give up their evil ways.

In short, no-one knew for sure. Only one thing was certain. Stone-sickness meant that life on the Edge would never be the same again.

The league ships were grounded. Sky-trade was at an end. With Undertown and New Sanctaphrax now cut off, the usurper Vox Verlix – the erstwhile cloudwatcher who had ousted the new Most High Academe of New Sanctaphrax – commissioned the building of the Great Mire Road to connect the twin cities to the Deepwoods. In order to complete the project he enlisted the help of both the fearsome shrykes and the Librarian Academics – a union of earth-scholars and disillusioned sky-scholars who had joined their ranks. The consequences were far-reaching.

In the Deepwoods permanent settlements began to spring up for the first time: the Eastern Roost of the shrykes, the Foundry Glade and the Goblin Nations, and far, far to the north-west, between the Silver Pastures and the Hundred Lakes, the Free Glades. In the Mire, a new settlement sprang up overnight, when the sky pirates scuttled all their sky ships together.

Meanwhile, back in Undertown and New Sanctaphrax, despite an uneasy temporary truce, the rift between the sky-scholar Guardians of Night and the Librarian Academics became greater than ever.

The Guardians of Night maintained that the answer to stone-sickness lay in the healing power of storms, believing that Midnight's Spike – at the top of the Sanctaphrax Tower of Night – would attract the electrical energy of passing storms and destroy the terrible pestilence. The Librarian Academics, on the other hand, believed not only that the cure must lie somewhere far out in the Deepwoods, but that, if struck, Midnight's

13

Spike would cause more harm than good.

As the years passed, the Guardians got the upper hand. Led by the notoriously brutal Most High Guardian, Orbix Xaxis, they imposed their will, manipulating the leagues, enslaving the Undertowners and driving the Librarian Academics, literally, underground – for the sewers of Undertown became their new refuge.

It is down here, in the dark, dank, dripping underground chambers, that an unassuming, yet adventurous, young under-librarian lives. He is thirteen. He is an orphan. When no-one is around, he likes nothing better than to sit at one of the many floating sumpwood desks and bury his head in a treatise-scroll – even though this is strictly forbidden to someone of his lowly status.

He assumes, wrongly, that no-one has ever seen him. However, his disobedience has been both noticed and noted. What is more, it is to have repercussions that no-one could ever have predicted.

The Deepwoods, the Stone Gardens, the Edgewater River. Undertown and Sanctaphrax. Names on a map.

Yet behind each name lie a thousand tales – tales that have been recorded in ancient scrolls, tales that have been passed down the generations by word of mouth – tales which even now are being told.

What follows is but one of those tales.

·CHAPTER ONE·

THE GREAT
STORM CHAMBER
LIBRARY

The young under-librarian awoke drenched in sweat. From all around, echoing down the tunnels of the Undertown sewers, came the sound of the piebald rats' shrill dawn chorus. How they knew the sun was rising over Undertown, high above them, was a mystery to Rook Barkwater. But they did know, and Rook was grateful to be awake. The other nineteen under-librarians in the small sleeping chamber twitched and stirred in their hammocks, but slept on. It would be another couple of hours before the tilderhorns sounded. Until then Rook had the sewers to himself.

He slipped out of the hammock, dressed quickly and stole across the cold floor. The oil lamp fixed to the damp, mossy wall flickered as he passed by. In the furthest hammock Millwist muttered in his sleep. Rook froze. It wouldn't do to be caught.

'For Sky's sake, don't wake up,' Rook whispered as Millwist scratched his nose. Then, with a small cry of anger or alarm, the youth rolled onto his side – and fell still.

Rook crept out of the chamber and into the gloom of the narrow corridor outside. The air was cold and clammy. His boots splashed in the puddles on the floor and water dripped down his neck.

When it rained in Undertown, the underground tunnels and pipes filled with water, and the librarian-scholars fought to keep it out of the network of sewers they called home. But still it seeped through the walls and dripped from every ceiling. It hissed on the wall lamps, sometimes extinguishing a flame completely. It fell on mattresses, on blankets, on weapons, clothes – and on the librarian-scholars themselves.

Rook shivered. The dream still echoed in his head. First came the wolves – always the wolves. White-collared. Bristling and baying. Their terrible yellow eyes flashing in the dark forest ...

His father was shouting for him to hide; his mother was screaming. He didn't know what to do. He was running this way, that way. Everywhere were flashing yellow eyes and the sharp, barked commands of the slave-takers.

Rook swallowed hard. It was a nightmare, but what came next was worse; far worse.

He was alone now in the dark woods. The howling of the slavers' wolf pack was receding into the distance. The slave-takers had gone – and taken his mother and father with them. Rook would never see them again. He was four years old, alone in the vastness of the Deepwoods – and something was coming towards him. Something huge . . .

And then . . .

Then he'd woken up, drenched in sweat, with the shrill sounds of piebald rats in his ears. Just like the time before – and the time before that. The nightmare would return every few weeks, always the same and for as far back as he could remember.

Rook took the left fork at the end of the corridor and went immediately left again; then, fifty strides further on, he turned sharp right into the opening to a low, narrow pipe.

Newcomers to the sewers were forever getting lost in the perplexing labyrinth of pipes and tunnels. But not Rook Barkwater. He knew every cistern, every chamber, every channel. He knew that the pipe he was in was a short cut to the Great Storm Chamber Library – and that even though he had grown tall since he first discovered

17

it, and now had to stoop and stumble his way along, it was still the quickest route.

Emerging at the far end, Rook looked round furtively. To his right, the broad Main Tunnel disappeared back into shadows. It was, he was pleased to see, deserted. To his left, it ended with a great, ornate arch, on the other side of which lay the chamber itself.

Rook took a step forwards and, as the cavernous library chamber opened up before him, his heart fluttered. No matter that he had seen it almost every day for the best part of a decade, the place never failed to amaze him.

The air was warm from the wood-burners, and wafted round in a gentle breeze by hundreds of softly fluttering wind-turners. The buoyant lecterns – which housed the vast library of precious barkscrolls and bound treatises – gently bobbed in their 'flocks', straining at the chains which secured them to the magnificent Blackwood Bridge below. The ornately carved bridge spanned the great, vaulted chamber, linking the two sides of the Grand Central Tunnel. Beside it was the older Lufwood Bridge and numerous gantries; below, the flowing waters of this, the largest of Undertown's sewers.

Rook stood for a moment at the entrance to the chamber, feeling the warmth seep into his bones. No dripping water or leaks of any kind were permitted here; nothing that could harm the precious library that so many earth-scholars had died to establish and protect.

The words of the ageing librarian, Alquix Venvax, came back to Rook. 'Remember, my lad,' he would say,

THE GREAT STORM CHAMBER LIBRARY

'this great library of ours represents just a fraction of the knowledge that lies out there in the Deepwoods. But it is precious. Never forget, Rook, that there are those who hate librarian academics and mistrust earth-scholarship; those who betrayed us and persecuted us, who blame us for stone-sickness and have forced us to seek refuge down here, far from the light of the sun. For every treatise produced, one librarian has suffered to write it, while another has died defending it. But we shall not give up. Librarian Knights elect will continue to travel to the Deepwoods, to gather invaluable information and increase our knowledge of the Edge. One day, my lad, it will be your turn.'

Rook crept out of the tunnel and onto the Blackwood Bridge, keeping his head down behind the balustrade. There was someone on the adjacent bridge, which was unusual for so early in the morning – and though it was probably just a lugtroll there to clean, Rook didn't want to take any chances.

Unconsciously, yet unavoidably, he counted off the mooring winch-rings as he passed. It was something every under-librarian did automatically, for those who made an error about which buoyant lectern was at the end of which chain did not last long in the Great Storm Chamber.

Rook's experience led him unerringly to the seventeenth lectern, where he knew he'd find one treatise in particular. *A Study of Banderbears' Behaviour in Their Natural Habitat*, it was called. Of all the countless leatherbound works in the library, this one was special; special for a very simple reason.

Rook Barkwater owed his life to the treatise, and he could never forget it.

Having checked that the lugtroll was definitely not spying on him, Rook gripped the winch-wheel and began turning it slowly round. Link by link, the chain wound its way round the central axle and the buoyant sumpwood lectern came lower. When it was at the same level as the mounting platform, Rook ratcheted the brake-lever across, and climbed aboard.

'Careful!' he whispered nervously, as the lectern dipped and swayed. He sat himself down on the bench and gripped the desk firmly. The last thing he wanted to do was keel over backwards and fall into the sluggish water of the underground river. At this time of day, there were no raft-hands to drag him out – and he was a hopeless swimmer.

The honey-coloured wood felt warm and silky to the touch. In the warm, dry conditions of the library chamber a well-seasoned piece of sumpwood timber was twice as light as air. However, as with all timbers of the first order of buoyant wood, the minutest shift in temperature or humidity could destabilize the timber – and so the sumpwood lecterns bobbed and jittered constantly, making sitting at one for any length of time an art in itself.

'Stop wobbling about, you stupid thing,' Rook told the lectern sternly. He shifted his position on the bench. The violent lurching eased. 'That's better,' he said. 'Now, just hold still while I . . .'

Squinting into the bright spherical light above the

lectern, Rook reached up and pulled a large, bound volume from the uppermost shelf of the floating lectern. It was the one about bander-bears. As he laid the treatise out on the desk before him, he felt a familiar surge of excitement, tinged with just a hint of fear. He opened it up at random.

His head bowed forwards. His eyes narrowed in concentration. No longer was he sitting at a floating lectern, in a vaulted chamber, deep down underground . . .

Instead, Rook was *up there* – in the open, in the vast, mysterious Deepwoods, with no walls, no tunnels and no ceiling but the sky itself. The air was cool and filled with the sound of bird-cry and rodent-screech . . .

He turned his attention to the treatise. *The yodelled communication cry*, he read, *is meant for one specific bander-bear alone. None, not even those who may be nearer, will answer a call intended for another. In this respect it is as if a name had been used. However, because, throughout my treatise-voyage, I never managed to get close enough to one to fully decipher the language, it is impossible to know for sure.*

Rook looked up. He could hear in his head the banderbear yodel, almost as if he had once heard one for himself . . .

One matter appears certain. It seems to be impossible for any banderbear to deceive any other about his/her identity. It is perhaps this fact that makes banderbears such solitary animals. Since their individuality cannot come from anonymity in a crowd, it must come from isolation from that crowd.

The further my travels take me . . .

Rook looked up from the neat script for a second time and stared into mid air. '*The further my travels take me . . .*' The words thrilled him. How he would love to explore the endless Deepwoods for himself, to spend time with banderbears, to hear their plaintive yodelling by the light of the full moon . . .

And then it struck him.

Of course! he thought, and smiled bitterly. Today wasn't just any old day. It was the day of the Announcement Ceremony, when three apprentice librarians would be selected to complete their education far off in the Deepwoods, at Lake Landing.

Rook wanted so, so much to be selected himself – but he knew that, despite Alquix Venvax's encouraging words, this would never happen. He was a foundling, a nobody. He'd been discovered, lost and alone, wandering through the Deepwoods, by the great Varis Lodd – or so he'd been told. Varis, daughter of the High Librarian, Fenbrus Lodd, was the author of the treatise Rook now held in his hands.

If she hadn't been out in the Deepwoods studying banderbears, she would never have stumbled across the abandoned child with no real memories – apart from his name, and a recurring nightmare of slave-takers and wolves and . . .

Yes, Rook Barkwater did indeed owe his life to this particular bound treatise.

Varis Lodd had brought him back to the sewers of Undertown along with her treatise on banderbears, and left him here to be raised by the librarian-scholars. The old librarian professor, Alquix Venvax, had befriended the sad, lonely little boy and done what he could, but Rook was well aware that an orphan with no family connections would never be more than an under-librarian. His lot was to remain down in the great library chamber, tending the buoyant lecterns and serving the professors and their apprentices.

Unlike Felix. Rook smiled to himself. If *he* couldn't go to Lake Landing, then at least Felix could.

Felix Lodd was Varis Lodd's baby brother – though he wasn't much of a baby any more. He was tall for his age, powerfully-built and athletic. Quick to smile and slow to anger, what he lacked in brains, he made up for in the size of his heart.

Felix was an apprentice and had made up his mind to look after the small orphan his sister had found. Rook sometimes thought Felix felt guilty that his beloved sister, whom he idolized, had simply left Rook with the librarian-scholars to fend for himself. It didn't matter. They were friends, best friends. Felix fought the apprentices who tried to bully Rook, and Rook helped Felix with those studies the older boy found difficult. Together they made a strong team. And now all the hard work was about to pay off, for Felix was one of the favourites to be picked to go to Lake Landing and complete his education. Rook felt so proud. One day, he might even be sitting at this lectern with Felix's treatise in his hand.

He picked up the volume and was just reaching up to return it to the high shelf when a bellowing voice echoed angrily round the great chamber.

'You, there!'

Rook froze. Surely he couldn't have been spotted. Not today. Whoever it was must be shouting at that lugtroll on the Lufwood Bridge.

'*Rook Barkwater!*'

Rook groaned. Steadying himself, he slid the treatise back into place and turned slowly round. That was when he first realized how high up he was. With all the violent dipping and swaying of the lectern when he'd first boarded, the brake-lever must have shifted, for the chain securing the lectern had completely unwound. Now he was trapped, far up in the air on the buoyant lectern, which was floating higher from the Blackwood Bridge than any of the others. It was no wonder he'd been spotted. Rook peered down and swallowed unhappily. Why did it have to be Ledmus Squinx who had done the spotting?

A fastidious, flabby individual with small pink eyes and bushy side-whiskers, Squinx was one of the library's various under-professors. He was unpopular, and with good reason – for Ledmus Squinx was both overbearing and vain. He liked order, and he liked comfort and – as he'd grown older – he'd also discovered a distinct aptitude for throwing his (increasing) weight around.

'Will you get down here, now!' he bellowed. Rook stared down at the portly, red-faced individual. His hands were on his hips; his lips were sneering. They both knew that Rook couldn't get down without the under-professor's help.

'I – I can't, sir.'

'Then you shouldn't be up there in the first place, should you?' said Squinx triumphantly. Rook hung his head. 'Should you?' he rasped.

'N-no, sir,' said Rook.

'No, sir!' Squinx barked back. 'You should not. Do you know how many rules and regulations you have broken, Rook?' He raised his left hand and began counting off the fingers. 'One, the buoyant lecterns are not to be used in the hours between lights-out and the tilderhorn call. Two, the buoyant lecterns are not to be used unless another is present to operate the winch. *Three, under no circumstances whatsoever,*' he hissed, speaking each word slowly and clearly, '*is an under-librarian ever to board a buoyant lectern.*' He smiled unpleasantly. 'Do I need to go on?'

'No, sir,' said Rook. 'Sorry, sir, but—'

'Be still,' Squinx snapped. He turned his attention

to the winch-wheel, which he turned round and round – puffing noisily as he did so – until the buoyant lectern was once again level with the mounting platform. 'Now, get out,' he ordered.

Rook stepped onto the Blackwood Bridge. Squinx seized him by both arms and pushed his face so close that their noses were almost touching.

'I will not tolerate such disobedience,' he thundered. 'Such insubordination. Such a flagrant disregard for the rules.' He took a deep breath. 'Your behaviour, Rook, has been totally unacceptable. How dare you even *think* of reading the library treatises! They are not for the likes of you.' He spat out the words with contempt. 'You! A mere under-librarian!'

'But . . . but, sir—'

'Silence!' Squinx shrieked. 'First I catch you flouting the library's most serious rules, and now you have the bare-faced cheek to answer back! Is there no end to your audacity? I'll have you sent to a punishment cell. I'll have you clapped in irons and flogged. I'll—'

'Is there some problem, Squinx?' a frail yet imperious voice interjected.

The under-professor turned. Rook looked up. It was Alquix Venvax, the ageing librarian professor. He pushed his glasses up his nose with a bony finger and peered at the under-professor.

'Problem, Squinx?' he repeated.

'Nothing I can't handle,' said Squinx, puffing out his chest.

Alquix nodded. 'I'm glad to hear it, Squinx. Very

glad.' He paused. 'Though something troubles me.'

'Sir?' said Squinx.

'Yes, something I thought I overheard,' said Alquix. 'Something about imprisonment cells and being clapped in irons. And . . . what was it? Ah, yes, being flogged!'

Squinx's flabby face turned from red to purple and beads of sweat began oozing from every pore. 'I . . . I . . . I . . .' he blustered.

The professor smiled. 'I'm sure I don't have to remind you, Squinx that, as an *under*-professor, you are in no position to hand out punishments.' He scratched at his right ear thoughtfully. 'Indeed, I believe that attempting to do so is itself a punishable offence . . .'

'I . . . I . . . that is, I didn't intend . . .' Squinx mumbled feverishly, and Rook had to bite into his lower lip to prevent himself from smiling. It was wonderful to see the bullying under-professor squirm.

'But, sir,' Squinx protested indignantly as he gathered his thoughts. 'He has broken rule after rule after rule.' His voice grew more confident. 'I caught him up on a buoyant lectern, reading, no less. He was reading an academic treatise. He—'

Alquix turned on Rook. 'You were doing *what*?' he said. 'Well, this puts a totally different complexion on the matter, doesn't it? Reading indeed!' He turned back to the now smugly beaming under-professor. 'I'll deal with this, Squinx. You may go.'

As the portly Ledmus Squinx waddled off, Rook waited nervously for Alquix to return his attention to him. The professor had seemed genuinely angry. This was unusual and Rook wondered whether, this time, he had gone too far. When the professor did finally turn to face him, however, his eyes were twinkling.

'Rook! Rook!' he said. 'Reading treatises again, eh? What are we going to do with you?'

'I'm sorry, sir,' said Rook. 'It's just that—'

'I know, Rook, I know,' the professor interrupted. 'The thirst for knowledge is a powerful force. But in future...' He paused and shook his head earnestly. Rook held his breath. 'In future,' he repeated, 'just don't get caught!'

He chuckled. Rook laughed too. The next moment the professor's face grew serious once more.

'You shouldn't be here anyway,' he said. 'The buoyant lecterns are closed. Had you forgotten that the Announcement Ceremony is to take place today?'

Just then the tilderhorns echoed round the cavernous chamber. It was seven hours.

'Oh, no,' Rook groaned. 'It's Felix's big day, and I promised to help him get ready. I mustn't let him down.'

'Calm down, Rook,' the professor said. 'If I know Felix Lodd, he'll still be fast asleep in his hammock.'

'Precisely!' said Rook. 'I said I'd wake him!'

'Did you now?' said the professor, smiling kindly. 'Go, then,' he said. 'If you hurry, you should both make it back here in time.'

'Thank you, Professor,' said Rook as he scurried back across the bridge.

'Oh, and Rook!' the professor called after him. 'While you're about it, smarten your*self* up a bit, lad.'

'Yes, sir,' Rook called back. 'And thank you, sir.'

He left the Storm Chamber, ducked down and darted back into the narrow pipe. As the darkness wrapped itself around him once again, his mood also darkened.

The memory of his nightmare came back to him: the snarls of woodwolves and the cries of slave-takers. And the terrible, terrible feeling of being alone . . .

And with Felix gone, he'd be alone again. A small, guilty thought crept into his mind. *What if Felix isn't picked? What if he oversleeps and . . .*

'No!' Rook slapped a fist to his temple. 'No! Felix is my friend!'

· CHAPTER TWO ·

THE SEWERS

Pushing past the thick hammelhornskin door-hanging, Rook entered the sleeping chamber. Unlike the damp, spartan under-librarians' dormitory, the room was warm and cosy, for Felix Lodd enjoyed all the comforts of a senior apprentice. There was a wood-burning stove in the corner, woven hangings on the wall and straw matting on the floor. The tilderhorns trumpeted the last wake-up call as Rook approached the quilted hammock with its plump pillows and warm fleece blankets.

Rook stared down at his friend. He looked so contented, so carefree and, judging by the smile tugging at the corners of his mouth, as if he were having a pleasant dream. It seemed almost a shame to wake him.

'Felix,' said Rook urgently. He shook him by the shoulders. 'Felix, get up.'

Felix's eyes snapped open. 'What? What?' He peered up. 'Rook, is that you?' He smiled and stretched lazily. 'What time is it?'

'It's late, Felix—' Rook began.

'I was having the most amazing dream,' Felix interrupted him. 'I was flying, Rook. Flying above the Deepwoods! Just imagine! Flying up there in the clean, clear air! It was such an incredible feeling – swooping this way and that, skimming the tops of the trees ... Until I hit turbulence and went into a tailspin.' His eyes narrowed. 'That must have been when you woke me up.'

Rook shook his head. 'You've forgotten, haven't you?' he said.

Felix yawned. 'Forgotten what?' he said.

'What day it is today! It's the Announcement Ceremony.'

Felix sprang out of the hammock, scattering pillows and cushions, and upending a small ornate lamp. 'The Announcement Ceremony!' he exclaimed. 'I thought it was tomorrow.' He looked round the sleeping chamber. 'Curse this stupid place!' he thundered, pulling his robes from the heavy leadwood chest beneath the hammock. 'There's no dawn, no dusk. How can anyone keep track of the time down here?'

'Don't worry,' Rook assured him. 'The last tilderhorn has only just sounded. If we hurry we can still make it to the Lufwood Bridge before the Professor of Darkness begins the oath – although all the best places will be taken.'

'I don't care if they are,' said Felix, fumbling to unknot his formal sash. 'The Announcement Ceremony can't come too soon for me. I'm dying to get out of this rain-soaked sewer and feel the wind on my face, to breathe in clean, fresh air . . .'

'Let me,' said Rook, taking the sash from his friend and deftly unknotting it. He handed it back to Felix, who was now struggling into the heavy robes of a senior apprentice.

Rook smiled sadly. This was the last time he would be able to help his friend out of some scrape or other – for today, the Professor of Darkness was bound to announce that Felix Lodd would be sent off to Lake Landing to complete his studies. There, Felix would have to look after himself; making sure that his work was submitted on time, that his robes were clean and mended, and that he didn't oversleep on important occasions. He wouldn't have Rook to look after him.

Then again, he'd soon make friends out there in the Free Glades because, wherever he went and whatever he did, Felix couldn't help being popular and the centre of attention. Just like his sister before him, Felix was about to set off on a great adventure and make a name for himself up there in the world of fresh air and sunlight. And he, Rook, would be left alone.

Felix tied the sash around his waist and stood back. Rook looked him up and down. It never failed to amaze him! Just a few minutes earlier, Felix had been snoring his head off. Now he stood before him

looking magnificent in
his ceremonial robes,
as if he had taken
hours, not minutes,
preparing.

'How do I look?'
he said.

Rook smiled.
'You'll do,' he said.

'Earth and Sky
be praised!' said
Felix. He picked
up two lanterns,
handing one
to Rook. 'Right,
then. Let's get
to the Lufwood
Bridge. They'll
be expecting
me.'

'Quiet, Felix! I'm
trying to listen.' Rook
stepped closer to the tunnel entrance he'd stopped
beside and motioned Felix to be still with a flap of his
hand. 'I thought I heard something,' he whispered. He
raised his lantern and pointed down the narrow, dripping pipe to his right. 'In there.'

Felix came closer. His eyes narrowed. 'Do you think
it's a—' he mouthed the word – 'muglump?'

'It sounded like one to me,' Rook replied softly.

Felix nodded. That was good enough for him. Rook was second to none when it came to identifying the numerous parasites and predators that lurked in the network of sewers. He drew his sword and, pushing Rook firmly to one side, advanced into the pipe.

'But, Felix . . .' said Rook as, head down, he trotted after him. 'What about the ceremony?'

'It'll just have to wait,' Felix told him. 'This is more important.' He continued along the pipe, pausing at the first fork he came to and listening, before storming on.

Rook struggled to keep up. 'Wait a moment,' he panted, as Felix took a third turning. 'Felix—'

'Shut up, Rook!' Felix hissed. 'If a muglump *has* broken into our sewers from Screetown, then none of us are safe.'

'Couldn't we just report it and leave it to the sewer patrols?' said Rook.

'Sewer patrols?' said Felix, and snorted. 'That useless bunch can't even keep the rats at bay, let alone a fully grown muglump on a blood-hunt.'

'But—'

'*Ssh!*' He stopped at a junction where five tunnels intersected, and crouched down. It was cold, dank. All around, the air echoed with the sound of dripping water. 'There it is,' Felix whispered the next moment.

Rook cocked his head to one side. Yes, he could hear it, too – the soft, whistling hiss of the creature's breathing and the *squelch-squelch-squelch* of its paw-pads. It sounded like a large one.

Lantern raised, Felix followed the noises into the tunnel opposite and continued. Rook followed him. He was trembling nervously. What if Felix was right? What if it *was* on a blood-hunt?

Although they could be vicious when cornered, the muglumps which infested the Undertown sewers were generally less aggressive than their Mire cousins. Perhaps it was due to the lack of direct sunlight. Or perhaps, the change in their diet – the piebald rats they now feasted on were both plumper and more plentiful than the bony oozefish of the Mire. Whatever. As a rule, the sewer-muglumps kept themselves to themselves. But every once in a while, one of their number would develop an insatiable appetite for blood that would draw it into the main sewers in search of larger prey. A blood-hunt. Stories of the havoc such muglumps could wreak were legion amongst the scholars.

'This way,' said Felix grimly as he turned abruptly right. 'I can *smell* it.'

'But Felix,' Rook protested. 'This tunnel, it's . . .'

Felix ignored him. The muglump was near, he was sure. It was time to close in. At a trot now, with his sword out in front of him like a bayonet, he charged down the tunnel. He was going to rid the sewers of this foul creature that had developed a taste for librarian blood once and for all.

Rook did his best to keep up. Raising his head, he saw that Felix had almost reached the end of the tunnel.

'Felix, be careful!' he shouted. 'It's a dead— *Aargh!*' he

cried as his foot slipped, his ankle turned and he came crashing down to the floor of the tunnel. '—end,' he muttered.

He pulled himself up. 'Felix?' he called. Then a second time, louder, 'Felix!' Still nothing. 'Felix, what's—'

'It must be here *some*where!' came Felix's voice, frustration turning to anger in his voice.

'Felix?' Rook shouted. 'Hang on! I'm coming . . .' Limping slightly, he hurried on as fast as he could. His breath came in puffy clouds. Water dripped down his neck. He pulled his dagger from its sheath. 'Felix, are you all right?' he asked anxiously.

'Dead end,' said Felix. His voice was flat. 'Where did it go?'

Rook reached the end of the tunnel and looked into the cistern it had led to. Felix was standing at the far side, his back turned away.

'FELIX! WATCH OUT!' Rook bellowed. 'ABOVE YOU!'

Felix spun round. He looked up into the shadows above his head and found himself staring into the yellow eyes and slavering crimson mouth of the muglump.

It was huge – with a swollen belly, a long, whiplash tail and six thick-set limbs. It was standing on the ceiling, its body tensed, its rapier claws glinting.

'Come on, then, you hideous monstrosity,' Felix challenged it through clenched teeth.

The creature's nasal-flaps fluttered as it sniffed at the air and a long glistening tongue licked round its lips. Its eyes narrowed. It drew back, ready to pounce.

Felix brandished his sword menacingly. 'Guard the exit, Rook,' he said. 'This one isn't going to escape.'

Rook took up a position at the end of the pipe. He

gripped his dagger tenaciously – although he couldn't help wondering how much use it would be against the muglump's thirty terrible blades if the creature *did* turn on him.

Eyeing Felix's sword warily, the muglump retreated. Walking slowly backwards, it crossed the ceiling – *squelch, squelch, squelch*. Rook swallowed nervously. It was heading for the exit pipe; it was heading for *him*.

'It's all right, Rook,' Felix reassured him. 'I'll get it. Just keep your nerve, and—'

Just then the muglump flipped down from the ceiling, twisted in mid air and landed on the ground directly in front of Rook. It glared at him, nasal-flaps rasping loudly, and snorted with fury.

Felix bounded across the cistern, his sword slicing through the air. Rook raised his dagger and held his ground – only to be batted aside the next instant by a mighty blow from the creature's whiplash tail. He fell heavily to the ground. The muglump bowled past him and into the tunnel.

'Don't let it get away!' Felix yelled.

Rook pulled himself up and sent the dagger flying through the air after the retreating muglump. With a rasping *crunch*, the gleaming blade severed the long, prehensile tail in one curving slash and embedded itself at the top of the creature's right hind-leg.

The muglump froze, and howled with agonizing pain. Then it turned, and Rook felt the creature's furious gaze burning into him.

'Well done, Rook,' came Felix's voice from behind him. 'Now move out of the way, and let me finish the job off.'

Wounded it may have been, but the muglump seemed no slower on five legs than on six. Before Felix had gone a dozen strides, the muglump had reached the end of the tunnel and disappeared.

'This time you've got away!' Felix roared after it. 'Next time you will not be so lucky! That, my evil friend, I guarantee!'

Rook poked at the severed tail with his boot. The question was, when would that 'next time' be? After all, Felix was about to be sent off to Lake Landing, where blood-crazed muglumps would be the last thing on his mind.

At that moment, from far away in the depths of the underground sewers, there came the roar of a cheering crowd. It throbbed along the tunnels, drowning out the noise of the dripping water. Felix turned to Rook. 'The Announcement Ceremony,' he said. 'It's started. Quickly, Rook, we must hurry. I'll never live it down if I miss my own name being announced!'

They had by now reached the end of the narrow pipe. Felix looked up and down the adjoining tunnel. 'Left, I think.'

'No,' said Rook. 'We'll go right. I know a quicker way.'

40

And he dashed off down the tunnel. 'Follow me,' he called back.

Rook skidded round into an abandoned, unlit pipe to his left. Felix followed, close on his heels. The pipe was old and cracked, with pools of water and jagged debris lying all along the floor. Nightspider webs – thick and soggy – wrapped themselves round the two youths' faces as they splashed and stumbled on.

'Are you sure this is – *ppttt, ppttt* – the right way?' said Felix, spitting out the cobwebs as he spoke. 'I can't hear the crowds any more.'

'That's because they've stopped cheering,' said Rook. 'Your father'll already be doing his stuff. Trust me, Felix. Have I ever let you down before?'

'No,' said Felix. He shook his head slowly. 'No, Rook, you haven't. I'm going to miss you, you know.'

Rook made no reply. He couldn't. The lump in his throat wouldn't let him.

'You're right!' Felix exclaimed a moment later as the deep, resonant voice of the High Librarian filtered down into the pipe. 'I'd know that voice anywhere.'

'Welcome!' cried Fenbrus Lodd. 'Welcome to the Great Storm Chamber Library, librarian academics of every echelon, on this, the occasion of the Announcement . . .'

'We sound near,' said Felix.

'We *are* near,' said Rook. 'A little bit further and ... yes, here we are.' He darted off into a broader pipe which, fifty strides on, abruptly emerged into the Grand Central Tunnel. Rook sighed with relief. They'd made it. The arched entrance to the Great Storm Chamber stood before them.

'Come on,' said Felix grimly. 'There's probably only standing room left.'

Rook looked ahead at the vast crowds who had gathered to witness the Announcement Ceremony. They were spilling out of the Storm Chamber and jostling for position. 'We'll be lucky to get beyond the door,' he said.

'No problem,' said Felix. 'Mind your backs!' he shouted good-naturedly. 'Make way for an apprentice with an appointment at Lake Landing!'

CHAPTER THREE

THE ANNOUNCEMENT CEREMONY

With so many crammed together in the great chamber – packing the Blackwood Bridge, clinging to the jutting gantries and perched on the skittish buoyant lecterns – the place was warmer than ever. Both Felix and Rook were soon dripping with sweat, and when their wet clothes began to dry they also began to steam.

Having forged their way right to the front of the crowd on the Blackwood Bridge, Rook and Felix stood on the lower rail of the carved balustrade and looked across to the smaller Lufwood Bridge. Below them, the channel of water – sluggish after so long without a decent downpour outside – was covered with rafts, each one weighed down with still more spectators and held in place by the raft-hands' hooked poles.

'They're all there,' Felix noted, jerking his chin towards the stage on the Lufwood Bridge.

Rook nodded. Seated on high-backed chairs on either side of the High Librarian's speaking-balcony, from which Fenbrus Lodd was addressing the crowd, were the Professors of Light and Darkness, Ulbus Vespius and Tallus Penitax. Both were former sky-scholars who, appalled by the behaviour of the Guardians of Night, had decided to throw in their lot with the Librarian Academics. Flanking them, six on either side, were the elders of the library.

Fenbrus Lodd's voice echoed round the hushed chamber. 'Never has the Council of Three had such a hard task selecting those who are to journey to Lake Landing. Not, I should add, because there was a lack of suitable candidates, but rather the opposite. Each of your library elders put up an excellent contender, and argued well in his or her favour . . .'

Rook looked at the dozen venerable individuals, one after the other. Their backgrounds were wildly varied. Some were brilliant earth-scholars who had returned from exile to help with the new underground library; others had been eminent sky-scholars who, like the Professors of Darkness and Light themselves, had changed sides when the evil Guardians of Night took over Sanctaphrax – and then there were those whose histories were an absolute secret. His gaze fell on Alquix Venvax. The kindly professor who had taken him under his wing was a case in point. His past was a mystery.

'As always,' the High Librarian continued, 'the short-list has been whittled down to the three individuals who we, the Council of Three, consider best suited to the task ahead . . .'

Rook glanced round at Felix. His face was glowing with keen expectation. The pair of them had talked often about what being selected would involve. First the journey, through Undertown, over the Great Mire Road and on into the Deepwoods, aided by those loyal to the librarian-scholars. Then, after a period of intense study (which Felix usually chose to gloss over) the building of his own sky-craft. Finally Felix's dreams of flying were to come true.

'. . . sacred, but also arduous,' the High Librarian was saying. His voice dropped. 'And deeply perilous. Those of you who are selected must fight against over-confidence, for that is your worst enemy. You must remain on your guard. The world outside is a dangerous place.'

Just then Rook's and Alquix Venvax's eyes met. The professor acknowledged the young under-librarian with a slight nod. Rook nodded back, and hoped Alquix hadn't noticed how red his cheeks had become. The professor, he'd heard, was intending to take him on as his permanent personal assistant when he came of age. Rook knew he should be grateful – it was, after all, what most under-librarians dreamed of. But for Rook, the thought of spending the rest of his life down in the airless, sunless underground system of tunnels and chambers was, instead, an absolute nightmare.

'And so, Edge scholars, one and all,' Fenbrus Lodd proclaimed, his voice laden with occasion, 'the time has come for the Announcement.'

The chamber fell still. All that could be heard was a soft, distant dripping which echoed round the vaulted ceiling and, like great wings beating, the flutter of the wind-turners. All eyes fell on the scroll which the High Librarian, Fenbrus Lodd, now unfurled before them.

'The first Librarian Knight elect shall be Stob Lummus,' he announced.

The news was greeted with clapping and cheering, and the traditional *whoop-whoop-whooping* of the apprentices, while the professors nodded approvingly. As Stob Lummus was a brilliant scholar, his selection came as no surprise to them – although a couple of the older, wiser academics present noted that he would soon learn that barkscroll-learning alone was not enough to ensure success. Rook and Felix looked down to see a stocky youth with a broad back and a shock of thick, dark hair being hoisted up onto his neighbours' shoulders.

'That must be him,' said Felix, peering down more closely. He was feeling a little uneasy not to have been announced first. 'Stob Lummus,' he said finally, and shrugged. 'I don't think I know him.'

Rook frowned. '*I* might,' he said thoughtfully. 'From down in the Eastern Reaches. I think he's the son of that big guard in the sewer patrol – you know, the one with the scar . . .'

'The son of a guard, eh?' said Felix. He stared across at his own father. There was a time when the other apprentices had accused him of being at an unfair advantage with so eminent an academic as his father. Felix didn't see it that way. If anything, being the son of the High Librarian and brother to the famous Varis Lodd meant that everyone seemed to expect great things of him. He had to be twice as good at everything as anyone else. Sometimes he just didn't think he was up to it. He often saw disappointment in the eyes of his tutors. Only Rook continued to have absolute faith in his friend.

'Your turn next,' he whispered.

Felix nodded, but made no reply. As Stob Lummus reached the side of the stage, Fenbrus Lodd raised the scroll for a second time. Once again, the chamber fell into a silence that seemed to quiver with expectation.

'The second Librarian Knight elect shall be . . .' Felix swallowed hard. Rook bit into his lower lip. 'Magda Burlix.'

There was a sharp intake of breath from, it seemed, every onlooker present. The shocked gasp echoed round the chamber walls. The next moment, as the person in question revealed herself, the crowd split itself into two. Half of them raised their hands and clapped; the other half kept their hands in their pockets and turned to their neighbours to express their surprise.

Magda Burlix, tall with piercing green eyes and three thick plaits, emerged from one of the rafts. She was hauled up onto the Lufwood Bridge, where she took her place beside Stob Lummus.

From the back of the chamber came the sound of booing. But the clapping grew louder to drown it out, and a lone voice from near the Central Tunnel cried out, 'Another Varis Lodd!'

Those in favour of the announcement cheered gleefully. Those against fell silent, for how could they reject Magda Burlix's selection without also dismissing the finest, bravest, cleverest Librarian Knight ever to have been ennobled?

Felix stared directly ahead, fighting back the tears. With such a father and such a sister, how could he fail? Yet if he did, how could he ever show his face again? He turned to Rook and seized him by the sleeve. 'I'm not going to make it, am I?' he said. 'Am I, Rook? They're not going to announce my name.'

'Of course they are,' said Rook. 'There's no-one here who is better than you, Felix. At one-to-one combat, you're unbeaten. At swordplay, you're the best. At pummelball and parajousting . . .'

Felix shook his head. 'It's the studying,' he said. 'It's always let me down. The learning. The memorizing. Without your help I wouldn't even have got this far.'

'Nonsense,' said Rook reassuringly. 'Besides, who needs books when they fight as well as you do?'

Felix nodded. 'I suppose you're right,' he said. He paused and looked at Rook properly. 'Do you think I'm being foolish?'

'No, not foolish,' said Rook. 'But you're worrying needlessly. There's one perfectly good reason your name hasn't been announced yet.'

'There is?' said Felix.

'Yes,' said Rook and smiled. 'They're saving the best till last.'

For the third time, an expectant hush fell over the great chamber. The High Librarian scratched at his thick, bushy beard and returned his attention to the scroll.

'The third Librarian Knight elect . . .' Fenbrus paused and looked round. For a fleeting moment his gaze rested on the spot on the Blackwood Bridge where the two friends were standing.

Rook sighed sadly. This was it, then. Felix's selection would be announced and the two of them, who had once been like brothers, would be separated, probably for

ever. Felix would leave for Lake Landing that evening –
while he, Rook, would remain underground. 'I'll miss
you,' he whispered.

'Same here,' Felix whispered back.

Fenbrus Lodd returned his attention to the scroll
before him. '. . . will be . . .'

As one, the entire assembled gathering held its breath.
The High Librarian cleared his throat. He looked up
again. 'Rook Barkwater.'

For a moment there was complete silence in the chamber. No-one, but no-one, could believe what he or she
had just heard.

Rook Barkwater?

The youth wasn't even an apprentice! A mere under-
librarian, that's all *he* was; a lectern-tender, a
chain-turner . . . How could such a lowly individual
have been accorded so high an honour? It was incredible. It was unheard of.

Low muttering grew in volume until the whole
chamber was in uproar. The gantries and bridges
trembled and, as the atmosphere grew more heated and

steamy, so the buoyant lecterns dipped and swayed
wildly. Several senior apprentices fell into the water, and
had to be retrieved by the raft-hands.

Dazed, Rook looked along the line of academics on the
Lufwood Bridge. He saw Tallus Penitax, the Professor of
Darkness, looking at him levelly, his brows knitted and
his heavy arms folded. He saw Alquix Venvax nodding
enthusiastically – and he remembered his professor
telling him to smarten himself up. Now he knew why.
The fact was, however, that the chase for the muglump
had left him looking even scruffier than usual. Still, there
was nothing to be done.

Rook climbed down from the balustrade, head in a
whirl and knees knocking, and turned to go back along
the Blackwood Bridge. The rowdy crowd parted before
him. Their faces, shocked and questioning, were a blur
to Rook. As he stumbled on, murmurs and whispers
filled the air.

'An under-librarian!' said one. 'What next? A sewer
cleaner?'

'I, for one, have never heard of him,' said another.

'Apparently he's Varis Lodd's foundling,' said a third scornfully.

'And a friend of that fool son of the High Librarian!' added someone else.

On the Lufwood Bridge at last, Rook advanced slowly towards the stage, where Ulbus Vespius, Tallus Penitax and Fenbrus Lodd stood waiting in a triangle. Following Stob and Magda's lead, Rook went from one to the other. Each of the venerable academics congratulated each of the librarian knights elect and presented objects to help them with the task ahead.

Ulbus Vespius was handing out pairs of pale yellow stones. 'Sky-crystals,' he told Rook. 'Keep them in separate pockets, for they glow when close to each other. And if you rub them together, they spark.'

'Thank you, sir,' said Rook. 'Thank you.' He moved on.

The Professor of Darkness was next. Having congratulated Magda, he turned to the bashful youth.

'Well done,' he said gruffly, and leaned forward to tie a folded square of glistening black material around Rook's neck like a scarf. 'The Cover of Darkness is woven from the finest silk that nightspiders can produce,' he explained. 'Open it up and wrap it round you when you need either to hide away or travel unseen.'

Once again, Rook gave thanks and moved on. Fenbrus Lodd, High Librarian of the Great Storm Chamber, stood before him.

'Congratulations, lad,' he said, and reached down to

place a talisman over Rook's head. 'It is a bloodoak tooth – engraved with your name,' he added. 'It will offer you some protection from the dangers of the Deepwoods.'

Rook looked down at the pointed claw-like object which gleamed in the lamplight. 'Thank you,' he said uncertainly. 'But . . .'

'But?' said Fenbrus.

'Please, sir,' Rook mumbled. 'It's just . . . It should be Felix going, not me,' he said. 'Surely there's been a mistake.'

Fenbrus took a step forwards and gripped Rook by the arms. 'There has been no mistake,' he said. 'Even though he is my own son, I cannot pretend that Felix is cut out for the task ahead. Certainly, he has the boldness, the courage and the strength required, but he has no natural aptitude for study – and without that, his other qualities count for nought.'

'But—' Rook said for a second time.

'Enough,' Fenbrus interrupted him. 'The decision was unanimous.' He smiled. 'Though given the powerful arguments put forward by your proposer, that was hardly a surprise.'

Rook nodded. 'Professor Venvax has always been good to me,' he said.

The High Librarian frowned. 'I'm sure he has – yet it was not he who offered you up for selection.'

Rook was confused. 'It wasn't?' he said.

'No, it was not,' came a voice from behind him. Rook turned to see Alquix Venvax himself standing there. 'Indeed, if it had been down to me alone, you would have become my personal assistant—'

'It was *I* who put your name forward for selection.' The Professor of Darkness stepped forwards. He looked quite different in the formal ceremonial robes of his office, rather than the usual harness and jerkin of a sky-flyer. His dark, attentive eyes darted this way and that, seemingly missing nothing.

'You?' said Rook, surprised – and blushed at how insolent he must have sounded. 'I mean . . . thank you, sir,' he added.

The Professor of Darkness nodded. 'I've had my eye on you for some while now, Rook,' he said. 'Your perseverance and rigour have impressed me greatly – even though your willingness to bend the rules can, at times, be a little alarming.'

Rook's eyes widened. The professor clearly knew all about his reading the treatises.

'Remember, Rook. While such behaviour was under-standable in an under-librarian, it is completely unacceptable in a librarian knight elect. I shall continue to keep an eye on you.' His eyebrows came together sternly. 'Do not disappoint me, Rook.'

'I won't,' Rook assured him.

The professor nodded approvingly. 'You have a long and difficult journey ahead of you. The treatise you will produce is precious, for it is only by librarian-academics constantly adding to our knowledge of the Edge that we will keep the dark ignorance of the Guardians of Night at bay – and in due course, Earth and Sky willing, discover the cure to stone-sickness. If you are to return safely and successfully, Rook, you must travel in secret and trust no-one. A single careless word, and you could all perish!'

Just then a dozen tilderhorns trumpeted loudly, announcing that it was time for the three young hopefuls to take the Scholarship Oath. Rook took his place between the others.

The High Librarian raised his head. 'Do you, Stob Lummus, Magda Burlix and Rook Barkwater, swear to serve Edge Scholarship, both Earth and Sky, for the good of all?'

Three voices rang out in response. With his eyes fixed on the High Librarian's face, however, Rook was aware of no-one but himself. He heard the words come out of his mouth – words he'd always longed to say, but never dared to imagine that he ever would.

'With my heart and my head, I do.'

The Most High Guardian of Night, Orbix Xaxis, was standing on one of the uppermost gantries of the Tower of Night. A tall, imposing figure, he was wearing the heavy black robes of public office – and the dark glasses and metal mask of his own private fears. The glasses, he hoped, would repel any who would try to curse him with the evil eye, while the mask – which had a filter of phraxdust behind the muzzle – purified the germ-laden air he breathed.

From below him there came the clanking and clunking of the mounted swivel telescopes turning this way and that as the Guardians scanned the early morning sky for any sign of illicit skycraft in flight. Sky flight, both in Sanctaphrax and Undertown, was strictly forbidden.

Xaxis stared out into open sky. The high winds and driving rain which had been forecast only the day before had, once again, failed to materialize. 'Surely a storm must come soon,' he muttered to himself. He looked up at Midnight's Spike, the tall, elegant lightning conductor which pointed up to the sky from the top of the tower, and shook his head. 'Fifty years, and nothing. But soon. Soon a storm is bound to come,' he hissed, 'and when it does, the great Sanctaphrax rock will be healed, cured, restored . . .' His eyes glinted unpleasantly behind the dark glasses. 'And when *that* happens—'

Just then there was a knock at the door. Xaxis turned and, with a flourish of his cape, stepped back through the open window and into his reception chamber.

'Enter,' he called, his imperious voice muffled somewhat by the mask.

MIDNIGHT'S SPIKE

The door opened, and a youth dressed in the black robes of the Guardians of Night walked in. He was pallid, angular, with shadowy rings beneath his violet eyes and his hair shorn to a dark stubble.

'Ah, Xanth,' said Orbix, recognizing the youth at once. 'What brings you here? Has the execution taken place already?'

'It has, sir – but that is not the reason for my visit.' He paused. There was something deeply disturbing about never being able to see the Most High Guardian's eyes. It was only his rasping voice that gave any clue as to what he was thinking.

'Well?' Orbix demanded.

'I have information,' said Xanth simply.

Orbix nodded. Xanth Filatine was, without doubt, the most promising apprentice to have come his way in many years. Now that Orbix had prised him away from that obese fop, Vox Verlix, the youth was shaping up well. 'Information?' he said. 'What information?'

'It concerns the librarian knights,' he said, and spat on the floor. 'A recently captured prisoner has just revealed some interesting facts about them under interrogation.'

'Go on,' said Orbix, rubbing his gloved hands together.

'They are about to send three more apprentice treatise scholars off to the Deepwoods. Tomorrow morning, when—'

'Then we must seize them.' Orbix smiled behind the metal mask. 'Three more traitors to add to the hanging gantries.'

'If you please, sir,' said Xanth, his nasal voice little more than a whisper, 'I think I may have a better idea.'

Orbix glowered at the youth. He didn't like his plans being questioned. 'A *better* idea?' he growled.

'Well, not better, as such,' said Xanth, back-tracking. 'But an alternative that you might like to consider.'

'Go on,' said Orbix.

'Sir, if the renegades were followed, in secret, this could be the chance we have been waiting for to uncover the entire network of traitors. We could expose each and every enemy of the Tower of Night operating between Undertown and the so-called *Free* Glades.'

'But—' Orbix began.

'As I see it, the choice is this,' Xanth went on hurriedly. 'The three apprentices now. Or the whole treacherous set-up tomorrow.'

Orbix raised an eyebrow. 'And who might be the spy to carry out such a task?' he asked.

Xanth lowered his head modestly.

'I see,' said Orbix. He tapped thoughtfully on the muzzle of the mask with the tips of his bony fingers.

The proposal was interesting, very interesting. For so long now, he had dreamed of capturing those two turn-coats, Ulbus Vespius and Tallus Penitax, the treacherous Professors of Light and Darkness – and torturing them until they repented for going over to the other side and begged for his forgiveness. He *would* forgive them, of course. He would forgive all those who fell into his clutches – even Fenbrus Lodd.

And then he would have them executed.

'Very well, Xanth,' he said at last. 'I give you my permission to go.'

'Thank you, sir. Thank you,' said Xanth, emotion sounding in his voice for the first time since their meeting had begun. 'You won't regret your decision, sir. I give my word.'

'I hope not, Xanth,' came the icy response. 'Indeed, I make you this promise. If you should let me down, then it is *you* who will live to regret my decision.'

With Orbix Xaxis's doomladen words echoing round his head, Xanth left the chamber and headed back down the flights of stairs. Hood raised and gown wrapped close about him, he kept to the shadows and out of sight. Past the look-out gantries he went; past the guards' quarters and great halls, the laboratories and kitchens, and on down into the dark, dismal dungeons in the lower reaches of the sinister Tower of Night.

All round him he heard the low, whimpering moan of the prisoners. Hundreds of them, there were – earth-scholars, sky pirates, suspected spies and traitors, even Guardians who had fallen from favour. Each one had been locked up, pending a trial which would take years to come – and almost certainly end up with an execution. In the meantime, they had to remain in their cells – if cell was the right word for the precarious ledges which jutted out into the vast atrium at the centre of the tower.

Xanth stopped on a half-landing, where one of the descending flights of stairs became two, and turned to the door facing him. He slid the round spy-hole cover to one side and peered through. The prisoner was still sitting in exactly the same position as when Xanth had left him, nearly two hours earlier.

'It's me,' he hissed. 'I'm back.'

The hunched figure did not move.

'You were right,' said Xanth, louder now. 'It worked.' Still the prisoner did not stir. Xanth frowned. 'I thought you might be interested in my good news,' he said peevishly.

The figure turned and stared back at the spy-hole. He was old. His eyes were sunken; his cheeks hollow. His thick, grey beard and thinning hair were dark with years of filth. He raised one shaggy eyebrow. 'Interested?' he said. 'Aye, Xanth, I suppose I am.' He looked round his cell and shook his head wearily. The small ledge, sticking out into the cavernous, echoing atrium, had no walls, yet escape was impossible. Apart from the door, which was kept securely bolted from the outside, the only way out was down – down to certain death on the ground, far below. He turned back to the spy-hole. 'But I am also envious beyond words.'

Xanth swallowed with embarrassment. Here, deep down in the stinking bowels of the atrium, the cell was about as bad as it could be. There was a table where, being an academic, the prisoner was forced to do work for the Guardians, and a filthy straw mattress. And that was it. For as long as Xanth had been alive, and many, many long years before that, the cell had been the prisoner's entire world.

'I . . . I'm so sorry,' said Xanth. 'I didn't think.'

'You didn't think,' he murmured. 'How ironic that is, Xanth, for I do little else *but* think. I think of everything that has happened – of what I have lost, of what has been taken from me . . .' He paused, and when he looked up again he was smiling. 'You will enjoy the Deepwoods, Xanth. I know you will. It is dangerous there, of course, with more perils than you could imagine. Yet it is a wondrous place – exciting, beautiful . . .'

Xanth nodded enthusiastically. It was, after all, their long conversations about the endless forest which had triggered his interest in the Deepwoods in the first place. They'd talked about woodtroll paths and reed-eel beds, about waif country and (Xanth's favourite) about sacred Riverrise, high up in the distant mountains. Yet it was a place the prisoner would only ever visit again in his memory, for Xanth knew that the Most High Guardian of Night considered him too important ever to be released – and no-one had ever escaped from the dungeons of the Tower of Night.

Just then a pair of soiled ratbirds landed on the corner

of the prisoner's sleeping ledge. He flapped his thin, grimy hands at them, sending them screeching back into the air. 'And stay gone!' he shouted after them. 'I'm not dead yet.' He snorted. 'There'll be time enough to pick my bones clean when I am. Eh, Xanth?'

The young apprentice Guardian winced uneasily. 'Please don't talk like that,' he said. 'Something'll turn up. I know it will . . .'

'Hush now, Xanth,' the prisoner cautioned. 'Such words are treason. If you do not wish to end up on your own dungeon ledge, you'd better be careful.' He returned his attention to the barkscroll. 'I will be thinking of you,' he said.

The following morning Rook Barkwater stood in the cold, damp dormitory, stuffing all his belongings – which were few – into a backpack. He untied and reknotted the black scarf around his neck. He inspected the talisman. He rubbed the two sky-crystals together and watched the sparks tumble down to the floor, where they fizzed and disappeared.

'Where is Felix?' he wondered. He hadn't laid eyes on him since the moment his own name had been announced from the Lufwood Bridge. He had found his sleeping chamber empty, the hammock unslept in – and none of the other senior apprentices seemed to have seen him. Rook was confused. Surely, desperately disappointed as he was, Felix wouldn't let him leave without saying goodbye.

Would he?

As he pushed the last of his meagre belongings into the backpack and tightened the drawstring, Rook sighed unhappily. Just then there came a noise from the end of the long thin room, and the door burst open. Rook spun round.

'Felix,' he said as a figure appeared. 'At last! I was beginning to think . . .' He fell still. It was not Felix at all.

'Come on, Rook,' said Stob Lummus impatiently. 'Aren't you ready yet?'

'We've been waiting for simply ages,' added Magda Burlix, and pursed her lips primly. 'There's still a lot to be done before we can depart.'

Rook pulled the backpack shut and swung it up onto his shoulder. As he did so, he noticed something shiny which had been lying on the hammock beneath his backpack. Rook gasped. It was Felix's ceremonial sword.

'Thank you, Felix,' he whispered, as he belted it round his waist and trotted after the others. 'And fare you well, wherever you may be.'

·CHAPTER FOUR·

THE GREAT MIRE ROAD

It was late afternoon before the three young librarian knights elect were ready. First, they had to be fitted with their respective outfits. A long, flowing cape for Magda Burlix, with little bundles of bright materials hanging in bunches amidst clusters of shiny pins and thimbles of all sizes.

'Finest silks from the workshops of Undertown,' she smiled, turning to look at herself in the mirror. 'Something to suit every shryke-matron. How about you, madam? Can I interest you in twenty rolls of this very fine spider-silk?'

Rook smiled, but Stob Lummus, the other librarian, turned away. 'It won't be so funny when you're on the Mire road surrounded by shryke guards, Magda,' he said sharply. Stob adjusted the tall, conical hat of a timber trader, and pulled the rather moth-eaten tilder coat on over the heavy sample-laden waistcoat he wore.

'As for you!' He turned to Rook, contempt plain in his dark brown eyes and curling upper lip. 'Don't encourage her, *under*-librarian!'

Rook turned away, his face burning, and fumbled with the straps of his tool harness.

'What a natural knife-sharpener you make,' sneered Stob. 'Must run in the family.'

Rook didn't rise to the bait. As Felix had so often told him, 'You're equal to any and better than most.' Good old Felix!

Rook sighed as he thought of his old friend. He wouldn't like to guess how many times Felix had come to his aid over the years, defending him against overbearing professors and aggressive apprentices – for bullies came in all shapes and sizes.

'Ready?' It was the Professor of Darkness. He looked strained and tired. 'Here are your papers. Stob, you are a timber merchant from the Foundry Glade. Magda, you are a silk trader carrying samples to the Eastern Roost. And you, my boy,' said the professor, laying a hand on Rook's shoulder, 'you are a lowly knife-sharpener and tool-mender. Slip away quietly now – and look out for the bloodoak pendants. Those who wear them are friends to the librarian knights and will protect and guide you. The first of your contacts will make themselves known to you at the tollgate to the Great Mire Road. Sky speed, and may Earth protect you.'

Stob stepped forwards.

'No,' said the professor. 'Rook, you lead the way. You know the tunnels better than anyone.'

Stob shot Rook a black look.

'It's this way,' Rook told the others some time later as he led them through the labyrinth of underground sewage tunnels. He was heading for an overflow pipe in the boom-docks which, in times of heavy rain, emptied directly into the Edgewater River. It was not the closest to the Great Mire Road tollgate but, being so well concealed by the overhead jetties, it was considered by the Professor of Darkness to be the safest.

One after the other, the three of them emerged into the eerie half-light of shadows and setting sun. The air was cold, and took Rook by surprise. He swallowed it in great greedy lungfuls. Compared with the stale, tepid atmosphere of the sewers they had left behind, it tasted wonderfully fresh – even here, on the muddy shoreline of the sluggish river.

To their right stood a tall pillar. A single piece of cloth, nailed to its side, fluttered in the rising breeze.

'Look at that,' Rook murmured.

Stob frowned. 'I believe it's a posting-pole,' he said. 'I've read about them somewhere. Before the Edge was blighted with stone-sickness, sky ship captains with berths to spare would advertise—'

'Not that,' Rook interrupted. He nodded past the pillar at the huge sun, deep crimson and pulsating. '*That,*' he murmured in awe. 'It's been so long . . .'

Magda, who had herself been standing with her mouth open, shook her head. 'It's incredible, isn't it?' she said. 'I mean, I knew the sun was up there above us the whole time, but actually to see it – to feel it—'

'But you mustn't look at it directly,' Stob interrupted stiffly. 'Ever. I read that it can blind you if you stare for too long, even when it's this low in the sky . . .'

'The colour of the clouds,' Rook whispered reverently. 'And the way they glow! They're so beautiful.'

'They make my spider-silk samples look dull in comparison,' said Magda, nodding.

'What nonsense,' said Stob. 'Sunsets are just dust particles in upper sky . . .'

'Read that somewhere, did you?' said Magda, lightly.

Stob nodded. 'If you must know, it was in an old sky-scholar scroll I uncovered in—' He heard Magda's sigh of irritation and stopped himself. 'We should be making tracks,' he said. He strode off, not looking back.

Magda followed. 'Come on, Rook,' she called back gently. 'We mustn't get separated.'

'Coming,' said Rook. Reluctantly, he dragged himself away from the dazzling evening sky.

Rook's senses were on fire and, as he followed the other two up a rotting wooden flight of stairs to the quayside promenade, along a winding alleyway and onto the main thoroughfare which led to the beginning of the Great Mire Road, he was bombarded with sights, sounds, smells – and distant memories which tugged at his feelings. The cool caress of night air coming in from open sky. The smudge and twinkle of the first emerging stars. The smells of roast meats and strange spices from the ramshackle stalls they passed. Goblins shouting down to passing cloddertrogs, timber wagons creaking along narrow alleys and boots clattering on the cobbled streets. By the time the massive lamplit towers of the Great Mire Road gateway came into view, Stob, Magda and Rook were walking in the midst of a large and growing crowd, streaming both to and from the road's great entrance.

'Busy 'ere this evening, innit, Maz?' said a voice behind them.

'You can say that again,' came the reply.

'I said, it's busy here this evening . . .'

'Oh, Sisal, you are a one!'

Rook glanced round to see two grinning mobgnomes with a bundle of costumes, robes and frock coats on hangers draped over their left arms, hurrying past them. To their left was a gnokgoblin sitting astride a prowlgrin which was pulling a low cart, laden with boxes labelled FINEST PEWTER CUTLERY. Behind him an officious-looking lugtroll was shouting out orders at half a dozen cloddertrogs who were staggering along beneath the weight of a long, heavy roll of red and purple tapestry. And following them, a contingent of gyle goblins bearing pallets of gleaming flagons, goblets and urns above their heads . . .

Nobody paid any heed to the sullen timber merchant, the young silk-seller or the lowly knife-sharpener who followed close on their footsteps. Rook felt overwhelmed yet exhilarated to be a part of all this great activity. From every corner of Undertown, merchants and dealers were converging on the Great Mire Road. For though some of the more heavy industry had shifted to the Foundry Glade, where wood-fuel was cheap – and labour cheaper still – the majority of manufactured goods were still produced in the traditional workshops and factories of Undertown. On the other side they would barter and sell their wares in the Eastern Roost.

'Mind your backs!' roared a rough voice from near the gateway. 'Coming through.'

Ahead of him, Rook saw the crowds part as an approaching hammelhorn-drawn wagon rolled into view. It was long and flat – and followed by two others. On the bench at the front of each one were two seated leaguesmen and a swarthy flat-head goblin, who stood on the driving platform, holding a knot of reins with one hand and cracking a whip with the other. Rook craned his neck to see what load was being carried beneath the huge tarpaulins. Raw materials of some kind, that much was certain, for everything manufactured in Undertown – from bracelets to bricks – was made from materials brought in from outside.

'It's timber,' Rook heard Stob telling Magda in that bossy, rather haughty voice of his. 'Ironwood, by the look of it. No doubt bound for the Sanctaphrax forest,' he continued. 'Sheer madness, if you ask me, but then –' his voice dropped to a low whisper – 'that's the Guardians of Night for you.'

'*Ssh!*' Magda warned him under her breath 'There are spies everywhere,' she breathed.

Stob's eyes narrowed. Even though he knew she was right, he didn't like to be told. And as the third load of ironwood rumbled past, and the departing crowd surged forwards once again, Stob marched ahead, demanding that the others keep up.

Magda turned to Rook, rolled her eyes and smiled conspiratorially. Rook increased his pace to keep up with her.

'The Guardians,' he whispered. 'Do you think they know what we're doing?'

Magda shrugged. 'I wouldn't be surprised,' she said. 'But knowing and *finding* are two different things!' she added fiercely.

'What about the Most High Academe?' asked Rook. 'They say he has an army of goblin mercenaries on duty day and night, just to hunt down librarian knights . . .'

Magda tossed her head back contemptuously. 'The Most High Academe, Vox Verlix, that great sack of oak-wine – *hah*! He's finished.' She paused. 'Of course, you

71

know it's him who's responsible for that.' She pointed to the tall towers of the Mire road looming up ahead of them.

Rook gasped. 'He built *that!*'

Magda nodded. 'Oh, yes,' she said. 'After stone-sickness put an end to sky-trade, he designed and supervised the building of the Great Mire Road so that we humble merchants of Undertown could trade with the Deepwoods. Clever person, old Vox. At least, he was once. Too clever! Mother Scab-beak and the Shryke Sisterhood seized control of it, and there was nothing he could do to stop them.'

'What about his goblin mercenaries?' asked Rook.

'Them? They're worse than the shrykes. Vox recruited them to guard the slaves he used to build the Great Mire Road, and they ended up holding him to ransom. He has to pay them off constantly. Otherwise they'd throw him out of that fancy palace of his – and he knows it. The goblins and the shrykes have made an alliance to control the trade between Undertown and the Deepwoods, and Vox Verlix, the so-called Most High Academe, is nothing more than their puppet. Anyway, it's not him we have to worry about,' Magda added darkly. 'It's the Guardians of Night who are really dangerous.'

Rook shivered and adjusted the tool-harness on his back. It suddenly felt very heavy.

Magda shook her head. 'It was also Vox Verlix who designed the Tower of Night for the Guardians,' she said. 'It was supposed to tap the power of a passing storm and thereby heal the great floating rock.' She stopped and looked over her shoulder. 'You can see it over there in the distance. Evil-looking monstrosity.'

Rook nodded, and glanced back. There, huge and threatening, was the great wooden structure, towering high above the rooftops of even the tallest Undertown buildings. Its narrow spire – Midnight's Spike – pointed up accusingly at the sky.

'And it was Vox,' she went on, turning back, 'who, when that same great floating rock began to crumble and sink, was forced by the Guardians to keep it shored up with timbers. Hundreds, thousands of ironwood timbers. The Sanctaphrax Forest.'

'Yes, I know about that,' said Rook, remembering his studies. It's that vast wooden scaffold of pillars and crossbeams that keeps the floating rock from sinking right down to the ground, isn't it?'

'Precisely,' said Magda. 'According to many scholars, that must never be allowed to happen. If the floating rock touches the ground, they say, it would mean that the power of the storm would pass straight through the stricken rock to the ground beneath, failing to heal it. Hence the so-called *forest* – which, unlike the Tower of Night and the Mire road, will go on being built for ever,' she added, 'for the lower the rock sinks, the more timbers are needed to support it. Stob is right. It *is* madness – Careful, Rook!'

Too late. Rook walked slap-bang into an oncoming tufted goblin. There was a *thud*, followed by a *crash*, followed by the sound of round objects clattering over the cobbles and loud, angry swearing. Rook, who had been looking back at the angular Tower of Night silhouetted against the darkening sky, spun round. The goblin was lying on his back, dazed and cursing loudly, with Magda crouching down next to him. The crate he had dropped had upturned and its contents – a consignment of choicest woodapples – were rolling noisily over the cobbled street in all directions. As for Stob, he was nowhere to be seen.

Rook's heart began to pound. He was meant to be travelling as inconspicuously as possible, yet here he was drawing attention, not only to himself, but also to Magda. A small crowd had collected round the ranting goblin. If the guards were to get wind of what was going on, he ran the risk of sabotaging the entire trip before they even got properly started.

'I'm so sorry,' he said as he scurried about, retrieving the woodapples. 'It was entirely my fault. I wasn't looking where I was going.'

'Yeah, well,' said the tufted goblin, making a great show of dipping his finger into the soft red flesh of a shattered woodapple. 'That's all very well, but what about the fruit what's got smashed up? I'm just a poor fruit vendor . . .' He left the words hanging in mid air.

'I . . . I'll make good the loss, of course,' said Rook

uneasily. He looked up at Magda. 'Won't we?'

Without a word, Magda reached into her cloak and pulled out a leather pouch. She loosened the drawstring. 'Here,' she said, placing a small gold piece into the goblin's palm. 'This is for the damaged fruit.' The goblin nodded, his eyes glinting craftily. 'And this,' she said, as she added a second coin, 'is for any bumps or bruises suffered.' She stood up, yanked the goblin to his feet and smiled fiercely. 'I trust the matter is settled, then,' she said.

'Y-yes, I suppose so,' the goblin stammered. 'Though—'

'Excellent,' Magda announced. She turned and, with Rook in tow, strode back off into the crowd.

'You handled that very . . . confidently,' said Rook.

Magda tossed her plaits back and laughed. 'I have three older brothers,' she explained. 'I've had to learn how to hold my own.'

Rook smiled. He was growing to like this travelling companion. Although at first she had seemed imposing, abrupt – abrasive even – now he was beginning to see her in a different light. She was practical, she was forthright, she spoke her mind and acted decisively. Rook realized, now, why she had been selected to go to the Free Glades. In comparison, Stob seemed cold, aloof, bookish ... He frowned. 'Where *is* Stob?' he wondered out loud.

Magda shook her head. 'That's what I was just asking myself,' she said, and looked round. 'We must stick together.'

They were, by now, almost at the entrance to the Great Mire Road, with the gateway towers reaching far up above their heads. If everything went as planned, then someone would make themselves known to them – someone who would guide them safely through the toll-gate. Rook fingered his bloodoak tooth and searched the crowd for anyone wearing something similar.

Stob was nowhere to be seen, and the large square in front of the tollgate was thronging. The noise was colossal, and the smells! Everything from the sour stench of pickled tripweed barrels to the overpowering sweetness of vats of barkcat-musk perfume. Here, where the in-trade and out-trade converged, were merchants and pedlars, prowlgrin-riders and hammelhorn-drivers, carts, carriages and cargo of every description.

There were armed guards and tally-shrykes, smugglers and slavers, food vendors, bar-tenders, entrepreneurs and money-lenders. There were creatures and characters from every corner of the Edge – lugtrolls, gabtrolls, woodtrolls, cloddertrogs and termagants, nightwaifs and flitterwaifs, and goblins of every description. And there, standing in the shadows of a tall loading-derrick, his body half turned away, was Stob Lummus himself.

'He's talking to someone,' Rook hissed. His voice

dropped. 'It must be our contact.' And he went to step forwards, only to find Magda's firm grip on his arm holding him back.

'I'm not so sure,' she said. 'Listen.'

Rook cocked his head to one side and concentrated on the gruff voice coming from the depths of the shadows. 'What was that? Bloodoak *what*?' the voice complained tetchily. 'You must speak up!'

'I said,' he heard Stob replying in a sibilant stage-whisper, 'that is an interesting charm you're wearing.

Bloodoak tooth, if I'm not mistaken—'

'What?' demanded the voice, and Rook caught the flash of something metallic. 'What's it got to do with you?'

Magda shook her head. 'Surely that can't be our contact,' she said.

'Indeed it's not, missy,' came a sing-song voice behind her. '*I* am.' Both Magda and Rook turned to see a dumpy gnokgoblin wearing a long cape and head scarf, and carrying a covered basket on one of her stubby arms. Around her neck glinted an ornate pendant, the centre-piece of which was a glistening red tooth.

'My name is Tegan,' she said. 'Your friend has made an unfortunate, not to say foolish, mistake—'

'He's no friend of mine,' Magda cut in sharply.

'Friend, companion, fellow-traveller,' said Tegan, 'the precise nature of your relationship is unimportant. All that matters is that he is in danger.' She shook her head and tutted with concern. 'This could be serious,' she said. 'Very serious. You must go and get him before he gives all of us away. Quickly, now.'

Neither Magda nor Rook needed to be told twice. They darted across the square, dodging through the streaming crowds, and into the shadows at the bottom of the loading-derrick.

'There you are, Stob!' cried Rook, grabbing one of his arms. 'We've been looking everywhere for you,' said Magda, as she took hold of the other. 'Off we go!'

'No, no,' said Stob urgently, and tried to shake them off. His voice lowered to a conspiratorial whisper. 'I've found our first contact,' he said.

Rook and Magda glanced round at the old woodtroll who was standing beside them. He was plump and bandy-legged, and the plaits in his beard had turned white. He had a brass ear-trumpet raised to one ear, while round his neck were clustered trinkets and lucky charms of all shapes and sizes. A dullish brown tusk on a leather cord nestled in the white whiskers.

'No, you haven't,' said Magda.

'Trouble is,' Stob said, 'he's a bit deaf.'

'I heard that!' said the woodtroll indignantly.

'So are you, Stob!' Magda said in a clipped whisper. 'I'm telling you, he's *not* the contact. Now, *come on*.' With that, she and Rook tightened their grip and frogmarched Stob away.

'Here!' the woodtroll called after them. 'What's this all about?'

Magda turned to Stob questioningly. Stob shrugged. 'Didn't you see it?' he said. 'The pendant – a bloodoak tooth on a leather strip—'

'That was no bloodoak tooth,' said Magda. 'It was a whitecollar woodwolf fang.' She tutted. 'Call yourself a librarian scholar!'

Even as he heard her accusing words, Rook realized that he, too, might just as easily have been fooled. At a glance, in the jostling crowd, the wolf fang could easily be confused with a bloodoak tooth. Stob's big mistake had been to approach the old woodtroll rather than wait to be approached.

'You made it, then,' the gnokgoblin said to them when they arrived back by her side. 'Well done. I was beginning to worry.'

'Yes,' said Magda. 'Though no thanks to—'

'Who is this?' said Stob, butting in. He was feeling both foolish and resentful. 'Can we trust her?'

Tegan nodded sagely. 'You are wise to be sceptical,' she said. 'For "Trust no-one" is as good a motto as any for you to stick to on your long journey.'

'You still haven't given us a reason for trusting you,' said Stob rudely.

Without saying a word, the gnokgoblin reached forwards and fingered the carved bloodoak tooth round his neck, then nodded towards the two others. 'Rather a coincidence for three travellers to be wearing the same earth-studies talisman, don't you think?' she said. 'Unless Fenbrus Lodd is now handing them out to all and sundry.'

'No,' Stob conceded. 'So far as I know, they are given only to librarian knights elect, and their supporters.'

'Then nothing has changed,' said Tegan. She opened the front of her cape to reveal her own ornate talisman.

'You?' said Stob, surprised. 'You're our contact?'

'You seem surprised,' said the gnokgoblin. 'Over the years I have done my best to be useful to scholars and academics of every persuasion. Acting as a counsellor here, a guide there...' Her voice took on an icy edge. 'Anything, rather than allow the Edge to slide into the dark oblivion those cohorts of the Tower of Night would foist upon us all.'

'Well said,' Magda agreed.

The gnokgoblin looked around anxiously. 'We have already been standing here for too long. It's not safe.' She turned back to them and her face broke into a smile. 'The three of you have got a long and difficult journey ahead of you, but with a little luck and a lot of perseverance, I just know you're going to succeed.'

Rook suddenly felt buoyed up by the gnokgoblin's confidence, and grinned from ear to ear. He could hardly wait to get going.

'Right, then,' said Tegan. 'It's high time we saw about your tally-discs. Keep close together – and let me do all the talking.'

As they approached the Great Mire Road, Rook saw that there was a row of tally-huts and barriers strung out in a line between the huge towers. Individual queues led to each one. The gnokgoblin led them straight to the tally-hut closest to the left-hand tower.

Ahead, on an ornately carved throne, sat a large shryke matron, bedecked in jewels and rich fabrics. On either side of the throne sprouted enormous carved claws which barred the way through. The shryke eyed each trader with yellow, unblinking eyes, before scrutinizing the tattered, much-thumbed papers handed to her.

'Pass!' Her voice rasped out as she flicked the lever at her side with an evil-looking talon. The carved claws clicked open and the trader walked through. 'Next!'

'Pass!' *Click.* 'Next! Pass!' *Click.* 'Next!'

Rook jumped. To his surprise, he realized that Stob and Magda were through. It was his turn. His heart leaped into his mouth.

'Remember,' Tegan whispered in his ear. 'Let me do the talking.'

'*Next!*' The shryke's voice was shrill with irritation. Tegan pushed Rook forward. Somehow, Rook made his legs work. With a trembling hand, he offered up his false documents, trying not to look at the yellow eyes that seemed to be boring into his skull. What if there was some mistake with his papers? What if the shryke asked him about his so-called line of business? What did Rook know about knife-sharpening? A cold panic began to build in the pit of his stomach.

'Knife-sharpener?' The shryke cocked her large head to one side. The feathers at her neck ruffled, the jewels clinked, her terrible curved beak came towards Rook's down-turned face. 'Don't look old enough to play with knives, do he?' the shryke cackled nastily. 'Well, sonny? Goblin stolen your tongue?'

Tegan stepped forward. 'It's his first time,' she smiled. 'Obviously he's overcome with the beauty of your plumage, Sister Sagsplit.'

The shryke laughed. 'Tegan, you old charmer. Is he with you?'

Tegan nodded.

'I might have known,' said the shryke. 'Through you go.'

The talon flicked the lever. Rook took his papers and tally-disc, and stumbled through the opening claw-stile. Magda and Stob were waiting on the other side.

'What kept you?' Magda sounded panicky.

'Stopped for a chat, no doubt,' said Stob smugly.

'Shut up, Stob,' said Magda. She clasped Rook's hand. 'Are you all right? You look very pale.'

'I'm fine,' said Rook shakily. 'It's just, I've never seen a shryke before. They're so . . . so . . .'

'You'll see plenty more on the Mire road,' said Tegan, motioning them forward.

'*You?* Don't you mean *we*?' said Magda.

'Yeah, I thought you were coming with us,' said Stob.

'My place is here,' Tegan explained. 'My role is to get travellers safely through the tollgate tally-huts and onto the Great Mire Road. Others will make themselves known to you along the way.' She gave them each a brief, but heartfelt hug. 'Take care, beware and well may you fare, my dears,' she said. And with that, she was gone.

The three young librarian knights elect suddenly felt very alone. From behind them, there came the loud noise of clattering and chattering as a contingent of rowdy mobgnomes lugging a vast range of ironware products, from buckets and bellows to wrought-iron railings, drew closer and overtook them. Without saying a word to one another – but instinctively aware that there was safety in numbers – Stob and Magda attached themselves to the back of the group, and Rook brought up the rear.

Ever since the young under-librarian's name had

THE GREAT MIRE ROAD

echoed round the high vaulted ceiling of the Great Storm Chamber, Rook Barkwater had felt he was in a dream, scarcely able to believe the events unfolding before him. Now, as he stared ahead at the magnificent raised road, with its ironwood pylons and huge floating lufwood barges; with its look-out posts, its toll-towers and its blazing beacons snaking away into the distance far ahead, his head reeled and his body tingled with excitement.

'This is it,' he whispered softly. 'There's no turning back now. The greatest adventure of my life has already begun.'

Back at the tally-hut, there was a soft *click* as the claw-stile opened once more. An angular figure in dark robes slipped through. As he lowered his hood, the moon glinted on high cheekbones and closely cropped hair.

CHAPTER FIVE

DEADBOLT VULPOON

They had been walking for hours over the slippery boarded walkway. All around them traders, merchants and itinerant labourers just like themselves trudged on, backs bent under heavy burdens, eyes staring fixedly down. Few spoke, and when they did, it was in whispers. It was dangerous to attract attention on the Great Mire Road.

Rook glanced up. Ahead, the timber walkway snaked off into the distance like some gigantic hover worm. To their left and right, the Mire mud glistened in the fading light.

'Keep your eyes down!' Stob's whisper was urgent and threatening.

'Remember,' said Magda softly, placing a hand on Rook's shoulder. 'To look directly into a shryke guard's eyes is punishable by death.'

Rook shuddered. Just then, ahead of them, he heard

the clicking sound of clawed feet on the wooden boards and the brittle crack of a bone-flail. Shryke guards were approaching.

Rook's heart missed a beat.

'Steady,' Stob hissed. 'We mustn't draw attention to ourselves. Just keep moving. And you—' he jabbed Rook nastily in the back – 'keep your eyes to yourself!'

'It's all right,' whispered Magda. 'Here, take my hand, Rook.'

Rook grasped Magda's hand gratefully, fighting the urge to turn tail and flee.

The clawed feet clicked nearer. Ahead, the slow-moving crowd seemed to melt away into the shadows cast by the blazing beacons that were strung out high above them at hundred-stride intervals along the way. Rook couldn't help himself. He glanced up.

There ahead of him, staring back with cruel, yellow unblinking eyes, was a tall mottled shryke guard, resplendent in burnished metal breast-plate and great curved beaked helmet. A razor-sharp talon moved to her side, where the vicious-looking bone-flail was strapped. With a rustle of feathers, the guard drew the flail. Rook was transfixed with fright. He looked down instantly and squeezed Magda's hand with all his might. He heard Magda gasp.

'How *dare* you!' The screech pierced the air like a dart.

Rook closed his eyes and hunched his shoulders, waiting for the blow he felt must surely come.

'Mercy, mercy,' a goblin's frightened voice cried out pitifully. 'I didn't mean to . . . I beg you. I—'

The bone-flail cracked to life in the evening air, followed by the sound of a skull shattering. Rook opened one eye. In front of him, in the harsh glare of an overhead beacon, a small goblin lay at the shryke's feet. A pool of blood spilled out across the surrounding boards.

'Goblin scum!' the shryke squawked, and behind her two other guards clacked their beaks with amusement.

The shryke swung the flail over her shoulder, and the three of them strode on. Magda pulled Rook to one side as they passed. He felt faint. Rook had witnessed, and experienced, violence before – the viciousness of an angry professor, the brutality of the fights that had occasionally broken out amongst the apprentices and under-librarians . . .

But this. This was different. It was a cold violence, callous and passionless – and all the more shocking for that.

'That was close,' said Stob quietly, behind them. 'Come on, now. Keep moving, or we'll never make it to the toll-tower. There's a rest platform there,' he added.

Rook glanced down at the body on the road and, with a jolt, recognized the pack on the hapless goblin's back.

The goblin had been a knife-grinder, just like himself.
Hands were now grasping the body, dragging it into the
shadows. Rook heard a distant muffled thud as something landed far below in the soft Mire mud. All that was
left of the goblin was a small blood-red stain in the
wood, which marked what had happened. It occurred to
Rook that, along the length of the Great Mire Road, he
had seen many such stains.

Rook turned to Magda. 'This is a terrible place,' he
said weakly.

'Courage, Rook,' said Magda kindly. 'We can stop for
the night at the rest platform. There'll be someone there
to meet us, I'm sure.'

Rook stopped. 'Couldn't we just stay here? Night's
closing in, the road seems to be getting more and more
slippery – and I'm so hungry.'

'We keep on to the toll-tower,' said Stob firmly. 'Then
we stop for something to eat. Rook!' he snapped. 'Do
keep up.'

Rook was motionless, rigid. His eyes and mouth were
open wide, his face drained of all colour. He had seen
something hanging from a great beacon-pole, just up
ahead.

'What's the matter?' said Magda. 'Rook, what is it?'

Rook pointed. Magda looked round – and gasped. Her
hand shot up to her mouth.

'Earth and Sky,' Stob groaned as he, too, saw what
Rook had seen. 'That is . . . dis-*gus*-ting,' he murmured.

Rook shuddered. 'Why do they do it? What could
possibly justify *that*?'

He stared up at the hang-
ing-cage. It was a mesh of
interlocking bars, shaped
like a sphere and suspended from
a gantry fixed to the top of
the tall, fluted ironwood
beacon-pole. There was a
dead body inside it, its limbs
contorted, its head bathed
in shadows. A growing
flock of white ravens was
flapping round, landing
on the bars and pecking
fiercely through the gaps.

All at once the corpse
slumped forwards. The
largest white raven of all gave
a loud *kraaak*, beat the other
birds away and stabbed at
the head, once, twice.

Rook screwed his eyes shut, but too late to avoid seeing the unfortunate creature's dead eyes being plucked
out of its skull. One. Two. The sudden jerkiness of the
movement ... A strand of something glistened in the
yellow lamplight. Rook abruptly bent over double as if
he'd been struck a blow to the belly and retched emptily
as he staggered over the bloodstained boards.

'Come on, now,' Magda said gently. 'Pull yourself
together.' Then, supporting him with her arm, she handed
Rook her water-container. 'Drink some of this,' she said.

'That's it. Now, breathe deeply. In, out. In, out . . .'

Slowly, Rook's legs stopped shaking, his heart quietened, and the choking feelings of nausea began to subside. 'You were right, Rook,' he heard Magda saying in a quavering voice. 'This is indeed a terrible place.' They rejoined the slow-moving file of travellers on the Mire road, and continued in silence.

With the toll-tower no more than a hundred strides away now and the wind coming from the west, the acrid smoke from the tilder-fat beacon at its top blew back along the Mire road into their faces. It made Rook's eyes water. It made his heart pound. After all, if no-one appeared soon to help them through this stage of their journey, they would have to deal with the shryke toll-guards on their own – and having just seen what they were capable of . . .

'I am a knife-sharpener, if it pleases you,' he practised breathlessly. 'A knife-sharpener from the Goblin Glades – I mean, *Nations*. The Goblin *Nations*. That's it. I'm a knife-sharpener from the Goblin Nations.'

In the event, the imposing shryke at the desk took their money, stamped their papers and waved them on without even raising her crested head. Rook kept his eyes firmly on his feet, which were now aching from the hours of walking. Presenting their papers was clearly a mere formality, he realized, important only when it was *not* done – for if the shryke guards ever found a trader or merchant without the most up-to-date stamps during one of their random inspections, the punishment was both swift and severe.

Rook didn't want to think about it. He followed the other two out onto a wide landing of lufwood planks, crammed with numerous stalls. Run by mobgnomes and gabtrolls they were, slaughterers, woodtrolls and gnokgoblins – each one vying with his or her neighbour for the passing trade.

There were lucky charms for sale: talismans, amulets and birth-stones. There were crossbows and long-bows, daggers and clubs. There were purses, baskets and bags. There were potions and poultices, tinctures and salves. There were street plans for newcomers to Undertown and charts of the endless forest (often hopelessly inaccurate, though none who purchased them would ever find their way back to complain) for those who hoped to travel in the Deepwoods.

And there were food stalls. Lots of them, each one laden with delicacies from all parts of the Edge. There were gnokgoblin meatloaves on offer, woodtroll tilder sausages, and sweetbreads cooked to a traditional cloddertrog recipe. There were pies and pastries, puddings and tarts; honey-soaked milkcakes and slices of candied oaksap. In short, there was something for everyone, whatever their taste, and the air was filled with an intoxicating mixture of aromas – sweet, rich, juicy, creamy, tangy – all mingling together in the brazier-warmed air.

Yet Rook was no longer hungry. His appetite had been lost to the memory of that dead prisoner in the cage, with his torn flesh and his stolen eyes.

'You must try to eat,' said Magda.

Rook shook his head mutely.

'Then I'll get something for you,' she said. 'For later.'

'As you wish,' said Rook wearily. It was sleep he needed, not food.

'There are hammock shelters and sleeping pallets close by,' came a soft, yet penetrating voice by his side. 'If you require, I can take you there.'

Rook looked down to find a short, wiry waif standing by his side. With his pale, almost luminous skin and his huge bat-like ears, he looked like a greywaif, or possibly a night-waif . . .

'A *night*waif,' the character confirmed. 'Greywaifs are generally larger and—' he gestured towards his mouth – 'they have those rubbery barbels hanging down from round here . . .' He frowned. 'But you're right, Rook. And I apologize. My name is Partifule.'

Rook scowled. He'd always found the mind-reading ability of waifs – whatever their variety – deeply disturbing. It made him feel exposed, vulnerable – and how could you ever trust a creature that made you feel like that?

Partifule sighed. 'That is our curse,' he said. 'In waif country, reading the minds of others is essential for our survival; a gift to enable us to see through the darkness. Here, however, it is a curse – spoiling every friendship and turning so many of us into spies who sell their services to the highest bidder.'

And you? Rook wondered with a shudder. How much have you been paid to spy on us?

Partifule sighed a second time. 'I give my services for free,' he said. 'And I am no spy. Perhaps *this* will help you to trust me.' He pulled his cape apart and there, nestling in the folds of the shirt beneath, was a red bloodoak tooth hanging from a delicate silver chain. 'I have been assigned the task of guarding you all while you sleep this first night. You must be fully rested for what lies ahead.' And he added, in response to Rook's unspoken question, 'The Twilight Woods.'

Rook smiled. For the first time that day he felt himself relax. Stob and Magda returned from the stalls, food wrapped in small, neat bundles. Magda handed one to Rook, who put it in his pocket.

'Who's that?' Stob demanded, his voice cold and imperious.

'Partifule, at your service,' came the reply and, for a second time, he revealed the bloodoak tooth.

'He's going to show us where we can bed down for the night,' Rook explained, 'and keep watch while we sleep.'

'Is he now?' said Stob. 'And slit our throats while we're snoring, eh?'

'Stob,' said Magda, sounding angry and embarrassed. 'He's wearing the tooth.' She turned to the nightwaif. 'Greetings, Partifule,' she said as she shook the creature's damp, bony hand. 'And apologies for our companion's rudeness.'

'Better safe than sorry,' Stob muttered.

'Indeed,' Partifule agreed. 'And, of course, Stob, you must feel free to spend the night on watch with me,' he said. 'I'd welcome the company.'

Stob made no verbal reply, but from the amused expression that played around the nightwaif's face, Rook knew that he had *thought* something back.

'Come on, then,' said Partifule. 'Stick together. It's just over here.'

They picked their way through the crowds gathered round the stalls, and across the landing to its outer edge. There, Partifule showed them the long, covered stall, with hammocks strung from its beams. To the right were row upon row of pallets, each one padded with a thick mattress of straw.

'Hammock shelter or sleeping pallet?' Magda asked Rook.

'Oh, a sleeping pallet, definitely,' said Rook. He gazed up into the speckled inky blackness above him. 'I've wanted to sleep out under the starry canopy of the sky for so long—'

'Well, now's your chance,' Partifule broke in. 'In fact, you should all be settling down for the night. It's almost midnight and you've got a long day ahead of you.'

None of the three young librarian knights elect needed any persuasion. It had been a long, draining day. Before Partifule had even taken up his look-out position at the end of his pallet, Stob, Magda and Rook were settling down to sleep.

Rook was just dozing off when, above the coughs and snores of the sleepers all around him, he heard a voice.

'Wa-ter,' it rasped. '*Waooooh*-ter.'

Rook got up slowly and picked his way through the pallets to the very edge of the landing. There, in front of him, were two hanging-cages next to each other. His blood turned cold in his veins. The first contained a bleached skeleton, with one bony hand reaching out of the cage pleadingly and the skull resting against the bars, its jaws set in a permanent grimace. The second cage appeared to be empty.

'Wa-ter.'

There was the voice again, but weaker now. Rook cautiously approached the cages. The skeleton couldn't have spoken, which meant ... He peered up into the shadows within the second cage, and gasped. It wasn't empty after all.

'Wa-ter,' the voice repeated.

Rook hurriedly unclipped the leather water-bottle from his belt and held it up – but although he stretched as high as possible, he couldn't reach the cage. 'Here,' he called. 'Here's some water.'

'Water?' said the voice.

'Yes, here below you,' said Rook. For a moment

 nothing happened. Then a great ham of a hand shot out from the bottom of the cage and grabbed the water-bottle. 'You're welcome,' said Rook, as he watched the hand and the water-bottle disappear back inside the cage.

There came the sound of slurping and swallowing – followed by a loud burp. The empty water-container dropped out of the cage and fell at Rook's feet. He bent down to retrieve it.

'Forgive me,' came the voice from above his head, weak still, but less rasping. 'But my need was indeed great.' The hand descended for a second time. 'And if you had a little something to eat, too . . .'

Rook searched his pockets, and found the bundle Magda had given him. He'd forgotten even to open it. He passed the warm package up to the waiting hand. The sound of hungry chomping and chewing filled the air.

'Mmm . . . mmmfff . . . Delicious – though perhaps it could do with a little extra salt.' He peered down at Rook and winked. 'You saved my life, young fellow.' He nodded towards the skeleton in the next cage. 'I did not wish to end up like my neighbour.'

Rook noticed the harsh edge to the voice. This was someone who was used to giving orders. He peered more closely inside the shadowy cage. Behind the bars, bathed in dark shadows and flickering lamp-light, was a hulking great figure, so immense that he was forced to crouch in the cage. Dressed in a frock coat, breeches and a tattered tricorn hat, he had dark curly hair, bushy eyebrows and a thick, black beard with what looked – Rook realized with a gasp – like ratbird skulls plaited into it. Bulging eyes glared out from the tangled bird's-nest of hair like two snowbird eggs.

Rook felt a surge of excitement. 'Are . . . are you a sky pirate?' he asked hesitantly.

A throaty laugh went up. 'Aye, lad. Long ago. A sky pirate captain, no less.' He paused. 'Not that that means anything these days – not since the Edge was stricken with stone-sickness.'

'A *sky pirate captain*,' Rook whispered in awe, and felt tingles of excitement running up and down his spine. What must it be like, he wondered, to have sailed in a sky pirate ship, with the sun in your face and the wind in your hair? He had often read, late into the night at the lecterns of the underground library, of the Great Voyages of Exploration into the darkest Deepwoods and the fearful dangers encountered there; of the series of Noble Flights out into Open Sky itself – and, of course, all about the fierce and terrible battles the sky pirates had fought with the wicked leaguesmen in their determination to keep the skies open for free trade.

Ships with names like *Galerider*, *Stormchaser*, *Windcutter*, *Edgedancer* and the *Great Sky Whale*, sailed by legendary sky pirate captains. Ice Fox, Wind Jackal, Cloud Wolf. And, perhaps the most famous of them all, the great Captain Twig himself.

Rook stared more closely at the caged captain. Could *this* be the fabled Twig? Had the popular young captain he'd read so much about become the huge hairy hulk before him?

'Are you Captain—' he began.

'Vulpoon,' the sky pirate captain answered, his voice low, hushed. 'Deadbolt Vulpoon. But keep it to yourself.'

Rook frowned. *Vulpoon*. There was something familiar about it.

A little smile played around the captain's eyes. 'I see you recognize my name,' he said, unable to keep the pride from his voice. His voice dropped to a whisper. 'Those flea-ridden featherballs that captured me had no idea the size of the fish they had landed. If they had, I wouldn't be talking to you now.' The sky pirate captain laughed. 'If they knew it was Deadbolt Vulpoon in this stinking cage, they'd cart me off to the Wig-Wig Arena in the Eastern Roost faster than a three-master in a sky-storm.' He played with one of the skulls in his thick beard. 'Instead, they've left me to waste away like a common Mire raider.'

'Can I help?' asked Rook.

'Thank you, lad, for the thought,' said the pirate, 'but unless you have the cage key of a shryke-sister, I'm done for like an oozefish on a mudflat.' He stroked his beard. 'There is one thing . . .'

'Name it,' said Rook.

'You could stay and talk a while. Three days and three nights I've been here, and you're the first who hasn't been too frightened of shrykes to approach the cage.' He paused. 'Yours will probably be the last kind voice I'll ever hear.'

'Of course,' said Rook. 'It would be an honour.' He slipped back into the nearby shadows and crouched down. 'So, what was it like?' he asked. 'Skysailing.'

'Skysailing?' said Vulpoon, and sighed with deep longing. 'Only the most incredible experience in the world, lad,' he said. 'Nothing compares to the feel of soaring up into the air and speeding across the sky, with the full sails creaking, the hull-weights whistling and the flight-rock – sensitive to every change in temperature – now rising, now falling. Angle, speed and balance, that's what it was all about.' He paused. 'Until the flight-rocks began to fall to the stone-sickness, that is.'

Rook stared at the sky pirate captain's crestfallen face.

'A terrible time, it was,' he continued. 'Of course, we'd known what was happening to the new floating rock of Sanctaphrax for some time. The loss of buoyancy. The gradual disintegration ... But we made no connection between the plight of the New Sanctaphrax rock and our own precious flight-rocks. That was soon to change. First off, news started coming in of large, heavy traders simply crashing out of the sky. The broad tug boats followed, with league ships and patrol boats soon also becoming useless. The leagues fell into decline and the skies above Undertown emptied. A terrible time it was, lad. Terrible.

'At first, we sky pirates did very well out of the situation. Night after night, we would carry out raids on the Great Mire Road, knowing that none would be able to follow us. What was more, we became the main means of transportation for fleeing Undertowners—' he rubbed his forefinger and thumb together – 'for a price.' He sighed noisily. 'And then it happened.'

Rook waited expectantly. Vulpoon scratched beneath his chin.

'We thought we were clever,' he said. 'We thought that by keeping our distance from New Sanctaphrax we would avoid the sickness. But we were wrong. Whether it travelled in on the wind, or had simply been incubating inside the stone, we'll never know . . . It was on the third day of the fourth quarter that the *Cloudbreaker* – one of the oldest and finest double-masters ever to have been built; a real beauty – just fell out of the sky like a speared ratbird and crash-landed in the Deepwoods below. Stone-sickness had finally caught up with us.

'Something had to be done if we were not all to go the same way, one by one. We had to convene to make plans. I dispatched a flock of ratbirds bearing word that an assembly was to be held at Wilderness Lair at the next full moon.' He sighed. 'And it was there, clinging to the underside of the jutting Edgelands rock like a collection of rock-limpets, that we decided to scuttle the entire fleet together—'

'The Armada of the Dead,' Rook gasped.

'You've heard of it, then?' said Vulpoon.

'Of course,' said Rook. 'Everyone has.' He didn't

mention *what* he'd heard – that it had become a renegade outpost attracting every dissident, runaway and more notorious denizen of the Mire.

Vulpoon was nodding sagely. 'What a night that was,' he murmured. 'We sailed together, that final time, across the sky from the misty Edgelands to the desolation of the Mire. And there, as one, we descended. All round us, a flock of white ravens flapped and screeched at the giants in their midst. We landed on the soft, sinking mud . . .' He looked up. 'That was nigh on thirty-five years since – and we're still there.'

Rook stared out across the mudflats of the Mire. 'It seems so very bleak,' he said.

'We get by,' said Vulpoon. 'A fleet of sky pirate ships was a pretty good basis for a settlement. And what we don't have, we go out and get.' A broad grin spread from ear to ear, revealing gums which bore more gaps than teeth. 'The occasional raid on the Great Mire Road. The odd skirmish with the shrykes . . .' He chuckled. 'There aren't many who haven't heard the name of Captain Deadbolt Vulpo—'

'*Thunderbolt!*' Rook blurted out. 'Thunderbolt Vulpoon. *That* was the name I was trying to remember.'

'He was my father,' the sky pirate captain said quietly. 'Executed in cold blood by the shrykes – those murderous, verminous, *pestilential* creatures. By Sky, how I'd like to wring every one of their scraggy necks.'

'The shrykes killed him,' Rook murmured.

'Aye, lad, in that evil Wig-Wig Arena of theirs,' he said. 'Yet it was a noble death, an honourable death – for he died that another might be saved.'

'He did?'

Deadbolt Vulpoon nodded, and wiped a tear from the corner of his eye. 'You may not have heard of him, but it was a certain Captain Twig they were actually after.'

'Oh, but I *have* heard of him,' said Rook. 'The young foundling, raised by Deepwoods woodtrolls, who was to become the most famous sky pirate captain of all time. Who has not heard of him?'

'Yes, well,' said Vulpoon, and puffed up his chest – as far as the confines of the cage would allow. 'Perhaps not *the* most famous.' He paused. 'Anyway, Twig'd been sentenced to death by the shrykes for some heinous crime, so he had. They were about to throw him to the bloodthirsty wig-wigs, when my father intervened – and sacrificed himself instead.'

'He must have been very brave,' said Rook.

Deadbolt Vulpoon sniffed, and wiped the corner of his other eye. 'Oh, he was,' he said. 'He certainly was.' He paused. 'If only there had been something left of him to bury, something to remember him by. But . . . well, I'm sure I don't need to tell you about wig-wigs. By the time they'd finished, there wasn't a scrap remaining.'

Rook nodded sympathetically and left a respectful pause before asking what he really wanted to know. 'And this Captain Twig?' he said. 'What happened to him? Is he with you at the Armada of the Dead? Or . . .'

'Or?' said Vulpoon.

'Or could those stories about him be true?' said Rook. 'That he alone refused to scuttle his ship. That he sailed off, back into the Deepwoods. That he lives there still, alone, unwashed and in total silence, wandering endlessly by day and sleeping in caterbird cocoons by night.'

'He did sail off into the Deepwoods,' Vulpoon concurred gruffly. 'As for the rest, I don't know. I've heard stories, of course. There have been sightings. *Soundings*, even – for some have returned with tales of him singing to the moon.' He shrugged. 'You have to take most of what you hear with a pinch of salt.' He looked up. His eyes narrowed. 'Shrykes,' he whispered urgently. 'You'd better make yourself scarce.'

'Shrykes!' Rook jumped. He turned and saw three of them, all bedecked in gaudy ornamentation, striding across the platform towards them. Rook shrank back into the shadows.

One of them cracked a flail ominously. Three pairs of

yellow eyes seemed to cut through the darkness and bore into Rook's. He held his breath.

'Not long now, Mire scum!' the lead shryke taunted. 'Where are your friends now?' She threw back her head and gave a cruel, screeching laugh.

Then, as one, the three of them turned and clicked back across the landing.

'*Phew*,' Rook murmured. 'I thought . . .'

'You were lucky just then,' said Deadbolt Vulpoon. 'But you must leave now. Thank you for the food and drink,' he whispered. 'And for listening.'

'It was nothing,' Rook replied. 'Good luck,' he murmured awkwardly.

Rook walked back to the sleeping pallets with a heavy heart, his parting words mocking him with their inadequacy. 'Good luck', indeed! What could he have been thinking? Magda rolled over and muttered something in her sleep, and next to her Stob snored noisily. Rook laid his head down on the soft mattress of straw and fell gratefully to sleep.

·CHAPTER SIX·

THE SKY
PIRATE RAID

At first Rook's sleep was deep and dreamless. He was warm beneath the thick blankets and the straw was wonderfully soft. Later, however, a cold wind gathered. It plucked at his bedding and sent dark clouds scudding across the moon. The light seemed to be flashing – on, off, on, off – now bathing Rook's face in silver, now plunging it into darkness. His eyelids flickered.

He was on a sky ship; a huge vessel with two masts and a great brass harpoon at its prow. He was standing at the helm, with the wind in his hair and the sun in his eyes.

'More lift, Master Midshipman,' came a voice. It was the captain, a foppish creature with jewelled clothes and a great waxed moustache, and – Rook realized with a start – he was giving orders to *him*.

'Aye-aye, Captain,' he said and, with nimble fingers playing over the rows of bone-handled levers, he raised the hanging weights and adjusted the sails with the expertise of someone who had *the touch*.

'Thirty-five degrees to starboard!' the captain barked.

The sky ship soared and around him its crew cheered and called out to one another. Rook felt a surge of exhilaration. The shouts and cries of the sky pirates rose, getting louder and louder and—

'Wake up!' came an insistent voice.

Rook stirred. The dream began to fade. No, he thought muzzily, he didn't want to be dragged away. He was enjoying it all too much – the sensation of flight, his sudden expertise with the flight-levers . . .

'Wake up, *all* of you!' the voice insisted.

Rook's eyes snapped open. The sky ship disappeared – yet the sound of its crew seemed louder than ever. He turned to Partifule, who was shaking the snoring Stob roughly by the shoulders. 'Wh-what's happening,' he murmured.

'It's a raid,' the nightwaif whispered back. 'A sky-pirate raid.'

Rook was on his feet at once. 'It is?' he said. He peered into the darkness. Sure enough, figures with flaming torches were shinning up ropes attached to grappling-irons and swarming onto the landing near the cages. 'But this is fantastic!' Rook gasped. 'They've come to rescue Deadbolt Vulpoon.'

'Fantastic for your friend Vulpoon if he does manage to escape,' Partifule said. 'Not so great for the rest of us if the shrykes go into one of their rage-frenzies. Like creatures possessed, they are, screeching, screaming,

107

spitting, slashing out at anything that moves . . . Rook!' he called out, as the youth hurried off. 'Come back!'

'I must help!' Rook called back.

'ROOK!' Magda shouted, as he disappeared into the shadowy and chaotic scene unfolding over by the hanging-cages.

Stob sat bolt upright, and looked round, bleary-eyed, startled. 'What? What?' he said.

'Oh, nothing,' said Magda. 'Nothing at all. Except we're in the middle of a sky-pirate raid. And the shrykes are about to go crazy. Oh, and Rook's decided he wants a better view.'

Stob jumped up from his pallet. 'Why didn't anyone wake me before?' he demanded.

Magda rolled her eyes impatiently.

'Never mind all that now,' said Partifule. 'We must get as far away from here as possible. *All* of us.' He stared back towards the cages, ears fluttering. 'I . . . I can hear Rook,' he said.

'Let's just go on without him,' said Stob. 'I can't think why an under-librarian was selected in the first place. Insolent, sloppy, disobedient—'

'Stob, be quiet,' Magda snapped. 'I'll go and get him.' And before anyone could stop her, she dashed off.

Unaware of the discord he was generating amongst his fellow-travellers, Rook darted ahead from shadow to shadow. All round him, the roaring sky pirates were homing in on the cage where Deadbolt Vulpoon was imprisoned. One had already shinned up the fluted column and had used a long pikestaff to jam the chain and stop it from swinging. A second, at the very top, acted as look-out. Meanwhile, two more sky pirates – one, a brawny giant with thick, matted hair and an eye-patch; the other (on his shoulders) an angular individual with steel-framed, half-moon glasses – were standing directly beneath the cage. All round them, a dozen or more pirates formed a protective circle, their weapons glinting in the intermittent moonlight like the horns of a phalanx of hammelhorns. The raid must have been well-planned.

Rook listened, spellbound, to the flood of muttered expletives as the bespectacled sky pirate picked at the lock of the cage door with the long, thin blade of his knife. All at once there was a click.

'At last!' he exclaimed, but his triumph was drowned out by the wail of a loud klaxon splitting the air, and the look-out's bellowed warning.

109

'Shrykes!'

The effect that single word had on the scene was both immediate and absolute. Bystanders and spectators on the landing turned away from the spectacle of the sky-pirate breakout, some taking cover, others dashing this way, that way, desperate to escape, yet terrified of running slap-bang into the oncoming shrykes – while those who had been trying to sleep through the raid, now picked up their bedding and fled for their lives.

Back on the road, the merchants and traders who had decided to journey through the night were suddenly thrown into turmoil. Those on foot scurried into the shadows and concealed themselves and their wares; those on wagons and carts shouted at their hammel-horns and prowlgrins, and the sound of cracking whips rose up above the klaxon wail and panicked screaming. There were crashes and collisions, cries of anger and groans of dismay as the carts keeled over and spilt their loads. And underneath it all, the rhythmic screeching of the shrykes advancing down the Great Mire Road towards the landing.

'Fifty strides and counting!' the look-out cried, then added, 'I'm getting out of here.'

Rook stood rooted to the spot. He watched, mouth open and eyes unblinking, as the cage door flew back and Deadbolt Vulpoon himself squeezed his body through the narrow opening and dropped heavily to the boards below. He was free, Rook realized, his heart fluttering. The old sky pirate was free!

All at once an anguished cry rang out. Louder than the

klaxon, louder than the crowd, louder even than the shrieking shrykes. 'Spatch!' roared the voice.

It was the huge sky pirate with the eye-patch. He crouched down beside the companion who, only a moment before, had been on his shoulders. Now he was dead. A single crossbow bolt had shattered one of the half-moons of his glasses and lodged itself behind his eye.

'Oh, Spatch, my friend,' he wailed. '*Spatch!*'

'Come, Logg.' It was the captain himself. He laid a hand on the sky pirate's shoulder. 'There is nothing more we can do for him. We must leave before the rest of us taste the shrykes' weapons.'

'I'm not leaving Spatch here,' came the belligerent reply as he hoisted the limp body up onto his massive shoulders. 'He deserves a proper burial, so he does.'

'As you wish,' said Vulpoon. He raised his head and looked round at the expectant sky pirates, all waiting for his command. 'What are you waiting for, you mangy mire-rats? Let's get out of here!'

As one, the sky pirates turned on their heels – only to find their escape route cut off. The shryke guards had surrounded the landing on all sides and were closing in. The sky pirates had no choice but to fight.

'Forget what I said!' Vulpoon roared. 'ATTACK!'

The air abruptly shook with an explosion of noise as the sky pirates and the shrykes fell on one another. The shrykes swung their bone-flails, and fought with beak and claw, crossbow and evil spiked scythes. The pirates battled back with cutlass and pike and baked mire-mud slingshots that hissed like angry hover worms as they cut through the air.

The fight was short and vicious.

A crossbow bolt whistled past Rook's ear. He came to his senses, wild excitement turning to cold, stomach-churning fear. He flung himself behind an upturned cart, its cargo of heavy stone jars strewn around it.

In front of him two sky pirates – one tall and thin, one short and portly – stood back to back, battling with two shrykes. The pirates' swords glinted and clanged. The shrykes' claws flashed, their beaks gnashed. It looked as if the sky pirates were tiring when – as if to some unspoken command – both of them lunged forwards. Their attackers were skewered simultaneously. The sky pirates withdrew their swords and turned to face a fresh onslaught.

There were dead shrykes everywhere, but those who fell were instantly replaced by more of the frenzied bird-creatures, answering the klaxon-call and streaming down the Great Mire Road.

'Take the balustrades!' Rook heard Vulpoon bellow, and looked round to see the sky pirate captain fighting off two shrykes at the same time. 'And *keep* them,' he grunted as first one, then the other shryke fell lifeless to the ground. 'We all leave together,' Vulpoon cried. 'When *I* give the word.'

Just then Rook saw the flash of crimson and yellow feathers as a tall, muscular shryke guard emerged from the shadows behind Vulpoon. She was wearing a gleaming breast-plate and a plumed helmet. A spiked scythe was raised above her head.

'Captain!' screamed Rook, leaping to his feet.

Just in time, the sky pirate captain dodged sharply to his left. The scythe struck the wooden boards and stuck fast. Vulpoon swung his heavy cutlass. With an ear-piercing screech, the shryke hawked and spat. A glistening boll of saliva flew through the air and splattered into his face. Crying out in disgust, Vulpoon staggered backwards in the direction of the cart.

Rook gasped with surprise. This was no ordinary shryke guard, he realized. With her bright plumage and her stature, she must be one of the elite Shryke Sisterhood.

'Deadbolt Vulpoon!' the shryke-sister screeched, as she advanced towards him in a hissing whirr of bared talons. 'The great Deadbolt Vulpoon! Let's see how great you are now!'

Vulpoon was dazed and half-blinded. The shryke-sister contemptuously knocked his sword away. Then, balancing on one clawed foot, she slashed at his arm with the other.

'I'll rip out your heart!' she shrieked. 'And devour it!'

There was blood seeping through the sleeve of Vulpoon's jacket and dripping down the hand which clasped his sword. The sky pirate slumped to his knees in front of the upturned cart.

It was all but over.

Vulpoon had no sword. The shryke – eyes blazing, unblinking – approached with her razor-sharp talons outstretched.

'Fool,' she shrieked. 'Did you truly believe we were

unaware of who you are? Did you? You, great captain, were the bait to lure them here.' She nodded back to the battle for the balustrade continuing behind them. 'With you dead, they'll give up, and I will have rid the Edge of you and your sky pirate scum once and for all.'

Vulpoon made no reply. He was utterly defenceless. The shryke-sister seemed to enjoy toying with him.

'No longer shall I be a mere shryke-sister,' she screamed. 'I shall return to the Eastern Roost victorious and claim my reward.' She paused. 'Mother Hinnytalon of the Eastern Roost. It has a nice ring to it, don't you think,' she said, and shrieked with raucous laughter. 'There is only one thing standing between me and my goal,' she added. Her gaze hardened and fixed itself on Vulpoon. She raised her claws, ready to strike. 'You.'

'Wrong!' Rook cried out as he sprang to his feet, a heavy pot clutched tightly in his shaking hands raised high above his head.

Looking up at the cart, the shryke was stunned into inaction for a split second – and that was all it took. With a grunt of effort, Rook brought the heavy pot crashing down onto the shryke's head. It smashed into the helmet and shattered, sending pieces flying through the air, and the shryke staggering backwards.

Vulpoon made a lunge for his sword. In one graceful movement he straightened up and swung it round in a low, rising sweep, beheading the creature with a single blow. The plumed helmet clattered to the ground, while the head it had once protected bounced across the landing, beak agape and eyes bulging with surprise.

Vulpoon turned. His jaw dropped. 'You,' he said. 'Again.'

Just then a second voice called out. 'Rook. Quickly!' It was Magda. 'Come on,' she said through clenched teeth. 'We must leave now.'

'That is the second time you have saved me,' Vulpoon said. 'What did you say your name was?

'Rook Barkwater, if it pleases you,' said Rook.

'It pleases me well, lad,' the sky pirate captain said. 'Rook Barkwater. I will never forget what you have done for me this night.' He nodded towards Magda. 'But your friend is right,' he said. 'You must leave now.'

'Captain,' roared a voice from behind him, and a swarthy individual grabbed at his arm. 'The balustrade is clear. Come quickly before more shryke reinforcements arrive.'

With the sky pirate pulling Vulpoon in one direction, and Magda dragging Rook away in the other, their gaze met for one last time.

'Fare you well, Rook Barkwater,' the captain called out.

'Goodbye, Captain,' Rook called back.

He and Magda hurried back to the sleeping stall to find Stob and Partifule sitting up on the driving seat of a sturdy hammelhorn-drawn cart.

'Where did you get that?' asked Magda.

'We found it abandoned,' said Stob. 'Lying on its side—'

'Just jump up,' Partifule shouted out urgently.

Magda and Rook leaped onto the back of the cart. Stob cracked the whip and the hammelhorn plodded off along the road as fast as it could, leaving the sky pirates and the shryke guards far behind them. The shuffling walkers on the road jostled and jumped out of their way, but the shrykes – hurrying to the landing where the battle still seemed to rage – paid them no heed.

As they rumbled on over the boards, the shouting grew distant and the klaxon-wail faded to nothing. Still they continued, driving on through darkness, mile after mile. Their pace slowed as they became snagged at the back of a convoy of heavy wagons. The darkest hour came and went. Soft strands of light threaded their way up from the horizon as the sun prepared to rise.

Rook's head spun. More had happened to him during that last day than would normally occur in an entire year. Yet they had made it. He turned to Magda and smiled. 'Do you think the worst is behind us?' he asked.

Stob glanced round. 'That shows how much you know, under-librarian,' he snarled unkindly. He turned back and nodded up ahead. 'Look.'

Rook climbed to his feet to get a better view. Although the sky was, for the most part, still swathed in impenetrable darkness, directly in front of them was a curious golden half-light, like the glow from a giant tilder-oil lamp.

'What is it?' asked Rook.

'Need you ask?' said Stob.

'We are approaching the Twilight Woods,' said Partifule, his voice hushed and reverent. 'Which, my young friends,' he continued, 'is the most treacherous and perilous place in all the Edge.'

·CHAPTER SEVEN·

THE TWILIGHT WOODS

The waif pulled gently at the reins, and the great lumbering hammelhorn snorted and came to a halt. It shook its shaggy head, with its immense curling horns, and waited patiently. Partifule got down from the wagon.

Rook sat up, suddenly wide awake, and looked around. The unfamiliar, eerie light bathed everything in a golden glow. A straggle of gnokgoblins pulling hand-carts clattered past, their heads down, their faces grim.

'Why have we stopped?' said Rook.

'Search me,' said Stob beside him, stifling a yawn.

'I must leave you now,' said Partifule.

Magda gasped. The waif turned to her, took her hand and gazed deeply into her eyes, listening to her thoughts. 'You will reach Lake Landing,' he said. 'Of that I am convinced. From the little time I have spent with you all, I have been impressed with your determination, your bravery –' he turned to Rook – 'your compassion.'

'And we with yours,' said Magda softly.

Partifule nodded and lowered his head. 'I have already come closer to the Twilight Woods than I like.' He looked up ahead at the line of trees, bathed in their alluring half-light, which signified the end of the Mire and the beginning of the treacherous woods. 'Even at this distance, the twilight glow fills my head with the strangest visions . . . and voices . . .' He shook his head. 'And for a waif, that is dangerous indeed.'

'Go, then,' said Magda. 'And thank you.'

'Yes, thank you, Partifule,' said Rook.

The pair of them turned to Stob. 'Thanks,' he muttered. Partifule nodded to each of them in turn. 'Ahead of you lies great danger. But you will not be alone. There is a guide waiting for you in the Eastern Roost. He is one of the greatest and bravest of us all. You will be in good hands, believe me.'

He turned away, tears welling in his dark eyes. His ears fluttered. 'Earth and Sky be with you,' he said softly. 'Farewell.'

As they approached the tally-hut, Rook could see the road ahead disappearing into the Twilight Woods. It shimmered and swayed, as if under water, before losing itself in the miasmic gloom beyond. Where it did so, Rook noticed that the very construction of the road seemed to alter.

It became narrow beyond the tally-hut, and the balustrades seemed to be closer together. They curved up like the bars of a cage. Above, there were two long cables – one on each side of the road – slung through great hanging hoops and snaking off into the distance.

The gnokgoblins emerged from the tally-hut with lengths of rope, which they threw over the cable-hooks above their heads. Then they attached both ends to their belts.

'Knot them firmly!' screeched a shryke guard, looking on. 'And keep moving, if you know what's good for you.'

Alone amongst the creatures of the Edge, shrykes were impervious to the effects of the treacherous forest. Their double eyelids ensured that its seductive visions had no power over them. It was this immunity which had enabled them to build the Great Mire Road, and now meant that any who crossed the Twilight Woods were dependent on the callous and unpredictable bird-creatures for safe passage.

'Next!' came the rasping voice of a tally-hen from the hut.

Rook, Stob and Magda got down from the cart and entered the hut. A large speckled tally-hen sat in the dimly lit interior behind an ornately carved lectern. She looked up.

'Three is it?' she squawked. 'That'll be nine gold pieces for the rope and three more for the cart. Hurry up, hurry up! Haven't got all day . . .'

Magda paid and the shryke handed them each a length of rope from a sack hanging from the side of the lectern, and a scrap of barkpaper with a symbol scrawled on it in brown ink.

'For the cart!' she snapped as Rook took it gingerly from her talons. 'Next!'

Outside, a shryke guard met them and snatched the barkpaper from Rook. She examined it with unblinking yellow eyes, handed it back and clicked her bone-flail. A second shryke appeared and climbed up into the driver's seat. With a vicious snap of the reins, she drove the hammelhorn on. The wagon clattered off along the timbered road and into the Twilight Woods in a cloud of glittering dust.

'Central Market, Holding Pens,' squawked the guard. 'It'll be waiting for you there.' She jerked her head to one side. 'Well, what are you waiting for?'

Magda stepped forward. She flung her rope up into the air and over the cable-hook. Stob and Rook followed suit. Rook flushed crimson as he fumbled with his leash-rope, making the knots round his belt as tight as possible.

'Tie them firmly!' commanded the guard. 'And keep moving.'

With a deep breath Rook plunged into the rippling twilight after the others. He felt the rope go taut and tug on him. Straining with exertion, he pushed on; the hook, rasping on the cable above, like a leadwood anchor-weight, pulling him back. Every movement was an effort. Every step, an achievement.

He struggled after the other two. Up ahead, the gnokgoblins laboured with their handcarts, their ropes swaying as they pulled at them. Behind him, Rook could see a small group of cloddertrogs milling round the tally-hut.

'Keep moving!' screeched the guard behind him. 'If one stops, you all stop! Any hold-ups and you'll be cut loose! Remember!'

Rook pressed resolutely on. Soon his lungs were on fire, his legs ached and he found himself gulping in the thick, humid air as fast as he could. His head was swimming, and everything swayed and swirled in front of his eyes. I can't keep going! he thought, fear churning in the pit of his stomach.

Behind him, the cloddertrogs panted and groaned. In front, Stob's back shimmered, sometimes close, sometimes impossibly far away. Then, just as Rook thought he was going to faint with exhaustion and be trampled on by the following cloddertrogs, the panic and fatigue suddenly seemed to disappear. He felt strength returning to his limbs. The rope seemed less like an anchor and more like a string holding a balloon. A sense of elation began to course through his body.

It was, Rook thought, like being immersed in a pool of warm, golden water which swirled round his body and made him feel oddly buoyant. It poured into his ears, his eyes, his nose, drowning out the grunts and groans of the cloddertrogs and turning the toasted-almond scented air to shimmering liquid. And when he went to speak, it filled his mouth with forgotten tastes of his earliest childhood, before the slave-takers had stolen his parents away – oak-flake rusks, smoky woodbee honey, delberry linctus . . .

There were voices too, calling from the shadowy depths. 'Come,' they called, their honeyed tones matching the thick, dappled light. 'Rook. *Rook!*'

Rook trembled. That voice, so familiar . . . He felt his throat aching with loss, with longing. 'Mother?' he said tremulously. 'Is that you?'

The woods swallowed up his words. Ahead of him, he was dimly aware of Stob waving his arms and laughing hysterically, and of Magda's great, gulping sobs. 'Keep moving,' he told himself. 'Keep moving.'

Rook tried to clear his mind, to ignore the voices and just look ahead – but the Twilight Woods seemed to have a hypnotic hold over him that he could not shake free.

He found himself looking into the endless expanse of golden forest. The trees, sparkling with a strange sepia dust, creaked and groaned with age as the soft, warm breeze stirred their branches. The air twisted and sighed. Something – or someone – flitted between the shadowy tree-trunks.

All at once a strange, spectral figure was emerging from the gloom. Rook stared with fascinated horror as it approached the road. Mounted on a prowlgrin, the apparition wore the tarnished antique armour of an ancient Knight Academic. It was as if an illustration in one of the library scrolls had come to life. The gauges and pipes, bolts and levers covering the rusting armour were all there; even in the twilight Rook could make

them out quite clearly. He reached out and tapped Stob on the shoulder.

'Do you see it?' Rook called. Stob kept on walking and made no reply. Rook hurried after him. 'A Knight Academic! Stob! Out there in the woods! He's getting closer!'

'Shut up and keep moving!' Stob growled back. 'Or a shryke guard will cut you loose. You heard what they said.'

'He's right, Rook,' Magda called back. Her voice was thick from crying. 'It'll soon be over if we just keep moving and don't lose our heads.'

Rook glanced back; the knight had vanished. He could hear muffled sighs and taunting whispers and, whichever way he looked, he caught sight of movement out of the corner of his eye – though when he tried to focus in on it, the movement ceased and he saw nothing.

Was anything real in the Twilight Woods? he wondered. Or was it inhabited solely by phantasms and ghosts – the spirits of those who had fallen victim to the seductive charms of the dimly lit forest?

Just then there was a loud *crash*. One of the gnok-goblins' handcarts had overturned, sending its cargo of metal pots clattering and clanging across the narrow road. The group came to a halt, twisting round on their leash-ropes as they attempted to right the cart and rescue its spilt contents. Soon they were all hopelessly tangled, and shouting at each other.

'Turn *this* way, Morkbuff!' wheezed their elderly leader. 'You, Pegg! Help him out . . . No, not like that!'

Magda, Stob and Rook came to a halt a few strides away. Behind them, the cloddertrogs approached.

'Keep moving!' they bellowed.

'We can't!' Rook called back. 'Or we'll get caught up with that lot.' He pointed at the tangle of goblins.

Another handcart crashed over.

'Somebody *do* something!' shouted Stob above the din.

'That's really helpful!' said Magda. 'What do you suggest?'

Around them, the Twilight Woods seemed to be listening. From the shadows, Rook was aware of movement. The Knight Academic reappeared.

'Look,' he whispered excitedly to the other two. 'He's back.'

They followed Rook's gaze.

'He's not the only one,' said Stob.

Sure enough, other figures were emerging from the shadowy gloom, as if drawn by the gnokgoblins' commotion. Rook shuddered. There were ragged, half-dead trogs, skeletal leaguesmen, several desperate-looking goblins, some with missing limbs and many bearing terrible wounds. They stood all round them; hollow-eyed, staring, silent.

The gnokgoblins saw the ghostly crowd they had attracted and fell still. The two groups watched each other in absolute silence; the living and the undead.

Despite the clammy heat, Rook felt icy sweat run over his face, into his eyes, down his back. 'This is a dreadful place,' he whispered.

Suddenly, there came the sound of furious screeching and squawking, and a squadron of shryke guards appeared through the gloom, glittering dust flying in their wake. Just as suddenly, the ghostly apparitions melted back into the woods.

'What's going on?' squawked the shrykes' leader, an imposing female with bright yellow plumage and a purple crest. 'Why is no-one moving?'

Everybody started talking at once.

'Silence!' roared the shryke, the feathers round her neck ruffling ominously. 'Twilight-crazy, the lot of you!' She turned to her second-in-command. 'Clear this featherless vermin off my road, Magclaw, and get the rest moving!'

'You heard what Sister Featherslash said!' rasped Magclaw, with a click of her bone-flail. 'Cut them loose! Now!'

The gnokgoblins began wailing, and Rook flinched as the shrykes began slashing at the snarled ropes with their razor-sharp scythes. The ropes fell to the ground.

The shrykes chased the weeping goblins into the woods.

'Get moving, the rest of you!' ordered Sister Featherslash. 'I'm sure you've all got important business in the beautiful Eastern Roost!' She cackled unpleasantly. 'If you ever get there.'

Magda, Stob and Rook set off quickly.

'I don't care what the Eastern Roost is like, it can't be worse than this,' said Magda. 'Can it?'

'Just keep moving,' said Stob. 'And try not to think about it.'

Rook looked back over his shoulder. In the eerie, dappled light, the elderly gnokgoblin was sitting on a tree-root, waving his arms and protesting loudly to thin air.

CHAPTER EIGHT

THE EASTERN ROOST

Out of the swirling twilight loomed a lufwood tree, so enormous that a gateway had been tunnelled through the middle of its vast trunk. It straddled the road, separating the Twilight Woods from the Eastern Roost beyond. High up, above the arched entrance, the cable to which the leash-ropes were attached came to an end.

Two shryke guards stood sentry, one on either side of the gateway. 'Untie your ropes!' one of them commanded harshly as Magda, Stob and Rook approached.

They quickly did as they were told. Already, the cloddertrogs were arriving behind them.

'Proceed by the Lower Levels to the Central Market!' barked the other guard. 'The upper roosts are for shrykes only.' Her yellow eyes glinted menacingly. 'You have been warned!'

Rook's head was beginning to clear as the strange,

penetrating atmosphere of the Twilight Woods released its grip. He squinted into the gloom beyond the Lufwood Gate.

The first thing that struck him was the smell. Beneath the roasting pinecoffee and sizzling tilder sausages, beneath the odours and scents, of leatherware, incense and the greasy smell of oil lamps, there was another smell. A rank and rancid smell. A smell that, as the wind stirred, grew more pungent, then less – but never faded completely.

Rook shivered.

'We're going to be fine,' Magda whispered, and squeezed his hand reassuringly. 'If we all stick together. We must head for the Central Market.'

Rook nodded. It wasn't only his sense of smell which had become so acute. After the sensory deprivation and confusion of the Twilight Woods, his senses were blazing. The air felt greasy, dirty. He could taste it in his mouth. His ears heard every screech, every squeal; every barked order and crack of the whip – every heartrending cry of despair. And as for his eyes . . .

'I've never seen anything like it,' Rook muttered, as they started along one of a series of walkways strung out between the trees, which led deeper and deeper into the thronging city.

Lights. Colour. Faces. Movement . . . Everywhere he looked, Rook was bombarded by a confusing mass of strange and disturbing sights. It was like a great patchwork quilt which, as he passed through it, threw up image after individual image.

A caged banderbear. A chained vulpoon. Tethered rotsuckers. Betting posts and gambling tables. Itinerants hawking lucky charms. A pair of shrykes, their flails clacking. Two more – one armed with a great studded club. An animated argument between a gnokgoblin and a cloddertrog. A lost woodtroll, screaming for its mother. Leather dealers, paper merchants, chandlers and coopers. Refreshment stalls selling snacks and beverages that Rook didn't even know existed. What was a wood-toad shake? Or a hot-bod? And what in Sky's name might gloamglozer tea taste of?

'It's this way,' he heard Stob saying, pointing up at a painted sign above their heads.

They descended three flights of rickety steps, zig-zagging downwards until they arrived at a bustling walkway in the trees. Burdened with its heavy load of merchants and marketeers, goblins, trogs and trolls streaming in both directions, the walkway dipped and bounced, creaking ominously as it swayed. Rook gripped the safety-rail anxiously.

'Don't look down,' Magda whispered, sensing Rook's nervousness.

But Rook couldn't help himself. He peered down into the depths below. Three levels beneath him, in the dark, acrid gloom, was the forest floor. It shimmered and writhed as if the earth itself were somehow alive. With a jolt, Rook realized that that was precisely what it was – for the forest floor was a living mass of tiny orange creatures.

'Wig-wigs,' he muttered uneasily.

Although he'd never seen one before, Rook had read about them in Varis Lodd's treatise on banderbears. They hunted in huge packs and could devour a creature as big as a banderbear in an instant – flesh, hair, bones, tusks; everything. Rook shuddered as it occurred to him that this vast city in the trees – the Eastern Roost – must provide an abundance of food for so many bloodthirsty scavengers to have congregated underneath. Giddy with forebod-ing, he gripped the rail tightly.

'Come on, knife-grinder,' said Stob nastily. 'We don't have time for sightseeing.'

He pushed Rook roughly in the back and strode off along the walkway. Magda and a trembling Rook followed.

As the Central Market drew closer, the walkway grew broader – though no less congested. It became louder than ever and, with all the constant coming and going and general milling about, the three librarian apprentices were hard pushed to fight their way through.

'Stick together,' Stob called back as he reached the narrow entrance to the market.

'Easier said than done,' Magda grumbled, as the surging crowd threatened to separate them.' Hold my hand, Stob,' she said. 'And you, too, Rook.'

With Stob in front, the three of them forged onwards. The gateway came closer. They were shuffling now, with bodies all round them, pressing in tightly. Through the archway and . . . inside.

Rook took a deep breath as the crowd released its grip. He looked round at the others and smiled. They had made it to the Central Market.

Built on a platform which was supported by a scaffolding of trees, sawn off where they stood, the Central Market was open to the elements. The starry canopy looked almost close enough to touch as the stars shimmered in the heat thrown off by the braziers and spits.

THE CENTRAL MARKET OF THE EASTERN ROOST

Rook took out the scrap of barkpaper the shryke had given them and examined it.

'Now what?' said Stob, looking around.

'We find the cart,' said Magda, and then . . .'

'Yes?' said Stob meanly.

'One thing at a time,' said Magda, frowning and looking around. 'Over there, I think.'

They made their way across the bustling Central Market. There was everything there, and more – stuffed, pickled, roasted and tanned; woven, gilded and carved. They passed slaughterers with their hammelhorn enclosures and overflowing displays of leatherwear; woodtrolls at their timber stalls and goblin tinkers and ironmongers, all bargaining, bartering and hawking their wares. And as they got close to the Holding Pens, they became aware also of the constant flow of shryke-driven carts and heavy wagons arriving from the Twilight Woods. The drivers waved flaming torches to ward off the wig-wigs before climbing the swaying ramp that snaked up to the Central Market platform where the wagon owners waited anxiously by the stalls.

Rook stared in amazement at the sprawling Holding Pens before him. The atmosphere was urgent – and smelly. A vast sea of carts and wagons, and pack-animals tugging on their leashes, guarded by burly, sullen shrykes, was waiting to be reclaimed. The air resounded with discordant cries and voices raised in protest.

'But half my cargo has been stolen!' shouted a gnokgoblin.

'I've lost two hammelhorns!' a cloddertrog complained.

'Shryke tax!' laughed one of the guards. 'Perhaps you'd like to take your wagon through the Twilight Woods yourself next time? No? Didn't think so!' She cackled unpleasantly.

'Typical shryke robbery,' moaned a goblin as he barged past Rook. 'Just 'cause they're not affected by the Twilight Woods, they think they can rob us blind!'

Magda matched a sign above one of the pens with the scrawl on the barkpaper. 'Here!' she shouted excitedly to the other two. 'Over here!'

Stob and Rook joined her as she presented the paper to a scruffy, bored-looking shryke leaning against a fencepost.

'Over there,' said the shryke, waving a talon.

In the corner of the pen was a small, broken-down cart with a thin, ill-looking prowlgrin in harness.

'But that's not our cart,' Magda protested. 'Ours was a four-seater, pulled by a hammelhorn . . .'

'Take it or leave it,' sneered the shryke. She yawned and inspected her talons.

'They'll take it, mistress. A thousand thank-yous,' came a squeaky voice. A small, tatty shryke-mate stepped forward and took Magda by the arm.

'But—' said Magda.

'No *buts*, my child,' squeaked the shryke-mate. 'We have urgent business, and we mustn't take up any more of the generous mistress's valuable time.'

He bowed low to the shryke guard and ushered

Magda away. The other two followed.

'What's the big idea?' said Stob, grabbing the shryke-mate's puny wing and pulling the grasping talons from Magda's arm.

The shryke-mate cringed. 'A thousand apologies,' he whispered. 'But we can't speak here. It's too dangerous. Follow me.'

He reached inside his filthy tunic and flashed a bloodoak-tooth pendant at Stob, before turning and hurrying into the crowd.

'Wait for us!' said Stob. 'Come on, you two. Stop dithering! You heard what the shryke said.'

Magda and Rook exchanged quizzical glances before following Stob as he pushed through the crowd after the small, scruffy figure of the shryke-mate.

They caught up with him by a stall in the slaughterers area. Everything – from tooled amulets, breast-plates and leather gauntlets, to great hanging carcasses of hammelhorn, woodhog and tilder – was on offer. Stob stood at the middle of it all, scratching his head and looking round.

'He was here one second and gone the next,' he muttered angrily. 'Hey, you there!' he said, turning to a short, flame-haired slaughterer who was laying out smoked tilder hams on a nearby table. 'Did you see him? A mangy little shryke-mate . . .'

The slaughterer turned his back on Stob and looked right and left furtively.

'I said—' Stob's voice was raised in anger.

'I heard what you said,' the slaughterer replied softly,

without turning. 'You'll find Hekkle round the back, behind the curtain. And don't let appearances deceive you.'

Stob pushed rudely past the slaughterer and pulled aside the leather curtain at the back of the stall to reveal a small concealed chamber behind. Magda and Rook went with him.

'Thank you,' whispered Rook as they passed the slaughterer.

'Good luck,' came the gruff reply.

Sitting by a small lufwood stove on a tilderskin rug, was the shryke-mate. As the curtain fell back into place, the flames of the burning lufwood bathed everything in a soft purple glow.

'Please, my brave and intrepid friends,' said the shryke, 'be seated. We must hurry, for every moment you spend here in the Eastern Roost your lives are in danger.'

'Well, this place of yours looks nice and cosy,' said Stob, casually reaching out to stroke a hammelhornskin wall-hanging. As his fingers touched the fur, it instantly bristled, becoming as sharp as needles to the touch. 'Ouch!' he cried out in alarm.

'Don't be fooled,' said the shryke. 'There are shryke guards all around us, and they raid the lower roosts constantly, on the look-out for contraband or...' He hesitated. 'Spies.'

Rook gulped. Was that what they were to these terrifying feathered creatures? He remembered the terrible cages on the Mire road and suddenly felt very weak.

'Are you the guide we were told would meet us?' asked Magda.

Stob, sucking his finger, looked at the shryke-mate with open contempt.

'Indeed I am, most merciful mistress, indeed I am,' trilled the shryke-mate. 'My name is Hekkle, and you do me a thousand honours to allow me to serve you.'

'Yes, yes,' said Stob. 'But if we're in danger, why are we standing around here?'

'Patience, brave master,' said Hekkle, rummaging in a large trunk in the corner, 'and I will explain everything.'

Rook dropped to his knees. His head felt strangely light, and the lufwood glow was making him sleepy.

'The Eastern Roost is a closed city, my brave friends,' said Hekkle, pulling a bundle of dark robes from the trunk and laying them out. 'For visitors, there is only one way in and one way out and that, as you have seen, is by the eastern Lufwood Gate. The Undertown merchants – such as you pretend to be – arrive, sell their wares and return on the Great Mire Road back to Undertown, bearing the goods from the Deepwoods they have bought in the Central Market.'

'So, how do we get out of this accursed city and into the Deepwoods?' asked Stob impatiently.

'Only shrykes may leave or enter the Eastern Roost on the Deepwoods side of the city,' Hekkle continued. 'That way, merciful master, the Shryke Sisterhood controls all the trade between Undertown and the Deepwoods settlements. It's beautifully simple. The shrykes buy goods from the Deepwoods and bring them into the Roost, where they trade them for Undertown goods, which they use to buy more Deepwoods goods – thus making a profit from Undertowners and Deepwooders alike. That is why there is no way through the Eastern Roost for anyone who isn't a shryke.'

'So, you're saying we're trapped here?' said Magda, a hint of panic in her voice. 'That the only way out is back to Undertown the way we came?'

'No, not quite, merciful mistress,' said Hekkle, returning to the trunk.

'Then how *do* we get out of the Roost and into the Deepwoods?' Stob persisted.

'Simple,' said Hekkle, turning round. 'If only shrykes are permitted to leave by the western Deepwoods Gate, then you shall become shrykes!'

He held up three crude feathered masks, each with a curved, serrated beak and black staring eye-sockets.

'You can't be serious,' scoffed Stob. 'It'll never work!'

'Oh, but it has before,' said Hekkle, his voice suddenly serious and with a brittle, harsh edge to it. 'And it will again.' Looking at the three earnest faces in front of him, he suddenly laughed. 'You, my fine brave friends, will be sooth-sisters – the venerated priestesses of the Golden Nest. Here are your robes.' He held up the heavy black garments, plain and drab compared to the gaudy costumes most shrykes loved. 'And here are your masks.' He handed them each a feathered head-dress. 'Hurry now. Time is short.'

They put Hekkle's costumes on over their merchants' clothes, fastening up the robes at the front and securing the masks on their heads. Hekkle slipped out of the room, returning a moment later with a burnished milk-wood mirror.

Rook turned and looked at himself. In the heavy robes and ornate mask he looked the part – but for one thing. 'But, Hekkle,' he began, his voice muffled beneath the beaked mask. 'The eyes. Surely our eyes will give us away. I mean, look. They're not yellow, or fierce-looking, or—'

'Silly me, oh merciful master,' laughed Hekkle. 'I was forgetting. Here, take these. No self-respecting sooth-sister would dream of appearing in public without them.'

He handed Rook a pair of spectacles with thick, black lenses. Rook put them on over his mask with difficulty, and clipped the nose-piece onto the false beak.

'But I can't see a thing!' he protested. 'Of course not,' chuckled Hekkle indulgently. 'Sooth-sisters only permit themselves to look upon the clutch of eggs in the Golden Nest, laid by the Roost Mother herself. The rest of the time, they wear spectacles of coal-glass to blot out impure sights.'

'But if we can't see—' began Rook.

'That's what *I'm* here for,' said Hekkle, bowing low. 'I shall be your guide. All sooth-sisters have them – at the end of a golden chain. But I must warn you.' Hekkle was suddenly solemn again, the harsh edge back in his voice. 'On no account are you to remove the spectacles. Just keep silent, and trust me. For if we are caught, the penalty for impersonating a shryke – and a sooth-sister at that – is terrible indeed, brave friends.'

'What is it?' Stob asked, trying to hide the nervousness in his voice.

'Roasting,' said Hekkle simply. 'Roasting alive, on a spit in the Central Market. Now, let's go.'

When Rook thought back to the ensuing journey to the Deepwoods Gate of the Eastern Roost, he could scarcely believe he had survived the terrifying experience. The sound of his own breathing inside the mask, the inky blackness of the coal-glass spectacles and the noises of the upper roosts – unfamiliar, and all the more sinister for that – haunted him in dreams for months afterwards.

They were climbing, climbing, constantly climbing. Even inside the mask, Rook sensed the air becoming fresher the higher they went. The cacophony of the lower roosts receded, to be replaced with the strange disturbing calls of the shrykes promenading along the upper walkways. There were coos, shrieks, and odd staccato throat-throbbings which built up to a sudden hooting scream.

'Steady,' whispered Hekkle, leading them on the end of his golden chain, like a tame lemkin. 'The sisters are just singing to one another. Nothing to worry about.'

But the sounds made Rook's blood run cold. How long had they been walking? In his growing panic it seemed like hours – although it could only have been minutes; half an hour at the most. He wanted to ask Hekkle, but he knew that it would be madness to utter so much as a single word. Behind him, Stob trod on the backs of his heels, and Rook bit his lip hard.

'Steady, your gracious holinesses,' cooed Hekkle, then, in a louder voice, 'Make way for the sooth-sisters! Make way!'

Rook was aware of the clattering of claws on the wooden walkway as respectful shryke-matrons moved aside.

'Give our blessings to the Golden Nest,' came a harsh shryke voice.

'May the egg-clutch prosper, sisters,' came another.

'Fruitful hatching!'

The calls sounded all round them. Rook's heart was thumping like a hammer. He battled to control his churning stomach and the panic rising in his throat.

'The sooth-sisters bless you,' called Hekkle in his sing-song voice. 'The sooth-sisters bless you.' He whispered urgently out of the side of his beak, 'We're nearly there. Keep together. One more walkway and we'll be at the prowlgrin corral beside the Deepwoods Gate.'

Stob stepped on the back of Rook's heel again. Rook stumbled heavily, the jolt almost dislodging his heavy coal-black spectacles. He screwed up his left eye as daylight flooded through a gap that had opened up between the mask and the lens. He felt the spectacles wobble on the beak.

'Careful, sister!' came a piercing voice.

Out of the corner of his eye Rook glimpsed a tall, imposing shryke-matron bedecked in finery, sitting on a raised bench and flanked on either side by smaller, but no less gaudy, companions. He was suddenly aware of a familiar overpowering stench. The shryke-matron's plumage ruffled and she let out a contented squawk as an acrid white shryke-dropping fell through the hole beneath her and down onto the lower roosts below.

'That's better,' she said, turning to her companion. 'Now, you were saying, Talonclaw . . .'

'Oh, yes,' said the shryke next to her, also letting a

sour-smelling spurt of droppings go. 'The sky pirate cut off her head with one blow. Leastways, that's what I heard.'

'Come now, sisters.' Hekkle's voice had that hard edge back in it. He pulled at Rook's robes. 'We must get to the prowlgrin corrals. We have nesting materials to gather in the Deepwoods, remember.'

Rook forced himself to put one foot in front of the other. He hunched his shoulders, convinced that the piercing yellow eyes of the shryke-matron seated on the ornate latrine would unmask him at any moment.

'Wait!' The matron's raucous cry rang out.

Rook froze. The spectacles rattled on the bridge of his beak. The matron rose from her seat and adjusted her skirts. Rook scarcely dared breathe. Behind him, the other two were rooted to the spot. The matron approached and Rook shut his eyes tight.

'May blessings attend your nest-building,' said the shryke-matron and bowed. Rook inclined his head gingerly in response, praying the spectacles would stay in place. The matron turned and her talons clicked on the wooden boards as she and her companions walked away.

'Quickly now.' Hekkle's voice sounded urgently in his ear. 'Before they return!'

They hurried on in a nightmare of tension and uncertainty, Rook catching glimpses of evil shryke faces as they made their way to the Deepwoods Gate, all the time in terror of his spectacles falling from his mask. The acrid smell of shryke droppings gave way to the warm, musty smell of prowlgrins. Rook could hear their soft, throaty purrs as they neared the corrals. It sounded strangely reassuring.

Hekkle guided them down a gangplank, and Rook could feel the heat given off by the roosting prowlgrins. He peered out of the side of his spectacles. The creatures were all round them, perching on broad branches and looking down on the newcomers with their sad, doleful eyes. Hekkle reached up and untied one of them. He passed the tether to Magda.

'Climb up,' he said. 'And take the reins. She won't move until you kick her.'

With Hekkle's help, Magda tentatively pulled herself up onto the prowlgrin's back, taking care not to let the shryke-mask slip. She reached round the harness for the reins and gripped them tightly. On either side, Rook and Stob did the same. Finally, Hekkle jumped up onto his own prowlgrin and pulled the great beast round.

'Kick!' he cried.

All four of them jabbed their heels into the prowl-grins' sides. The prowlgrins moved off, thrusting away from the broad perch with their hind-legs and clinging onto the one ahead with their fore-claws. Following the lead of Hekkle's prowlgrin, they clambered down onto a walkway. Rook glimpsed a large gateway up ahead.

'We're approaching the guard tower,' said Hekkle, reining in his prowlgrin. The others did the same. All four prowlgrins slowed to a sedate lope, placing their fore-paws down and swinging their hind-legs forward.

At the end of the long walkway, the guard tower came closer.

'What are we going to do?' said Magda.

'Nothing,' said Hekkle. 'Remember, you are sooth-sisters. You do not need to talk to mere guards. I shall speak for you.'

As they reached the guard tower, a tawny shryke with a rusty lance stepped forwards. Hekkle approached her. Rook, Magda and Stob stood apart and aloof, their heads raised imperiously, blind behind their spectacles.

'You heard me,' Rook heard Hekkle saying sternly a moment later. 'We seek nesting materials for the Golden Nest.' His voice dropped. 'Do you *dare* to stand in the sooth-sisters' way?'

'No, no,' the shryke guard said. 'Pass through.' She put her lance to her side, clicked her heels and bowed her head. Hekkle led his prowlgrin past. The others – keeping as rigid as possible as their prowlgrins lurched – followed close behind. Rook held his breath. He could only pray that the guard would neither see behind the spectacles nor hear the noisy hammering of his heart.

Step by faltering step, they left the Eastern Roost and entered the Deepwoods. The moment the last of them had crossed the boundary separating the two, Hekkle kicked his prowlgrin into action. The others followed suit, and all four of them hurtled off into the great forest, leaping from branch to branch.

'*Wahoo!*' Rook screeched, with a mixture of elation and relief. '*Waahoooo!*'

Hekkle laughed. 'Well done, brave friends,' he said. 'You have done well.'

'You are a brave guide,' said Rook. He glanced back over his shoulder. The guard tower had disappeared from view. 'We made it!' he gasped, and he tore off his shryke-mask, glasses and heavy robes and tossed them to the air.

Magda did the same. 'At last,' she sighed, tears of relief welling up in her eyes.

Stob pulled off his own mask and held it before him. 'I think I made a pretty convincing sooth-sister,' he said. 'Even if I do say so myself— *Whoooah!*' he cried out as his prowlgrin stumbled, and he almost lost his grip.

He gripped the reins tightly with both hands. The shryke-mask slipped from his fingers and bounced through the branches, down to the forest floor below. He noticed the others staring at him. 'What?' he said. '*What?*'

Back at the guard tower the shryke guard was receiving a second visitor, a callow youth with a dark stubble covering his scalp sitting astride a prowlgrin.

He had pulled back his hood and thrust a pass under the guard's beak.

'See here,' he said quietly. 'The gloamglozer seal of the Most High Guardian of Night. And here. The thumbprint of Vox Verlix. And here, the crossed-feather stamp of the Shryke Sisterhood. I trust that is authority enough for you. Well, is it?'

'Yes, sir. Sorry, sir,' the guard said, scraping her feet furiously. It was not proving to be her day. 'What was it you wanted to know?'

Xanth ran his fingertips lightly over his shaven skull. 'I asked whether any had recently passed this way?'

'Three sooth-sisters, sir,' said the guard, 'and an accompanying shryke-mate.'

'*Mm-hmm*,' said the youth. 'And did they say where they were bound?'

'On a nesting expedition,' said the guard promptly.

Xanth snorted. 'An expedition to the Free Glades more like,' he said.

The guard cocked her head in puzzlement. 'But shrykes don't go to the Free Glades,' she said.

'Precisely,' said Xanth. He turned away and tugged at the reins. The prowlgrin grunted, sniffed the air and was off, leaping from branch to branch.

Xanth held on tightly. He didn't look back.

·CHAPTER NINE·

THE DEEPWOODS

The four riders rode on hard into the Deepwoods, leaving the Eastern Roost far behind them. With the wind in their hair and their stomachs in their mouths, Stob, Magda and Rook clung desperately onto the reins as their prowlgrins – sure-footed, yet breathtakingly swift – hurtled on from branch to branch through the trees. For more than an hour they continued like this, neither pausing for breath nor descending to the forest floor. It was late afternoon by the time Hekkle finally signalled that he considered it safe to leave the trees.

'Are you sure?' Stob called back uneasily. 'What about the wig-wigs?'

'They seldom stray this far from the roosts,' Hekkle reassured him. 'Besides, you must be getting tired. It's much easier riding on the ground.'

Neither Magda nor Rook needed telling twice. The lurching, jolting ride had left the pair of them exhausted.

With a sharp kick and a downward tug on the reins, they began the long descent to the forest floor below. Hekkle followed them. Seeing that no harm had befallen his companions, and not wishing to be left behind, Stob came down close behind him.

Rook soon got into the rhythm of moving with his prowlgrin as it loped steadily forwards. 'I can hardly believe it,' he called across to Magda. 'All those long years spent down under the ground. You know, I must have dreamed about the Deepwoods almost every single night. And now, here I am.' He sighed. 'It's even more wonderful than I imagined.'

Massive, ancient trees rose up out of the forest floor like great pillars. Some were ridged, some were fluted, some were covered in great bulbous lumps and nodules – all of them were tall, reaching up through the green, shadowy air to find light above the dense canopy of leaves. Occasionally, the trees would thin out, allowing dazzling shafts of sunlight to slice down through the air and encouraging shrubs and bushes to grow below. There were combbushes humming in the soft breeze, clamshrubs snapping their shell-like flowers, and hairy-ivy, spiralling up round the thick tree-trunks and glittering like tinsel. And, as they pounded on, Rook saw the alluring turquoise glow of a lullabee glade far to his left.

'It's all so beautiful!' he cried out.

'. . . so beautiful!' his echo cried back.

There was a feverish rustling in a nearby bush and Rook caught a glimpse of something moving out of the

corner of his eye. He looked round to
see a small furry creature with deep
blue fur and wide, startled eyes
bounding across the leafy forest floor
to a tall lufwood tree, and scurrying
up into its branches.

'A wild lemkin!' said Magda. 'Oh,
how sweet.'

Oakbells and tinkleberries filled the air with soft,
jangling music. A scentball fungus exploded, sending its
spores flying and filling the air with a sweet, flowery
perfume. A flock of cheepwits flew up into the air in a
loud explosion of flapping, and fluttered away.

'Wonderful!' bellowed Rook. 'It's all *wonderful*!'

'. . . *wonderful* . . . *derful* . . . *ful* . . .'

'Yes, wonderful, brave master,' came Hekkle's voice
by his side. 'But the Deepwoods is also treacherous.
More treacherous than you could believe. It is unwise to
draw attention to ourselves. We must travel discreetly,
silently, and remain vigilant at all times . . .'

Rook nodded absent-mindedly. They were passing
through a dappled glade of smaller trees – dewdrop
trees, their pearl-like leaves glistening in the yellowing
sunlight; weeping-willoaks and brackenpines. And
there, scurrying across the ground before him, a comical
family of weezits in a long line, largest at the front down
to smallest at the back, each one clutching the tail of the
one in front in its mouth.

'. . . And never become separated from the others,' he
heard Hekkle saying. Rook looked round. 'On no

account are you ever to wander off on your own, do you understand?'

'Yes,' said Rook. 'Yes, I do.'

Hekkle shook his head. 'I hope for your sake, brave master, that you truly do.' He reined in his prowlgrin and stopped beside an aged and ailing tree with sparse foliage, crumbling bark and the scars of many storms and lightning bolts. 'Hold my prowlgrin steady,' he told Rook.

Rook did so. Magda and Stob caught up, and the three of them watched Hekkle remove his backpack, climb onto the prowlgrin's back and reach up towards a rotten knot-hole high up on the trunk. He dangled a single talon down inside.

No-one spoke. No-one moved. Throughout their journey through the Deepwoods, Hekkle had stopped innumerable times just like this, and they had learned not to disturb him.

Sometimes he had stopped by fallen logs and broken branches and, having listened intently – head cocked and feathers quivering – had torn into the bark to reveal plump, pale grubs wriggling beneath. Once he had paused and scraped at the leaves beneath his feet – and discovered a nestful of squirming red worms. Another time he had thrust his beak into the soft, powdery wood of a rotting lullabee tree, and emerged with a fat caterpillar skewered on the end. Each new addition had ended up with the others in Hekkle's forage sack.

Stob leaned forwards. 'What's he doing now?' he whispered into Magda's ear.

Magda shrugged.

Since taking up his position on the prowlgrin's back, Hekkle had remained completely still – apart from the one talon. *Scritch scritch scritch.* The needle-sharp point of the claw scraped lightly at the swollen bark around the edge of the hole. *Scritch scritch scritch.*

Stob shook his head impatiently. Rook craned his neck to see better.

Scritch scritch . . .

All at once there was a loud scrabbling sound from inside the tree, a flash of pale orange from the entrance to the hole and Rook gasped as a set of vicious, glinting mandibles snapped shut around the curving talon. Hekkle did not flinch. Rook held the prowlgrin harness tight and watched intently as the shryke-mate slowly and smoothly drew his hooked talon away from the hole.

The creature came with it. It was sleek, with varnished armour, and multi-segmented like a string of mire-pearls. A pair of delicate white legs waved from each segment. Suddenly, perhaps sensing that it was exposed and wishing to return to the darkness, the creature squirmed and released its hold. But Hekkle was too quick for it. Stabbing into the hole with its beak it dragged the entire creature out – all stride and a half of it – and shook it until it fell still. Then, jumping down and loosening the drawstring to his forage sack, he dropped it in on top of the rest.

'A skewbald thousandfoot,' said Hekkle. 'Delicious . . .'

'Delicious?' said Stob. 'You mean you *eat* them?'

'Of course, brave master,' said Hekkle. 'The forest is full of food. It's just a matter of knowing where to look.'

Rook blanched. He'd assumed that Hekkle was simply collecting interesting specimens, perhaps to sell to the scholars in the Free Glades. 'Are you intending to *eat* all the stuff you've collected in that sack?' he asked.

'Of course, brave master,' said Hekkle and chuckled throatily. He swung the backpack over his shoulders and mounted his prowlgrin. 'The sun's getting low,' he said. 'We must make camp before darkness falls. Stay close, and keep your eyes peeled. We need to find a specially sturdy tree to rest up for the night. Then we can see about that meal.'

'I can't wait,' muttered Rook weakly.

'You first,' said Stob meanly, thrusting the skewer with the gimpelgrub on it into Rook's face.

Rook shuddered queasily. He was sure he'd just seen it wriggle.

'He doesn't have to if he doesn't want to,' said Magda.

'Oh, but I'm so hungry!'

'Eat!' chuckled Hekkle. 'Eat! I prefer them raw, but they're equally good cooked. Go on, it won't bite!'

'I'm not so sure,' said Rook, holding up the bright red fleshy grub. He closed his eyes, opened his mouth and bit down hard . . .

'I never thought I'd say it,' Rook said, 'but that was delicious.'

'Even the thousandfoot?' said Hekkle.

'*Especially* the thousandfoot,' said Rook, licking his fingers. 'In fact, is there any more?'

Hekkle poked about inside the hanging-stove. 'No,' he said at last. 'It's all gone. *Everything's* gone.'

'Pity,' said Rook and Stob together, and laughed.

They'd come across the tree just as the last rays of the sinking sun were being extinguished from the forest floor. It was a huge, spreading leadwood, with a gnarled grey trunk and broad, horizontal branches. As the prowlgrins had carried them up into the tree – leaping and grasping, leaping and grasping – so the sun had reappeared, treacly yellow and comfortingly warm.

High up in the tree, they had dismounted and Hekkle had tethered the prowlgrins to the stout branch they were perching on. Having travelled all day, the weary creatures were soon asleep. Hekkle had led the others up to the broad branches above the roosting prowlgrins and given the three young librarians the tasks which, as they journeyed further, were to become a daily routine.

Magda and Rook collected kindling and logs. Hekkle secured the hanging metal stove he had been carrying on his back to an overhanging branch. Stob tied up their three hammocks. Then, when they returned, Rook laid a fire inside the round stove, which Magda lit, using her sky-crystals. Meanwhile, Hekkle prepared the contents of his forage sack for cooking – washing, slicing, spicing and finally, when the fire was hot enough, placing them

on skewers which he slid into the glowing stove.

The flames had died down now, and the embers of the various pieces of wood that Rook and Magda had collected flickered with colour – now red, now purple, now turquoise – and gave off both sweet aromatic smells and the sound of soothing lullabies.

Magda yawned. 'I'm going to sleep well tonight,' she said.

'It's time you all got some sleep,' said Hekkle. 'Get into your hammocks, brave masters and mistress. I shall roost in the branches above your heads and sleep with one eye open. We shall be making an early start in the morning.'

Stob, Magda and Rook pulled themselves up and laid their weary bodies down in the swinging hammocks. The heat from the glowing stove warmed the chill air.

'Haven't you forgotten something?' Hekkle said, as he looked down from his perch. 'The Covers of Darkness will keep you safe from prying eyes.'

As one, the three librarian knights elect remembered the gift they had received from the Professor of Darkness. They sat up and untied the scarves from around their necks. Rook watched Stob and Magda unfold the flimsy material, wrap it around themselves and their hammocks – and disappear. With fumbling fingers, he opened up his own scarf. The nightspider-silk was as soft and fine as gossamer, and almost weightless. As he went to drape it over himself, the wind caught it, making it dance in the air like a shadow.

'Secure it to the rope by your head,' Hekkle instructed him. 'That's it.'

Rook lay back in the soft hammock, arms behind his head and looked upwards. Though concealing him totally, the cover was see-through, and Rook stared up into the canopy of angular leaves far above his head, silhouetted against the milky moonlit sky beyond. All round him, curious sounds filled the air. The screech of woodowls and razorflits. The coughing of fromps and squealing of quarms. And far, far away in the distance, the sound of a banderbear yodelling to another. Feeling warm, safe and secure, Rook smiled happily. 'I know that Hekkle said the forest can be treacherous,' he said quietly, 'but to me the Deepwoods still seems a wonderful, magical place . . .'

'Particularly after the horrors of the terrible Eastern Roost,' said Magda drowsily.

'Just think,' said Rook. 'One day, when we've completed our studies and set out on our treatise-voyages, we'll fly over these woods.'

Magda stifled a tired yawn. 'I'm thinking of looking at the life-cycle of the woodmoth,' she murmured.

'Woodmoths?' said Rook. 'I'm going to study banderbears.' The curious yodelling sound repeated, fainter and farther away. 'I can't wait . . .'

'Go to sleep,' said Stob.

'Well said, Master Stob,' said Hekkle. 'We've got a long day ahead of us.' He fluffed up his feathers against the rising wind. 'Goodnight, brave masters, goodnight brave mistress,' he said. 'And sleep well.'

'Night-night,' came Stob's sleepy voice.

'Goodnight, Hekkle,' said Rook.

Magda, already half-asleep, muttered softly and rolled over.

Six days they travelled – six long, arduous days of hard riding. After the initial thrill of being inside the dark, mysterious forest, even Rook's enthusiasm was beginning to wane. The going was tough and, when it rained at night, they climbed out of their hammocks the following morning feeling more tired and achy than when they had turned in. But with their destination still far off, they had no choice but to continue, no matter how weary they felt.

Hekkle urged them on as best he could, encouraging and reassuring them, producing delicious food night after night and praising the contributions they were beginning to make to the forage sack. But the un-remitting pressure of the long, difficult journey through the Deepwoods was taking its toll. Stob and Magda bickered constantly, while Rook's sleep was increasingly troubled.

On that sixth evening, as they tucked into their supper of grubs and fungus, the atmosphere was oppressive. Stob was in a foul mood, Magda was tearful, while Rook – who had drifted off to sleep and fallen from his prowl-grin earlier that day – was nursing a badly bruised knee.

'Any more for any more?' said Hekkle, offering round a tray of toasted ironwood bugs. The young librarians all declined. Hekkle looked at them fondly. 'You are doing so well,' he said.

Stob snorted.

'Believe me,' said Hekkle. 'I have never guided a more determined and courageous group through the Deepwoods than your good selves. Our progress has been phenomenal.' He clacked his beak. 'So much so that you'll be pleased to know our journey is coming to its end.'

'It is?' said Rook eagerly.

Hekkle nodded. 'We are getting close to the Silver Pastures,' he confirmed. His face grew serious and the familiar harsh tone to his voice returned. 'But I must tell you that this is the most perilous part of our expedition.'

Magda sniffed miserably.

'Naturally,' muttered Stob sullenly.

'This area attracts the most dangerous of creatures,' Hekkle went on. 'The pastures – and indeed the densely populated Free Glades beyond – offer rich pickings. From sun-up tomorrow, we must be extra vigilant. But fear not. We shall not fail – not having come so far.'

That night Rook slept worse than ever. Every squawk, every screech, every whispered breath of wind permeated his fitful sleep and turned his dreams to nightmares – to *the* nightmare.

'Mother! Father!' he cried out, but his voice was whisked away unheard as the slave-takers carried them both off. The whitecollar wolves snarled and howled. The slavers cackled. Rook turned away, trying to shut out the horrors of what had just taken place, when . . .

'No!' he screamed.

There it was again. Looming out of the darkness; something huge, something terrifying. Reaching towards him. Closer, closer . . .

'NO!' he screamed.

Rook's eyes snapped open. He sat bolt upright.

'It's all right, brave master,' came Hekkle's voice. The shryke was perched above the hammock, looking down at the youth sympathetically.

'H-Hekkle,' said Rook. 'Did I wake you?'

'No, brave master,' said Hekkle. 'Stob's snoring woke me hours ago.' He smiled kindly. 'Get up and get ready,' he said. 'The end is almost in sight.'

Despite Hekkle's words, the atmosphere that morning remained tense. They packed up quickly and in silence, and set off before the sun had risen high enough to strike the forest floor. On they travelled, through the morning and into the afternoon without once stopping.

'What about the forage sack?' asked Rook.

Hekkle smiled. 'Tonight you will feast on something grander,' he said. 'Hammelhorn, perhaps. Or if you're lucky, oakbuck.'

Rook peered ahead into the shadows and shook his head. 'It all still looks the same,' he said. 'How can you tell that the Silver Pastures are near?'

Hekkle's eyes narrowed and his head-feathers quivered. 'I can sense it, Master Rook,' he said quietly. He shuddered. 'Believe me, the pastures are not far now.'

As they journeyed further, the prowlgrins began to grow skittish. They snorted; they rolled their eyes. They pawed the ground and tossed their heads. Once, Rook's prowlgrin bolted, and it was only Hekkle's speedy re-actions that prevented him from being whisked off into the endless forest alone.

'I thought I saw something out there,' said Magda a while later. 'Something watching us . . .'

Hekkle reined his prowlgrin in, and listened intently. 'Courage, Mistress Magda,' he said at last. 'It's probably just woodhogs scratching for oaktruffles. But we'd better move on quickly, just in case.'

Magda tried to smile bravely. So did the others. But as dark, purple-edged clouds moved in across the low sun, plunging the forest into shadow, their hearts beat fast.

In a loud hiss and a flash of yellow and green, a hover worm emerged from the undergrowth to their left and sped across their path, causing the prowlgrins to rear up in panic.

'Steady,' said Hekkle. 'Keep your nerve.'

Rook glanced round him constantly, his head jerking this way, that way, as he searched the shadows for whatever it was lurking just out of sight. His eyes focused in on a dark shape sliding off behind a tree. He shivered.

Crack.

'What was that?' gasped Stob.

'Stay calm, brave master,' said Hekkle. 'Fear amplifies the slightest of sounds.'

Crack.

'There it was again,' said Stob. He looked round nervously. 'From over there.'

Hekkle nodded. 'Stay close together,' he whispered. He kicked his prowlgrin's sides, urging it into a loping canter. The others did the same.

Crack.

The sound was behind them now, and fainter. 'I think we lost it,' said Hekkle, easing up. 'But just in case, no-one must make another sound until we get to the Silver Pastures—'

All at once something whistled over their heads. There was a thud and the sound of splintering wood. And there, inches from where Magda sat on her jittery prowlgrin, was a flint-tipped spear, embedded in the trunk of a great lufwood tree.

Magda screamed. Stob held on desperately as his prowlgrin reared up and squealed. A second spear flew past, hitting the forest floor and scattering the iron-wood cones which lay there.

'Take to the trees!' Hekkle cried. 'And try not to get separated!'

But it was no use. All round them the air suddenly pulsed with the sound of low, guttural voices grunting in unison, throwing the prowlgrins into a panic.

'Urrgh. Aargh. Urrgh. Aargh. Urrgh. Aargh.'

The prowlgrins leaped around in alarm – and there was nothing their riders could do to bring them back under control. A second flurry of spears flew through the air.

'Urrgh. Aargh. Urrgh. Aargh. Urrgh. Aargh.'

'Rook! Stob!' shouted Magda, as her prowlgrin thrashed about, trying its best to dislodge her. 'It won't climb! I can't make it—' She screamed as the prowlgrin suddenly bolted. 'Help!' she cried out. 'Help!'

'Hold on!' Rook called to her.

He yanked the reins and tried to steer his own prowl-grin after her. But the creature had a mind of its own and, before he could do a thing about it, had tossed him off its back and leaped up into the low-slung branches of a huge ironwood tree.

'Stick together!' he heard Hekkle shouting.

Rook rolled over and looked round. Magda's faint voice floated back through from the shadows. Stob and Hekkle were nowhere to be seen.

'Urrgh. Aargh. Urrgh. Aargh. Urrgh. Aargh.'

Heart pounding, Rook looked up to see his prowlgrin perched on a branch of the ironwood tree above. He struggled to his feet, and cried out as searing pain shot through his injured knee. He fell to the ground again. 'Here, boy,' he whispered. 'Come here, boy.'

The prowlgrin watched him from the branch, with wide, terrified eyes. Rook gritted his teeth. There was nothing for it. If the prowlgrin wouldn't come to him, then he would have to go to the prowlgrin.

Head down, he began dragging himself across the forest floor to the foot of the ironwood tree. His knee felt as if there were a knife lodged beneath his knee-cap, jarring with every movement he made. Closer. Closer . . .

'*Urrgh. Aargh. Urrgh. Aargh. Urrgh. Aargh.*'

All at once another spear whistled through the air. It struck the prowlgrin in its side. With a low moan, the creature dropped like an ironwood cone, hit the ground with a thud – and fell still.

Rook froze. What now?

'*Urrgh. Aargh. Urrgh. Aargh. Urrgh. Aargh.*'

The chanting was louder than ever. It seemed to be coming from every direction. Rook was on his own – wounded and frightened. He couldn't run. He couldn't hide. And something huge was coming towards him . . . With a surge of panic mixed with nausea, Rook suddenly realized that it was as if his nightmare were actually coming true.

Then he saw it. Tall, brutal, half-formed – it looked like a larger, fiercer and much, much uglier version of a clod-dertrog. Its huge, blunt face was mottled and scarred. The flat nose sniffed the air, the heavy jutting brow frowned over deep-set, red eyes that scanned the gloom of the forest floor.

Rook shrank back down into the soft leaf-cover on the ground and held his breath. His only hope was that it did not see him.

'*Urrgh!*' it grunted over its shoulder, and was joined by another trog with jagged, yellow nails and long matted hair.

'*Aargh!*' its companion responded. It pulled a spear from the giant quiver slung across its shoulder and brandished it in the air. '*Aargh!*'

From all round came replies, and out of the shadows emerged more of the hulking great trogs. Rook trembled with terror. Each of the creatures had skulls – whole strings of them – tied on leather thongs around its neck. They rattled as the trogs walked, jaws grinning and empty eye-sockets staring out in all directions.

'*AARGH!*'

The first trog had spotted him. Their eyes met.

'No, no, no,' Rook muttered as he desperately tried to scuttle away on his backside, dragging himself along with his scrabbling hands.

The creature advanced unhurriedly. It drew back its heavy, muscular arm and threw the spear.

Rook ducked.

It whistled past him, and on into the tangled under-growth behind. The creature drew another spear and lumbered forwards, the necklace of skulls rattling. Its mouth opened to reveal a set of long, wolf-like teeth.

'*AARGH!*' it roared.

A sharp pain shot up from Rook's injured knee. He collapsed. It was no good. There was nothing he could do. He could feel the pounding feet vibrating through the ground beneath him, he could smell rancid fat. The facets of the flint spear glinted in the dappled light as the trog raised it, ready to strike.

'AARGH!'

Rook closed his eyes. So this was how his nightmare ended, he thought bitterly.

Just then, from behind him, there came the sound of furious scratching, followed by a loud whirring noise. The trog cried out.

Rook looked round to see a dense swarm of small, silver-black angular creatures emerging from the undergrowth where the stray spear had landed. Despite the perilousness of his situation, the instincts of a true earth-scholar were awakened in him. With their long, pointed

noses
and stubby
triangular
wings, they were
clearly related to the
ratbirds which had once
roosted in the bowels of the
great sky ships. Like the ratbirds,
they flew in flocks. Unlike their
harmless, scavenging cousins, however,
these small, vicious creatures seemed to be
hunters.

Wheeling through the air in a great cloud, the countless silvery creatures flapped in perfect synchronization. When one turned, they all turned. Together, they resembled nothing so much as a billowing sheet, tossing and turning in the wind.

'*AARGH!*' bellowed the trog.

The flock switched in mid air, and swooped down towards it. Roaring loudly, the trog swiped at them with its spear. Several of the tiny creatures plummeted to the ground – but with so many, the loss of half a dozen of their number meant nothing.

'*AARG—*'

As Rook stared, fascination replacing fear, the flock struck. It engulfed the trog in an instant. The sound of gnashing and slurping filled the air – but only for an instant.

The next, the creatures flapped back into the air, squealing loudly.

Rook felt the icy fear return. The flock had stripped the hapless trog to the bone. Where he had been standing a moment before, there now stood a white skeleton and empty, grinning skull which, as Rook watched, fell to the ground in a heap of bones. The gruesome necklace of skulls lay among them. The spear dropped down on top of them all.

At the sight of what had happened to their leader, the others let out a howl of alarm.

'*Aargh!*' they screamed. '*Urrgh!*' And they turned on their heels and hurtled back into the forest.

The flock of tiny, blood-crazed creatures wheeled round in the air – looking, for a moment, like a vast sky ship with billowing sails – before turning as one, and speeding off after the fleeing trogs.

For a moment Rook could not move. His breath came in short, jerky gasps. Beside him lay one of the small creatures, its neck broken. He picked it up. It was small – smaller than the palm of his hand and scaly. Four razor-sharp teeth protruded from its slack jaws.

Rook trembled. On their own, the creatures were nothing, yet when they swarmed they were transformed into a huge, fearsome predator.

Rook memorized every detail of the tiny creature, fascinated and repelled in equal measure. If he ever got back to the library, he would describe it and name it, and perhaps one day a young under-librarian would pick up his treatise and read about it, and wonder . . . He would call it a snicket.

Slowly and painfully, using one of the discarded spears which littered the forest floor for support, Rook climbed to his feet. He stared round into the gloomy shadows. Whichever way he turned, the forest looked the same. He sighed. He'd escaped the primitive skull-trogs, and the snickets – only to find himself lost and alone in the depths of the Deepwoods.

Back in the underground library, he had often wondered why so many of those who had written about the Deepwoods described it as *endless*. Of course it isn't endless, he would say. You can see that from the map. Look, here it becomes the Edgelands, and here it borders the Twilight Woods ... After a week tramping through the forest, however, 'endless' seemed exactly the right word. It was so vast that anyone lost could wander for ever, and never find a way out.

Too frightened to call for his missing companions, Rook set off, orientating himself as best he could by the distant glow of the sun. His knee throbbed and, now that the dangers had passed, he was left feeling weak with hunger. He stumbled on, glancing round constantly, try-ing not to cry out as the forest sounds seemed to grow more and more sinister with every step he took. 'Stay calm,' he told himself.

But what was that? It sounded like footsteps – and they were coming towards him.

'It's all right,' he whispered, his voice breathless with rising fear. 'Don't panic.'

Yes. Yes. They were definitely footsteps. Heavy, sure-footed. Had one of the terrible skulltrogs come back to finish him off? He crouched down behind a vast trunk, festooned with hairy-ivy, and peered out tensely. The foliage parted and—

'Hekkle!' Rook cried.

'Master Rook!' the shryke exclaimed. 'Can it truly be you? Oh, brave master, praise be to Earth and Sky!' Rook climbed awkwardly to his feet. 'But you're hurt! What have you done?'

'It's my knee,' said Rook.

Hekkle dismounted and trotted towards him. Crouching down, he inspected it closely. 'It's swollen,' he said at last. 'But nothing too serious. Sit down for a moment, and I'll fix it up.'

Rook slumped back heavily to the ground. Hekkle removed a pot of green salve and a length of bandage from his backpack and began treating the knee.

'Did you see the flying creatures?' said Rook. 'Thousands of them, there were. They stripped that giant trog to the bone in a second.'

Hekkle nodded as he rubbed the salve into the joint. 'And not only him,' he said darkly.

Rook took a sharp intake of breath. 'You mean . . .? Stob . . . Magda . . .'

Hekkle looked up. 'I meant the other trogs,' he said. 'The brave master and mistress are safe,' he said. 'They are waiting for us at the edge of the Silver Pastures.'

'Praise be to Earth and Sky, indeed,' Rook breathed.

'There,' said Hekkle, as he knotted the ends of the bandage securely. 'Now, let's get you up onto my prowlgrin.'

173

They set off at a brisk trot, with Hekkle at the front holding the reins, and Rook behind, gripping the saddle tightly. As they loped on, the trees around them began to thin out. A head wind, blowing into their faces, sent the dark clouds scudding away across the sky, and for the first time that day, as warm shafts of sunlight flooded the forest floor, Rook began to feel optimistic about what lay ahead.

'Not far now,' said Hekkle. He pointed to a line of tall lufwoods. 'Those trees mark the edge of the pastures.'

Rook grinned. They had made it. The next moment his happiness was complete. 'And look!' he cried out. 'Magda and Stob!'

'You're right, brave master,' said Hekkle. 'But . . . Oh, no!' His feathers ruffled and his eyes nearly popped out of his head. 'What is *that*?'

'What? What?' said Rook. He looked intently for any sign of danger, but could see none. Stob and Magda had dismounted next to a long log, tethered the prowlgrins to a nearby lufwood tree and were standing with their backs turned away, looking out across the pastures beyond. 'What is it?' said Rook. He was suddenly frightened.

Hekkle flicked the reins and kicked into the prowl-grin's side. 'Watch out, Master Stob!' he shrieked as they pounded across the ground, but the wind whipped his warning away. 'Mistress Magda!'

'What was that?' said Magda.

Stob shrugged. 'I didn't hear anything,' he said, sitting down on the log.

Magda turned. 'Look,' she said excitedly. 'It's Hekkle. And he's got Rook with him!'

Stob frowned. 'Why are they galloping like that? And waving their arms? You don't suppose any of those horrible trog things are . . . ?'

Magda jumped up onto the log for a better view. 'I don't think so,' she said. 'There's nothing chasing them.' She cupped her hands to her mouth. 'What's wrong?' she cried out. 'Are you all right?'

'Stop waving, brave mistress!' Hekkle screeched back. 'And get out of there! Both of you!'

Rook knew Hekkle well enough to understand that Magda and Stob must be in terrible danger. 'Run for your lives!' he screamed. 'NOW!'

All at once there was an ominous rumble and a loud hiss. The ground shook. The dead leaves flew up. A pair of fromps skittered across the ground and away.

Rook stared ahead in horror and disbelief as the log on which Stob sat and Magda stood quivered, swung round and abruptly reared up into the air. It writhed. It swayed. It opened at one end, revealing sharp fangs and a dark, cavernous throat – and howled and wheezed with a bloodthirsty rage.

'Stob,' Rook gasped. 'Magda . . .'

· C H A P T E R   T E N ·

THE SILVER PASTURES

Rook stared in horror as the enormous thrashing creature rose up on a cushion of air spurting from rows of knot-like ducts the length of its huge mossy body.

'A logworm!' Hekkle shouted. 'Save yourselves!' He kicked his prowlgrin hard with his heels.

Stob fell heavily just behind the hovering logworm, and remained motionless where he lay. Magda landed with a thud beside the tethered prowlgrins, which twisted and reared in panic as the logworm swung round in mid air.

'Stob!' Magda screamed as the creature's great gaping maw lurched towards her fallen companion. 'Watch out!'

The logworm instantly turned towards the sound of her voice. Magda screamed. The prowlgrins thrashed about, screeching and howling and rolling their eyes in terror. The logworm's ring of green eyes focused on the terrified creatures.

'For pity's sake, Magda!' shouted Rook from behind Hekkle. 'Get out of there . . .'

His voice was drowned out by a deafeningly loud hissing. The logworm's huge mouth was sucking in air with tremendous force. A flurry of leaves and cones disappeared inside the creature as it came down low, and advanced on Magda and the terrified prowlgrins. They squealed and screeched and fought against the tunnel of swirling air, while Magda gripped their straining tether-ropes desperately.

'Magda . . .' Rook gasped.

Hekkle brought their prowlgrin to a skidding halt, leaped from its back and raced towards her. 'Brave mistress!' he called and seized her tightly by the wrist. Her cloak billowed out in the twisting air as he dragged her away to safety, just in time.

There was loud *crack* as the first of the tethers snapped under the unrelenting pressure, and one of the squealing prowlgrins barrelled back towards the cavernous mouth of the logworm. It disappeared inside. With a hideous crunching sound, the log-worm's body arched and shivered as it squashed the life out of its still squealing prey.

Hekkle, dragging Magda with him, reached Stob and plucked at his shirt. 'Get up, brave master,' he said. 'Get up!'

The librarian apprentice groaned.

Just then there was another *crack*, and the second

screaming prowlgrin disappeared. The logworm belched thunderously.

Hekkle and Magda pulled Stob to his feet, and stumbled away from the writhing monster. Rook kicked into the sides of his panic-stricken mount.

'Come on, boy,' he said. 'They need our help— *Whoooah!*' he cried out.

The terrified prowlgrin let out an ear-splitting screech and reared up. At the sound, the logworm turned on them, and Rook found himself staring straight down the creature's blood-red throat. Its circle of green eyes fixed him with a malevolent intensity. With a sinister hiss, the logworm lurched towards them, sucking in everything in its way in huge, convulsive gulps.

Rook felt the prowlgrin being dragged backwards. It was like being caught inside a whirlwind. He tugged at the reins in a furious attempt to yank the creature out of the traction-like spiral of air which was drawing them closer and closer to the terrible gaping mouth. Suddenly, with a loud *crack*, the harness snapped. The reins came away in his hands.

'No,' he groaned, tossing the useless bits of tilder-leather to the ground, and hanging on grimly round the creature's neck.

'Pick on someone your own size!' Hekkle's voice shrieked and, turning, Rook caught sight of the puny shryke-mate – feathers fluffed up and eyes glinting – beating the ground furiously with a lullabee branch. Distracted, the huge logworm roared with rage and twisted round to confront the shryke. Twigs, leaves, rocks and earth were thrown high up into the air.

Suddenly free, the prowlgrin tore off as fast as its powerful legs could take it. Rook held on desperately as they thundered through the suddenly thinning lufwood trees and on into the brilliant light and vast spaces of the Silver Pastures themselves.

Rook felt a great wave of relief wash over him. Vast and softly undulating, the pastures were spectacular. The silvery grey-green was broken only by the thick streaks of the black and brown herds of migrating hammelhorn and tilder, which stretched out as far as the eye could see.

The wide sky, cloudless now, was dotted with birds in flight – a flock of snowbirds, a cluster of cheepwits, songteals twittering loudly, a gladehawk hovering and waiting to dive and, far, far in the distance, a solitary caterbird flapping sedately. Below, the huge herds moved slowly through the pastures. The air was filled with the warm, musty smell of their thick fur mingling with the mouthwatering scent of crushed grass. Their deep lowing rumbled sonorously . . .

A loud hiss cut through the air directly behind him. The logworm! Rook kicked his heels into the galloping prowl-grin, not daring to look back. The huge beast had followed them out into this vast sea of grass. Ahead, a large herd of shaggy hammelhorns trumpeted loudly and, turning on their heels, stampeded off in a cloud of dust.

The logworm was almost on top of them. Rook could feel the twisting air tugging at his cape, his trousers, his hair, and making the prowlgrin pant with exertion.

'Faster! Faster!' Rook cried out in desperation. 'Don't give up now!' The prowlgrin snorted helplessly. It had done all it could; it could do no more. Clinging on tightly, Rook leaned forwards. 'You did your best,' he whispered.

The prowlgrin stumbled. Rook cried out. They crashed into the soft, herb-scented grass, Rook tumbling clear of his mount. The gaping maw of the logworm loomed over them, closer, closer . . .

'No!' he screamed. 'Not like this!'

All at once Rook caught sight of a blur of movement out of the corner of his eye. The next moment something struck him hard, knocking the air from his lungs, and – in a flurry of grasping hands, glinting wood and flapping sails – he was plucked from the ground.

Rook gasped. He was soaring up, up, up into the sky.

'Just in time, friend,' came a voice from behind him. Rook craned his neck round. He was on a skycraft! He was actually flying! There, astride a narrow seat behind him, was the pilot – a young, slightly built slaughterer, dressed in flight-suit and goggles. The skycraft lurched to the left. 'Stay still, friend,' he said firmly. 'She's not used to passengers.'

Rook turned back, scarcely able to believe what was happening. He wrapped his arms round the neck of the skycraft's roughly hewn figurehead and clung on tightly, his heart bubbling with joy.

Flying!

Far below, there came a long howl of despair. Rook looked down to see the brave yet hapless prowlgrin disappear inside the voracious log-like creature. A last plaintive squeal rose up through the air. Then nothing. Rook shuddered, and almost lost his grip on the figurehead.

'*Whooah*, steady there, friend!' the pilot shouted. 'First time in the air?'

Rook nodded and tried not to look down.

At that moment the fragile skycraft hit a pocket of turbulent air. It bucked and dipped, and went into a nose-dive. The slaughterer pilot's hands darted forwards and began tugging at a series of ropes, raising weights and shifting the sails round, while his feet balanced the craft with thin, curved stirrups. Rook gasped, stomach in his mouth, as the ground spiralled towards them.

'I know, I know,' the slaughterer muttered through clenched teeth, as he tugged on two of the ropes at the same time. 'You're not built for two, are you, old girl?'

The skycraft abruptly pulled out of the dive and soared back into the sky – only to be struck by a ferocious gust of wind slamming into its side. Rook's

stomach did a somersault as the buffeting crosswind threatened at any moment to send them into another terrifying spin. The patched sails billowed in and out; this side, that side . . .

'Help!' Rook shouted out despite himself, his cry whipped away on the battering wind. He glanced behind him.

With his jaw set grimly, the young slaughterer was gripping the steering-handles tightly. The skycraft juddered violently, threatening to shake itself to pieces at any moment.

'Easy, girl!' he coaxed as, balancing in the stirrups, he wrestled with the tangle of ropes.

Rook held his breath.

Slowly, slowly – his brow furrowed with concentration – the slaughterer brought the skycraft round. His feet were poised, ready for the moment when the wind struck them from the back. Rook gripped the carved wood with white-knuckled ferocity . . .

All at once the skycraft gave a violent shudder. The wind was directly behind them. The sails billowed, the ropes strained. With a terrible lurch – and an ominous crunch – the skycraft hurtled forwards like an arrow.

Nothing could have prepared Rook for the sudden burst of speed. It threw him back, snatched his breath away and plucked at the corners of his mouth. He screwed his eyes tightly shut.

'*Whup! Whup! Wahoo!*' he heard a moment later. He frowned in disbelief. Was the slaughterer seriously enjoying this – or had the young pilot gone mad with fear?

Rook risked another glance over his shoulder. Although they were travelling at breakneck speed, and at an alarmingly steep angle, the slaughterer did seem to be in control. Standing up in the stirrups, he was pulling in the sail-ropes one by one, reducing the bulge of the individual sails, while at the same time keeping the fragile craft expertly balanced. *'Whup! Whup! Wahoo!'* he cried out again. He *was* enjoying himself.

Ahead of him, Rook spotted a tall tower; a mass of roughly hewn timber that seemed to sprout from the pastures like a colossal wooden needle. Just below the point, Rook could make out a series of rough gantries and primitive walkways bedecked with lanterns that, even in the light of the pastures, seemed to be glowing.

'That's my beauty, I knew you could do it,' the slaughterer muttered under his breath. 'Nearly there . . . Nearly there . . .' He tugged on a thick, plaited black rope above his head, and the sail to Rook's left rose.

The effect was instantaneous. Instead of continuing forwards, the skycraft went into a slow, coiling turn, arcing through the air like a woodmaple-seed on the wind. Once round the tall needle of the tower it flew, then descended, inch perfect onto a rough plank gantry where the skycraft touched down.

Rook slumped forwards, exhilarated and exhausted in equal measure. The slaughterer tore off his goggles and leaped from the seat, his face bursting with pride. 'Yes,' he smiled, and stroked the skycraft's carved prow. 'I knew you wouldn't fail me.' He looked suddenly thoughtful. 'What does the Professor of Darkness know?' he said. 'More than a single pilot on a skycraft. Can't be done, eh? Well, we've shown him, haven't we, *Woodwasp*, old girl?' He patted the figurehead affectionately.

Rook tapped him on the shoulder. 'My name's Rook Barkwater, and I want to thank you from the bottom of my heart,' he began. He paused. 'Did you say *Professor of Darkness*? Are you also an apprentice?'

The slaughterer looked down and laughed. 'I, Knuckle, an apprentice?' he said. 'No. Just a simple herder, me. The professor is a . . . an acquaintance of mine.' He turned to face Rook, as if only now seeing him for the first time.

'But you fly so well,' said Rook. 'Who taught you, if not the masters of Lake Landing?'

'I taught myself,' said Knuckle. He patted the skycraft lovingly. 'Built her from scratch, I did. 'Course, I'd be the first to admit that she's not the most beautiful skycraft ever to fly, but the *Woodwasp* here is a remarkable creature. Obedient. Sensitive. Responsive . . .'

Rook was intrigued. 'You're talking about it as though it was alive,' he said.

'Aye, well, that's the secret of skycraft flight in a nutshell,' said Knuckle earnestly. 'You treat your skycraft like a friend – with love, with tenderness, with respect – and she'll return the favour tenfold. When I saw you in trouble with that logworm, it was the *Woodwasp* herself who urged me to try to rescue you. "We can do it!" she told me. "The two of us together!" And she was right.'

'And thank Earth and Sky for that,' said Rook softly. 'Without you both, I would have perished.'

Suddenly, from all around, came the sound of voices. Rook looked out from the gantry to see half a dozen or so skycraft – each one piloted by a single pilot – looping down through the air towards them. Like Knuckle, they seemed to be slaughterers, flame-haired and clad in leather flight-suits. They waved down enthusiastically.

'That was amazing, Knuckle!' shouted one.

'The most incredible piece of flying I've ever seen!' shouted another.

'And with two people on board!' said a third, awestruck. 'If I hadn't seen it with my own eyes, I'd never have believed it possible!'

One by one, they landed their own skycraft on gantries below them, dismounted, and clambered up swaying ladders to join them. Knuckle bowed his head.

'It was nothing,' he said, modest, almost shy. 'It's all down to the *Woodwasp* here, the little beauty—'

'But you are an excellent pilot,' Rook butted in. He turned to the others. 'The way he swooped down and plucked me from the jaws of the logworm. The way he battled with the air-pockets and gale-force winds . . .' He shook his head with admiration. 'You should have seen it!' He glanced back towards the young slaughterer. 'Knuckle, here, was magnificent! He saved my life!'

'And who are *you*?' asked a short, sinewy slaughterer as he stepped forwards.

'Looks like a merchant to me,' came a voice.

'Probably one of those apprentices,' came another.

'He *is* an apprentice,' Knuckle answered for him. 'His name is Rook Barkwater.'

Rook nodded. 'I was travelling with two other apprentices,' he said. 'A shryke guide was taking us to the Free Glades. Have you seen them? Do you know if they're all right?'

'A shryke?' said Knuckle, and screwed up his nose.

The others muttered under their breath. Shrykes were clearly not popular among the group of slaughterers.

'This one's not like the others,' Rook assured them. 'He's kind, thoughtful—'

'Yeah, yeah, and I'm a tilder sausage,' came a loud voice, and they all laughed.

'You certainly fly like a tilder sausage,' said someone else. The laughter got louder.

Knuckle turned to Rook. 'Come,' he said, taking Rook by the arm. 'We'll get a better view from the west gantry. Perhaps we can spot your friends from there.'

*

187

Rook gasped as he peered down from the west gantry of the tower. On the ground, far below him, the herds of tilder and hammel-horn looked like woodants in the failing light. He clutched the balustrade nervously.

'It's so high,' he trembled.

'Wouldn't be much use for looking out of if it weren't,' said Knuckle.

'I know,' said Rook queasily. 'But does it have to sway like that?'

'The wind's getting up,' said Knuckle, and he scanned the sky thoughtfully. 'Looks like a sky-storm's brewing.'

Rook frowned. He turned to Knuckle. 'A sky-storm?' he said. 'With thunder and ball-lightning?'

Knuckle chuckled. 'Yeah, and hailstones the size of your fist if you're lucky.'

'The size of your fist,' Rook said softly.

The slaughterer looked at him quizzically. 'Are you telling me you've never seen a sky-storm before?'

Rook shook his head. 'Not that I remember,' he said

wistfully. 'I grew up in an underground world of pipes and chambers – dripping, enclosed, illuminated with artificial light . . .' He turned, tilted his head back and was bathed in the golden shafts of warm sunlight. 'Not like this. And as for the weather,' he said, turning back to Knuckle. 'Everything I know, I learned from barkscrolls and treatises.'

'So you've never smelt the whiff of toasted almonds in the air when lightning strikes? Nor heard the earth tremble as the thunder explodes? Nor felt the soft, icy kiss of a snowflake landing on your nose . . .?' He paused, suddenly noticing the blush spreading over Rook's cheeks. 'But I envy you, Rook Barkwater. It must be wonderful to have the chance to experience all these things for the first time – and be old enough to really appreciate them.'

Rook smiled. He hadn't thought of it like that.

'Now, let's see if we can spot these friends of yours,' Knuckle went on. 'They'll be making their way on foot if the logworm got your prowlgrins.'

'I hope so,' said Rook, following the slaughterer's gaze out across the silvery plains, over the heads of the grazing hammelhorns.

'That's where you came from,' he said. 'The Eastern Roost. If you look carefully, you can just see the top of the Roost Spike.'

Rook nodded. The sun was deep orange now and low in the sky, casting the trees in darkness. The spike stood out like a needle point and, as he watched, a light came on at its top. Knuckle's arm swung further round.

'Over there are the Goblin Nations,' he said. 'And there, due south, is the Foundry Glade. See how the sky is darker in that whole area? That's the filthy smoke constantly belching out from their factory chimneys.'

Rook could see the heavy black clouds, tinged with red, far in the distance. 'It looks like a terrible place,' he observed.

'Take my advice, friend,' said Knuckle earnestly. 'The Foundry Glade is no place for the likes of us. Ten times worse than Undertown, so they say – a place of fiery furnaces and slaves—'

'Slaves?' said Rook, shocked.

'And worse,' said Knuckle darkly. 'Not at all like the *Free* Glades.' The slaughterer smiled. 'Now the Free Glades are a sight to see, believe me!'

'Which way *are* the Free Glades?' said Rook.

Knuckle turned him round, till Rook was standing with his back to the sinking sun. 'Over there,' he said. 'Just beyond that ridge of ironwood trees; the most beautiful place in all the Edgelands.'

'So close?' said Rook, trembling with excitement. As he peered into the darkness, he was filled with a mixture of happiness and sadness. Overjoyed to discover that he had almost reached his destination, he had momentarily forgotten that his companions were not with him . . .

'Rook!' The voice echoed up on the swirling wind from the other side of the tower. '*Rook!*'

'Magda?' said Rook, hurrying to see. He clutched the rough wooden balustrade and looked down. A group of ant-like slaughterers were staring up. When Rook's head appeared they all started waving and pointing and shouting at once. 'Come down!' 'Come here!' 'Your friends . . .' And three individuals from the crowd were pushed forwards.

Rook cried out with joy. 'Magda!' he shouted. 'Stob! Hekkle!' And he turned on his heels, clambered down the ladders leading on to the walkways, and finally hurried down a creaking zigzag staircase.

'Rook!' Magda cried as he emerged at the bottom, and she rushed forwards to hug him, before bursting into tears. 'We . . . we thought we'd lost you for certain,' she sobbed. 'Then we saw that slaughterer swooping down . . .'

'And I thought I spotted you clinging on, brave master,' said Hekkle.

'You did,' Rook beamed and turned to Knuckle, who had followed him down. 'Knuckle, here, saved my life.'

Hekkle turned to him. 'You are a true friend of earth-and sky-studies,' he said.

Knuckle nodded uncertainly. Talking to a shryke clearly felt strange to him. 'Thanks,' he muttered. 'I just did what anyone else would have done.'

Magda broke away from Rook, and wrapped her arms tightly round the startled slaughterer. 'You're too modest, Knuckle!' she said. 'Thank you and thank you and thank you again,' she said, planting three kisses on his forehead.

The other slaughterers roared approvingly. Knuckle blushed, his normally red skin turning a deep shade of purple.

Hekkle's voice rose above the hub-bub. 'It is time we left,' he said. Ignoring the protests and politely declining the offers of refreshment and a bed for the night, he raised his hands and appealed for quiet. 'Tonight,' he began. The slaughter-ers fell still. 'Tonight we will sup, dine and sleep in the Free Glades.'

A cheer went up. And as Hekkle led his small party away, the slaughterers waved and cried out. 'Good luck!' they shouted. And, 'Earth and Sky be with you!' And, 'Don't forget us!'

Rook turned. 'Never!' he shouted back. 'I'll never for-get you! Farewell, Knuckle! Farewell!'

The sun had set by now, and the colours on the horizon behind them had become muted and shrunk away to a thin, pale ribbon of light. Above their heads the stars were coming out and, as they climbed the steep ridge of ironwood trees, the first of the night creatures were already calling to one another in the darkness.

'The Free Glades,' Rook breathed. 'So close.'

'Not long now,' said Hekkle.

Though on a gentle incline, the ridge seemed to continue for ever. Each time they reached what they thought was the top, the slope continued upwards. The moon rose and shone down brightly. Rook wiped his glistening forehead. 'It's further than I thought,' he said. 'Knuckle made it sound so—'

'*Sshhh!*' Hekkle stopped and cocked his head to one side. 'Can you hear that?' he whispered.

Rook listened. 'Oh, no,' he groaned as, from his right, he heard the unmistakable – and terrifyingly familiar – sound of hissing. 'It can't be.'

'A logworm,' Magda gasped.

'I'm afraid so,' Hekkle whispered nervously. 'The woods all round the pastures are infested with the brutes. The pickings are just too good.'

'What shall we do, Hekkle?' whispered Stob.

Rook noticed that his apprentice companion's voice had lost its usual arrogant tone.

'Find a tree,' whispered Hekkle, 'and climb as swiftly and silently as you can. Go, now!'

They did as they were told. Quickly, noiselessly, they scaled an ironwood tree and crouched in its huge branches, like ratbirds, beneath their cloaks of nightspider-silk. The hissing grew louder as the logworm approached, and a flurry of leaves rose up in the air. The next moment its great slavering snout poked out from between the trees; its eyes and teeth glinted in the moonlight.

They held their breath and remained as still as their pounding hearts and trembling bodies would allow. Rook willed the creature to go.

Please, please, please . . .

All at once it grew darker as a cloud fell across the moon. Rook glanced down. Something was flapping past.

'Snickets!' he gasped.

'So that's what they're called,' he heard Stob mutter beside him.

The logworm hissed louder, and turned in their direction. Rook shrank back. Below them, the whirring swarm of snickets was spiralling up through the darkness like a great arrow-head. As it approached, the moon burst forth again and shone down brightly on the countless silver-black beating wings. The snickets were heading straight for them.

Rook groaned. If the logworm didn't get them, the snickets would. And when they were so close to their journey's end . . .

All at once and with no warning, the logworm swerved round to face the swarm. Rook gasped as the logworm convulsed.

The
snickets
were
being
sucked
up into the vast, dark tunnel of the logworm.

It writhed and wriggled, sucking in more and more of the little creatures, its high-pitched hiss sounding like a great kettle letting off steam. As the last of the swarm disappeared inside the logworm, Rook turned to Hekkle.

'It's destroyed them all,' he said.

'On the contrary, brave master,' said Hekkle. 'Things in the Deepwoods are seldom what they seem.'

'But—' Rook began.

Just then the logworm let out a deafening cry of pain. The sound echoed round the trees, making the leaves tremble, and Rook felt the hairs on the back of his neck stand on end. As he watched, transfixed, the entire logworm seemed to disappear before his eyes. The snickets were consuming it from within, each and every scrap! For a moment the vast swarm resembled the great hovering log it had just devoured. Then, as if at some unseen signal, the snickets twisted round in the air – no longer together, but singly and in pairs – and fluttered off in all directions.

Legs shaking, Rook climbed down from the ironwood tree. 'I . . . I don't understand,' he said. 'Why did the swarm disperse like that?'

Hekkle clambered down and stood beside Rook. 'Their feeding frenzy is over,' he said. 'They will only swarm again when their hunger once more drives them to it.' He laughed humourlessly. 'Now it is the turn of other creatures to feed,' he said. 'Many of their number will be picked off by predators.'

Rook shook his head in wonder. He'd read so much about the delicate balance of life in the Deepwoods, about the constant battle between predators and their prey. Now he was experiencing it first hand. It was fascinating how it all slotted together. How no single creature seemed ever to get the upper hand. How victor became victim and victim became victor, and the whole violent yet intricate process continued for ever and ever.

He thought of the treatise that lay ahead, and the banderbears he wanted to study. They, at least, were gentle creatures. Noble. Humble. Loyal. At least, that was what everyone believed – even Varis Lodd. Soon he wanted to find out for himself . . .

'Come, brave friends,' said Hekkle, setting off up the ridge once more. 'We're almost there.'

Stob and Magda followed. Rook brought up the rear, his heart thumping with expectation. As they approached the brow, he almost expected it to give way to yet another slope, and another one beyond that.

This time, however, they really had reached the top. The ground fell away before them, and in front – spread out in all their magnificence – were the Free Glades. To their right was a pool of honey-coloured lamplight. To their left, a flickering circle of burning torches, and beyond that, the low red glow of furnaces. Whilst far in the distance, shimmering like silver beneath the moon, were three lakes. In the centre of the largest one, twinkling brightly, was a tall, spired building, bedecked with coloured lights. It was there that, for the months of study which lay ahead, they were to stay.

'Lake Landing!' said Rook, pointing. 'Our new home.'

CHAPTER ELEVEN

STORMHORNET

Lake Landing

Spirits soaring, Rook, Magda and Stob raced down the steep incline, with Hekkle flapping behind them, clucking noisily. 'Careful, brave masters!' he called out breathlessly. 'Not so fast, brave mistress!'

They emerged from the trees onto a track – flattened and hardened by the passing of countless booted feet and wooden wheels – and there in front of them, like some magnificent jewel-encrusted tapestry, were the glades themselves.

Rook's pulse quickened as he looked round in wonder. In the moonlight, the diverse dwelling places of the numerous Free Glade denizens were picked out in luminous silver and long, sharp shadows. The three apprentices stopped and stared. The air was filled with smells and sounds. The tang of leather, the odour of stale beer, the aromatic scent of spices and herbs. And Rook could hear the buzz of distant voices – joyful voices, and singing and laughter. Hekkle bustled up behind them and tried to catch his breath. The feathers on his neck stood up in a ragged ruff and his thin pointed beak quivered. 'Over there, that's where the webfoot goblins live.' He nodded towards a group of huts floating on shimmering marshland to their left. 'Great eel-fishers,' he said, 'but not too particular in their personal habits. And those,' he said, pointing over his right shoulder to a tall, steep, pockmarked hill, 'are the cloddertrog caves. Now, they're really a sight to see. They say whole clans live in a single cave together; sometimes hundreds of them—'

All at once there was a clatter of hoofs behind them. They turned to see two gnokgoblins on prowlgrins approaching. Both the goblins and their mounts wore tooled-leather armour; the gnokgoblins carried long ironwood lances and large crescent-shaped shields. One stopped and, standing tall in his saddle, scanned the area. The other rode towards them.

'Advance and identify yourselves,' he barked.

Hekkle stepped forwards and produced the bloodoak-tooth medallion, which he held up. 'Friends of Earth and Sky,' he said.

Rook and the others revealed their medallions, too. The guard nodded. Up close, Rook noticed that the burnished leather of his armour was pitted and scratched with the scars of battle.

Just then a third guard appeared. 'Hey, Glock, Steg,' he shouted. 'Marauders have been sighted up in the Northern Fringes. We're needed there at once.'

The guard turned back to Hekkle and his three charges. 'Pass, friends,' he said, 'and fare you well.'

He tugged the reins, kicked hard, and galloped off after the others, his prowlgrin throwing up clods of earth with each bound.

'The Free Glades are beautiful and peaceful, brave friends,' said Hekkle. 'But many a brave soul has had to lay down his life to keep them that way. Come, let us continue to Lake Landing.'

They walked down a broad set of steps lit by huge, floating lanterns, and passed by a towering copse of dark trees, immense against the slate-grey sky.

'Who lives there?' said Rook.

'Waifs,' answered Hekkle. 'That is Waif Glen. Only the invited may go there, for the ways of waifs are secretive and mysterious, even here in the Free Glades.'

'And what's that?' said Rook excitedly, turning to his right.

In the distance, rows of lights illuminated narrow streets and the windows of clusters of ornate buildings – some broad and squat with spreading roofs; others tall, thin and topped with elegant towers.

Hekkle turned. 'That, brave master, is New Undertown. You'll find it very different from the old one. There is a welcome to be found for all in New Undertown – a hearty meal, and a free hammock in the hive-huts for those who want it.'

'Hive-huts?' said Rook excitedly. 'You mean those buildings over there – the ones that look like helmets?'

'That's right, brave master, they're—' Hekkle began.

'And what in Earth and Sky's name is *that* called?' said Rook, pointing at the tall, angular building with latticed walls and a high spire which dominated New Undertown.

'It's the Lufwood Tower, brave master,' said Hekkle. 'It's like Vox Verlix's palace in Old Undertown – except all are free to go there and speak their minds in its meeting chamber.'

'Can we visit the waifs? And the hive-huts?' said Rook eagerly. 'And the Lufwood Tower?'

'Oh, Master Rook!' Hekkle laughed and held up his hands in submission. 'Enough! Enough! There'll be time for all that, but first we *must* get to Lake Landing.'

Rook blushed. 'I'm sorry,' he said. 'It's just all so . . . so . . .' He swung his arms round in a wide arc. 'So . . .'

'Get a move on!' said Stob grumpily. 'I'm tired, and so is Magda.' Magda shrugged and smiled, but Rook noticed the dark rings under her eyes.

'Believe me,' said Hekkle, 'the best is still to come.' He took Rook by the hand. 'Come, brave master.'

They continued past Waif Glen, and the Leadwood Copse beyond. Behind them, the sounds of New Undertown receded and, as the moon rose higher in the indigo sky, the air grew strangely still.

Rook's eyes darted round – but he kept his questions to himself. There were flowers with huge white blooms, swaying in the silvery light. There were black and yellow birds in the branches, chirruping to the moon. The grass hissed. The path crunched. They came to an archway of sweet-scented woodjasmine, stepped through and . . .

'Oh, my!' gasped Rook.

Before them lay a lake. It was vast and still, and, like a giant mirror, reflected everything in it perfectly. Birds skimming its surface. The trees fringing its banks. And the huge moon, shining down out of the inky sky so brightly.

On a broad platform at the centre of the lake – wreathed in mist and twinkling with a thousand lanterns – was a tall, sprawling building, jagged against the sky. It had pointed turrets, jutting walkways, arch-windowed walls and long, sloping roofs.

Rook shook his head in amazement. 'I've never seen anywhere so beautiful,' he said softly. 'Even in my dreams.'

'The Lake Landing Academy,' said Hekkle. 'The jewel of the Free Glades, and beacon of hope to all who love and value freedom.'

LAKE LANDING

But no-one was listening to the shryke guide's words any more. One after the other, as if in a trance, the three young apprentices walked slowly down to the water's edge and climbed onto the long narrow jetty which crossed the lake to the landing of vast lufwood planks.

As Rook stepped onto the great central platform, something caught his eye and he looked up to see a small skycraft with a gleaming prow and snow-white billowing sails approaching. His heart skipped a beat. It was the most beautiful sight yet. The moonlight played on the ornately carved figurehead and sleek curves of the skycraft's body. The dark greens and browns of the young pilot's flight-suit contrasted with the warm gold of his wooden arm-plates and leg-guards. The skycraft's sails seemed to flow through the night air like liquid silver as it circled the landing. It was joined silently by another craft, and then another, and another.

One by one, they swooped down out of the sky in perfect formation, before touching down lightly on the landing-stage, side by side. Rook stared at the four young apprentices as they climbed down from their craft, and shook his head in awe.

'I'll never be able to fly that well,' he said.

'Yes, you will, brave master,' said Hekkle, coming up behind him. 'Trust me. You're not the first young apprentice who's stood awestruck on Lake Landing, full of self-doubt. Believe me, though, you'll learn.'

'But—' Rook began.

Hekkle clacked his beak softly. 'No "buts", brave master. From the first moment I clapped eyes on you, back in the Eastern Roost, I knew you were special. Sky-spirit and earth-sense, I call it.'

Rook blushed deep pink.

'They'll teach you well here at Lake Landing, but you've got something already – something that no amount of teaching can give you. Always remember that.'

Rook smiled awkwardly. 'Thank you, Hekkle,' he said. 'Thank you for everything. I'll miss you . . .'

'Welcome!' came a rather shrill voice from the far side of the landing. 'The new apprentices, is it? My, my, but you look fit to drop! Yes, yes, you certainly do, and no mistake!'

Rook turned to see a small, shabbily dressed gnok-goblin with a wrinkled face and stubby legs striding towards Stob and Magda, one hand clutching his robes, the other pressed against his heart in greeting. Rook went over to join them.

Stob had already taken control. 'Ah, my good fellow,' he said. 'See to our bags, would you, and then take us to the High Master of Lake Landing. I think he'll be interested to see us.'

'Indeed!' said the gnokgoblin, his face crumpling with amusement. He made no move towards the bags. 'Interested to see you, yes, indeed!'

Stob frowned. 'Well?' he said imperiously.

Hekkle turned to him. 'I don't think you quite under-stand, brave master,' he began.

'It's all right,' said Rook awkwardly, moving for-wards. 'We can carry our own bags. After all, we've carried them this far.'

'Leave them, Rook,' said Stob sharply. 'A fine place
this is! Upstart servants who refuse to do as they're told.
Wait till the High Master hears of this!'

'I think,' said Hekkle quietly, 'he just has.'

'Stay out of this, Hekkle,' said Stob rudely, before
rounding on the smiling gnokgoblin. 'Now, tell me your
name this instant, you impudent wretch!'

Just then, as the gnokgoblin lowered
his hands, Rook noticed the gold chain
around his neck, glinting from
beneath the simple robes. Each of
the heavy links was in the shape of
twisted leaves and feathers.

'Why, certainly, my fine, young
and rather over-tired apprentice,'
the gnokgoblin said. 'I am
Parsimmon, High Master of Lake Landing.'

Stob turned a bright shade of crimson. 'I . . . I . . .' he
stuttered.

But the High Master waved his apologies aside. 'You
must be tired and hungry, all of you,' he said. 'Come
inside and I'll show you your sleeping cabins. Then I'll
take you to the upper refectory. There is food and drink
waiting and . . .' He looked up. 'But what have we here?
I was expecting only three, indeed I was. And yet, and
yet . . .'

Stob, Magda and Rook turned to see a wiry figure
with close-cropped hair crossing the walkway towards
them. 'He's not with us, your Most Highness, sir,' said
Stob, regaining the power of speech.

Parsimmon beckoned to the figure to approach. 'Welcome, welcome,' he said genially. 'And who might you be?'

'Xanth,' said the youth. He rubbed his hand over his scalp. 'Xanth Filatine. Sole survivor from the latest group of apprentices to set forth from the Great Storm Chamber Library.' He pulled a bloodoak-tooth pendant from his tattered gown and thrust it forward defiantly.

Rook noticed the youth's hands shaking. He frowned. There was something about this young apprentice that made him feel uneasy.

'They sent another group after us?' said Stob suspiciously. 'So soon?'

Xanth nodded. 'Word came back that you'd been lost in a shryke raid. The professors decided to despatch a second contingent of apprentices immediately.'

Stob humphed.

'I'm sure the professors know what they're doing,' said Hekkle.

'So, what happened to the others?' Stob demanded of the youth.

Xanth shook his head sadly. 'Dead,' he said quietly. 'All dead.' He swallowed noisily with choking emotion. 'I'm the only one who made it.'

Rook listened closely. Perhaps he had been too harsh.

'Bron Turnstone,' Xanth went on, his voice cracking with emotion. 'Ignis Gimlet. And our brave woodtroll guide, Rufus Snetterbark. A logworm got them all . . .'

'I don't know those names,' said Parsimmon, 'but it is always a terrible tragedy to lose any of our brave apprentices. And as you can see,' he said, nodding towards Rook and the others, 'this contingent did make it – which makes the losses all the more tragic.'

Xanth nodded silently and lowered his head. Tears welled up in his eyes.

'But *you* made it, Xanth Filatine,' said Parsimmon kindly. 'The journey to the Free Glades is never an easy one. Few are lucky enough to get through. And those who do . . .' He clapped the four new arrivals reassuringly on the shoulder. 'You are very precious to us. We will teach you everything we know, and send you off on your treatise-voyage, so that you may add to our deepening knowledge of the Edge.' His eyes sparkled brightly. 'Yes, yes,' he said. 'Very precious, indeed.'

The Woodtroll Workshop

'Damn and blast!' Rook shouted, and sucked at his painfully throbbing thumb.

Stob chuckled. 'A fine way for a young scholar to talk,' he said.

'Another splinter?' came Magda's sympathetic voice. She was standing by her own workbench.

'Yes,' said Rook, wearily inspecting his hands. Apart from the jagged splinter – which he managed to pull from his thumb with his teeth – his hands were grazed, scarred and bruised black and blue. He looked bleakly at the huge sumpwood log clamped into the vice before him. Despite weeks of work, what should by now have been an elegant skycraft prow, was still no more than a shapeless lump. 'I'll never get the hang of this,' he muttered miserably.

Around them, the timber yards hummed with activity. Convoys of tall-sided log-carts swayed past the long, thatched woodsheds, the musky odour of the sweating hammelhorns pulling them mixing with the peppery scent of sawdust. Cloddertrog wagoneers shouted down to the woodtroll carpenters, while groups of woodtroll tree-fellers queued good-naturedly at the huge, ever-busy grindstones to sharpen their axes. Rook gazed out of the open-sided workshop at the cluster of woodtroll villages in the distance and let out a deep sigh.

'Don't give up,' said Magda.

Rook glanced over towards his friend. Her own prow was coming along beautifully. The wood was smooth and the figurehead was slowly taking on the appearance of a delicate woodmoth, with its bulging eyes and coiled feelers. Stob, too, had created something recognizable. A hammelhorn, stolid and lifelike. He was using a fine rasp to shape the long, curling horns. While Xanth – who was at his usual workbench apart from the others at the far end of the thatched workshop – was the farthest advanced of them all. With its long, crumpled snout and swept-back wings, the ratbird he had carved from the sumpwood was almost complete.

Oakley Gruffbark, the woodtroll master, his thick orange hair twisted into the traditional woodtroll tufts, stood beside him, running his leathery hands over the wood and inspecting the workmanship closely. 'Well, young'un, it's an unusual creature to carve, and that's the truth,' he was saying. 'Yet it seems to come from the heart . . .'

Stob snorted. 'A ratbird,' Rook heard him muttering scornfully. 'I wonder what *that* says about his heart?'

Rook said nothing. He'd distrusted Xanth at first, but the young apprentice kept himself to himself and, with his haunted-looking eyes and polite, quiet voice, Rook found it hard to dislike him. At least, Rook thought, Xanth had thought of *something* to carve. He picked up a plane from the workbench and attacked the lump of wood with a sudden fury. The air filled with muttered oaths, and a flurry of pale wood-shavings.

'Stupid! . . . Blasted! . . . Accursed!'

'No, no, no! That'll never do, Master Rook, indeed it won't!' came Gruffbark's urgent voice as he hurried over to his bench. He snatched the plane away. 'You must *feel* your wood, Master Rook,' he said. '*Know* it. Study it intimately, until you are familiar with every mark of its swirling grain, with the intricate pattern of knots, with the natural curve of its sweeping shape.' He paused. 'Only then will you find the creature hiding within . . .'

Rook looked up angrily, his eyes filling with tears. 'But I can't!' he said. 'There's nothing there!' Oakley shook his tufted head sympathetically. 'All those dreams of flying I've had, and I'm never even going to leave this workshop! It's hopeless! Useless! And so am I!'

The woodtroll's face creased into a warm smile. He fixed the youth with his deep, dark eyes and took his hands in his own. 'But there *is* something there, Rook,' he said patiently. 'Open your ears and your eyes, and let the wood speak to you.'

Rook shook his head mutely. The words meant nothing to him.

'It's getting late, and you're tired, young'un,' said Oakley. He clapped his hands together. 'Class dismissed.'

Rook turned and walked stiffly away. Outside, the parties of axe-carrying fellers and teams of carpenters were wandering out of the timber yards and off down the woodtroll paths towards their villages – and supper. Small groups passed him by, laughing and joking in the evening twilight glow. Magda caught him up and put her arm round his shoulders. 'You'll feel better after supper,' she said. 'I think it's your favourite tonight. Tilder stew.'

Magda was right on both counts. It *was* tilder stew, which *was* Rook's favourite. The upper refectory was busy tonight. Several visiting professors sat at the central table. A huge translucent spindlebug – the stew clearly visible digesting in his stomach – was in conversation with a tiny waif, her large ears flapping delicately as she ate. Parsimmon sat listening indulgently, his usual supper of barkbread and water untouched in front of him.

Rook, too, had little appetite. He stirred at the stew absent-mindedly, the spoon never leaving the bowl. He looked round at the others on the circular outer table, all tucking in hungrily. There were Magda and Stob, sharing a joke; and groups of other apprentices, loud and swaggering, at different stages in their learning; and Xanth, alone as usual, watching everything but saying nothing.

Rook sighed. If he couldn't even carve his prow, then how would he ever learn to fly?

A painful lump rose in his throat, which he could not swallow away. His eyes smarted and watered. He pushed the bowl back, climbed from the bench and quietly left the refectory. With the door closed behind him, he clambered down the circular staircase of the Academy Tower, passing the round doors of the sleeping cabins as he went, and on through the dark wooden colonnades where the skycraft lessons took place.

At the edge of the landing platform Rook stared out across the dark waters of the lake, his heart weary. The air was thick and heavy, smudging the stars and sliver of new moon, and muffling the night sounds coming from the Deepwoods beyond. Black, forbidding stormclouds rolled in from the north-west, making the air darker, denser – and charging it with a crackling force that made Rook's skin tingle.

The sky splintered and flashed as fine tendrils of lightning spread out across the darkness; the water shimmered with a pale green phosphorescence and, out of the corner of his eye, Rook caught sight of something darting across the lake. He couldn't quite make it out. The air seemed as heavy as a liquid and the lake blacker than it had ever looked before.

There it was again, a flash of yellow and red. And a perfect circular ripple spread out across the dark surface of the lake, growing in front of Rook's eyes, larger and larger, before fading away.

Suddenly, close by, there was the hum of swiftly beating wings – and Rook saw it. A large, insect-like creature with an angular head and a long, slender body striped yellow and red. As he watched, it swooped and dived, sipping at the luminous water before looping back up into the air. Another perfect ripple spread out.

Rook was entranced. His heart soared and bubbled. The little creature was so graceful, so elegant – so perfect.

And as he stared, unblinking, it was as though he too were flying beside it, darting down to the surface of the water and soaring back up again. His stomach turned somersaults. His head spun. He opened his mouth, and laughed and laughed and laughed . . .

The following morning, after a deep dreamless sleep, Rook skipped breakfast and hurried to the timber yards before the others had even emerged from their sleeping cabins. He hugged the great slab of wood.

'Perfect,' he whispered, and his body tingled with the feelings of the previous evening.

With mallet and chisel, Rook began to shape the wood. Although it was still dark, he worked swiftly and confidently, and without a break. And each time when, for a moment, he was unsure what to do next, he would close his eyes and stroke the wood gently, for Oakley

Gruffbark was right. The wood *was* telling him what to do.

The rough form of the skycraft began to take shape: the narrow seat, the fixed keel and, at the front, the raised figurehead. Although lacking any fine detail, the angular head of the creature was already clearly recognizable. He was working on the curved neck when he heard footsteps approaching. The first woodtrolls must be arriving from the surrounding villages.

Rook felt a hand on his shoulder. 'Early start, young'un?' said Oakley, his rubbery face creasing with amusement. 'That's what I like to see. Now, what do we have here?' He raised his lantern and held it up to the wood. For the first time, Rook saw the carved prow clearly. A smile tugged at the corners of his mouth.

'I think I've found it,' he said.

'I think you have,' said Oakley. 'Do you know what it is?'

Rook shook his head.

'Why, young'un, it's a stormhornet,' Oakley told him. 'And you don't see many of them, I can tell you.'

Rook's heart fluttered.

He lay his hands on the roughly hewn head of the creature. '*Stormhornet*,' he whispered.

The Gardens of Light

Click click click click . . .

The rhythmical sound of claw on stone came closer. Rook looked up from the bubbling pot in front of him, to see their tutor – an ancient spindlebug, already in his third century – tottering towards them. He was picking his way along one of the narrow, raised walkways which formed a winding network throughout the glowing underground cavern. A laden tray was gripped tightly in his claws.

Weeks after he had first set foot inside them, Rook still couldn't get over the Gardens of Light. Hidden deep below the huge Ironwood Glade, the vast illuminated cavern was one of the most spectacular wonders in all the Free Glades. It was here that the great glassy spindle-bugs grew the astonishing glowing fungus, the light from which shimmered on the cavern walls high above their heads and lent everything an eerie, yet ethereal beauty. Rook could have spent hours just gazing at the hypnotic shifting lights – if it wasn't for the varnishing.

'Nice glass of tea, Master Rook?' The ancient spindle-bug's voice, as thin and reedy as his long glass legs, snapped Rook out of his daydream. Tweezel towered above him.

'Thank you, sir,' said Rook, taking the glass of thin, amber liquid.

The spindlebug passed the tray to Magda, Stob and finally Xanth, who accepted the last glass with the faintest trace of a smile playing on his thin lips. Xanth really seemed to like Tweezel, Rook noticed. Although the young apprentice was still quiet and reserved, the spindlebug seemed somehow able to get him to relax. Rook never could work out how.

Perhaps it was the old creature's quaint formality; the way he insisted they stop and drink his strange scented tea, bowing to each other after each sip, but saying nothing – not a single word – until the glass was empty. Or perhaps it was the long conversations the two of them had together about long-ago times, as the apprentices stirred the little pots of varnish over the small brass burners, adding a pinch of oak pepper here and a dash of wormdust there.

Rook would listen in as Tweezel told Xanth about places with strange names, like the Palace of Shadows and the Viaduct Steps, and tell stories of a young girl called Maris, whom the old creature had loved like a daughter. They spoke quietly, politely, never raising their voices. Rook couldn't always make out the details, and when he tried to join in, Xanth would smile and Tweezel would say, in that thin voice of his, 'Time for a nice glass of tea, I think, my dear scholars.'

They finished their glasses and bowed. The spindle-bug inspected their varnish pots.

'Not bad, Master Rook, but be careful not to overheat your varnish. It does so thin it, I find – and with quite tiresome results.'

Rook nodded. It was strange to think, looking at the clear, bubbling mixture in front of him, that without it there would be no sky-flight. The sumpwood of the sky-craft, once coated with the meticulously prepared and applied varnish, gained the enhanced buoyancy that made wood-flight possible. Some said that it was Tweezel himself who had invented the varnish, but whether this was true or not, all accepted that the spindlebug was the greatest authority on varnish and its preparation in all the Deepwoods.

'What shall we do with you, Mistress Magda? We can't have lumps, now, can we?'

Magda sighed. Varnish was proving far trickier than she'd ever expected.

'And as for you, Master Stob!' Tweezel tutted, peering into the apprentice's blackened, sticky varnish pot. 'I think you'd better start again. To the milking field with you!'

Stob groaned, and with a dark look at Rook and Xanth he picked up a tin pail and a pair of heavy gloves, and stomped off towards a field of glowing fungus, several walkways below.

'Now, Xanth, my dear young scholar.' The spindle-bug's antennae quivered as he peered down at the glistening brass pot. 'I do believe you're done! Quite remarkable! I have never seen a more perfect varnish, and at only the fiftieth attempt! You, Master Xanth, will be the first to varnish your skycraft. Congratulations! You've made an old spindlebug very happy!'

Xanth smiled and looked down modestly. Rook was pleased for his classmate – though he couldn't help also feeling a little jealous. He was still months away from making a perfect varnish for *his* skycraft.

Just then there was a high-pitched scream, followed by a string of loud curses.

'Not again!' said Tweezel, trilling with irritation. 'Follow me, everyone.'

Rook, Magda and Xanth clicked the lids over their burners and followed the spindlebug off the laboratory ledge and down the stone walkway towards the fungus fields. As they rounded a corner, they saw him.

Covered with glue and upside down, Stob was stuck halfway up the cavern wall. Ten feet below him, snuffling amongst the glowing toadstools, a huge slime-mole swayed from side to side, its translucent body bulging and sloshing with mole-glue. The sight of the glistening creatures' jelly-like bodies always made Rook's stomach lurch queasily – and milking them was one of his least favourite tasks. But without mole-glue there would be no varnish, and without varnish there would be no wood-flight, and without wood-flight . . .

'Master Stob!' said Tweezel, his reedy voice sharp with vexation. 'Don't tell me. You did it again, didn't you? You milked it . . .'

'Yes,' said Stob weakly. 'From the wrong end.'

The Slaughterers Camp

'Behave yourselves, you stupid things!' came Magda's angry voice. 'Oh, no! Not again!'

Rook turned to see his friend hopelessly entangled in the gossamer light spider-silk sails. 'You've got to watch out for the crosswind, Magda,' he called over his shoulder, as he concentrated on controlling his own sails, which were billowing up into the warm air like two large, unruly kites.

He tugged on the silk cord in his right hand and the loft-sail gently folded in on itself. Then, having waited a split second, he swung his left arm round in a wide arc, playing out cord to the nether-sail. It, too, folded gracefully in on itself, and fell silently to the ground.

'How do you *do* that?' said Magda. She looked at the two neatly folded sails beside Rook, then at the tangled mess of cord and spider-silk wrapped round her own arms and trailing in the dust, and sighed deeply.

'You look like a bedraggled snowbird,' laughed Stob. He was sitting at a table eating tilder steaks with two flame-red slaughterers, who laughed good-naturedly with him.

In front of them the huge fire crackled in the vast iron brazier, throwing heat high into the clearing and warming the long family hammocks slung from the trees above.

Rook loved the slaughterers camp almost as much as the Gardens of Light. Especially at this time of day, when the evening shadows grew long, the camp fires were replenished and, one by one, the slaughterer families woke up and poked their flame-red heads from their hammocks to greet the new night. Soon, the communal breakfast would begin. Rook's stomach gurgled in anticipation of tilder steaks and honey-coated hammel-horn hams. But first, he must try to disentangle his poor friend.

He turned back to Magda, crouched down, and began gently tugging at the knotted ropes.

'Careful, now. Careful,' came a voice from behind him. It was Brisket, the slaughterer who had been assigned to teach the four apprentices all about sail-setting and ropecraft. 'Don't want to weaken the fibres now, do we?' he said. 'Let me have a look.'

Rook stood back. Brisket kneeled down and began teasing the ropes loose with one hand, while – taking care not to snag it – easing the sailcloth free with the other. Rook watched closely. Even though the slaughterer was little older than himself, his every move-ment revealed a lifetime of experience.

'My word, mistress!' he was saying. 'You really have got yourself in a tangle this time, haven't you?'

'I just don't understand it,' said Magda, her voice tear-ful and cross. 'I thought I was doing everything right.'

'Sail-setting is a difficult business,' said Brisket.

'But I did what you taught me,' said Magda. 'I threw out the loft-sail slowly, just as you said.'

'But you threw out into a crosswind,' Rook blurted out, stopping himself when he saw the hurt look on Magda's face.

'Rook's got a point,' said Brisket softly as he carefully folded Magda's sails. 'You must feel what the sail is telling you through the cord. You must watch how the wind shapes it, and let your movements flow. Never fight the sails, Mistress Magda.'

'But it's so hard,' said Magda disconsolately.

'I know, I know,' said Brisket understandingly. 'Get Master Rook here to help you. He's got the touch, and no mistake.' He paused, and tugged at a last knotted cord. The knot undid, the cord slid free. 'There, Mistress Magda,' said Brisket, handing her the sails. 'That's all for today. Now, who's for breakfast?'

Stob, Magda and Rook sat at a long table, which was weighed down by the sumptious spread of food laid out upon it. A little way off, Xanth stood practising his ropecraft. With one lazy movement, he lassoed the great curling horn of a hammelhorn which stood chewing the cud at the far side of its enclosure.

'Show off,' said Stob, and grabbed another huge steak from the platter before them.

'You'll turn into a hammelhorn if you eat any more,' said Magda.

Rook looked across at Xanth. Thanks to his success in varnishing, the young apprentice had gained a head start on the others. He'd already mastered sail-setting and was close to passing ropecraft. Despite this, Rook didn't feel jealous. Rather, he felt sorry for him. It was Xanth's haunted expression and quiet, lonely manner that touched him.

'Oh, he's all right,' he said to Stob, and turned back to his steaming tilder stew.

By now the communal tables were bursting with hungry, happy slaughterers, toasting the new night with mugs of woodale and bursting into song. Stob joined in, raising his mug high in the air.

Stob, Rook noticed, loved the slaughterers camp even more than he did. The arrogant, surly Stob he knew seemed to disappear in the company of slaughterers. He relaxed and become almost playful. For their part, the slaughterers had taken to Stob, treating the young apprentice like some sort of prize hammelhorn, to be fed and patted on the back.

Just then there was a loud cry from above their heads. Rook looked up. There, an arm waving in greeting, was Knuckle astride the *Woodwasp*, bearing down on them in a series of exquisitely executed loops. He had a lasso in his hand, which he was swinging round and round.

Lower he came, swooping down past the communal hammocks strung out between the ironwood trees, over the hammelhorn pens and tanning vats. When he was no more than a dozen strides away, he flicked his wrist forward. The rope coiled down like a striking woodcobra and circled Stob's raised hand. Knuckle jerked the lasso. The slip-knot tightened around the mug of woodale – which abruptly flew out of Stob's grasp and up into the air.

'Hey!' shouted Stob indignantly.

Knuckle smiled and took a gulp from the mug. 'Delicious!' he called down as he brought the little sky-craft in to land. 'Thanks, friend,' he said, handing the empty mug to Stob. 'I was feeling rather thirsty.'

Stob looked at the slaughterer for an instant – then a broad smile broke across his face and he threw back his head and roared with laughter. The slaughterers around them joined in.

'It's good to see you, Rook,' said Knuckle, sitting down next to him and helping himself to Rook's tilder stew. 'You look more grown-up each time I see you. You'll be off on your treatise-voyage in no time, I'll be bound.'

Rook smiled. 'If I can master ropecraft half as well as you, I hope to,' he said. 'The *Stormhornet*'s varnished, rigged and tethered at Lake Landing, just waiting to be flown – if the masters ever let me, that is.'

'Oh, they'll let you all right,' laughed Knuckle, his mouth full of stew. 'From what I hear, you're a natural, just like your friend Xanth over there.' He paused. A smile played on his lips. 'A stormhornet, eh? A rare creature, by all accounts. Swift and graceful, and with a sting in its tail; a harbinger of mighty storms brewing far off.' He clapped Rook on the shoulder. 'It's a fine name, Rook, my friend. A fine name!'

The Naming Rite

'We are assembled here, over Earth and under Sky, to welcome four apprentices to the Academy's long list of brave librarian knights, so we are,' announced Parsimmon, the High Master of the Lake Landing Academy. Behind him, the mighty Ironwood Glade cast its reflection in the glassy lake; above, the sky glowed a deep gold. The air was heavy and still.

Rook's heart give a little leap. He was standing in a line with Magda, Stob and Xanth. Before them, at the centre of a long, raised lufwood platform, stood Parsimmon, flanked on both sides by the tutors who had guided them through their long, arduous months of learning: Oakley Gruffbark, the wise and patient woodtroll, his tufted hair blazing a brilliant orange in the evening light; Tweezel, the ancient spindlebug, leaning on an ironwood staff and wheezing softly; and Brisket, the flame-red slaughterer, dressed in a heavy hammel-hornskin coat, with a length of rope coiled over one shoulder.

'You have done well, my young apprentices,' Parsimmon continued. 'Very well. For though many months more will pass before you are ready to depart on your treatise-voyages, this evening marks the completion of the first stage of your studies.' He turned to the row of skycraft, tethered to heavy rings at the back of the stage. 'You have carved your skycraft exquisitely, taking care to heed what the wood told you. You have prepared your varnish and applied it with care, to give them the gift of flight. You have rigged them with sails of finest woodspider-silk, tamed by your touch, and you have mastered ropecraft, to tether them and bring you safely back to earth. Well done, my fine young librarian knights!'

Rook lowered his head modestly. The tutors murmured their approval. Rook nudged Xanth and smiled. Xanth looked round and, for an instant, Rook thought he saw a flicker of sadness in his friend's eyes before he returned the smile.

'It is time,' Parsimmon continued, 'for you to name your skycraft which, tomorrow, you will fly for the first time.'

'At last,' Rook heard Stob mutter under his breath.

Magda felt for Rook's hand and squeezed it tightly. 'We did it,' she whispered.

Rook nodded, and looked up into the twilight sky, his eyes wide and heart singing. It was indeed a perfect evening, with the sun warm, the wind gentle, and small clouds rolling across the sky like orange and purple balls of fluff. The water of the lake ruffled like velvet.

226

'Step forward, Magda Burlix,' said Parsimmon.

Magda left the line. She climbed up onto the stage, shook the High Master's hand and crossed over to where her skycraft was tethered beside the others. She laid her hands upon the gently bobbing figurehead.

'By Earth and Sky, your name shall be *Woodmoth*,' she said, reciting the words she had been practising. 'Together, we shall set forth into the Deepwoods and return with a treatise entitled, *The Iridescence of Midnight Woodmoth Wings*.' She bowed her head and returned to her place in the line.

'Step forward, Stob Lummus,' said Parsimmon.

Stob came up and rested his hands on the ridged, curling horns of his figurehead. 'By Earth and Sky, your name shall be *Hammelhorn*,' he said in a loud, confident voice. 'Together, we shall set forth into the Deepwoods and return with a treatise entitled, *A Study of the Growth Rings of the Coppertree*.

As Xanth stepped forwards, he glanced round at Rook. He looked oddly troubled; sheepish, almost. Rook smiled at his friend encouragingly, but the expression in Xanth's eyes remained sad, haunted.

'By Earth and Sky, your name shall be *Ratbird*,' Xanth announced, his hands shaking as they clasped the creature's carved snout. 'Together, we shall set forth into the Deepwoods . . .' His head lowered and the thick hair which had grown unchecked since his arrival at Lake Landing flopped down over his eyes. His voice dropped. 'And return with a treatise entitled . . .' A faraway look came into his eyes as he raised his head. '*A Witnessing of the Hatching of a Caterbird from its Cocoon.*'

It was Rook's turn. He stepped up onto the stage, his heart bursting with pride and excitement, and walked slowly towards his skycraft. 'By Earth and Sky, your name shall be *Stormhornet*,' he said. 'Together we shall set forth into the Deepwoods and return with a treatise entitled, *An Eyewitness Account of the Mythical Great Convocation of Banderbears.*'

All four apprentices raised their right hands and touched their bloodoak pendants with their left. Then, heads raised and voices carrying across the dark waters of the lake, they announced in unison, 'This we pledge to do, or perish in the attempt.'

Sure enough, hanging from the iron hook outside his cabin was a great leather flight-suit with pockets and loops, as yet unfilled with equipment. Wooden log-shields... straps beside it. With trembling fingers, Rook eased them and, fumbling clumsily, pulled the soft, burnished flight-suit on over... for his first flight. He was about to go... his new goggles. Rook dashed down the lower walkway to join his companions on the landing.

'Where are our Skycrafts?' he asked breathlessly.

'Over there,' said Magda, nodding towards the four...

Rook grinned. They... The...

...few more minutes went...

...wrench... pains towards the timber...

So where is our flight-instructor?

...not all about us more like, said...

·CHAPTER TWELVE·

FLIGHT

Rook was awoken by shafts of light streaming through the grille of his sleeping-cabin door. He threw off his tilderwool blanket and flung the door open. 'Magda,' he called. 'Magda, are you up yet?'

'Down here, sleepy head,' came Magda's reply.

Screwing up his eyes against the light, Rook squinted down at the landing below. There, resplendent in their green flight-suits, goggles and golden wood-armour, stood Magda, Xanth and Stob.

'Why didn't you wake me?' Rook called angrily.

'We tried,' said Stob. 'But you were dead to the world, believe me.'

Rook scratched his head. He'd had the old familiar nightmare again the previous night, and had woken in the half-light of early dawn, exhausted. He must have nodded off again.

'Come and join us,' said Xanth. 'Your flight-suit's by your door.'

Sure enough, hanging from the iron hook outside his cabin was a green leather flight-suit with pockets and loops, as yet unfilled with equipment. Wooden leg-shields and arm-protectors dangled from their cord straps beside it. With trembling fingers Rook seized them and, fumbling clumsily, pulled the soft, burnished flight-suit on over his night clothes. His first flight! He was about to go on his first flight! Pausing only to adjust his new goggles, Rook dashed down the tower walkway to join his companions on the landing.

'Where are our skycraft?' he asked breathlessly.

'Over there,' said Magda, nodding towards the four skycraft, still tethered to the back of the lufwood stage.

There, gently bobbing in the breeze, was the *Ratbird*, the *Hammelhorn*, the *Woodmoth* – and the *Stormhornet*. Rook grinned. 'They look good, don't they?' he said.

'They'll look even better up in the sky,' said Stob. 'Where's our flight instructor? I thought he'd be here by now.'

'Patience,' said Magda. 'We've waited long enough. A few more minutes won't make any difference.'

As the early dawn mist began to lift over the lake, and the sounds of hammelhorn carts rumbling down the woodtroll paths towards the timber yards echoed through the air like distant thunder, the apprentices began to get impatient.

'Sunrise, the High Master said, didn't he?' said Stob. 'So where is our flight instructor?'

'Perhaps he overslept, whoever he is,' said Xanth.

'Forgotten all about us, more like,' said Stob irritably.

'Well, I'm not going to stand for it. How about you three?'

The others shrugged.

'Just once round the lake and back again,' Stob said. 'It can't do any harm. Who's up for it?'

'Me,' said Rook and Xanth together.

Magda nodded. 'All right,' she said quietly.

Rook ran to the *Stormhornet*. Now that it had been decided, he couldn't wait to be up in the sky. He released the tether, jumped up onto the saddle and, feet in the stirrups, grasped the two wooden rope-handles.

With nimble fingers, he raised the loft-sail and lowered the nether-sail – keeping a hold of the upper nether-sail rope as he did so. The two sails billowed out in front of him, just as they had so many times before, when he had been perched on top of the training block. This time, however, his craft was not secured to the ground.

With a tremble and a sigh, the elegant *Stormhornet* rose from the platform. For a second, it hovered there, its sails fluttering and flight-weights swaying.

231

Then, as the wind took it, Rook pulled on the pinner-rope, and the skycraft suddenly came to life and surged upwards into the crisp morning air.

Nothing could have prepared Rook for the thrill which raced through his body as the skycraft climbed ever higher. Not the buoyant lecterns, nor riding the prowlgrins as they leaped from tree to tree – nor even his brief flight with Knuckle. This time, he was in control. The *Stormhornet* responded to his every movement, dipping and swooping, rising and looping, utterly obedient to his command. It was exhilarating. It was awesome.

Once round the lake, Stob had said, yet now he was air-borne, Rook had no intention of landing so soon. He looked round at the others. Stob was some way to his left, his flight steady and arrow-straight, the heavy hammelhorn prow seemingly butting its way through the currents of air. Magda, in contrast, seemed almost to be fluttering; this way and that she went, darting through the air, catching each gust and eddy for just a moment before changing course. Rook realigned the weights and sails, pulled the pinner-rope to his left and swooped down towards her. As their eyes met, they both burst out laughing.

'Isn't this the best thing ever?' said Rook, his voice snatched away on the wind.

'Incredible!' Magda shouted back.

Xanth, sleek and poised on the *Ratbird*, swooped down low over the lake, his trailing flight-weights skimming the still surface. Rook gasped at the elegance of his friend's flight. Xanth twitched the ropes and flew off, laughing.

Standing up in the stirrups, and tugging hard on the pinner-rope, Rook gave chase. Up to the top of the trees they flew, then, twisting round, they hurtled down, down like stones, before pulling out at the last moment, skimming the water again, and soaring back into the sky.

Xanth glanced round, his face glowing with excitement.

'*Whup! Whup! Wahoo!*' Rook cried.

'*Wahoo!*' Xanth bellowed and, turning away, darted back off towards the trees, looping the loop twice as he went.

This time Rook did not follow. Pulling the *Stormhornet* round, he flew back across the lake.

All at once he heard a cry of alarm, and spun round to see Stob and the *Hammelhorn* hurtling straight towards a great ironwood tree on the far edge of the lake. His hands were a blur of movement as they leaped around the ropes and levers, but the *Hammelhorn* was not responding. With a sickening crunch, the skycraft struck the tree's massive trunk, and fell.

Rook gasped and, distracted, let go of his own sail-ropes. The next moment he felt a heavy drag below him. Looking down, he saw, to his horror, that the nether-sail was half immersed in water. Desperately, he tried to raise it, while at the same time giving full head to the loft-sail. But it was no use. With a loud splash, the *Stormhornet* struck the lake.

The icy water snatched Rook's breath away and

chilled him instantly to the bone. He struggled desperately upwards, fighting against the weight of his wet clothes, and emerged next to the *Stormhornet*, which was bobbing about on the surface, pinned down by its sodden sails. Gasping with relief, Rook grabbed hold of the tether-rope, and clung on tightly.

Overhead, Magda seemed to stall. Her sails collapsed and the *Woodmoth* lurched to one side. With a shrill scream, she tumbled down towards the lake. There was a resounding *splash*, followed, seconds later, by coughing and spluttering as Magda surfaced beside Rook.

'It's all your fault, Rook!' she laughed. 'You put me off!'

The *Woodmoth* dropped slowly down towards the surface of the lake, landing close to the base of the ironwood tree where a disgruntled Stob sat rubbing his head ruefully.

Xanth swooped in from overhead. 'Are you two all right?' he called. 'It's a bit cold for a swim, if you ask me.' He flew off with a laugh, circling the lake effortlessly on the soaring *Ratbird*, before turning back towards Lake Landing.

'Just look at him,' said Magda. 'He makes it look so easy.' She shook her head. 'Who'd have thought it, eh? Quiet little Xanth, the best flyer of us all.'

'Beginner's luck,' said Rook, and smiled. 'I'll race you to the landing, come on!'

He and Magda splashed through the cold water, with Magda soon pulling in front. Ahead of them, Xanth was coming in to land, the *Ratbird* – sleek and swift – tilting into the wind.

'He's coming in too fast,' said Rook.

'Oh, he'll be all right,' Magda called back. 'Look at him, he's in control.'

The skycraft swooped low in an elegant arc and descended steeply. Just as it did so, a lone figure emerged from the Landing Tower and strode across the lufwood decking. At the sight of the figure, Xanth seemed to check his descent. The *Ratbird* reared up, its sails collapsed and the smooth arc turned into an ugly tumble. The next moment the skycraft crashed heavily into the landing, splintering its slender mast and throwing its rider clear.

Rook and Magda kicked out for the landing. The figure was crouching over the stricken body of their friend as they approached. At the same time Stob was running from the far edge of the lake, dragging the *Hammelhorn* behind him. Wet, breathless and shivering from the cold, Magda and Rook heaved themselves up onto the landing. Behind them, their skycraft bobbed on the water.

'Is he all right?' asked Magda.

'He'll live,' said the figure, without looking up. 'But

he's broken his leg badly. This is one apprentice who won't be flying again for a long time to come.'

Xanth groaned and opened his eyes. 'It hurts,' he said miserably.

'It's all my fault!' said Stob, running up, red-faced and with tears in his eyes. 'We were waiting for the flight instructor, but he didn't show up, so I thought it wouldn't do any harm just to take a short flight round the lake and back.' He shook his head. 'If I'd only known it would end like this . . .' He sank to his knees and grasped Xanth's hand. 'I'm sorry, Xanth. We should have waited for that stupid flight instructor. Now we'll have to postpone our first lesson.'

'I don't think so,' said the figure, standing up and turning to face them. '*I* am your "stupid" flight instructor.'

Stob groaned; he'd done it again.

'Perhaps you've heard of me,' she said. 'My name is Varis Lodd.'

Rook's jaw dropped. So this was the great Varis Lodd. Felix's sister. The librarian knight who had rescued him from the Deepwoods all those years ago. He wondered whether he should say something to her . . . Then again, he thought, she didn't even seem to recognize him – and why should she? He'd been a child of four when she'd rescued him, and she hadn't seen him since. He bit his tongue.

'And as for your first lesson . . .' Varis was saying. She paused and looked along the line of apprentices, one red-faced, one open-mouthed and one shivering; and at Xanth, prostrate on the landing, and moaning with pain. 'You have just learned it.'

As the moon peeked up above the horizon, broad and creamy yellow, Rook soared into the sky. Below him on Lake Landing, Varis Lodd and Parsimmon grew smaller and smaller.

Far to his left, a great caterbird, its black plumage and huge curved beak magnificent in the moonlight, flapped slowly across the sky. Xanth would have loved the sight. Rook remembered his friend's proposed treatise and wondered whether he would ever achieve his dreams. Poor Xanth. Even now, six long months after the terrible crash, he still walked with the aid of a stick, and had become even quieter and more haunted-looking, if that were possible.

Rook had always made a point of seeking Xanth out and including him in all the talk of sail-craft, flight-signing and wind-riding that accompanied their flight training. But there was no escaping the fact that, when-ever he, Magda and Stob took to the air, Xanth was left behind, his pale face and dark eyes betraying his hurt and disappointment.

Tonight had been especially tough for Xanth because it was the night of their final flight. After this, Magda, Stob and Rook would be fully-fledged librarian knights,

ready to embark on their
treatise-voyages. The thrill
of it coursed through
Rook's body as
he realigned the
sails and pulled
hard on the
pinner-
rope. The
skycraft shifted round,
swooped down lower in the
sky and skirted the fringes of
the vast island of light and prosperity nestling in the
dark, mysterious Deepwoods.

'The Free Glades,' he whispered, as he steered the little
craft over each of the three glistening lakes in turn, past
the towering Ironwood Glade and back down towards
New Undertown.

He skimmed over the Lufwood Tower, the building
that had so impressed him when he first arrived in the
glades: how long ago that now seemed! Over the hive-
huts and the tufted goblins' long-houses he flew, and
round the gyle-goblin colony where small groups of the
bulbous-nosed goblins were wending their way home
from the surrounding fields – back to their Grossmother
and a supper of sweet gyle honey.

The moon rose higher. Tacking expertly against the gathering wind, Rook swooped down over the Tarry-vine Tavern, meeting-place for creatures from the farthest corners of the Deepwoods. How he'd loved sitting in its dark corners, listening to the tales of the old times, before stone-sickness, when the great sky ships had sailed the skies.

And now, here he was, in his own skycraft, with the moonlight in *his* eyes and the wind in *his* hair. He smiled, re-jigged the sails, stood up in the stirrups and flew up high over the tavern and beyond.

There were the timber yards, and the woodtroll villages beyond. 'Farewell, Oakley,' he whispered, remembering the kindly, tufty-haired old woodtroll. 'And thank you.'

There, beneath the huge Ironwood Glade, was the entrance to the Gardens of Light. How many times, labouring over his varnish stove, had he dreamed of this very night. But now the time had come, he knew he would miss the beautiful shimmering gardens – and his ancient spindlebug tutor. 'Farewell, Tweezel!' Rook whispered.

239

And there, shrouded in a fine red mist, the slaughter-ers camp. The huge fires were blazing beneath the sleeping hammocks, already swaying with waking slaughterers, making ready for a hard night's work. Rook could almost taste the spicy tilder sausages he'd eaten so many times. 'Farewell, Brisket!' he whispered. 'Enjoy your breakfast, kind master.'

He coaxed his craft into a long, slow turn, and headed back towards Lake Landing. In the distance, the Silver Pastures glistened in the moonlight. They'd never looked more beautiful, thought Rook. 'Farewell, Knuckle – my friend,' he said softly.

As he approached the Central Lake, Rook spotted Magda and Stob circling the landing, waiting for him to join them for their final descent. They, too, had been say-ing their last goodbyes. A lump came to Rook's throat.

There was heavy, arrogant Stob on his solid *Hammelhorn*. Quick to anger, slow to forgive – but now, Rook realized, for all his faults, like an older brother to him. And Magda, serious, sensitive Magda, on her *Woodmoth*, fluttering delicately on the wind. She was like a sister, sharing his triumphs and disasters alike, and always ready with a word of encouragement or a sympathetic look.

The three of them twisted down through the air in perfect harmony, furling their sails gracefully as they came lower, and landing in front of their flight instructor and the High Master soundlessly.

'Well done, all of you,' Varis Lodd said quietly. 'That was magnificent.'

Glowing with pleasure at her words of praise, Rook smiled. He remembered how haughty and aloof he had initially thought Varis Lodd to be. Yet how wrong he'd been. On that first morning, as she had turned and walked away, he'd run after her, keen to announce himself.

'I'm Rook Barkwater,' he had told her.

And she had turned, placed a hand on his shoulder and smiled warmly. 'I know,' she'd said. 'I'd know those deep blue eyes anywhere. But look at you! What a fine young apprentice you've turned into. Go and get your skycraft, Rook Barkwater, and then we shall have lunch together at my table.'

Ever since that moment Rook had felt close to her, as if the bond between them – established all those years ago when Varis had discovered him in the Deepwoods – had never been broken. Sometimes she reminded him of Felix, humorous and playful. At other times she could be as earnest and exacting as Alquix Venvax. Throughout it all, however, she had always been there for Rook; teaching him well and spurring him on to ever greater feats of achievement. And now here he was, standing before her, having completed the final flight of his studies.

'You are all now ready,' she said, bowing her head formally. 'It is time for you to embark on your treatise-voyages, friends of Earth and Sky.'

Parsimmon bowed his head in turn. 'Good luck in all your travels, and may you return safely to us in the Free Glades, my dear, precious librarian knights.'

Rook's heart was thumping fit to burst. He felt like

shouting out, with relief, with joy and anticipation, but instead he followed Stob and Magda's lead, bowing low and saying quietly, 'By Earth and Sky, we shall not fail you.'

Just then the heavy creaking sound of rough wheels on the lufwood decking interrupted the quiet ceremony, as a hammelhorn cart drew up, accompanied by two Free Glade guards on prowlgrins. Rook looked round.

A young apprentice lay groaning softly in the back of the cart, a dark stain spreading across the knife-grinder robes he wore. Parsimmon hurried over.

'We found him on the Northern Fringes,' the first guard, a gnokgoblin, reported, saluting the High Master. 'He says he was one of a group of apprentices from Undertown ambushed by shrykes. Says they knew they were coming.'

'Is this true?' said Parsimmon, kneeling down beside the stricken apprentice.

'Yes, master,' the apprentice whispered, his face pinched and white from the pain. 'They picked us out in the Eastern Roost, surrounded us on the upper gangways, and hacked us down, one by one . . .'

Parsimmon patted his hand. 'There, there, the journey is a terrible one indeed, but you have made it. That's the important thing. We will look after you now. You are very precious to us.' He motioned to the guards. 'Take him to the tower, and fetch Tweezel – we don't want to lose this brave young apprentice.'

The guards hurried off. Varis walked stiffly over to Parsimmon. 'I don't like it,' she said tersely. 'That is the third group that has been ambushed. We can't afford these losses, High Master. The Guardians of Night are growing stronger. I sense their hand in this.'

Parsimmon nodded sagely. 'You may be right, my dear Varis, but that is a matter for the Free Glades Council and our masters back in Old Undertown. Tonight, let us salute our brave young friends here, and talk no more about it.' He turned to Magda, Stob and Rook. 'Go now,' he said. 'Supper awaits you in the upper refectory.'

As he turned to follow the others, Rook caught sight of Xanth, half-hidden in shadow, his face ashen, his lips thin and bloodless. Their eyes met. 'Xanth,' Rook called out.

Xanth looked away shiftily.

'Xanth!' he called, louder.

'Come and join us.'

'Leave him,' said Magda. 'He knows where to find us if he wants to. He must be feeling pretty miserable at the moment – wishing his leg would mend, wishing he was us.'

Rook nodded. But though he knew Magda's words made sense, he didn't believe them. It wasn't sadness or regret, or even envy, that he had seen in Xanth's eyes.

It was guilt.

CHAPTER THIRTEEN

THE FOUNDRY GLADE

After a wild storm that raged through the night and late into the morning, the weather had finally cleared around noon. In its wake came fluffy white clouds which scudded across the gleaming sky, seemingly buffing it up as they passed, while down in the Deepwoods, it looked to Rook as if every leaf of every tree glinting in the shafts of silvery sunlight had been freshly waxed and polished.

He steered his skycraft expertly round a great lullabee tree and on low over the jagged thickets of razorthorn beyond, his heart racing with the excitement of it all. He could hardly believe it; so soon after his final flight as an apprentice, here he was with the great Varis Lodd and his best friend, Knuckle the slaughterer, flying through the Deepwoods on a raid!

Darting swiftly and silently through the dappled light of the forest, the three skycraft – the *Windhawk*,

Woodwasp and *Stormhornet* – kept low in amongst the towering trees. Rook's hands played with the rope-handles, coaxing the skycraft this way and that, up, down and from side to side. It was difficult flying, demanding his constant attention.

Every so often – more from nervousness than necessity – his hand would pat his flight-suit, checking that all the unfamiliar items of flight paraphernalia were still in place: his grappling-hook and a coil of rope; his water-flask and – Sky and Earth forbid he should ever need it – his lufwood box, courtesy of Tweezel the spindlebug, with its bandages, potions and salves. On his chest he wore his telescope, compass and scales; at his side, his knife, Felix's ornate sword and, slung through a leather loop on his belt, one of the small razor-sharp axes carried by all skycraft pilots. Now he felt like a real librarian knight, equipped for any eventuality. If only the uneasy fluttering in the pit of his stomach would go away.

Dense forest ahead, Varis Lodd signalled to her two companions and, as one, she, Knuckle and Rook soared up high into the air and burst through the forest canopy.

Rook gasped with wonder as the tops of the trees spread out all round him. He stood up in his carved stirrups and, with the warm wind in his face, gave the *Stormhornet* full sail. The skycraft trembled for a moment before throwing Rook back in his seat and leaping forwards.

Stay low, Varis signalled silently. It was important that they weren't spotted.

Rook pulled at the looped pinner-rope. The

Stormhornet swooped down obediently, and skimmed over the top of the watery forest, just like its yellow and red striped namesake that Rook had watched skimming the surface of the lake. How long ago that seemed now. Rook's thoughts began to wander.

He went back to the previous evening when, just as he had been about to turn in for the night, he had heard a light *tap-tap-tap* on the door of his sleeping cabin. It was Varis Lodd, her flight-suit fully equipped and a loaded crossbow at her side.

'Come with me,' she'd said. 'I have something to tell you.'

He had followed her down to Lake Landing, where Knuckle was waiting for them, twirling his lasso. Below them, the dark, turbulent waters of the lake surged and swelled; above, dark, boiling clouds tumbled in from the west. Varis had turned to address them both, her face sombre, her voice trembling with emotion. Rook had never seen her so upset.

'Your young friend, Xanth, approached me this evening,' she began. 'Since his injury, he's made himself useful by, shall we say, gathering information.'

'Spying?' said Rook, faintly shocked.

'You could call it that,' said Varis. 'In our war against the Guardians of Night and their allies, we need to be vigilant. Anyway, young Xanth had disturbing news.'

'Go on,' said Knuckle, letting the rope fall.

'Slavery has returned to the Foundry Glade.'

Knuckle shook his head bitterly. 'Will the Foundry Master never learn?'

Varis put a hand on the slaughterer's shoulder. 'Like you, Knuckle here lost his family to slave-takers,' she said to Rook. 'We thought we'd taught them and their goblin allies a lesson last time we raided, but it seems they're back to their old ways.'

'These slaves,' Rook remembered asking, 'are they slaughterers? Gnokgoblins?'

And Varis had shaken her head. 'They're ...' She had turned to Rook, her eyes filled with a mixture of anger and sorrow.

'What?'

'Banderbears, Rook,' she had said. 'Banderbears.'

The *Stormhornet* juddered as the memory of Varis's words made his fingers tremble. Banderbears! How could anyone enslave such mighty, noble creatures? The very thought of it made his blood boil. Yet that is exactly what Hemuel Spume, the Foundry Master, had done. What kind of an individual must he be to keep banderbears in chains?

'You love banderbears as much as I do,' Varis had said. 'I knew you'd want to help rescue them.'

'And Stob and Magda?' Rook had asked.

Varis had shaken her head. 'The fewer the better on this sort of raid,' she'd said. 'And you two are the best flyers in the Free Glades.' She had paused. 'If you're with me, we'll need to fly into the Foundry Glade under the noses of Spume's goblin guards, release the banderbears from their slave-hut and get away before we're discovered. It won't be easy.'

'We're with you,' Rook and Knuckle had both replied at the same time. It was then that Rook had first felt the fluttering in the pit of his stomach.

As the sun darkened and slid down towards the horizon, Rook felt the wind getting up once again. He trimmed his nether-sail and tightened his grip on the pinner-rope. Although the stiffening breeze would make their flight much quicker, it also made the skycraft skittish and wilful.

There it is, Knuckle signalled, signing the words quickly, thumb and forefinger coming together to form the unmistakable signal for *glade*.

Rook looked ahead. Far in the distance, he saw thick black smoke belching out of the tall foundry chimneys and staining the sky above with a dark smudge of filth. His heart missed a beat.

Tack down! Varis signalled urgently, the *Windhawk* darting back down into the forest.

Rook shifted the rope-handles, bringing in the nether-sail and letting out the loft-sail while, at the same time, shifting his balance in the stirrups and slowly raising the pinner-rope. He chewed his lower lip nervously. The *Stormhornet* dipped forwards and dived down through a break in the canopy of leaves. As it entered the protected shadowy half-light below, the wind immediately dropped and the delicate craft trembled and dropped. Rook's fingers darted round the ropes and levers. The skycraft righted itself and swooped on.

Varis flashed a quick signal – *Outstanding flying, Rook!* – and smiled.

Rook found himself grinning broadly, then flushed as blood rushed to his cheeks. He felt suddenly so proud that the great Varis Lodd should compliment him on his skill. He patted the *Stormhornet*'s prow. 'Well done,' he whispered.

The light began to fail as they journeyed on. Time and again, Rook had to swerve to avoid the trees and their great spreading branches which suddenly loomed up out of the gloom before him. Just ahead, he noticed an oily yellow light glowing between the trees.

Follow me, both of you, Varis signalled over her shoulder.

She flew steeply upwards and landed silently on the broad branch of a huge, ancient ironwood tree. Rook and Knuckle came down beside her. Varis signalled to the other two and pointed towards the source of the light ahead.

Rook unhooked his telescope and raised it to one eye. Peering through the overhanging branches, he studied the glade before him. Vast, sick, scarred, the clearing was like a great festering scab on the surface of the forest. It stank of sulphur, of pitch, of molten metal. It echoed to the percussive sounds of hammers clanking and wood being chopped; to the roar of the furnaces, to the whipcrack and barked commands of the goblin task-masters, and the synchronized crunch of spades and pickaxes digging deep down into the ore-pits.

Beneath it all, like a dark mournful choir, was the sonorous groaning of the labouring goblins. Rook trembled. What those poor, miserable creatures must be suffering to produce so terrible a sound . . .

Just then, cutting across the cacophony of heavy toil and deep despair, there came a long creak, followed by a dull thud. Rook swung his telescope round. A cloud of dust, billowing up at the edge of the great clearing, settled to reveal the latest felled tree lying on the ground where it had crashed down. Already, a team of goblins were scampering over its immense trunk, stripping it bare.

The beautiful forest! Rook signed.

Hemuel Spume, Varis signalled back, and drew a finger in a cutting motion across her throat.

Rook nodded.

Apart from the ash-heaps and earth-mounds which erupted from the bare earth like boils, there were also mountains of stripped logs, each one serving one of the foundries. Teams of stooped, bony goblins – their hooded robes tattered and their skin ingrained with years of grime – were removing the logs, one after the other, and dragging them with ropes and hooks towards

THE FOUNDRY GLADE

the foundries, and inside. Work-team after work-team, log after log – yet the tall, unsteady heaps never diminished in size, for no sooner was one tree-trunk removed, than it was replaced by another, newly felled, as the cancerous glade ate further and further into the surrounding forest.

Where are the banderbears? Rook signed, shoulders shrugging.

Knuckle tapped him on the shoulder and pointed.

A banderbear! Heart beating excitedly, Rook shifted his telescope round and homed in on the banderbear emerging from the bottom of the tall, bulbous foundry to his left. The sight shocked him to the marrow in his bones.

The poor creature, with its jutting ribs and sunken cheeks, looked half-starved. Its mossy fur was singed and lustre-less; all over its hunched, cringing body, bare patches of red-raw skin showed through. Shackled at its ankles and wrists, the bander-bear was being escorted by two goblins, each one armed with a long, heavy stick – which they used often and with obvious relish. The banderbear took the blows, nei-ther reacting nor resisting. And as Rook watched it slowly shuffling on towards the slave-hut, he realized that the creature's spirit had been crushed.

Five more banderbears appeared, one from each of the foundries. If anything, their condition was even worse than the first. None of them seemed able to move any faster, despite the vicious blows and angry oaths that rained down on them. One was limping badly. Another had an angry weeping burn on its shoulder. All of them were shivering violently, freezing cold now after their hours spent in the blistering heat.

Rook turned to Varis. Her eyes were blazing; her jaw clenched and unclenched. She gripped her crossbow in both hands. Rook – his pity turned to anger – felt for the dagger and sword at his belt, then looked back at the glade.

As he watched, the banderbears were led into the slave-hut and chained to the central pillars within. Despite the roof, the open-sided building offered no shelter from the biting wind, and the six shackled banderbears huddled together for warmth at the centre of the mattress of filthy straw, mute and trembling, their eyes lifeless and dull.

Rook scanned the glade through the telescope. It seemed almost empty. With the banderbears no longer stoking the furnaces, the foundries had fallen idle, and the last of the ore-workers, tree-fellers and log-pullers were disappearing inside their long-huts. The goblin guards followed them, laughing and joking.

Soon the only remaining individual to be seen was a lone guard, asleep at his post at the top of a look-out turret. An eerie silence descended over the Foundry Glade. Varis turned to Knuckle and Rook, her face suddenly serious.

Remember, she signalled. *We fly in, we fly out. No sound.*

Rook and Knuckle nodded.

Come, Varis motioned, raising her sails and flying up from the branch. *We're going in!*

As the *Stormhornet* rose up from the ironwood bough, the fluttering in Rook's stomach disappeared. Keeping close to Varis and Knuckle, he steered the skycraft through the last fringes of foliage, and into the desolation beyond. A calm, icy fury wrapped itself around him as he flew silently into the evil glade.

Varis and Rook swooped down over rows of long-huts and covered wagons, and hovered beside the banderbear slave-hut. At the same time Knuckle darted up towards the top of the look-out turret where the goblin guard was snoring noisily, winding the end of his lasso round his hand as he went. Rook watched as the slaughterer swooped in close and tossed the lasso. The spinning loop disappeared from view behind the parapet. Rook held his breath.

The next instant the lasso reappeared, a large bunch of keys held in its tightened knot. The sleeping guard had not stirred.

Well done, Rook signalled, awestruck by the slaughterer's skill.

Rook, Varis motioned urgently. *Here*. She threw one end of her tether-rope to him.

Rook caught it and secured it round the neck of the stormhornet figurehead, binding the two skycraft together.

Varis swung her feet round and dropped down from the skycraft to the ground.

The *Windhawk* bucked and lurched, tugging on its tether-rope. The *Stormhornet* reared up in protest. Rook shifted in the stirrups and gripped the straining pinner-rope grimly as he struggled to keep both skycraft balanced and ready for their getaway.

'Steady,' he whispered softly. 'Easy does it.'

Knuckle swooped down close to the ground, tossing the bunch of keys to Varis as he flew past, before soaring back into the sky to keep a look-out for goblin guards. Inside the slave-hut, Varis set to work.

There was a *click*, followed by the clatter of falling chains. Then a second *click* . . .

Above Rook's head, Knuckle was slowly circling, keeping his eyes peeled.

With a final click and clatter, the last shackle tumbled to the ground.

'Go,' Rook heard Varis urge the banderbears. 'You're free!'

The poor creatures seemed dazed at first, but slowly – agonizingly slowly it seemed to Rook, who was battling to keep Varis's skycraft steady – first one, then another ban-derbear, climbed gingerly to its feet. Slowly, cautiously, they emerged into the glade, followed by Varis.

'Make for the tree-line,' Varis urged the shuffling giants desperately.

At the same moment a muffled sound came from the line of covered wagons. Rook spun round, his heart racing. Something was wrong.

All at once, the tilderskin tarpaulins flew back to reveal row after row of armed goblin guards.

'It's a trap!' Knuckle bellowed down. 'Get out of there!'

As one, the long-haired goblins drew their jagged-tooth rapiers and, with a bloodcurdling battle-cry, sprang forward.

The banderbears threw back their heads, bared their fangs and howled. Rearing up on their huge hind-quarters they lunged forwards, blind with rage, their great, sabre-like claws slashing through the air, desperate to get to the safety and freedom of the forest.

'Leave the banderbears!' shouted a voice. 'It's Lodd that we're after!'

Rook turned back to see a thin, wizened individual with long, coiling side-whiskers, a pinched face and darting eyes standing alone on one of the wagons. It was Hemuel Spume himself! He banged his heavy staff noisily on the boards. *'Get me Varis Lodd!'* he screeched.

Varis let fly a bolt from her crossbow. It thudded into the side of the wagon, inches from Spume's head. The Foundry Master squealed and leaped for cover. Varis raced over to where Rook held her skycraft ready. The goblins advanced, brandishing swords and a heavily weighted net. The tether-rope leaped from Rook's hand just as Varis clasped the *Windhawk*'s prow, and the sky-craft lurched to the side, throwing her to the ground.

Rook groaned. From behind him there came a loud howl of derision from the gleeful goblins.

'We've got her now!' one of them shouted.

'The great Varis Lodd!' taunted another.

'That'll teach her to— *Unnkh!*'

Rook looked round quickly. One of the goblin guards was lying on the ground, a bolt sticking out of his chest. Two more were crouched down beside him. Above them, crossbow raised, was Knuckle, coming in for another attack.

'Unnkh!' A second goblin crashed to the ground, blood pouring from the bolt in his back.

'Rook,' came Varis's voice, as she struggled awkwardly to her feet. 'Rook, help me.'

Rook reached forwards and grabbed the *Windhawk*'s

tether-rope, wrapping it back round his hand. The weight of the second skycraft almost pulled his arm out of its socket. Wincing with pain, he held on grimly. 'Get on board!' he shouted at Varis. 'Quick!'

The guards screeched with rage and surged forwards. *'Imbeciles!'* Hemuel Spume's furious voice echoed.

Knuckle swooped down a third time. The crossbow bolt hissed.

Rook let go of the tether-rope as Varis grabbed hold of the *Windhawk*. It juddered and listed dangerously to one side as she pulled herself up and swung her leg over the seat. The next moment she realigned the sails and the skycraft soared up into the air. Rook's heart sang as he flew up beside her, scattering goblins on every side. 'We made it!' he cried out.

'Thanks to you, Rook,' Varis called back. 'You saved my life.'

Knuckle swooped in towards them. 'Let's get out of here!' he shouted.

'But what about the banderbears?' Rook shouted back. 'Did they escape?'

'See for yourself!' Knuckle pointed down to his left.

There, at the edge of the clearing, the banderbears were disappearing into the forest. The goblin guards hung nervously back from the huge beasts, while Spume shouted curses and waved his stick furiously at the skycraft.

'Shoot them down!' he screamed.

'Scatter!' barked Varis, as a flurry of crossbow bolts hurtled past them.

Rook broke away. He curved down low over the huts and away from the goblins, following the retreating banderbears towards the cover of the tree-line.

The last banderbear turned. It was the one Rook had seen emerging first from the foundries – a massive female, with odd black markings circling one eye and crossing her snout.

Their eyes met.

'Watch out!' shouted Varis, somewhere above him.

Rook glanced back to see a goblin crouched down on one knee beside one of the empty wagons. He had a long-bow in his hands, trained on the motionless banderbear's heart.

With a twang and a hiss the arrow shot through the air. Rook swerved in front of the banderbear.

There was a soft thud as the arrow embedded itself in Rook's shoulder. The pain shot down his arm. He cried out.

'Hold on!' screamed Varis, swooping down towards him.

The goblin was reaching into his quiver for a second arrow when the bolt from Knuckle's crossbow struck him between the eyes. He slumped to the ground. Varis reached over and made a grab for Rook's dangling tether-rope. Shoulders braced, she dragged the wounded young apprentice towards the safety of the tree-line.

'Wuh-wuh!' the banderbear cried after them, and lumbered into the forest.

'It's going to be all right,' Varis called breathlessly

across to Rook. Grunting with effort, she fastened the end of the tether-rope to the *Windhawk* figurehead, then realigned the sails. As they dodged in and out of the tall trees, several crossbow bolts fell short behind them. 'Hold on, Rook!' she cried. 'Hold on!'

'Hold on,' Rook murmured. 'Hold on . . .' He leaned forwards and wrapped his arms around the *Stormhornet*'s elegant neck. All round him, the sea of silver-green treetops flashed past in a blur. His eyes closed.

Knuckle flew in close beside them. 'He looks in a bad way,' he shouted into the wind.

'The arrow,' Varis shouted back. 'It will have been poisoned, if I know long-haired goblins. We've got to get him to Lake Landing as quickly as possible. If we don't, he'll die.'

·CHAPTER FOURTEEN·

FEVER

A faint, milky light poured through the grille of the sleeping-cabin door, dimly illuminating the small room and falling across the carved, golden wood of the bed-shelf, where a bony figure with a bandaged shoulder lay sleeping fitfully. Tossing and turning beneath the tilderwool blanket, the hollow-cheeked young librarian knight was drenched in sweat. His legs kicked the blanket back. His eyelids flickered.

Wolves. There were woodwolves all round him, their yellow eyes flashing like bright coals. Howling. Growling. And voices – angry voices, frightened voices – shouting, raging . . .

'No, no,' he whimpered, his arms flailing wildly.

Now he was on his own in the silence of the vast, shadowy forest, overwhelmed with grief. A four-year-old once again, he began sobbing – loudly, uncontrollably, tears welling up in his eyes . . . He was lost and alone – and so, so terribly cold.

It was the old nightmare.

Suddenly, something loomed towards him out of the shadows. Something huge. Something menacing, with glinting teeth and blazing eyes . . .

'There, there,' came a voice.

Rook's eyes fluttered and opened. His shoulder throbbed.

Tweezel was standing above him, a lantern raised in one hand and a cold, damp mist-leaf in the other, which he pressed to Rook's glistening brow. The great spindlebug's glass body seemed to fill the entire cabin.

'Keep fighting, brave master,' he said, his reedy voice hushed with sympathy. 'The fever will soon break.'

He reached across, plumped up Rook's pillow and pulled the blanket back over him. Rook closed his eyes.

When he opened them again, the spindlebug had gone – though the lantern, low and sputtering now, still glimmered from the desk opposite. Rook looked round the small, shadowy cabin with its lufwood panelling and simple carved furniture. From the moment Parsimmon had first shown him to it on his arrival at Lake Landing– now already more than a year since – Rook had felt safe and secure inside the cocoon-like timber cabin.

He stared up at the ceiling, his gaze following the narrow planks of wood into the corners and down the walls. The soft amber light of the flickering lantern was mirrored in the varnished wood. Rook's eyelids grew heavy. The straight lines between the panels twisted and blurred. The dull ache in his shoulder throbbed, sapping his strength and spreading through his body like a slow-burning forest fire.

His eyes closed. His breathing became low and regular as Rook fell into a deep, dreamless sleep. When he woke again, the fever had returned.

One moment he was burning up, his bed-clothes drenched and his skin blistering hot. The next, as if plunged into icy water, he was bitterly cold, huddled up in a tight ball in the middle of the bed-shelf, teeth chattering and body violently shivering.

Noises from outside permeated his dreams. The night cries of the nocturnal Deepwoods creatures, the hushed yet excited chatter of the apprentices hurrying past his door; sometimes the wind howling or rain pounding on the roof, sometimes the turbulent lake slapping and sloshing beneath him – and just once, the distant yodelling cry of a solitary banderbear.

Rook lost all sense of time. Was it night? Was it morning? How long had he lain there, now moaning softly, now thrashing fretfully about, as he fought the goblin poison that coursed through his veins?

'It's all right,' he heard. 'Don't try to speak.'

He slowly opened his eyes. The room swam.

'We've come to say goodbye,' came a soothing voice.

'Goodbye,' Rook repeated, his own voice a low rasping growl.

Before him, two round faces emerged from the shimmering golden shadows. His neck lolled from side to side as he tried to hold their gaze. The effort was too great.

His eyes fluttered shut. A hand clasped his own. It was cool and soft. With one last effort he opened his eyes once again, and there, looking down at him, was Magda. Behind her, Stob.

Rook tried to speak. 'Magda . . .' he whispered, his cracked lips barely moving. His eyes closed.

'Rook,' she whispered back, her own eyes filling with tears, 'Stob and I depart on our treatise-voyages tomorrow . . .' She broke down. 'Oh, Stob!' she cried. 'Do you think he can even hear us?'

'He's a fighter,' came Stob's gruff voice. 'He won't give in – and Tweezel's doing all he can. Come, let's leave him to rest.'

The two apprentices rose to go. 'Fare you well, Rook,' they said softly.

Rook's eyelids flickered. He felt a light kiss brush his fevered brow, the lips cool and dry, and smelled the pine-like scent of Magda's thick hair. His body was impossibly heavy.

There was a click of the catch as the door closed. Rook was alone again.

Night followed day followed night. Time after time, as evening fell and the milky light from outside grew dim, the spindlebug came to light the oil lantern. He bathed Rook and tucked him in; he put droplets of potent medicine under his tongue and applied oily herbal unguents to the angry wound, and bandaged it up with fresh strips of gauzy cloth.

Sometimes Rook would wake to find Tweezel fussing about him attentively; mostly, he would sleep through the spindlebug's tender ministrations.

'Rook, can you hear me?' Rook opened his eyes. He knew that voice. 'It's me, Rook. Xanth.'

'Xanth?' he murmured, and winced as the searing pain in his shoulder shot down his arm.

Xanth winced with him. His face was pale and drawn, and his dark sunken eyes looked more haunted than ever. He pushed his hair off his forehead and took a step closer to the bed. The lantern in his hand swung to and fro. 'I came to say goodbye, Rook,' he told him.

'Goodbye,' said Rook dully. 'You as well? Magda and Stob . . .'

Xanth laughed bitterly. 'Magda and Stob! How I envy them,' he said. He put his head in his hands. 'There'll be no treatise-voyage for me, Rook. My path leads away from the Deepwoods and back to New Sanctaphrax.'

'New Sanctaphrax?' Rook struggled to clear his head. Was this really happening – or was it all just a fever-induced dream? 'But why, Xanth?' he murmured.

The apprentice turned away, and Rook could just make out his hunched-up shoulders in the shadows. When he spoke, his voice was low and thick with emotion. 'You have been a good friend to me, Rook Barkwater,' he said. 'When others ignored me or made fun of me, you were there, defending me, encouraging me . . .' He hesitated. 'And I have repaid your friendship with lies and treachery.'

'But . . . but how?' asked Rook. 'I don't understand.'

'I am a spy, Rook,' said Xanth. 'I serve Orbix Xaxis, the Most High Guardian of Night. The librarian knights are my enemies.' His eyes narrowed. 'Why do you suppose no groups of apprentices have reached Lake Landing since I arrived? Because I betrayed them, Rook. And how did the goblins at the Foundry Glade know that Varis Lodd was going to pay them a visit, eh? Because I set the trap, that's how. Oh, but Rook . . .' Xanth turned and kneeled beside the bed-shelf. He clasped Rook's hand, his own hands trembling with emotion. 'If I'd known that you – one of only two people I have ever called friend – were going to be on that raid, I would have warned you, Rook. You've got to believe me!'

Rook pulled his hand away. 'You? You betrayed us?' he said weakly. 'After all we've been through together . . . Oh, Xanth, how could you?'

'Because I belong to the Guardians of Night,' said Xanth bitterly. 'They own me, body and soul. Try as I might, there is nothing I can do to get away from them. Don't you think I'd rather stay out here in the beautiful Deepwoods if I could?' He shook his head. 'It's not possible, Rook. I have gone too far. I have done too much damage. I cannot stay.' He sighed. 'I am as much a prisoner of the Tower of Night as my friend Cowlquape, to whom I must now return.'

Rook stared at Xanth through lowered lids. His temples pounded, his vision was blurred.

'It was Cowlquape who first filled my head with stories of the Deepwoods, and his adventures with Twig the sky pirate,' Xanth continued. 'Because of him, I had to come out here and see it all for myself – even if the only way I could do so was by becoming a spy.' He looked down miserably. 'I suppose I have betrayed you both.'

Rook turned away. The fever was returning with a savage intensity. Xanth? A traitor? He didn't want it to be true. Xanth was his friend. A deep sorrow mingled with the pain of his wound, and the shadows grew darker round his bed-shelf. Rook closed his eyes and let the fever wash over him.

Xanth looked down at the sleeping youth, and pulled the blanket up around his shoulders. 'Farewell, Rook,' he said. 'I doubt our paths will cross again.'

He stepped back, turned and crossed the floor to the circular doorway. He did not look back.

Fingers shaking with excitement, Rook dressed himself in the stiff, green leather flight-suit, secured the belt with its dagger and axe, and Felix's sword round his waist, swung the small backpack of provisions onto his shoulder and set off down the tower staircase. Although he was still a little weak, and his face was pale and drawn, with Tweezel's help he had managed to beat the goblin's poison. Now – two weeks after Stob and Magda had set forth – it was his turn to set off on his treatise-voyage.

Varis Lodd was at the foot of the tower to greet him. 'There were occasions,' she confessed, 'when I wondered if this day would ever come. But you made it, Rook. I'm so proud of you. And now, Librarian Knight,' she said, nodding towards the tethered *Stormhornet* which bobbed about at the back of the stage, 'your skycraft awaits.'

Rook stepped forward, wrapped his arms round the smooth wooden neck of the delicate creature and rubbed his cheek against its head. '*Stormhornet*,' he whispered. 'At last.'

Just then, from behind Rook, there came the sound of footsteps. He turned to see two figures approaching. One was Parsimmon, his tattered gown flapping. The other – tall, bearded and dressed in a black tunic – raised his hand in greeting. Rook's gaze fell upon the white crescent moon emblazoned across his chest.

'The Professor of Darkness!' he said, surprised.

'He arrived while you were ill, Rook, bearing news of Xanth's treachery,' said Varis. 'A bad business all round.'

Rook nodded sadly. The two figures drew close. The professor took Rook's hand and shook it firmly.

'Can this truly be the callow youth who once tended the buoyant lecterns on the Blackwood Bridge?' he said. His eyes twinkled. 'I can scarce believe it. Here you are, about to embark upon your treatise-voyage. We have groomed and trained you. Now it is your chance to contribute to the great canon of work already stored in the Storm Chamber Library. You have done well, Rook. Very well.' His expression clouded over. 'Though you have hardly been helped by a certain friend, I believe.'

'Xanth?' Rook faltered. It all seemed like a dream to him now, Xanth's confession and departure. He had tried to put it out of his mind.

'Xanth Filatine,' the professor said, 'is a traitor!'

'A traitor,' Rook whispered softly. 'He ... he came to my cabin when I was ill, just before he ... disappeared.'

'Fled back to his evil master, the Most High Guardian

of Night,' said the professor, shaking his head.

'Many good apprentices and their loyal guides have been lost because of that young wood-viper,' said Parsimmon sadly. 'But come, we are not here to talk of such things. Xanth Filatine will pay for his treachery soon enough. Now we shall celebrate the beginning of your great adventure, Master Rook.'

Rook nodded, but said nothing. He couldn't think of his former friend without a heavy ache of sadness forming in his chest. He tried to push the feelings away. Today was a day for celebration, not sadness, he told himself.

Varis stepped forwards. 'Rook, it is time for you to leave,' she said softly. As she spoke, the low sun rose up above the trees. She shielded her eyes with her hand. 'May your treatise-voyage be safe and fruitful.'

Rook looked up. He saw the professor, Parsimmon and Varis all smiling at him kindly. He smiled back. Beside him, the sails of the waiting *Stormhornet* fluttered in the light breeze.

Parsimmon nodded towards it. 'She's raring to go,' he said.

'And so am I!' said Rook, hardly daring to believe that the moment of his departure had finally arrived.

Checking his laden flight-suit and tightening the straps of his backpack, he turned away. He untethered the small craft and leaped into its saddle. The skittish *Stormhornet* bucked and lurched.

'Good luck, Rook!' said Varis.

Rook adjusted his goggles, took hold of the upper sail-rope and raised the loft-sail.

'Earth and Sky be with you, lad,' said the Professor of Darkness solemnly.

The nether-sail billowed out beneath him. The *Stormhornet* juddered upwards and hovered impatiently.

'And may you return successful from your treatise-voyage!' cried Parsimmon. 'Fare you well, Master Rook.'

'Fare you well!' shouted the others.

Rook pulled down sharply on the pinner-rope. The sails filled. The flight-weights swung. And Rook's heart soared as the skycraft flew steeply up into the cool, bright morning air.

'Farewell!' he shouted back.

Below him, Lake Landing quickly became smaller and smaller, and the three figures standing upon it – their arms waving and their faces turned up to the sky – grew so tiny, he could no longer see which was which.

'This is it,' Rook murmured happily, the fluttering back in the pit of his stomach as he skimmed the tops of the trees fringing the far side of the lake. Before him lay the vast, mysterious Deepwoods, rippling in the wind like an endless ocean.

As the leaves rushed past him in a blur of greens and blues, he imagined his completed treatise nestling beside Varis Lodd's masterpiece, on the seventeenth buoyant lectern of the Blackwood Bridge, deep down in the Great Storm Chamber Library. He could see the bound leather volume with its gold lettering: *An Eyewitness Account of the Mythical Great Convocation of Banderbears* . . .

Far off in the distance a flock of snowbirds wheeled up from the trees below and soared into the air, their white wings flashing brightly in the rising sun. Farther still, a rotsucker flapped across the hazy sky. Beneath it, clutched in its claws, the egg-shaped silhouette of a great caterbird cocoon swung back and forth.

Rook frowned as the immensity of the Deepwoods – and his task – struck him. He pushed all thoughts of the completed treatise from his head; this was no time for daydreaming. He had come a long way since that morning when Fenbrus Lodd, the High Librarian, had announced that he, Rook Barkwater, had been selected as a librarian knight elect. He had journeyed to Lake Landing. He had built the *Stormhornet* with his very own hands and learned to fly. Now, finally, he was setting forth on his treatise-voyage.

'At last,' he whispered, as he swooped down low over the leafy canopy. 'Now it all begins.'

·CHAPTER FIFTEEN·

WUMERU

Rain was falling as Rook stirred from his sleep. He was high up on a colossal branch of an ironwood tree. The canopy he'd rigged up in the branches above his head, before turning in the night before, had kept the worst of it off him. But his hammock and sleeping bag were damp, and would have to be aired later if they were not to end up mildewy and rank.

Rubbing the sleep from his eyes, Rook got up. He yawned. He stretched. His breath came in wispy twists of mist. Shivering with cold, he lit the hanging copper stove, placed a small saucepan of water on its flickering, blue flame and went to check on the *Stormhornet*, tethered securely to one of the huge branch's offshoots.

'I trust you are well rested,' he whispered to the little skycraft. 'And not too wet to fly.'

He ran his fingers over its smooth, varnished prow, over each and every knotted rope and tethered sail. A shower of tiny raindrops glistened as they fell from the silky material. He tightened the flight-weights. He greased the levers . . . Everything seemed to be in order.

Behind him, the water started to bubble.

Rook hurriedly rolled up his hammock and sleeping bag, folded away the waterproof canopy, and secured all three behind the *Stormhornet*'s saddle. Then, back at the hanging-stove, he removed the saucepan from the heat, carefully capped the flame and poured the boiling water into a mug. He stirred in three spoonfuls of dried charlock leaves and wrapped his hands around the piping-hot mug.

He looked out from his vantage point on the ironwood branch. The rain had all but stopped and the forest was beginning to fill with birdsong as the sheltering cheepwits and songteals emerged from their shadowy perches and leafy hollows. He heard a rustle of leaves, and looked down to see a family of woodfowl foraging for food far below.

Rook sighed. He, too, should eat – yet all he had left from the previous evening was a thick slice of baked loafsap, wrapped up neatly in a broad, waxy leaf.

As he opened the small green package, the musty odour of the pappy fruit filled his nostrils and, although his stomach rumbled hungrily, his appetite completely disappeared. 'Stop being so fussy,' he told himself, biting off a large chunk and chewing gamely.

He knew from Varis Lodd's woodlore lessons that the edible loafsap was both nutritious and filling. He knew also that it was unwise to set out on an empty stomach ... But the fruit was so unpalatable! Rook took a sip of the charlock tea and swallowed the whole mouthful of claggy pulp in one go. He grimaced. 'That'll do,' he said, tossing the half-eaten slice away. It landed with a soft *thud*. The woodfowl darted off in all directions, squawking with alarm.

Rook climbed to his feet, packed up the precious stove and untethered the *Stormhornet*. The sunlight pierced the thinning clouds and, shining down through the gaps in the trees, gleamed on the burnished green leather of his flight-suit. In the weeks that had passed since he'd first set off from Lake Landing the stiffness of the leather had gone, and the flight-suit had moulded itself to the shape of his body, fitting him now like an extra layer of skin.

Rook glanced round one last time to make sure he hadn't left anything behind. Then, shifting the sails and weights, and tugging on the pinner-rope, he launched the *Stormhornet* into the dappled, forest air. 'Perhaps today,' he whispered, just as he whispered every morning. His breath came in soft, puffy clouds. 'Perhaps today will be the day.'

Three months Rook had been journeying; three long, tiring months. By day, when not foraging for food and water, he would scour the Deepwoods for any tell-tale signs of a banderbear – a woven sleeping nest, branches newly stripped of fruit, or heavy footprints in the soft, boggy places beside woodland springs. By night, he would rest up in the tall branches of the great trees, lying in his hammock and listening out for the curious yodelling of the creatures.

So far, he had heard them on three occasions. Each time, when he had risen the following morning, he had set off in the direction of their calls, his heart beating with anticipation. He still recalled the intense thrill he had felt in the Foundry Glade, when he saw those first banderbears. Now, he couldn't wait to see more – free, healthy banderbears in their own habitat – but as the sun had moved across the sky and the shadows had lengthened, Rook had, each time, been forced to concede defeat. The elusive creatures were proving far more difficult to locate than he could ever have imagined.

Yet his journey had not consisted only of disappointments. There had been triumphs, too, along the way; achievements, discoveries – each one faithfully recorded in his treatise-log in his small, neat handwriting, and illustrated with detailed pictures and diagrams.

Today I came across deep, tell-tale scratches in the bark of an ancient lufwood tree where a banderbear had sharpened its claws. Some scratches looked fresh, others were covered with green moss, suggesting that the tree is a regular scratching-post. I am greatly encouraged.

Four days he had camped high up at the top of a neighbouring lufwood, keeping constant watch. No banderbear had appeared. On the morning of the fifth day he had packed up and, with a heavy heart, set off once more. That evening, having set up his hanging-stove and hammock, the *Stormhornet* tethered safely to a branch, he sharpened his stub of leadwood and recorded a new entry.

After abandoning the scratching-post, I flew all day. Just before midnight I spotted a small mound of oakgourd-peel beneath one of the tall, bell-shaped trees – surely the sign of a recently passing banderbear. My hopes were confirmed by the presence of a banderbear footprint. I sat up most of the night in a nearby ironwood tree, hoping the creature might return for the few fruits remaining.

But again, the creature let him down. His journey continued bright and early the following morning.

The days began to blur into one another, with weeks turning to months, and still no sight of the shy, retiring creatures. Rook grew lean, yet strong; his senses razor-sharp. He got to know the Deepwoods increasingly well. Its changing moods. Its shifting character. The plants and trees and creatures that dwelt in its dark, mysterious shadows. What to eat and what to shun. Its sounds. Its smells. And at night, he would record the fauna and flora he encountered.

Today I discovered a woodbee hive. I was successful in smoking the swarm out with a branch of smouldering lullabee wood. The honey was delicious in the charlock tea, turning it a surprising blue colour, like the sky before a storm . . .

I have just witnessed a halitoad stunning a fromp with a blast of its noxious breath, seizing the creature in its long, sticky tongue and swallowing it whole. The hideous beast then swelled to twice its size, before letting go a revolting belch. I stayed well hidden for an hour . . .

It has been a week of violent thunderstorms. Once, while I was taking shelter, an ironwood close by was struck by lightning and burst into flames. I heard an odd 'popping' sound, which turned out to be the tree's seedpods bursting open, and scattering their seeds far and wide. 'In death there is life,' as Tweezel would say. By Earth and Sky, the Deepwoods is a strange and wonderful place . . .

Today I witnessed something truly horrendous. Drawn towards it by the sound of desperate screeching and squealing, I came down in the air to see the unexpected spectacle of a hammelhorn, apparently in flight! Around its middle, gripping tightly, was a tarry-vine – the long, green, parasitic sidekick of the terrible bloodoak. The creature struggled, wriggled and writhed, but the tarry-vine was too strong for it. And when a second vine came to its aid, coiling round the hapless hammelhorn's neck, the struggle was over. The vines pulled the creature through the forest towards the gaping maw at the top of the bloodoak's thick, rubbery trunk. The ring of razor-sharp mandibles clattered loudly. With a sudden flick, the two vines released the hammelhorn, which dropped head-first down inside the great flesh-eating tree. The creature's muffled cries fell still. The vines turned red . . .

Rook lay the stubby twig of leadwood down. He was sitting cross-legged, high up in a spreading lullabee tree, his stove blazing, his hammock hanging absolutely motionless in the still, humid air. The moon shone down on his pinched, anxious-looking face. The hammelhorn had reminded him of his fellow apprentice.

'Are you safe, Stob?' he whispered. 'Have you found your coppertrees yet? Has your treatise work begun? Or . . .' He swallowed, and fought hard against the choking emotion which rose in his throat.

Just then, from above, Rook heard a soft scratching sound. He turned and looked up. Some way to his left, secured to the knobbly bark on the underside of a thick, horizontal branch, was what looked like a bunch of pine-grapes. Only the colour was different, parchment brown rather than purple – that, and the increasingly insistent scratching.

As Rook watched, one of the spherical pods split and opened. A small, bedraggled insect appeared at the papery entrance, crawled up onto the top of the branch and flapped its wings in the warm, moonlit air. The matted fur on its body dried and fluffed up. The wings thrummed softly as they stiffened.

'A woodmoth,' Rook whispered. 'First the hammelhorn. Now a woodmoth.' He smiled as memories of Magda flooded his thoughts.

Soon the first woodmoth was joined by others as the rest of the pods cracked open, one after the other, and the hatchlings emerged. Then, as the last of them climbed onto the branch and flapped its wings, the whole armada took to the air and fluttered through the shafts of moonlight.

Rook stared, unblinking, as the woodmoths performed their strange, exuberant dance – dipping and diving like autumn leaves in a blustery wind, their bright, iridescent wings sparkling like marsh-gems and black diamonds in the silvery light.

How Magda would have loved the sight, he thought, and smiled. Perhaps she already had. Perhaps her treatise was already finished... His face clouded over.

While his own was yet to begin.

Rook was thirsty. His canteen was empty and, apart from a little sticky juice which he'd sucked from the chewy flesh of a woodpear that morning, not a drop of liquid had passed his lips for almost two days. His head was throbbing. His vision was becoming blurred. His concentration strayed . . .

'*Wooah*, there!' he cried out, as the nether-sail snagged on a spike-bush branch and tipped the skycraft off-balance. Shocked by his own carelessness, Rook realigned the sails and raised the flight-weights. The *Stormhornet* lurched away from the danger unharmed and up above the tops of the trees. But Rook knew he'd had a lucky escape. He must find water before he blacked out completely.

As the sun beat down ferociously, Rook slipped back beneath the forest canopy and continued through the dappled trees, keeping low and close to the forest floor. He knew that sallowdrop trees, with their pale, pearly fronds, grew near running water, and that clouds of

woodmidges often collected above underground pools –
but he saw neither.

His mind was beginning to wander once more when,
from his right, there came the unmistakable sound of
babbling water. With a sudden burst of energy, Rook
manoeuvred the *Stormhornet* skilfully about, swooped
down through the air and round the cluster of tall
lullabee trees before him.

And there, at the far side of a small, sandy clearing,
bursting with lush vegetation, was a spring. It bubbled
up from rocks on the side of a slope, trickled over a
jutting lip of rock and splashed down into a deep green
pool below.

'Thank Sky and Earth,' Rook whispered to the
Stormhornet. 'At last.'

Yet he did not dare land. Not yet. Beautiful though this
welcome oasis looked, he knew it would also be a
perilous place, attracting some of the most dangerous
Deepwoods creatures there were: rapier-toothed wood-
cats, whitecollar wolves and, of course, wig-wigs which,
though they themselves never needed to drink, fre-
quented such places to prey on those that did.

Rook brought the skycraft down to land on a sturdy
branch high up in one of the ancient lullabees. He put his
telescope to his eye and, trying hard to ignore his dry
mouth and burning brow, focused in on the spring
below him.

As the time passed, several creatures appeared from
the surrounding forest to drink at the babbling pool. A
small herd of speckled tilder, a family of woodfowl, a

solitary woodhog boar, with long curving tusks and small, suspicious eyes. A hover worm flitted over the surface of the water, bowing its head and sipping delicately, as the jets of air expelled from tiny ducts the length of its underbelly hissed softly.

Finally Rook could wait no longer. He tethered the *Stormhornet* securely, scurried down the great bulbous trunk of the lullabee to the ground and, looking all about him, crept towards the bubbling spring.

There, he quickly dropped to his knees, cupped his hands, and drank mouthful after mouthful of the cold, clear water. He felt it coursing down his throat and filling his stomach. Immediately his head stopped pounding and his eyes cleared. He hastily filled his canteen and was about to return to the *Stormhornet* to continue on his way, when something caught his eye.

A footprint.

Rook gasped and, scarcely able to believe his good fortune, crouched down for a better look at the broad marking in the soft, damp sand at the water's edge. Although smaller than the print he had seen beside the oakgourd tree, from the arrangement of pads and claws, there could be no doubt. It was a banderbear footprint. What was more, the impression was sharply defined. It had been made recently.

Bursting with excitement, Rook leaped to his feet and inspected the whole clearing. In amongst the footprints of all the other thirsty creatures were more of the small banderbear tracks. Some were faded and worn, some as fresh as the one at the water's edge – the banderbear must have returned several times to drink over the last few days.

Turning away, he scaled the lullabee tree. 'This is the place,' he confided to the *Stormhornet*. 'We shall wait here for a banderbear to appear, no matter how long it takes.'

Rook stayed awake that night. All round him, the sounds of the night creatures filled the air. Coughing fromps. Squealing quarms. Chattering razorflits ... As the moon rose, blades of silver light cut through the surrounding trees, and speared the forest floor below. Rook's eyes were growing heavy when all at once, shortly before the dawn, he heard the sharp *crack* of a twig snapping in the shadows beneath him.

How could anything have got so close without me noticing? he wondered. He pointed his telescope down at the place where the noise had come from and adjusted the lens, until every leaf appeared in sharp focus. As he did so, the foliage trembled and abruptly parted, and out of the shadows stepped a tall, stocky creature.

It was a banderbear! Rook held his breath and tried not to tremble. He had finally found a wild banderbear!

The creature was truly magnificent, with bright eyes, sharp white tusks and long, gleaming claws. Though smaller than the banderbears he had seen at the Foundry Glade, it was nevertheless both tall and imposing and, given the half-starved appearance of those sorry

individuals, probably weighed more than them. As it lumbered towards the bubbling pool, its shiny coat gleamed – now dark brown, now pale green.

Rook watched it stoop down at the water's edge, lower its snout and begin lapping at the water. He was so excited, he could hardly breathe. His hands were trembling, his legs were shaking – he had difficulty keeping the telescope focused.

Just then there was a rustling in the leaves. The banderbear looked up, its delicate ears fluttering. It was probably just a fromp swinging through the trees, or a roosting woodfowl shifting position in its sleep. But the banderbear was taking no chances. As Rook watched, spellbound, the banderbear climbed to its feet and melted silently into the surrounding forest.

'Today,' Rook whispered, as he closed his telescope and clipped it back onto his flight-suit. 'Today *is* the day!'

The banderbear returned many times, and as the days passed, Rook observed it closely, keeping detailed notes of its behaviour and writing them up in his treatise-log. He recorded what time of day and night it appeared, and for how long. He documented each movement it made: every scratch, every gesture, every facial expression. And he drew pictures – dozens of them – trying to capture each individual characteristic of the creature: the curve of its tusks, the arch of its eyebrows, the grey mottled markings across its shoulders . . .

Several days into his vigil, Rook decided to track the

banderbear. As it lumbered off into the forest, he slipped the tether-rope of the *Stormhornet* and, keeping at a safe distance, flew after it. He was surprised how fast the creature travelled. Hovering silently up in the air, he watched it stop at a huge, spreading tree, and gorge itself on the dripping blue-black fruit which hung from its branches, before continuing on its way.

An idea formed in Rook's head. He swooped down and, keeping close to the tree, plucked an armful of the fruit. Then, having returned to the spring, he laid it out in small pile beside the bubbling water.

For the rest of the day – using a makeshift catapult to keep other visiting creatures away from the fruit – Rook made sure that the pile remained untouched, ready for the banderbear's return. When the banderbear did return – several hours later – it sniffed at the fruit suspiciously. Its ears fluttered wildly. It sniffed again.

'Go on,' Rook whispered urgently. The next moment he beamed broadly as the banderbear picked up the first piece of fruit in its sharp, yet delicate claws and bit into it. Gleaming red syrup dribbled down over its chin, and Rook noted the blissful expression – the drooping mouth and dreamy eyes – that passed across the creature's face.

When the first fruit was gone, it started on the second, then the third. It didn't stop until every last morsel had gone.

The following day Rook laid out more fruit. This time, however, when the banderbear came to eat it, he was crouched down on the ground behind the lullabee tree, watching it. Up so close, he realized just how enormous the creature was. Although clearly little more than an adolescent, it was already more than twice his own height and ten times as heavy, and from its shorter tusks and mane, Rook could tell it was a female.

It was four nights later when Rook plucked up the courage to take the next step. The banderbear returned at midnight to discover that no fruit had been left out for her. She sniffed round disappointedly and, with a low guttural groan, made do with a drink of spring water.

Heart in his mouth, Rook tentatively emerged from his hiding place. He held a piece of fruit in his trembling hands. The banderbear spun round, eyes wide and ears fluttering. For a terrible moment Rook thought she was about to turn on her heels and gallop back into the forest, never to return again now that her drinking place had been discovered.

'It's for you,' Rook whispered, holding his hands out.

The banderbear hesitated. She looked at the fruit, she looked at Rook, she looked back at the fruit – and something in her expression seemed to change, as if she had made the connection between the two.

Her right arm rose, and her great taloned paw fluttered by her chest. Rook held his breath. With her gaze fixed on Rook's eyes, the banderbear reached forwards and gingerly seized the fruit from his hand.

'Wuh-wuh,' she murmured.

Little by little as the weeks passed, Rook gained the confidence of the banderbear, until – by the time the ironwood's leaves were beginning to turn colour and fall – the two of them had become close. They foraged for food side by side. They watched out for one another. And at night Rook would help the banderbear build one of the great sleeping nests in the dense thickets of the forest floor. Intricately woven and expertly concealed, lined with moss and soft grasses and protected by branches of thornbush, the nests were spectacular constructions, and Rook could only marvel at the banderbear's skill.

He recorded everything in his treatise-log: the edible fruit and roots they ate, the building of the sleeping nests, the creature's finely tuned senses which enabled her to detect food, water, shelter, changes in the weather, danger ... And as the banderbear became more and more familiar to him, he began also to understand her language.

Rook had often read the part in Varis Lodd's seminal treatise – *A Study of Banderbears' Behaviour in Their Natural Habitat* – where she had outlined the possible meaning of some of the banderbears' more simple grunts and gestures. Varis had had to rely on observations taken from a distance. Now, closer to a banderbear in the wild than any librarian had come before, Rook was able to take the understanding of the subtle intricacies of their communication further.

As they journeyed together, he slowly began to master the banderbear's language and, though the creature appeared amused by his own attempts to communicate, they seemed to understand one another well enough. Rook loved the rough beauty of the language in which a tilt of the head or the shrug of the shoulders could convey so much.

'Wuh-wurreh-wum,' she told him, her head down and jaw jutting. *I am hungry, but step lightly for the air trembles.* (Beware, there is danger close by.)

'Weg-wuh-wurr,' she would growl, with one shoulder higher than the other and her ears flat against her head. *It is late, the new moon is a scythe, not a shield.* (I am anxious about proceeding further in the darkness.)

Even the creature's name was beautiful. Wumeru. *She with chipped tusk who walks in moonlight.*

Rook had never been so happy as he was now, spending every day and every night with the banderbear. He was becoming quite fluent now, and – he realized with a guilty jolt – so wrapped up in his life with Wumeru that he was neglecting his treatise-log. Still, there was always tomorrow. Or maybe the next day . . .

They were seated on the ground one late afternoon, sharing a supper of oaksaps and pinenuts. The dappled sunlight was golden orange. Wumeru turned towards him.

'Wuh-wurrah-wugh,' she grunted, and swept an arm round through the air. *The oaksap is sweet, the sun warms my body.*

'Wuh-wuh-wulloh,' Rook replied and cupped his hands together. *The pinenuts are good, my nose is fat.*

Wumeru's eyes crinkled with amusement. She leaned

forwards, her face coming close to Rook's.

'What?' he said. 'Did I say something funny? I simply meant that their smell is . . .'

The banderbear covered her mouth with her paw. He should be quiet. She touched Rook's chest and her own in turn, then, concentrating hard, she uttered a single word; low, faltering, but unmistakeable – a word, Rook knew *he* had never given her.

'Fr-uh-nz.'

Rook trembled. *Friends?* Where could she possibly have heard the word before?

Some nights later Rook woke with a start and looked up. The sky was clear and the moon was almost full. It shone down brightly on the forest, casting the treescape in silver and black. He climbed out of his hammock, high in the lufwood tree and looked down. Wumeru's sleeping nest was empty.

'Wumeru?' he called. 'Wuh-wurrah.' *Where are you?*

There was no reply. Rook walked along the branch to where the *Stormhornet* was tethered, and looked out across the dark forest.

And there she was, standing on a rocky incline not twenty strides away, motionless – apart from her fluttering ears – and staring intently at the distant horizon. Rook smiled and was about to call out his greetings, when he heard something that took his breath away.

Echoing across the night sky, came the yodelled cry of a distant banderbear. It was the first one Rook had heard since meeting his companion.

There it was again!

Wumeru! Rook recognized the name being called, and he felt a tingle run down his spine. The second banderbear was not merely calling out to any other; it was addressing his friend by name. *'Wumeru, Wumeru . . .'*

Over such a long distance, with the wind whipping half of the sounds away, it was difficult for Rook to make out exactly what the banderbear was saying. But he had no difficulty translating Wumeru's reply.

'Wuh-wuh. Wurruhma!' *I come, the full moon shines brightly; it is time at last.*

'Wumeru,' Rook called down, suddenly gripped by an

incredible sense of expectation. 'What's happening?'

But Wumeru ignored him. She had ears only for the other banderbear. From the distance, the yodelling continued.

'What's that?' Rook murmured. *Make haste . . . The Valley of a Thousand Echoes awaits . . .*

Shaking with excitement, he fumbled for his treatise-log and leadwood stub, and began to write the words down in a trembling hand. 'Valley of a Thousand Echoes,' he whispered. 'Wumeru,' he called and looked down. '*Wumeru?*'

He fell still. The rock where the banderbear had been standing was empty. His friend had gone.

Wumeru had abandoned him.

·CHAPTER SIXTEEN·

THE GREAT CONVOCATION

Rook quickly gathered his belongings together and stowed them on the *Stormhornet*. He couldn't lose the banderbear. Not now. He was all fingers and thumbs unhooking the hanging-stove and, as he was folding it away, the flame-cap came loose and tumbled down into the darkness below.

'Blast,' Rook muttered breathlessly. It would take for ever to find the thing again, and meanwhile Wumeru was getting farther and farther away . . . There was no choice. He would have to leave it.

Jumping astride the *Stormhornet*, he raised the sails, realigned the hanging weights and pulled on the pinner-rope, all in one smooth movement. The skycraft leaped from the branch, darted through the overhead canopy of leaves and soared off into the clear night sky beyond.

'Where are you?' Rook murmured, as he searched the forest floor ahead of him. The yodelling of the other banderbear had come from somewhere to the west – and that was where Rook set his course. Earth and Sky willing, Wumeru had headed off in the same direction. 'Where *are* you?' he whispered. 'You must be down there somewhere.'

Just then the trees began to thin beneath him, and Rook spotted his banderbear friend striding purposefully ahead. She was walking in an unwavering straight line, as if hypnotized. And as Rook caught up, he could hear her murmuring under her breath. The same sound, over and over – a word he didn't recognize.

'*Worrah, worrah . . .*'

'Not too close, now,' Rook whispered, patting the *Stormhornet*'s prow and raising the loft-sail. 'We don't want her to spot us. Not yet. Not until we know where she's heading.'

The *Stormhornet* slowed to little more than a hover, and Rook steered it gently to his right, where the forest was thicker and he could follow Wumeru without her seeing him. As he darted on from tree to tree – keeping to the shadows and taking care not to lose sight of her, even for a moment – Rook's hopes began to rise.

'The Valley of a Thousand Echoes,' he murmured. 'Is it too much to hope . . .? Could it be . . .? Could it actually be the place where the banderbears assemble? The Great Convocation?' He ran his fingers down the long, curved neck of the *Stormhornet*. 'Is that where Wumeru is heading?'

For several hours he flew on, keeping Wumeru constantly in sight. The other banderbear's yodel must certainly have been important; Rook had never seen his friend so determined. Usually she would amble slowly through the forest, leaving no trace of her passing. Tonight, as she blundered tirelessly on, she left a trail of trampled undergrowth and broken branches in her wake.

Suddenly the air was splintered with the sound of banderbears – seven or possibly eight of them, far ahead, yodelling in unison. '*Worrah, worrah, worrah, worrah . . . whoo!*'

It was the same sound that Wumeru herself had been chanting under her breath, and as the chorus of voices faded away, their calls were answered by others. Dozens of them. From every direction.

'*Worrah, worrah . . . whoo.*'

And from his right, louder than all the others, came Wumeru's answering cry. '*Worrah-whoo!*'

Rook's hopes soared. Surely it must be the convocation. What other reason could there be for so many of these solitary creatures to be gathering together in the forest?

'*Worrah-whoo!*' Wumeru called a second time, and Rook looked across to see that she had stopped some way up ahead on the crest of a rocky outcrop. Motionless save for her twitching ears, against the slate-grey sky the banderbear looked like a great boulder with a pair of cheepwits fluttering at its top.

Rook flew closer. 'Wumeru,' he called out. 'Wumeru, it's me.'

He landed the *Stormhornet* on the flat slab of rock just

behind her and jumped down. The banderbear turned to face him.

'Wuh-wuh,' said Rook, holding his open hand to his chest. *I woke alone. You abandoned me.* He sighed and touched his ear, then pointed down to the ground. 'Wurrah-wuh.' *Your parting words were silent, I followed you here.*

'Wuh!' grunted Wumeru, and sliced her claws down through the air like a great sword. Her eyes blazed. Her lips curled back, revealing her gleaming tusks and glinting fangs.

Nothing had prepared Rook for this. It was as if he were suddenly a stranger to her.

'But—' he began, his hands open in a gesture of supplication.

The banderbear let out a low, menacing growl that rose from the back of her throat. Could this strange, fearsome creature truly be gentle Wumeru, his friend? Never before had he heard her sound so full of rage. She lunged forwards and swiped at the air, her fangs bared.

'Wuh-wuh!' *No further! It is forbidden for you to follow my path!*

Rook took a step backwards, his hands still raised defensively. 'I'm sorry, Wumeru,' he said. 'I meant no harm.'

The banderbear grunted, turned and disappeared back into the trees. Rook watched her leave, a painful lump forming in his throat.

'What now?' he whispered, as he climbed back on to the *Stormhornet* and took to the air. As if in response, the yodelling voices echoed back.

'Worrah, worrah, worrah . . . whoo!'

Rook trembled. The banderbears were closer than ever. How could he resist their call? Yet dare he go on? If Wumeru discovered that he had followed her, there was no knowing what she would do. Then again, he could not leave. Not now. Not having come so far . . .

The yodelling grew louder. The ululating chanting rose and fell in waves.

Rook's mind was made up. Ever since he'd first picked up Varis Lodd's treatise in the library, he'd dreamed of this. He was a librarian knight, and this was the moment to prove it. He brought the *Stormhornet* down low, and landed on the sturdy branch of an iron-wood tree. He tied up the tether-rope tightly and scrambled down.

Keeping to the shadows, he passed the rocky out-crop where Wumeru had been standing and went on through the trees, following her trail of flattened undergrowth. Then, stepping cautiously ahead, he found himself on a high, jutting ledge which looked out over a bowl-shaped valley. At the very edge grew a tree – its roots clinging to the great fissured blocks of rock, its long, thick trunk curving out at an angle above the yawning chasm below.

Rook ran to the tree, climbed up and inched himself along its curved trunk out above the valley. All around him the low sound of chanting grew louder and louder . . .

'Sky above and Earth below!' he gasped as the scene abruptly opened up beneath him. 'There must be hundreds of them! *Thousands!*'

Rook shook his head in disbelief. Everywhere he looked there were banderbears gently swaying in the moonlit valley, each one calling out the same mesmeric chant: low, guttural, building at the back of the throat, only to soften into a long, tuneless moan. Some were alone, some in pairs, some in groups which grew bigger and smaller as the great lumbering creatures endlessly came together and drifted apart. Little by little, the chanting became synchronized, until the entire gathering was calling as one. The tree beneath him seemed to vibrate with the resonant booming.

'This is it,' Rook breathed. 'The Great Convocation of the Banderbears. I've *found* it.'

Gripping on tightly to the sloping tree-trunk with his legs, Rook rummaged in his backpack for the treatise-log and stub of leadwood. He had to capture every detail of the wondrous scene for his treatise.

Large groups constantly breaking up and reforming, he hurriedly scribbled down. *As if in some huge dance that every banderbear seems instinctively to understand . . . And the chanting – incredible, booming, resonant . . .*

From below him, the chanting grew in intensity. The tree trembled. And there was something else . . .

Hard to catch at first, but, yes, there it was again. Mingling with the overall chant, yet somehow distinct from it, single banderbear calls were rising and falling against the background throb. Rook could just make out snippets.

I, from the lone ridges of the twin peaks . . . I, from the high reaches of the mist-canyons . . . I from the sombre shadows of the ironwood groves . . . from the lullabee forests . . . from the deepest, darkest nightwoods . . .

Rook listened, transfixed, as the individual voices came and went.

The snow-passes of the lofty Edgelands . . . The fur-damp swampwood glades . . . The turbulent thornwoods . . .

It was as if he were listening to a map; a map of the Deepwoods in banderbear song. They were singing of their homes and, as their chants intermingled, they became one great shared description of all the places the banderbears knew. Below him was a living library, as rich as the concealed library of Old Undertown itself, kept alive in the memories of the banderbears and shared amongst them at this Great Convocation. Head swimming with the beauty of it all, Rook swooned . . .

The treatise-log slipped from his grasp. He lunged forwards desperately as it tumbled down, missed it, and lost his balance in the process. Suddenly, to his horror, he found himself falling from the tree – legs pedalling and arms flailing, as he hurtled towards the ground below.

The next instant he struck the hard, packed earth with a loud *thud*. Everything went black.

*

Rook's head spun. He felt a warm wind blowing across his body and sensed a bright light shining in his face.

Where am I? he wondered.

His head throbbed. Everything was blurred and shifting. His breath came in short, sharp gasps and, as his head began to clear, he let out a cry of surprise.

All around him was a towering circle of banderbears, glaring down at him furiously. Their huge tusks glinted, and there was fire in their eyes – yet not one of them made a sound. The Valley of a Thousand Echoes was in absolute silence.

Rook swallowed hard.

All at once a mountainous male banderbear with jet-black fur and thick, curling tusks, leaned down. Rook saw the great paws swoop down towards him and felt the cold, hard claws clutch his body. The creature's fur smelled musty, its breath sour.

'*Aaargh!*' he cried out, his stomach turning somersaults, as he was lifted into the air.

'Wuh!' the banderbear roared. *How dare you!* And Rook felt the great creature's indignation and rage trembling through its entire body as it gripped him tightly and cried out, 'Wuh-wurrah!'

He had never seen a banderbear so angry, so . . . so *vengeful*. Stiff with terror, Rook was rigid in the creature's grip, as the other banderbears took up the same, blood-chilling cry, until the whole valley echoed with their roaring.

'Wuh-wug-wurrugh?' the great black banderbear boomed out above the tumult. *Who dares to steal the echoes*

*of our valley and trespass on our sacred
convocation?*

'Wuh,' Rook replied, his
voice low and trembling.
'Wuh-woor.' Wriggling to free

his hand from the banderbear's crushing hold, he
touched his heart lightly. *I come as a friend. I mean no harm.*

The banderbear hesitated. His startled eyes inspected
Rook's face as if to say, *Who is this creature that knows the
secret language of banderbears?*

Rook sensed the creature's confusion. 'Wurrah-
wegga-weeg,' he said, his voice thin and warbling. *I am
a friend of banderbears. She with chipped tusk who walks in
moonlight and I have walked the same path.*

The banderbear's dark brow knitted and he looked
round at the crowd of banderbears, scouring the sea of
angry faces for Wumeru. When he caught sight of her,
his eyes narrowed. 'Wuh?' he growled menacingly. *Is
this true?*

Wumeru stepped forwards, head bowed and fluttering ears drooping. 'Wuh-wurroo. Wuh,' she said, without looking up. *My friend of the forest trail has brought only shame upon our companionship.* She turned away.

'Wumeru!' cried Rook desperately. 'Wumeru, *please*! I—'

The black banderbear raised him up high in the air once more. His grip tightened, his eyes grew cold. With Rook held aloft, he bellowed out loudly.

You, who have listened to words meant only for banderbears' ears, have committed the greatest sacrilege of all. Thief of our songs. Stealer of our chant. You must die!

Just then a solitary cry abruptly rose up above the gathering frenzy. 'WUH!' *STOP!*

The great black banderbear instantly froze. He looked round. Rook – dizzy and befuddled – could just make out a banderbear pushing through the crowd towards them.

'Wuh?' *Who speaks?* the black banderbear demanded.

The female stopped before him. 'Wuh-wuh. Wurrawoogh-weerlah,' she grunted, touching first her shoulder, then her chest. *I, Wuralo, who suffered much in the Foundry Glade. I know this one. He saved my life.*

With a start, Rook looked at the banderbear. She was heavier now than when he'd last seen her, and her coat was thick and glossy. But from her markings – the curious black line which circled one eye and crossed her snout – Rook knew that this was indeed the banderbear he had saved from the goblin's arrow.

The black banderbear hesitated. The female turned to

him and pressed her large, furry face up close to his.

'Wura-wuh-wurl!' *My heart cries for mercy. Spare him.* 'Wuh-wuh. Weera-weeg.' *I thought he fell to the poison-sticks. But he lives.*

'Wurra-woor-wuh,' Rook explained quietly. *I was indeed struck, yet my heart beat on. I carry the scar.* He opened the front of his shirt and pulled it back.

The black banderbear traced a claw delicately over the knot of healed skin. 'Wuh-wuh. Wurrh!' he cried. *It is true. You bear the mark of the poison-sticks.* He placed Rook down on the ground. *You risked your life for one of us?*

'Wuh-wurrel-lurragoom,' Rook explained. *I have loved banderbears from my first breath and will defend them to my last. I gladly risked my life in the Foundry Glade!*

The gathering of banderbears grunted softly and muttered beneath their breath.

'Wuh-wulla,' said Rook. *Believe me, I am a true friend of the banderbears!*

All at once, rising up above the general babble, a voice rang out. 'Wuh-wuh!'

Out of the corner of his eye Rook noticed a third banderbear approaching. She was old and stooped, her fur, silvery grey.

'Wurra-looma-weera-wuh,' she said, her voice cracked and frail. *I sense he speaks the truth. He is a friend of banderbears.*

The crowd, intrigued, turned and watched her walk up to the young intruder. A low murmur spread out through the ranks of attendant banderbears. The old, grey female leaned forwards and wrapped her great arms around him.

Rook smelled the warm, mossy scent of her fur, and felt her heart beating close to his. The sensation was extraordinary. He felt safe, protected, and found himself wishing that this comforting hug would never end.

At last, she released him and stared into his face, her dark eyes crinkling with affection. 'Wuh-wulla, wegeeral,' she whispered. *Friends until the last shadow of that final night.*

The surrounding banderbears grunted their approval. The black banderbear raised his great head. 'Wura-galuh-weer!' he proclaimed. *Gala, oldest of the old and wisest of the wise, has spoken. This is good enough for me.* 'Wuh-wurra-lowagh.' *We welcome you. You shall be Uralowa – he who took the poison-stick.*

The crowd of banderbears roared all the louder. Rook quivered with happiness. 'Thank you,' he said. 'Wuh!'

The black banderbear nodded earnestly. 'Wurrah-woor. Wuh-wuh.' *You are special. No others have witnessed our Great Convocation – save for one . . .*

Just then Rook sensed a movement behind him. He glanced back over his shoulder to see the great crowd of banderbears parting. A long, narrow passageway opened up between them and, as Rook peered down it, he saw a figure emerge from the other end and walk slowly towards him.

'What the—?' Rook whispered.

He stared at the figure, with his stooped shoulders and long, white matted hair and beard. His jerkin, trousers and boots were made from wild-leather, and stitched together with strips of thong. His threadbare hammelhornskin waistcoat flapped in the rising breeze. As he approached, Rook looked into the newcomer's face.

The skin was leathery and lined, every crease and every scar hinting at an episode in the stranger's past. But the eyes! Rook had never seen such eyes before. Marsh-gem green and crystal clear, they twinkled brightly in the moonlight, like the eyes of someone much younger.

He stopped in front of Rook. 'I believe this is yours,' he said.

Rook looked down to see his treatise-log clutched in the stranger's calloused hands. He reached out and took it gratefully. 'Th-thank you,' he said. 'But . . . who am I thanking?'

'My name is Twig,' came the reply. 'I used to be a sky pirate captain, a defender of Old Sanctaphrax. Now, like you, I am a friend of banderbears . . .' He smiled warmly, his eyes twinkling brighter than ever. 'Perhaps you've heard of me?'

·CHAPTER SEVENTEEN·

THE CAPTAIN'S TALE

It was a glorious morning, Rook. I'll never forget it. A morning which, after the ferocious storm which had raged throughout the previous night, many of us thought we'd never live to see.' Twig's eyes became dreamy; he shook his head slowly from side to side. 'I can scarcely believe that fifty years has gone by since then.'

Rook looked at Twig thoughtfully. Fifty years. That would make the sky pirate captain nearly seventy years old. So much had changed in the Edge in that time.

'The old days – oh, the stories I could tell you of the old days,' Twig was saying. 'But that is for another time. With the passing through of the great Mother Storm, the waters of the Edge were rejuvenated and the glistening air that morning pulsated with hope for a bright new future.'

Rook nodded. From the texts and scrolls in the Great

Storm Chamber Library he had learned about the birth of the new rock and the subsequent founding of New Sanctaphrax. And how Vox Verlix had taken over from the first High Academe – an obscure youth, not up to the task – and built the foundations of what was later to become the Tower of Night. Now, speaking to this strange, ragged old sky pirate captain, the dry accounts he'd read came vividly to life.

'My work there finally done,' Twig continued, 'I boarded the *Skyraider* and prepared to depart, for it was time for me to set a course for the Deepwoods, to collect those faithful members of my crew who were still at Riverrise, awaiting my return.'

'Riverrise,' Rook breathed.

'Aye, lad,' said Twig. 'That was where I'd left them. There was Maugin – the best stone pilot that ever tended a flight-rock. And Woodfish, a waterwaif with powers of hearing that were truly remarkable, even by waif standards. And Goom.' He smiled and looked round. 'Dear Goom, the bravest banderbear a captain could wish for. I promised them faithfully that I would return for them – and, on that fine morning so long ago, that was just what I intended to do.'

Rook and Twig were sitting side by side on the log of a fallen tree at the edge of the valley clearing. Before them, the Great Convocation was in full sway, with the vast crowd of banderbears mingling and chanting and sharing their knowledge of the Deepwoods, one with the other, as the first blush of dawn tinged the edges of the sky.

'I had a good crew to aid me in my quest,' Twig went on. 'I can see their faces almost as clearly as I can see yours now. There was Bogwitt, the flat-head goblin – just the type to have fighting by your side in a battle. And Tarp Hammelherd, the slaughterer I had rescued from the drinking dens of Undertown. And my quartermaster, Wingnut Sleet – his face hideously scarred by a lightning bolt.' He sighed. 'And the others. Teasel the mobgnome – good with ropes, I recall. Stile, the cook, with his twisted spine and awkward walk. Old Jervis, the gnok-goblin – not much use, but a cheery soul. And, of course, Grimlock. Who could forget Grimlock!'

'Grimlock?' said Rook.

'A giant of a brogtroll,' said Twig. 'Not the sharpest arrow in the quiver, perhaps, but strong as a team of hammelhorns.' He smiled to himself. 'Anyway . . . Where was I? Ah, yes. Pausing only to bid farewell to the Most High Academe and wish him luck, we set forth, with the wind in our sails and hope in our hearts.' He turned to Rook, his eyes twinkling brightly. 'I can still remember how warm upon my back the sun was, as we soared off over the Mire and on towards the Deepwoods.' He smiled broadly. 'And how high my spirits flew . . . Riverrise! I was returning to Riverrise!

Rook smiled with him, caught up in the enthusiasm of the old sky pirate captain.

'Of course,' Twig continued, his expression becoming serious, 'I knew it wasn't going to be easy. The voyage would be long and difficult. But I also knew that I needed to trust both my instincts and my senses.

Woodfish would be calling to me. I had to keep my mind focused so that I could follow his call.'

Twig's eyes had a faraway look in them as he went on. 'We sailed for several months,' he said, 'soon leaving woodtroll villages and goblin settlements far behind. Each morning I scanned the horizon and cleared my mind. All about us, the great Deepwoods stretched as far as the eye could see; dark, forbidding and endless. But we kept going, ever onwards, into the deepest, darkest places where the forest was so dense that no light penetrated. The air above it boiled with black, turbulent clouds and festering storms which buffeted and battered the *Skyraider* until it was as ragged and frayed as our nerves.'

Twig fell still. He put his head in his hands.

'What happened?' asked Rook. 'Did you hear the waif's call? Did you find Riverrise?'

Twig looked up, his eyes glistening. 'Nothing,' he said. 'I heard nothing but the taunting howl of the storms as they ripped through our sails – and the mocking silence of the Deepwoods during the lulls between.' He shivered. 'And worse . . .'

'Worse?' said Rook.

'The scream of Wingnut Sleet as a storm swept him from the quarterdeck, the last gasps of poor old Jervis, crushed by a falling section of rigging, and the incoherent babble of Teasel as he lost his mind and jumped from the mast into the blackness below. Stile, the old cook, died soon afterwards – of a broken heart, or so my crew said. And yet still we continued, because I couldn't give up, Rook. I couldn't. None of us could. You must understand.'

Rook patted the old sky pirate's tattered sleeve. 'I understand,' he whispered.

'Do you?' said Twig. 'Do you? Sixteen years we sailed, Rook. Sixteen long, lonely, frightening years, growing ragged, weary . . . defeated. And it was all my fault. I couldn't find my way back to Riverrise.' He looked up, his eyes shot with pain. 'I failed them, Rook. My crew . . . My friends . . .'

'You did your best,' said Rook.

'But my best just wasn't good enough,' said Twig bitterly. He shook his head. 'At last there were just four of us left. Bogwitt, Tarp Hammelherd, Grimlock – and myself. Flying the sky ship without a stone pilot had been difficult enough before, but now, with so few hands on board, it was all but impossible. To continue our search for Riverrise I needed to take on extra crew. So I turned back and set a course for a place I'd heard talked of in the woodtroll villages and rundown goblin hamlets we had passed through on our travels – a place that was said to be a beacon of hope in the darkness of the Deepwoods, offering a welcome to the weary and a haven to the lost—'

'The Free Glades!' Rook exclaimed. 'You visited the Free Glades!'

'That we did,' said Twig. 'New Undertown was no more than a collection of lufwood cabins back then, and the woodtroll villages were only just being established. But we did indeed find a welcome, at the Lake Landing Academy, from a young librarian by the name of Parsimmon—'

'Parsimmon,' Rook broke in excitedly. 'He's still there. Except he's the High Master now. He taught *me*.'

'Then you had a wise teacher, young Rook,' said Twig. 'I remember that evening well. We limped into the Free Glades and moored up at the Landing Tower. Caused a bit of a commotion, we did.' He smiled at the memory. 'I suppose we must have looked quite a sight to those young librarians, Parsimmon amongst them, who greeted us. Our clothes were no better than rags, and the poor old *Skyraider*'s hull was pitted and scarred, its sails in tatters. But they gathered round us and gawped, open-mouthed, until Parsimmon stepped forward and introduced himself.

'He said we looked as if we could do with a good meal and rest, and that we must dine with them in their refectory; and that he wouldn't take no for an answer! It was over supper – tilder stew and oakapple cider, as I recall – that we heard the terrible news, and realized why they were so surprised to see us.'

'What news?' asked Rook.

'Why, news of stone-sickness, of course,' said Twig. 'Parsimmon told me all about it. Both league ships and sky pirate ships were dropping out of the sky like stones, he said. Not a single flight from Old Sanctaphrax had reached the Free Glades for more than a year.

'The sickness had, it seemed, spread out from the stricken New Sanctaphrax rock. It was highly contagious, travelling from sky ship to sky ship like wild-fire. As the flight-rock of one sky ship crumbled, so the crew had to find work on another – infecting the flight-rock of the new ship as they did so. "The First Age of Flight was at an end" – those were his very words, and as I heard them I realized the awful truth.

'Though we had come to the Free Glades in desperate need of more crew-members, I could not risk taking anyone on board who might be contaminated. We had only escaped until then because we'd been out in the furthest parts of the Deepwoods for so long. I leaped up from the table, hurried back to the *Skyraider*, and departed at once.

'I called the crew together as soon as we'd left the Free Glades safely behind, and explained our situation. Tarp clapped me on the back, Bogwitt shook my hand and Grimlock almost broke my ribs with a great banderbear-hug. They all agreed they would stay with me in my search, even though, with just the four of us, it would be backbreaking work. Dear brave fellows, they were,' he said wistfully. 'Long gone now, of course.'

Twig looked into the distance for a long time, saying nothing. At last Rook asked, 'What happened?'

Twig's face grew sad. 'It was a stupid thing really. But deadly. You see, we needed provisions. So, not daring to venture into villages or settlements for fear of contamination, we scavenged in the Deepwoods themselves – for tilder and woodhog meat, fruits and roots we could dry or pickle, and twenty barrels of water which Grimlock, being so strong, managed to collect in a single afternoon.'

He shook his head miserably. 'It was the water which was to seal our fate, for poor, stupid Grimlock – Sky rest him – ignored that most important Deepwoods law of all. *Never drink from a still pool.* Grimlock had filled every single barrel with the same tainted water ... But it was *my* fault, not his!' he said, his eyes blazing. 'I was the captain. I should have checked; I should have known ...

'Before long, all of us had gone down with blackwater fever. I staved it off a while longer than the rest, but soon I too was held in its terrible grip. I vomited till my stomach was empty. I lost consciousness. How many days and nights I lay there on the deck, while the *Skyraider* drifted on across the Deepwoods unchecked, I will never know. Tossing and turning as the fever raged on, burning up one moment, shivering with bitter cold the next.'

Rook nodded sympathetically. He knew only too well how terrible a raging fever could be.

'It was daybreak when I finally came round. I sat up, my head spinning groggily, my stomach grumbling. A

cold, damp mist swirled
through the air. It clung
to my clothes, my hair,
my skin, and had covered
every surface of the
Skyraider with a fine coating of slippery wetness.
I struggled to my feet,
looked around.

'There were no trees beneath us now,
only rock; a vast, greasy-grey expanse, broken up into
broad, flat slabs with deep cracks between them. I knew
at once where I was, and my heart filled with dread. The
Edgelands; an eerie wasteland of mists and nightmares.

'It was in the Edgelands, many years before, that I had
come face to face with a horror I can scarcely bring
myself to share with you. For me, you see, Rook, the
Edgelands hold a particular terror, for it was there that I
met the gloamglozer – and lived to tell the tale.'

Rook gasped. 'The gloamglozer! But how? When . . . ?'

'One day I'll tell you the whole story,' said Twig. 'But
suffice to say, I survived, and vowed never to return to
that accursed place. Yet, as fate would have it, it was to
the Edgelands that the poor, battered old *Skyraider* had
carried me. I looked around.' Twig's eyes grew sad. 'The
Skyraider seemed deserted. My crew! Where were they? I
hadn't seen or heard any of them since wakening. I
called out, but there was no reply. I left the helm and
dashed to the fore-deck. And . . . and there they were. All
three of them . . .

'Oh, Rook,' he groaned. 'They were dead. Bogwitt. Tarp Hammelherd. Even poor Grimlock, great, powerful brogtroll that he was, had proved no match for black-water fever . . .' His voice faltered. 'Th-their bodies were sprawled out on the cold, wet deck, rigid in their death throes – arms reaching out, faces twisted with fear and horror. Each one of them had died a terrible death . . .' He swallowed hard. 'I performed the funeral rituals as best I could. It was the least I could do for a fine, loyal crew who had served me and the *Skyraider* so well . . .'

He fell still, and Rook watched as the tall, rugged sky pirate captain wiped a tear from his eyes. A lump formed in his own throat.

'You see, Rook, I had finally failed. There was nothing for it . . .' Twig took a deep breath. 'Sailing back to the Deepwoods was not an option. I could never have sailed the *Skyraider* single-handed,' he said. 'And so I tethered her to a great rocky outcrop that jutted out from the cliff-face, like some crouching demon, black against the sunrise, and left.'

'You mean, the *Skyraider* is still there!' gasped Rook.

'Aye, lad,' said Twig. 'If she hasn't rotted away or succumbed to stone-sickness in the meantime, then she *is* still there. A fine drizzle was falling the morning I bade her farewell. Despite what she'd been through, she looked magnificent, floating above that barren waste-land, a cruel reminder of all that had been lost.' He paused. 'The last sky ship . . .' Again Twig fell silent until – with a small sigh – he continued. 'Three days it took me to cross the treacherous Edgelands, and another two weeks before I chanced across a band of itinerant cloddertrogs who gave me food, drink and shelter. And I have wandered the Deepwoods ever since.

'Although there is now only me, and I am old and weary, I have never truly given up hope. I look for Riverrise on the horizon every morning when I wake, and I think of the friends I left there every evening when I lay myself down to sleep.

'I see their faces, Rook. Goom. Maugin. Woodfish. They are not angry with me. Sometimes I wish they were. The look of hope and trust in their eyes as they gaze upon me is a thousand times worse. I let them down, Rook,' he said. His voice broke. 'They believed in me ... My poor, lost friends ...' He held his head in his hands. 'I'm haunted by memories of all those I have known. The living and the dead, clustered together. Faces I'll never see again. My father. Tuntum. The old Professors of Light and Darkness. Hubble. Spooler. Spiker ...' He shook his head. 'And the Most High Academe of Sanctaphrax, the way he looked on that morning so long ago when my quest began, as he waved us goodbye ...'

Rook nodded. The captain's tale had come full circle.

'The excitement, touched with apprehension, in his smile. The pride in his stature. The hope in his eyes. He had once been my apprentice, and now he was the new Most High Academe of Sanctaphrax! How proud I was of him ...' He shook his head. 'Poor, dear Cowlquape—'

'Cowlquape?' said Rook, startled. 'But I know that name.'

'Yes, Cowlquape Pentephraxis,' said Twig bitterly. 'Murdered long ago by that tyrant, Vox Verlix. I learned the news at Lake Landing.'

With a shock, Xanth's words came back to Rook. *I am as much a prisoner of the Tower of Night as my friend Cowlquape, to whom I must now return*. Despite the fever raging at the time, he was sure that was what Xanth had said. *It was Cowlquape who first filled my head with stories of the Deepwoods, and his adventures with Twig the sky pirate . . .*

Rook leaped to his feet. Twig's friend and Xanth's prisoner were one and the same.

'So young,' Twig was saying, 'and I left him to rebuild Sanctaphrax on his own, to go on this failed quest. If only I had got to Riverrise, I could have returned to help him and perhaps he'd still be alive today.'

'But he is!' shouted Rook, unable to keep quiet a moment longer. A couple of banderbears glanced round curiously in mid yodel. Rook seized Twig by the arms. 'He's alive!' he exclaimed. 'Cowlquape is alive!'

The colour drained from Twig's face. His jaw dropped. 'Alive?' he gasped.

·CHAPTER EIGHTEEN·

SKYRAIDER

Twig stared at Rook in astonishment. 'But how do you know he's still alive?' he demanded. 'Parsimmon said . . . Let me see . . . Yes, even after all this time, I can remember what he told me. When I asked after Cowlquape the High Academe, he shook his head and said, "Vox Verlix is the Most High Academe now. Cowlquape's name has been stricken from the records. Murder, plain and simple, so it was – though you'll find few in New Sanctaphrax who dare say as much." Those were his very words—'

'But he *is* alive,' said Rook. 'A prisoner in the Tower of Night. A friend . . .' He paused, a sudden twinge of pain in his chest. 'At least, I thought he was my friend,' he murmured. 'He told me that he had seen Cowlquape in the Tower of Night – and that he was very much alive. He even said that Cowlquape spoke to him of you, Twig, and the adventures you'd shared.'

'He did?' said Twig. He was on his feet now, clutching both Rook's hands and staring hard into his eyes. Around them, the banderbears were falling silent in the light of the new dawn, as Twig's excited voice echoed round the valley. 'What is this Tower of Night you speak of?'

Rook shook his head. 'You've been out here for a long time, Captain Twig,' said Rook. 'Many things have changed since you left. Parsimmon told you of Vox Verlix becoming Most High Academe, but that was only the start.'

'Tell me,' said Twig. 'Tell me everything you know!'

Banderbears were crowding about them now, great mountains of fur topped by twitching ears.

'When Vox Verlix became Most High Academe, he ordered the construction of a tall tower on New Sanctaphrax, even as the rock began to crumble with sickness. From what I've heard, and read in the library, he claimed stone-sickness was a sign that the academics had grown soft and complacent and that he, Vox, would do something about it.'

'That Vox!' snarled Twig. 'He was a bad lot when I first knew him as a young apprentice in Old Sanctaphrax.'

'It gets worse,' said Rook. 'You see, Vox founded a sect of Knights Academic, whom he called the Guardians of Night. They enslaved Undertowners and forced them to work, not only on his accursed tower, but on his other great schemes as well. The Great Mire Road. And the Sanctaphrax Forest that props up the sick rock—'

Twig's eyes blazed. 'Slavery?' he said angrily. 'In Undertown?'

'Yes, I know,' said Rook. 'It was a terrible betrayal of the principles which Undertown was founded upon, and there were many who resisted. But the Guardians of Night were brutal. They ensured that the schemes were completed. Those Knights Academic who disagreed with Vox's plans split away and joined with the earth-scholars to found the Librarians Academic.' He paused. 'We live in hiding in the sewers of Undertown . . .'

'Librarians living in sewers.' Twig shook his head sadly. 'That it should have come to this. Vox Verlix the bully, master of New Sanctaphrax!'

'Not quite,' said Rook. 'There's a twist in the tale.'

'Go on,' said Twig.

'Well, Vox didn't realize what a monster he'd created when he established the Guardians of Night. Soon a leader emerged from their ranks, one Orbix Xaxis, who declared himself the Most High Guardian and took over the Tower of Night. Fearing for his life, Vox fled to an old palace in Undertown. The shrykes seized the opportunity to take full control of the Great Mire Road, and Vox was forced to rely on goblin mercenaries to hold on to what little power he had left in Undertown. These days, if the rumours are true, he spends his entire time alone in his dilapidated palace, too obese to leave his bed-chamber, drinking himself into a stupor each night with bottle after bottle of Oblivion.'

'Well, I, for one, am not in the least sorry for him,' said Twig. 'But tell me, Rook, what more do you know of this Tower of Night in which Cowlquape is held captive?'

Rook sighed. 'I know this much: they say no-one ever escapes from the Tower of Night. It is a vast, impenetrable fortress, with spiked gates and barred windows, rock-slings and harpoons, and great swivel catapults mounted on every jutting gantry. I've only seen it once myself, and that was from a distance, but I've heard stories from librarian knights who have seen it close up. Once, the great Varis Lodd even attacked it with a fleet of skycraft – but they proved no match for the tower's weapons.'

'Skycraft?' Twig said. 'Those little wooden things? I saw them at Lake Landing. No wonder they failed. Why, it'd be like woodmoths attacking a hammelhorn!'

'Armed guards patrol every corner of the tower,' Rook continued without a breath, 'each one trained to kill first and ask questions afterwards. The Tower of Night is impregnable. To attack it from the ground, you'd have to go through Screetown.' He shuddered. 'They say it's inhabited by strange, glistening creatures that constantly change their shape – rubble ghouls, they're called. And rock demons . . . And if you survived all that, there's the Sanctaphrax Forest – a mass of timber scaffolding that holds the rock up. It's infested with rotsuckers and razorflits, terrible creatures by all accounts. No, the only way to attack the tower is by air and, as you say, a skycraft is just too small—'

'But a sky ship isn't,' said Twig.

'A sky ship,' Rook breathed. All around them, the banderbears listened closely.

'Oh, Rook, lad,' said Twig, 'it would be like the old days when I sailed with my father, Cloud Wolf, on raids against those great over-stuffed league ships. The trick was to go in hard and fast, I remember, and be off again with whatever loot they had stashed away before they knew what had hit them. And that's what we shall do, Rook – in the *Skyraider*!'

'The *Skyraider*?' said Rook. 'But Twig, we don't have a crew.'

Just then there was flurry of movement behind them, and Rook turned to see the great female from the Foundry Glade, Wuralo, stepping forward. 'Wuh-wurra Tw-uh-ug-wuh,' she said, and raised a great paw to her chest. *I shall go with you, Captain Twig, friend of banderbears.*

Twig leaned forwards and clapped the great beast on the shoulders. 'Wuh-wuh,' he said, and swept his hand round in a languid arc. *Welcome! Friend!*

A second banderbear – a huge male with a deep scar in his shoulder – stepped up beside her. 'Wuh. Weega. Wuh-wuh.' *I, Weeg, shall also go with you.* 'Wurra-wuh!' He pointed to the skies, touched his scar and raised his head. *I served upon a sky pirate ship long ago, in the old days of which you speak.*

'Wuh-weelaru-waag!' boomed the giant black bander-bear. *I know nothing of flight, but I am strong! They call me Rummel: he who is stronger than ironwood.*

Rummel was immediately joined by three others:

Meeru and Loom – twin males who had once tended timber barges – and Molleen, a wiry old female who'd worked long ago as an assistant to a stone pilot. Her lopsided grin revealed several missing teeth and only one chipped tusk.

'Wuh-leela, wuh-rulawah,' she yodelled softly. *I can tend your flight-rock, Captain Twig, if you'll have an old bag of bones like me.*

'Wuh-wuh,' said Twig. *Welcome, Molleen. She, who is a friend of stone.* He took a step backwards, and raised his arms. 'Thank you, friends,' he said. 'From the bottom of my heart, I thank you all. But we have enough volunteers.' He turned to Rook. 'I think we've found our crew.'

'Wuh-wuh!' came an insistent voice, and Rook turned to see Wumeru forcing her way through the crowd of banderbears. *Take me! Take me!*

Twig smiled. 'And what experience of skysailing could you possibly have, my young friend?'

'Wuh,' said Wumeru, her great head hanging low. *None. But my youth is my strength. I am powerful and eager* . . .

'Thank you, young friend,' Twig began, 'but as I said before, we now have enough volunteers—'

'Wuh . . .' Wumeru faltered. She looked at Rook forlornly, imploringly. 'Wuh . . .'

Rook turned to Twig. 'We'll need a ship's cook,' he said. 'And Wumeru is an excellent forager, I can vouch for that.'

'Wumeru?' said Twig. 'You know each other?'

Rook nodded. 'We are friends,' he said.

Twig's face crinkled into a warm smile. 'Friendship with a banderbear is the greatest friendship there is,' he said, pulling a pendant – a discoloured banderbear tooth with a hole through its centre – from inside his hammel-hornskin waistcoat, and looking at it thoughtfully for a moment. '*I* know.' He turned to Wumeru. 'Welcome aboard,' he said. 'But I give you due warning. If you should ever serve up pickled tripweed, I shall have you sky-fired!'

Just then the rising sun broke through the high ridge of trees surrounding the valley and shone down brightly on the small group of waiting banderbears. Twig raised his head. 'Come, then, my brave crew,' he announced. 'Let us delay no longer. The *Skyraider* awaits us in the Edgelands.'

A roar of approval resounded all round the Valley of a

Thousand Echoes, and the cheering assembly of banderbears stepped aside to let Twig, Rook and the seven
volunteers pass between them.

'Cowlquape, my young friend,' Twig muttered under
his breath, 'I have lived too long with failure. This is one
quest that will not fail!'

They made excellent progress through the Deepwoods.
Never resting up for longer than an hour at a time, they
travelled by both day and night, orientating themselves
by the sun and the East Star as they headed north –
always north – through the deep, dark forest and on
towards the treacherous Edgelands.

Back in the saddle of the *Stormhornet*, Rook flitted
through the trees above Twig and the banderbears as the
group pressed on. The great creatures were speeding
through the forest silently and swiftly. And unlike
Wumeru who, as if in a trance when she was answering
the call to the Great Convocation, had battered her way
through the undergrowth leaving a trail of destruction
behind her, the banderbears left not a single sign of their
passing. Rook could only marvel at their agility, their
deftness, their stealth.

It struck him as strange that banderbears were such
solitary creatures, for together they worked so

cohesively and well. They each took it in turn to lead, falling back to be replaced by another when they tired; each kept an ear open and an eye out for any potential danger. Intrigued, Rook approached Wumeru during one of the short breaks they took to forage and take their bearings.

'Why *do* you live apart from one another?' he asked. 'You should form tribes. Work together. You're good at it!'

Wumeru looked up, ears fluttering wildly. 'Wuh-wuh. Wurra-waloo.' She slashed her paw through the air and tossed her head. *You are wrong. Banderbears can never live together. Together, we invite the fiercest predators. Alone, we can live longer, for we attract less attention.* She looked about her and smiled, her tusks glinting. 'Weeru-wuh!' *Though to be in a band like this, I almost wouldn't mind dying sooner.*

'Wug-wulla-wuh,' said Twig, approach-ing, his arms spread wide. *Don't speak of death, young Wumeru – though I am hon-oured to be facing it with you at my side.*

There was a rustle in the undergrowth and the huge figure of Rummel emerged, his arms full of branches of hyleberries. 'Wuh-wuh!' he grunted. *Quick, eat, for we must keep moving.*

They continued through the forest, Rook scouting ahead on the *Stormhornet* until, with a tug of the pinner-rope, he would twist elegantly round in the air and fly back the way he'd come, checking every inch along the strung-out line of banderbears. Weeg was currently leading the group, the great scar on his shoulder glinting in the half light. Meeru and Loom, walking side by side, followed some way behind. Shortly after them came Wuralo, her mottled shoulders hunched, and after her, the massive Rummel, with his strange, loping gait. There was then a long gap before Rook came to Wumeru who, though young, seemed to have less stamina than the others. Finally, after another long gap, he came to the stragglers: Molleen, who was older and slower than the rest, and Twig himself.

As Rook swooped down, the old sky pirate captain waved to him. Rook waved back, proud of the great captain's acknowledgement. And as he soared back into the air, he heard Twig murmuring words of encouragement to Molleen.

Not long now, old-timer. The flight-rock awaits your expert touch.

Darkness fell, but the banderbears – with Rook still up in the air above them – kept resolutely on. Through the night they journeyed, never easing up on their relentless pace, never making the slightest sound. The moon rose, crossed the sky and set far to their left. The sun came up, heating the damp, spongy earth and sending wisps of mist coiling up into the bright, glittering air.

All at once there came a yodelled cry from up ahead. It was Wuralo, now at the front of the line. *The Edgelands! We have reached the Edgelands!*

Twig yodelled back. *Wait for us. We'll soon be with you.*

Impatient to see the notorious Edgelands for himself, Rook gave full head to the skycraft sails and darted forward. Beneath him, the trees grew fewer and the undergrowth thinned. Silhouetted against the pale yellow sky ahead was Wuralo, looking back. She spotted the approaching skycraft and waved.

Rook signalled back and, shifting the weight-levers and sail-ropes, swooped down towards her. As he flew lower in the sky, the rising mist swirled around him, chilling him instantly to the bone. He landed on a flat slab next to the waiting banderbear, jumped down and wrapped the tether-rope round his hand.

'Wuh-wuh,' Wuralo greeted him. 'Wulloo-weg.' She hugged her arms tightly round her great stomach. *This place fills me with dread.*

Rook nodded as he looked around the broad expanse of greasy, grey rock. He had never been anywhere that made him feel so uneasy. Even the endless tunnels of the Undertown sewers, with their muglumps and vicious piebald rats, were nothing compared with the barren Edgelands.

It howled and sighed as the chill wind swept in from beyond the Edge and whistled along the cracks and gullies in the sprawling granite pavement. It clicked and whispered. It hummed and whined, as though it was alive. A sour, sulphurous odour snatched his breath away. His skin turned to clammy woodturkey-flesh as the coils of fetid mist wrapped themselves around him. The wind plucked at the *Stormhornet*, bobbing weightlessly by his side.

He saw Wumeru emerging from the woods, followed closely by Rummel, with Weeg and the twins – Meeru and Loom – behind him. Like Wuralo, they seemed deeply troubled by the eerie atmosphere of the bleak Edgelands, and clustered together for warmth and safety.

Twig and Molleen reached the desolate rockland last. Twig clapped a hand on Rook's shoulder. Rook could see he was trembling.

'I never thought I'd return to this terrible place,' said Twig, looking around uneasily. 'But somewhere out there the *Skyraider* is waiting for us. Follow me,' he said. 'And search the horizon for the great black demon crag!'

Twig strode off into the mist, with Rook by his side – the skycraft bobbing behind him as he slipped and slid over the treacherous rocks. The group of banderbears, still huddled together, followed close behind.

The wind continued to whine and whisper in Rook's ears and, as he trudged on, trying hard not to listen, wispy fingers of mist seemed to caress his face and stroke his hair.

'*Ugh!*' he groaned. 'This is a terrible, terrible place.'

'Courage, Rook,' said Twig. 'And keep looking for the crag.'

Rook strained to see through the dense, coiling mists. Ahead of them, the flat pavement seemed to stretch on for ever.

'Wait for the mists to clear,' said Twig. 'They will, if only for an instant – but that's all we'll need to spot our goal.' He pressed on. The wind howled round his ears, and strange voices seemed to snigger and jeer.

As Rook stumbled after him, the little skycraft at his side twisting and turning in the oncoming breeze, he could only pray that Twig was right. The mist closed in, blurring his vision and muffling his ears.

'Is everyone still here?' Twig called back.

'Wuh!' the banderbears replied with one voice. *We are all together*.

Occasionally, sudden squalls of turbulent air blew in, slamming into Rook's face and pitching him off balance. He would drop to the ground, clutching on tightly to the tether-rope, and wait for the wind to subside. The last time it happened, the air had cleared and, for the briefest of moments, he thought he caught a glimpse of the Edge itself. But then the mist had closed in again, and he'd been plunged back into whiteout blindness. 'I can't see a thing!' he called out nervously.

'It's all right, Rook,' said Twig. 'Trust me.'

Just then the mist thinned again, and Rook glimpsed

the cliff-edge a second time. Far in the distance a dark shape loomed. The mist thickened, and Rook lost sight of it. 'Did you see it, Captain?' he said excitedly. 'The crag!'

'I saw it,' said Twig. There was an odd catch in his voice. 'But I didn't see the *Skyraider*.'

They forged ahead in the face of the gusting wind and swirling mists, struggling to see more than a few feet ahead.

'I don't think I can go much further,' gasped Rook as he battled with the *Stormhornet*. Twig looked stooped and exhausted; the banderbears around him, bedraggled and miserable.

'We'll stop for a few moments,' shouted Twig above the howling wind.

The banderbears formed a huddle round Rook and the old sky pirate, offering a shield from the gale. Rook shivered unhappily. If only those mocking voices would stop, he would at least be able to think.

'We're lost, aren't we, Captain?' he said.

Twig didn't seem to hear him. He was gazing straight ahead. The wind had died down momentarily and the mist was rolling away. 'Look,' he said simply.

And there, looming above their heads, was the largest sky vessel Rook had ever seen. Its great battered prow alone was the size of twenty *Stormhornets*, its pitted, scarred hull as big as an Undertown tavern, while its mast towered up into the sky like a great ironwood pine. A mighty anchor chain descended to the black crag ahead, its dark bulk shielding the vessel in its lee.

'She's magnificent!' gasped Rook, then shook his head sadly as a thought struck him. No matter how wonderful it was to have created a wooden skycraft, the *Stormhornet* was, he realized, nothing compared with the *Skyraider*. The so-called Second Age of Flight, of which the librarian knights were so proud, was the merest shadow of what had existed before. So, so much had been lost.

'Come on, lad,' Twig called him, 'we have no time to lose. We must leave this accursed place! Take your skycraft and board the *Skyraider*. Throw down the rope-ladders and we'll climb aboard. Quick, now. Before the winds pick up again.'

Hurriedly Rook climbed onto the *Stormhornet* and took to the air. In moments, he was level with the battered balustrade of the mighty ship's foredeck. He secured the *Stormhornet* to the mast and jumped down to the deck. With trembling fingers, he untied the coiled rope-ladders and let them down. Instantly, the banderbears began clambering aboard, followed at last by Twig himself. As he set foot on the sky ship, the old sky pirate captain fell to his knees and kissed the deck.

'Thank Sky!' he whispered. 'I thought for a moment that I'd lost you.' He sprang to his feet. Suddenly, he no longer looked stooped. The years seemed to fall away, and a youthful glint came into his eyes. 'Come!' he cried. 'Let's get the *Skyraider* airborne!'

As one, the banderbears dispersed. Twig went with them. Rook was left on his own. He scuttled round the *Skyraider*, snooping into cupboards and locker-rooms, peering down below deck and watching the banderbears as they hurried this way and that, busily making the great sky pirate ship skyworthy.

Wumeru headed for the galleys below deck. Rummel unfurled the mainsail, checking it and double-checking it for any sign of major rents in the material. Wuralo saw to the ropes. Meeru and Loom climbed over the balustrades – one on the port side, one on the starboard side – and clambered round the hull-rigging beneath, ensuring that the hull-weights and rudder-wheel were all secure and in alignment. Weeg scaled the mast, inspecting the great wooden shaft for any trace of wood-rot or the tell-tale hairline fracture of timber fatigue as he climbed right up to the caternest at the very top.

From behind him Rook heard a hiss and a soft roar. Curious, he followed the sound, and stumbled across Twig himself – his head between the bars of the central cage – staring intently at the surface of the flight-rock. Beside him, adjusting the flames of the now blazing torches, was Molleen.

'Is it all right?' Rook asked.

Twig pulled away from the flight-rock and looked round. 'It shows no sign of the sickness,' he said.

'But that's wonderful news!' said Rook. 'We can fly!'

'Indeed we can,' said Twig. 'But we must make haste. For I fear the unseen sickness may already have struck.'

Rook frowned. 'But how?' he said.

Twig swept his arm round in a wide arc. 'Through the crew,' he said. 'You heard what they said. Most of them have had experience of life on board a sky ship. The danger is that one – or all – might be carrying the terrible sickness.'

Rook trembled uneasily. 'But how can we tell?' he said.

'We can't,' said Twig. 'Maybe the flight-rock has already been contaminated. Maybe not. Certainly, the closer we fly to the crumbling Sanctaphrax rock, the greater the risk. Make no mistake, Rook, this is a one-way voyage. The *Skyraider* won't be coming back. We must just hope and pray that it holds out long enough for us to make it to the Tower of Night.'

'Earth and Sky willing,' said Rook, his face pale and drawn.

'But cheer up, lad,' said Twig, clapping him on the shoulder. 'This is the beginning of a great adventure. Come with me.'

He turned away and, leaving Molleen to tend to the flight-rock, hurried round the narrow skirting-deck and up a short flight of stairs to the helm. He seized the great wheel and released the locking-lever. Then he tested the individual bone-handled flight-levers, one after the other, making sure that the ropes moved smoothly; raising and lowering the sails and hull-weights in preparation for take-off.

As he did so, the yodelled cries of the banderbear crew filled the air as, one by one, they announced that the various sections of the great sky pirate ship were just about in working order. When the last – Weeg – called down from the caternest that the mast was skyworthy, Twig clapped his hands together with glee.

'Prepare to launch!' he bellowed. 'Make ready to drop the anchor chain!'

'Wuh-wuh!' the banderbears bellowed back. *Aye-aye*.

With a mighty shudder and an ominous creak, the *Skyraider* began to lift up into the air. Twig let the heavy anchor chain fall away with a resounding *clang*.

'We shan't need that where we're going,' he called to the others.

The tattered sails billowed. The sky ship listed to one side and pulled away from the black crag. Higher and higher the great sky vessel flew, calmly, sedately, until, all at once, the wind caught it from behind and sent it soaring up into the air so fast that Rook's head spun and his stomach did somersaults.

'This is *amazing*!' he cried out. '*Incredible!* I can't believe that I'm actually flying on board a sky pirate ship!'

Twig chuckled. 'Neither can I, lad,' he said. 'Neither can I. Sky above, but I've missed it! The thrust of the sails, the sway of the weights – the wind in my hair. It's almost like the old days,' he said. 'As if I were a sky pirate once again.'

Rook turned to him, his eyes bright with excitement. 'But you *are*!' he said.

Twig nodded slowly, as his fingers danced over the flight-levers. 'Aye, Rook, I suppose I am,' he said. His brow furrowed. 'The *last* of the sky pirates.'

·CHAPTER NINETEEN·

THE TOWER
OF NIGHT

It was the darkest hour just before the dawn. A fine dew, glistening in the overhead lamplight, covered the surface of the crumbling Sanctaphrax rock. From a shadowy crevice came a soft, slurping noise. Something was stirring.

A long, glistening tentacle appeared, then another – and the two gripped the rock and pulled. A dripping, jelly-like creature emerged. Three small round bumps on the top of its head grew large, cracked open and eyed the surroundings suspiciously. The tentacles reached out again and dragged it forwards.

Where the creature passed, the rock behind was left bone-dry, and as it slipped and slid about, it began to swell. Larger it became, larger and larger until, with a hiss and a spurt, three rear-tentacles suddenly uncoiled and squirted a thick, oily substance over the rock behind it. It had drunk enough.

The rubble ghoul slithered back down between the cracks in the broken rock. Having sated its thirst, it was now hungry.

Far, far above, a hammerhead goblin was also hungry. Ravenous, in fact. And thirsty. And cold. He stamped his great booted feet and pulled his black robes up against the icy air which, so high up the towering building, was cold enough to cover the wood of the jutting gantry with a feathery coating of frost.

'Just you wait till I get my hands on you, Gobrat, you useless, squint-eyed little runt!' he growled, and his breath came in dense puffs of cloud which glowed and squirmed in the yellow light of the hanging oil lamps. He paced back and forwards, slapping his arms against each other in an attempt to get warm. 'Leaving me here to do your guard-duty!' he complained. He should have been relieved at nine hours the previous night; now, the first rays of early morning sun

340

were already lining the distant clouds with silver. 'All through the night I've been standing here!' he muttered angrily. 'I'll stove in your skull! I'll break every bone in your body! I'll— *Waaargh!*'

The heel of his boot skidded on an untouched patch of frost, and sent the goblin crashing to the floor. His heavy horned helmet came loose as his head slammed viciously down on the cold, hard wood with a loud *crack*!

Dazed, the hammerhead sat up. He saw the helmet scudding towards the edge of the gantry. Heart hammering furiously, he lunged forwards and grasped one of the helmet's curving horns just as it was about to tumble down from the high gantry.

'That was a close one,' he told himself grimly. 'You take care, now, Slab.' He climbed to his feet and put the helmet back on his head. If he'd lost it, the guard master would have clapped him in irons and thrown him into solitary confinement for a week as punishment.

Slab checked the rest of his equipment – the curved knife at his belt, the powerful-looking crossbow on his back, the heavy hooked pikestaff . . . Everything, he was relieved to discover, seemed to be in order.

Just then, in the distance, far below, came the sound of the bell at the top of Vox Verlix's Undertown palace tolling the hour. It was six. He'd now been on duty for eighteen hours! He stared out across the chasm of open sky as the sun slowly wobbled up above the horizon, shielding his eyes as the light grew dazzling. He looked down.

There, below, were the Stone Gardens, their once mighty rock-stacks now a mess of broken rubble littering the dead rock. Screetown and Undertown were wreathed in mist and, in the middle distance, the Great Mire Road was already teeming with countless tiny individuals as it wound its way back into the murky gloom and disappeared. For despite the bright start to the day, there were dark clouds rolling in from the Deepwoods far to the north-west, threatening rain, maybe even a lightning storm . . .

'A storm, after all this time.' Slab hawked and spat. 'That'd show those accursed librarian knights,' he growled. 'Think they're so clever, so they do – with their books and learning and their pathetic little skycraft.' He stared up into the great banks of cloud, praying for a lightning bolt to strike the top of the tower. 'But they'll learn one day. When Midnight's Spike heals the rock and we return to the skies, *then* they'll see—'

'Strength in night!' came a gruff voice behind him, and Slab turned to see a brawny, heavily tattooed flat-head who bore the scars of many a battle standing in front of him, his clenched right fist pressed against his breast-plate in ritual greeting.

'Ah, Bragknot, strength in night!' Slab replied, and saluted in response. 'Am I glad to see you. Gobrat never showed up, the little—'

'Gobrat's gone missing,' said Bragknot. 'No-one seems to know *where* he is.'

'Soused on woodgrog and slumped in some dark corner, if I know him,' Slab muttered bitterly. He yawned.

'Eighteen hours without a break I've been up here. *Eighteen* hours . . .'

Bragknot shrugged. 'It happens,' he mumbled unsympathetically and looked all around, scanning the townscape below and squinting into the distance. 'Quiet watch, was it?' he said. 'No problems?'

'None,' said Slab.

The flat-head nodded towards the great banks of cloud looming closer. 'Looks like rain,' he commented. 'Just my luck!'

'Yeah, well, I'll leave you to it,' said Slab. 'I'm off to get my head down.'

'You do that,' said Bragknot, turning towards him. 'I'll—' He gasped and looked back over Slab's shoulder. 'Sky above! What is *that*?'

Slab chuckled. 'I'm not falling for that one again,' he said.

'I mean it, Slab!' said Bragknot. 'It's . . . it's . . .' He grabbed the smirking hammerhead by the shoulders and twisted him round. 'Look!'

Slab's eyes widened. His jaw dropped. This time, Bragknot had not been playing one of his stupid games. There really was something there.

'It can't be,' he whispered, trembling with awe as a great ghostly vessel emerged from the cover of dark, swirling cloud.

Too young to have seen one before, Slab stood transfixed, staring in disbelief at the vast, solid sky ship as it swept gracefully down through the air towards them. With its huge billowing sails and massive hull, it was more awesome than he could ever have imagined.

'B-but how?' he faltered. 'How is it possible?' He shook his head. 'A sky ship still flying ... Where did it come from?'

'Never mind all that!' bellowed Bragknot. 'Sound the alarms! Raise the guard! Mount the harpoons! *Come on*, Slab! We must—'

Just then Slab heard a high-pitched whistle and a soft thud. He spun round. Bragknot stood there, swaying slowly back and forwards on the spot. He looked back at Slab, his eyes filled with fear and confusion as his fingers closed gingerly round the ironwood bolt lodged in the side of his neck. His throat gurgled. Blood gushed down over his black robe. The next moment he staggered backwards and toppled over the edge of the gantry, dropping down silently out of sight.

A second bolt whistled in over Slab's head and embedded itself in a broad crossbeam behind him. A third shattered the hanging-lamp. It was followed by a dozen or more arrows, hissing in through the air and quivering where they struck.

'To the gantries!' Slab roared. 'We're under attack!'

'What is it? . . . What's going on?' several voices cried out from above and below him.

'Over there!' shouted someone from an upper gantry, pointing into the cloud, now swirling round the tower.

'A sky ship!' bellowed another.

'It's turning this way!' shouted yet another, a telescope raised to his eye. 'And it's got heavy weaponry aboard!'

A loud rasping klaxon sounded, followed by another and another . . . Soon, the whole Tower of Night echoed to the clamour of the Guardians answering the call to arms.

Head down, Slab dashed back along the exposed gantry. Skidding awkwardly on the slippery wood, he tumbled in through the doorway. Behind him there was a flash and an almighty splintering *crash* as an incoming ball of flaming ironwood severed the jutting gantry and sent it hurtling down below. Had it landed a second earlier, he too would be hurtling down with it.

Slab climbed shakily to his feet. All round him the air was filled with bellowed orders and screeched commands. Doors banged and shutters slammed as section after section within the great tower was sealed off to prevent an invasion. Heavy boots pounded up and down stairs as well-armed, black-robed Guardians hastened to the west side of the tower to repel the great attacking sky ship.

In all the chaos and confusion no-one noticed a small skycraft as it swooped down through the dark, swirling mist on the far side of the tower.

With the cloud as cover, the sky ship spat out a flaming salvo at the Tower of Night. Gantries splintered and shattered; great holes appeared in the walls and, where the heavy balls of flaming ironwood penetrated, small fires broke out.

Inside the tower the Guardians of Night were in turmoil, with the guard masters barking out a stream of orders.

'Shove that broken beam back into place!'

'Douse that fire!'

'Load the harpoons!'

'Prime the catapults!'

While some effected makeshift repairs and others smothered the flames with water and sand, small groups ventured out onto the jutting weapon-platforms where the heavyweight weaponry stood on plinths, bolted to the floor. Working in threes, they took up their battle positions. At the harpoon-turrets, one jumped into the firing seat and primed the shooting mechanism, one loaded a harpoon into the long chamber, while the third grabbed the wheel at the side of the turret and began turning. Slowly, as the sequence of internal cogs moved, the whole mechanism swung round. Then, seizing a second wheel, he altered the angle of the long barrel until the huge harpoon was pointing directly at the attacking sky ship. At the swivel catapults a similar process was taking place. When the launch trajectory had been secured, the guards – two at a time – heaved enormous, heavy boulders into each of the ladle-shaped firing bowls.

'Fire!' roared a guard master. Then another, higher up, bellowed the same command. And another, and another.

'Fire! . . . Fire! . . . Fire!'

A volley of harpoons and rocks exploded from the Tower of Night and hurtled towards the sky ship. One of the harpoons struck the starboard bow; a second skittered across the lower deck. Further back, a boulder dealt a glancing blow to the stern. All would have shattered a small skycraft, but the mighty sky ship barely seemed to flinch.

The Guardians of Night reloaded. The *Skyraider* rose up higher in the sky. The harpoon-turrets and swivel catapults were realigned.

'*FIRE!*'

The second bombardment did even less harm than the first, with not a single harpoon or boulder meeting its target. Peering through their telescopes into the swirling cloud, the guard masters saw the bearded figure at the helm – resplendent in satin frock coat and tricorn hat – barking commands of his own. The main-sail billowed. The stern hull-weights dropped. Abruptly, the hovering sky ship soared upwards, returning fire as it did so.

'They're heading for Midnight's Spike,' someone cried.

'Defend the spike!'

'Defend her with your lives!'

'*FIRE!*'

A third salvo of rocks and harpoons soared into the sky, a single rock hitting amidships, where a lone banderbear feverishly tended the great flight-rock. The banderbears at the rear of the ship replied with a heavy bombardment of the flaming ironwood balls. The walls of the tower suffered more damage and one harpoon-turret was destroyed by a direct hit. Two Guardians – one up high on a look-out gantry and one on a weapon-platform some way below – were struck by arrows simultaneously. The pair of them keeled forwards and, one after the other, tumbled down through the air as in some strange and terrible dance.

'More fire-power!' roared a guard master.

'Reinforcements to the spike chamber at once!' bellowed another.

'Alert the Most High Guardian!'

'Call Orbix Xaxis!'

Slab crouched down on the boards and peered out through the shattered wall. He had neither harpoon-turrets nor swivel catapults up here at the look-out gantry, yet the death of his comrade-in-arms would be avenged. With trembling hands, he raised the sight of the crossbow to his eye, slid the ironwood bolt into place and ratcheted the string back.

'This is for Bragknot,' he muttered grimly.

The sky ship loomed up before him, thick clouds of mist swirling around it. Slab lowered his head. He took aim. For the briefest of moments, the sky ship drew level. He fired the crossbow.

There was a thump. A *twang*. The bolt shot into the air and disappeared into the thick misty cloud. Slab held his breath. The next instant, rising up above the cacophony of noise from the tower itself, there came an anguished yodelling cry and, as the cloud fleetingly thinned out, he saw a banderbear clutch at its heart and fall off the sky ship.

'Got you!' Slab snarled, as the great hairy beast tumbled down through the air. He raised the crossbow to his eye a second time. As he looked through the viewfinder, he saw three great flaming balls hurtling straight towards him.

Before he had a chance even to cry out, the ironwood balls struck – tearing apart the whole upper section of the tower and snuffing out the life of the hammerhead guard. The building shook from top to bottom. The sky ship rose higher, almost level with the great spike that topped the tower.

'They're using grappling-hooks!' screeched a guard from the base of the spike as a heavy three-pronged hook abruptly flew out from the *Skyraider* and hurtled towards it. 'They're trying to destroy Midnight's Spike!'

'Sacrilege!' bellowed another.

'Destroy the invaders!' roared yet another.

The Guardians intensified their efforts to repel the attacking sky ship with volley after volley of boulders and harpoons, arrows and crossbow bolts – and anything else they could lay their hands on. The air trembled with the din of battle. The *Skyraider* responded with arrows and crossbow bolts of its own, and the great flaming balls of ironwood which tore chunk after chunk from the dark tower. Numerous goblins, trogs and trolls in the black robes of the Guardians of Night plummeted to their deaths. Another grappling-iron clanged against Midnight's Spike. A second banderbear was struck . . .

On the other side of the tower the skycraft approached. Lightly, stealthily – like a woodmoth on the wing – it flitted up and down the great east wall, its rider looking for a place to enter. Finally he swooped down onto a small, jutting gantry, two-thirds of the way up, which appeared to be deserted.

The rider dismounted. As he tethered the skycraft securely to eye-hooks screwed into the wall, the weak milky sunlight penetrated the thick cloud and shone into his face. The youth – jaw set and brow creased with concentration – turned towards the small, dark entrance and disappeared inside.

*

As Rook peered into the gloom, the dark, menacing atmosphere assaulted his senses like a battering-ram slamming into locked fortress doors. It was dark within the tower despite the hanging-lamps, and the stench of death and rancid decay was overpowering. Rook faltered – numb, dumbstruck, incredulous that anyone could have created so evil a place.

He could hear voices, countless voices. Their muffled moans and feeble cries echoed in the darkness, a soft and terrible accompaniment to the bass rumbles and furious percussion of the battle raging far above him. 'Poor wretches,' Rook murmured. 'If only I could save you all.'

As his eyes grew accustomed to the gloom, he wrapped the cloak of nightspider-silk round his shoulders and ventured further into the tower. He found himself in a confusing labyrinth of narrow walkways and rickety flights of stairs sandwiched between the outer wall of the tower and an inner wall. At wild irregular angles, the wooden stairways zigzagged off in all directions – above and below him, and away to both sides. The sound of the hopeless, groaning prisoners grew louder, the foul stench more intense.

Rook's eyes followed the path of the walkway he was standing on. It led to a small, square landing, before doubling back on itself and rising steeply further up. At the far side of the landing, set into the shadowy inner wall of the tower, was a door.

Is that one of the cells? he wondered. There was only one way to find out.

Rook dashed up the stairs. On the landing, as he approached the heavy, wooden door, he saw what looked like markings. He pulled the sky-crystals from his pockets and, holding them together, used the pale light they emitted to examine the door more closely. Several names had been scratched crudely into hard wood: RILK TILDERHORN, LEMBEL FLITCH, REB MARWOOD, LOQUBAR AMSEL ... Each of them had a line gouged through them. Only the name at the bottom remained untouched.

'Finius Flabtrix,' Rook whispered. 'An academic, by the sound of him.'

There was a shuttered spy-hole in the door and heavy bolts at the top and bottom. Rook reached forwards, slid aside the spy-hole cover and quickly glanced inside. He couldn't make out anything in the blackness, but the stench intensified. Gingerly he reached up and drew the top bolt across; then the bottom bolt. Slowly he pushed the heavy door open and looked in.

With no walls, no chains, no bars, the cell was nothing like he had ever seen. A narrow set of steps led from the door down to a single ledge, which jutted out from the wall into a cavernous atrium beyond. Apart from the door which, when shut, formed a smooth, unbroken part of the inward-sloping wall, the only way out was to step off the ledge and tumble down through the fetid air to certain death below. Looking out into the atrium, Rook could make out countless other ledges, each connected by their own steps to individual cell doors.

Appalled, his gaze fell upon the individual at the corner of the ledge before him. Curled up in a foetal ball, he lay on a stinking mattress of straw, bony arms hugged round bonier legs; his robes in tatters, his breath uneven, rasping. Long, matted hair hung down over his face. In places it had fallen out in clumps, leaving angry scab-encrusted patches all over his scalp. His beard was thick and soiled; his skin was covered in grime and red, weeping sores – the result of scratching and scratching with his filthy, jagged nails to relieve the intolerable itching of the tick-lice which burrowed beneath the surface to lay their eggs.

'Finius? Finius Flabtrix,' said Rook softly, moving closer. '*Professor* Finius Flabtrix?'

The breathing quickened. The eyelids flickered and opened for an instant but, though the eyes stared in his direction, Rook knew that they had not seen him. They closed again.

'Not my fault,' the old professor murmured, his voice hoarse and faltering. 'Not my fault. Not my fault . . .'

'It's all right, I won't hurt you,' Rook whispered, tears welling up in his eyes.

The professor ignored him, lost in his own private torment. Rook turned and made his way carefully back up the stairs and out through the cell door. There was no time to lose; the *Skyraider* couldn't keep the Guardians occupied for ever. He *must* find Cowlquape and get out of this terrible place.

He hurried down another walkway, and saw a row of cell doors embedded in the inner wall. Quickly, by the

'THE DUNGEONS OF THE TOWER OF NIGHT'

glow from the sky-crystals, he checked the names scratched into each door: JUG-JUG ROMPERSTAMP, Rook read. ELDRICK SWILL. RAIN HAWK III. SILVIX ARMENIUS. GROLL . . . If the names were anything to go by, then the prisoners came from every walk of Edge life. Merchants and academics. Slaughterers, goblins and trolls. A former sky pirate . . .

At some, Rook simply read off the name and continued without stopping. At others, he paused to look through the spy-hole – though each time he did so, he wished that he had not. The abject creatures inside were too terrible to witness. Jabbering. Twitching. Deranged. Some rocked slowly back and forwards, some ranted and raved, some paced round and round mumbling beneath their breath, while others – the worst of them; those who had given up all hope – simply lay on the ledge, waiting for death to come and embrace them.

A fiery anger spread through Rook's body. Curse the Guardians of Night! he thought bitterly. 'The dungeons are an abomination! An affront to every living creature in the Edge – to life itself! Why, if I was ever uncertain whether the war between the librarian knights and the Guardians of Night was a just one, then here is the proof,' he told himself. 'This is truly a battle between good and evil!'

'Well said,' came a voice close by.

Rook jumped. 'Who's that?' he whispered.

'Over here,' said the voice.

Rook approached a cell door. He looked down. CODSAP was scratched into its heavy, dark wood.

'Open the door,' came the voice. 'Give it a good shove. A *really* good shove! Go on!'

Rook unbolted the door, and gave it a hard push. There was a thud, and a muffled cry. Rook's heart missed a beat. What had happened? What had he *done*? He thrust his head inside the doorway just in time to see a green, scaly creature tumbling back off the stairs and down into the yawning void of the great atrium.

'No!' Rook bellowed, his howl of anguish spinning round and round the rank air. 'I'm sorry! I . . .'

Suddenly, there was a voice, speaking to him inside his head. 'Thank you, thank you, friend, for releasing me when I lacked the courage to jump . . .' The voice fell still.

Rook flinched. How long had the poor creature waited on the stairs for someone to come and end his suffering? He slammed the door shut with a helpless fury, the clang echoing loudly through the tower.

'*Ouch*,' came a voice from the shadows, somewhere to his left. 'Oh, my poor head. I knew I shouldn't have had all that woodgrog. Is that you, Slab?'

Rook drew his knife and silently followed the direction of the voice. There, just ahead, slumped in the corner of a landing, head in hands, was a sleepy flat-head goblin in the black robes of a Guardian of Night, a crossbow and an empty jar by his side.

In an instant Rook grabbed the crossbow, kicked the jar away and thrust his knife at the goblin's throat.

'Y-y-you're not Slab,' he stammered. Rook could see the whites of his eyes as the goblin's frightened face

357

looked up into his. Wh-who are you?'

'Never mind who I am,' Rook whispered, stepping back and levelling the crossbow at the white gloam-glozer emblem on the goblin's chest. 'Who are *you*?'

'I'm Gobrat. I'm just a poor guard. A warder. Please don't hurt me.' He paused, a frown crossing his broad features. 'You're one of them librarian knights, ain't you? Oh, please have mercy, sir. I've never hurt no-one, honest I haven't.'

'And yet you wear the black robes of the Guardians of Night,' said Rook, a cold anger in his quiet voice.

'They took me in, sir, when I was starving in Undertown. I had nothing. They fed me and clothed me – but I'm just a poor goblin from the Edgewater slums at heart. Please don't kill me, sir.'

'A warder, you say,' said Rook.

'Yes, sir. I'm not proud of it, sir – but I does what I can for the poor wretches locked up here . . .'

Rook raised the crossbow to silence the flat-head. 'Take me to the cell of Cowlquape Pentephraxis and I'll spare your miserable life,' he said.

The goblin groaned. 'It'll be more than my life's worth if the High Master finds out I've led you to Cowlquape.'

'It'll be more than your life's worth if you don't,' said Rook, pulling back on the crossbow trigger.

'All right! All right!' The goblin got to his feet shakily. 'Follow me, sir, and be careful where you're pointing that there crossbow.'

Rook followed the flat-head through the endless maze of walkways and staircases, down into the depths of the

Tower of Night. As they continued, there was a loud
crashing sound from high up above the atrium,
and the stairs rattled as the tower shook.
'I suppose that's your lot
up there,' said Gobrat,
'causing all that
commotion.

It won't
do any good,
you know. You
never learn! Skycrafts
is no match for tower
weapons.'

'Just keep walking,' said
Rook, jabbing the
crossbow into
his back.
'How much

further?'
'Not far,' said
Gobrat, with a mirthless
laugh. 'We're almost at the
lower depths now, young sir.'

With the flat-head in front, they
made their way down a sloping flight of
stairs. Gobrat stopped at a heavily bolted door.

'Cowlquape Pentephraxis,' said Rook, reading off
the name. 'This is it!'

Gobrat scowled. 'There. Now take my advice and get out of here smartish. The guards will be swarming all round once they've dealt with your comrades, and now I've helped you, my life isn't worth an oakapple pip!' The goblin pulled off his robe and threw it to the ground. 'I suppose it's back to the Edgewater slums for old Gobrat – if the rubble ghouls don't get me.'

Rook waved the flat-head away. 'You've been of valuable service to the librarian knights,' he said. 'Fare you well, Gobrat.'

With the flat-head gone, Rook returned his attention to the cell door. Having checked that the stairs inside were clear, he slid the bolts across and pushed the door open.

'Is that you, Xanth?' came a cracked, frail voice.

'No, Professor,' said Rook. 'I'm a librarian knight. I've come to rescue you.'

He descended the stairs, down to the primitive, wooden ledge. Here in the depths of the tower, the stench was indescribable. The former Most High Academe of New Sanctaphrax looked up at him. His body was bent and painfully thin. His grey hair, long and unkempt, his robes thread-bare. Worst of all were his eyes. Filled with the memories of horrors too terrible to forget, they stared ahead, lifeless, dull, unblinking . . .

'Professor, we *must* leave now,' said Rook. 'Time is running out.'

'Leave . . .' Cowlquape murmured. 'Time . . .'

Rook leaned forwards and, taking the professor gently but firmly by the arm, hoisted him up onto his feet. Then, taking his weight – which wasn't much – he guided him up the stairs.

'Wait! Wait!' Cowlquape called urgently, and broke away. He returned to the ledge, grabbed a roll of papers and barkscrolls and thrust them under his arm. He looked at Rook, a little smile playing round his mouth. 'Now I am ready to leave,' he said.

Up at Midnight's Spike the battle raged on. The crew of the *Skyraider* was down to five now. Rummel, the huge, black banderbear, had fallen first, fatally wounded by Slab's crossbow bolt. Meeru was next to fall, skewered by one of the great harpoons and torn away from the sky ship. Mindless with grief, his brother Loom had thrown himself off the stern after his beloved twin.

But Twig hadn't time to mourn the loss of the three brave banderbear volunteers, for Molleen had yodelled to him to come at once to the flight-rock cage. Calling Wumeru over, and telling her to hold the helm steady, Twig hurried down to the old banderbear's side.

'Wuh-wuh!' *Look!* Molleen pointed at a livid scar in the glowing flight-rock. 'Wegga-lura-meeragul. Wuh!' *The rock is wounded. I thought the weapons of the Dark Ones had not hurt it – but look, Captain!*

Twig looked. Where the Guardians' rock had struck, a deep crater had formed. It was growing like an ulcer, eating away at the flight-rock.

'Contamination!' Twig gasped. 'We haven't much time. Do what you can, Molleen, but be prepared to abandon ship.' He hurried back to the helm.

Despite her best attempts to keep it buoyant – dousing the flight-lamps, drenching the rock with chilled sand and, with Wumeru now by her side, desperately operating the cooling-fans – the rock continued to disintegrate. The crater in its surface became wider, deeper, and a growing trickle of dusty particles showered down through the air.

'Give me as much time as you can!' Twig shouted across to Molleen. 'We can't abandon Rook now,' he added, mopping the beads of sweat from his forehead. His hands darted over the bone-handled levers in a furious blur as he carried out ever-finer adjustments to the sails and weights in an effort to keep the leaning, lurching sky ship from rolling right over.

But he was fighting a losing battle. With every passing

minute the flight-rock became less and less buoyant. If the *Skyraider* was to remain airborne, it would have to be made lighter.

'Weeg!' Twig bellowed. 'To the hull-rigging with you! I want you to cut the weights.'

'Wuh-wuh,' he shouted back. *Cut the weights, Captain? But we'll become unstable.*

'It's a chance we'll have to take,' Twig shouted back. 'Start with the klute-hull-weights, then the peri-hull-weights. And if that's not enough, move on to the prow- and stern-weights . . . Sky willing, it'll give us the lift we need.' He frowned. *'Now*, Weeg!'

Grunting unhappily, the lanky banderbear hurried off to carry out the commands. Twig fingered the various bone and wood amulets around his neck. Far below him, on the platform beneath Midnight's Spike, stood a figure in black robes, fluttering in the mist, with a curious muzzle-like mask covering most of his face.

'Wuh! Wuh!' Molleen cried out. *The flight-rock! It's broken in two!*

'Hold it steady!' Twig told her. 'Just a little bit longer—'

At that moment a lufwood-flare soared up from the other side of the tower and blazed in the sky far above their heads, a brightly glowing streak of purple.

Twig gritted his teeth. 'Thank Sky!' he whispered. 'It's the signal! Rook is waiting for us!'

Just then Weeg must have severed the first hull-weight, for the sky ship gave a sudden jolt and rose up several strides into the air. A salvo of harpoons sailed harmlessly beneath its hull.

'Hold tight, Cowlquape, old friend,' said Twig grimly. 'We're coming to get you.'

Down on the platform at the base of Midnight's Spike, Orbix Xaxis stared up at the bright purple light suspiciously. 'It must be some sort of signal,' he said. He looked across at the *Skyraider*; his eyes narrowed. 'While you, up there, were keeping us busy . . .' he said slowly, thoughtfully, 'there was something else afoot. I smell a rat . . .' He paused. 'The dungeons!'

'I'll check them at once,' said the sallow, shaven-headed youth by his side, dashing off as fast as he could down the broken flight of stairs.

'You, Banjax,' the Most High Guardian shouted at one of the guard masters close by. 'Take two dozen Guardians and scour the dungeons for intruders. No-one must get in or out!'

'At once, High Guardian,' Banjax replied, and the air resounded with the tramp of the Guardians' heavy boots on the wooden stairs.

The Most High Guardian looked back up at the *Skyraider*. The sky ship had pulled away from Midnight's Spike at last, and seemed to be heading round in a great circle. 'So you think you've tricked the Most High Guardian of Night, do you?' he hissed.

Twig gripped the main-sail lever grimly. With the flight-rock irreparably weakened, he was dependent on the great, tattered sail for lift. Slowly, carefully, battling against treacherous draughts of misty air, he brought the *Skyraider* round to the east side of the tower and began the long, perilous descent.

Wumeru cried out. 'Wuh-wuh. Roo-wuh-ook!'

Peering down, Twig saw Rook standing on a jutting gantry, a third of the way down, together with . . . Twig gasped. Could that be him? Could that stooped, grey-haired figure truly be his apprentice, Cowlquape? He looked so frail, so fragile – so old.

'Prepare to board!' he bellowed down.

Rook looked up and waved wildly. The sky ship sank lower. The gantry came closer.

'Wumeru!' Twig shouted. 'Wuh-weela-wurr.' *Help Cowlquape aboard.*

'Professor,' said Rook urgently, 'you'll have to jump.'

'Jump?' the ancient professor croaked. 'I think my jumping days are over.'

'Try,' said Rook. 'You must try.'

He looked up. The *Skyraider* was just above them now. As it came down lower, he stepped behind Cowlquape and seized him by the shoulders.

The sky ship drew level, but did not slow down . . .

'No, no, I can't . . .' Cowlquape trembled, the years of
being perched on the high prison ledge suddenly returning to him with full force as he looked down.

'Now!' shouted Twig.

Rook pushed Cowlquape off the gantry. At the same
time Wumeru leaned forwards, arms outstretched. She
caught the old professor in her great arms and lowered
him gently onto the deck. 'Wuh-wuh,' she said softly.
You're safe now.

Overjoyed, Twig locked the flight-levers and hurtled
down to the foredeck to greet his old friend. He rushed
up, arms open, and embraced him warmly.

'Cowlquape, Cowlquape,' he cried, his voice straining
with emotion. 'I can't tell you what it means to see you
again.'

'Nor I, you, Twig,' said Cowlquape. 'Nor I, you.'

At that moment the sky ship gave a sudden lurch. 'Hold on, old friend,' said Twig, pulling away. 'We're not quite safe yet. But fear not. I won't let you down.'

Back at the helm, Twig unlocked the levers and tried his best to right the stricken sky ship. 'Just a little bit longer,' he groaned, as it trembled and creaked.

'Wuh-wuh!' screamed Molleen. *The flight-rock's breaking up.*

Twig locked the helm and levers a second time, raced to the balustrade and bellowed down. 'The prow-weight, Weeg!' he roared. 'Then the stern-weight!'

'Wuh-wurra!' the banderbear shouted back. He'd already cut both of them free.

'The neben-hull-weights, then,' Twig shouted. 'Sever the neben-hull-weights – small, medium *and* large!'

Weeg made no reply, but the next moment the *Skyraider* leaped upwards abruptly, back past the gantry and – under Twig's expert guidance – soared round the tower and off into the cloudy sky.

As the sky ship sailed past, Orbix Xaxis – Most High Guardian of Night – raised his powerful, exquisitely tooled crossbow. He aimed it at the sky ship's helm, and fired.

Down on the gantry Rook untethered the *Stormhornet* and leaped into the saddle. Then, standing tall in the stirrups, he jerked the pinner-rope to his right, and rose up into the air – only to pull up sharply a moment later as the tether-rope went taut.

'*Ooof!*' he gasped as he was thrown forward in his seat.

Rather than soaring away from the gantry, the *Stormhornet* remained stuck, bobbing about in the air like a kite. Rook looked round. He had been careless. In his hurry, instead of reeling in the tether-rope and stowing it neatly, he had left it hanging loose. Now it was snagged on the gantry's jutting balustrade.

With trembling hands, Rook seized the rope. He tugged it and shook it for all he was worth – but the tether-rope was stuck fast. It would not budge. There was nothing for it but to land again, dismount and pull it free—

'Halt!'

The bellowed command cut through the air like a knife. Rook's heart missed a beat. He yanked desperately at the rope. It moved – but only a fraction, and wedged itself tighter than ever. A figure emerged from the doorway at the end of the gantry, crossbow in hand. He raised it to his eye. 'Halt, or I'll shoot!'

Rook stared at the wiry individual in the black uniform. Though his hair, shaved back to a shadowy stubble, was shorter than Rook had ever seen it before, the youth was unmistakable.

'Xanth,' he gasped.

Xanth lowered the crossbow. 'Rook? Rook Barkwater.' His dark eyes narrowed. 'Is that you?'

Rook raised his goggles. Their eyes met.

From behind Xanth came the sound of heavy boots pounding closer and closer. Rook's heart hammered furiously in his chest. Xanth stepped forwards.

'Please, Xanth,' said Rook quietly. 'For friendship's sake—'

The pounding of the boots grew louder. The unit of guards was almost upon them.

Xanth raised his crossbow and took aim. Rook closed his eyes.

There was a click, a *twang* and a whistle as the crossbow loosed its bolt and sent it speeding towards the *Stormhornet*. Rook froze. The next instant – with a soft *thwpp* – the bolt sliced through the tether-rope and the *Stormhornet* catapulted forward into the air.

Seizing control of the skycraft, Rook darted up and off into the swirling mists. He flicked the pinner-rope to the left and felt the *Stormhornet* gather speed beneath him. As he flew on, he glanced over his shoulder and glimpsed Xanth – his shaven head gleaming in the bright rising sun – standing in the middle of a large group of Guardians.

Had Xanth shot the bolt through the tether-rope on purpose, deliberately setting him free? Rook desperately wanted to think so. 'Thank you,' he whispered.

As he left the Tower of Night behind, he saw the *Skyraider* in the sky up in front. But something was wrong. It wasn't waiting for him. Instead, listing heavily to one side, it was gathering speed. Past Undertown it went, with the boom-docks ahead . . .

If it didn't change course, it would sail over the great jutting Edge itself, and be lost in Open Sky.

CHAPTER TWENTY

RETURN

Realigning the nether-sail, Rook stood up in the stir-rups and sped forwards. As he battled to get closer to the *Skyraider*, he realized just how bad the situation had become. The flight-rock seemed to be crumbling, with ever larger chunks falling down from the cage. What was more, without its hull-weights, the sky ship looked out of control and at the mercy of the turbulent wind that held it in its grip.

As the *Skyraider* careered over the boom-docks, Rook could see the banderbears abandoning ship. With their parawings strapped to their backs, they leaped off the balustrades, tugged their rip-cords and sailed down to the ground below – Old Molleen, with no flight-rock left to tend; Wuralo, the female whose life he had saved at the Foundry Glade; and Wumeru, his friend. Last to jump was Weeg. As he launched himself off from the deck, Rook saw that he was carrying a ragged bundle in his paws. He gasped.

It was Cowlquape, wrapped up in the banderbear's protective embrace, like a babe in arms. The pair of them were swooping down through the sky towards the boom-docks. Pulling on the pinner-sail, Rook set the *Stormhornet* on a path to meet them. A cloud rolled in and he lost sight of the distant *Skyraider*.

'I just hope they've all made it,' Rook murmured, as he approached the muddy shores of the boom-docks and swooped in to land.

He brought the *Stormhornet* down next to one of the great overflow pipes that would lead them back into the labyrinth of sewer tunnels. The banderbears were huddled together.

'Where's the captain?' called Rook, tethering the *Stormhornet* and rushing over. Cowlquape pointed at the clearing horizon. Rook's eyes followed the direction of his bony finger.

High up in the sky and far out beyond the Edge, the *Skyraider* was still airborne – but only just. With no weights left to balance it, the sky pirate ship was on its side, juddering as it sailed on. The useless weight-ropes dangled; the sails flapped in the gathering wind. Rook raised his telescope to his eye and focused in on the helm.

'I can see him!' he said, his voice breaking with emotion. 'Why doesn't he abandon her?'

Wumeru was suddenly by Rook's side. 'Wuh-wug. Weela-lugg.' *He is mortally wounded, a crossbow bolt in his back.* She hung her head. *He chooses to die with his sky ship.*

They stood there, side by side, arms raised to shield

their eyes from the sun, watching the great sky ship sailing away.

'He was so brave,' Rook trembled. 'So selfless . . .' Suddenly, the *Skyraider* was flying no longer. The buoyant flight-rock had died, and the sky ship was dropping out of the sky like a stone. Down it came, gathering speed as it fell, before – in the blink of an eye – disappearing below the Edge. Rook gasped. Tears welled in his eyes. 'Oh, Captain Twig,' he murmured.

Wumeru clapped her arm around his shoulder and squeezed warmly. 'Wuh-wuh,' she said. *Wumeru is truly sorry*.

Rook sniffed, and wiped his eyes on his sleeve. Captain Twig was gone. For ever.

He turned back to where Cowlquape, Weeg and Molleen stood waiting. 'Come,' he said, 'the librarian scholars will welcome us in the sewers. I know the way.'

He looked back at the Edge one last time, standing silently for a moment, and was about to turn away when he caught sight of something out of the corner of his eye. Something huge. Something flapping . . . He squinted into the misty distance. It was a bird. A magnificent black and white bird with vast wings and a long, spreading tail.

'What's that?' Rook breathed.

'Why, it's a caterbird,' said Cowlquape. 'I do believe it's a caterbird!'

'It's magnificent,' said Rook. 'But wait . . . What's it got in its claws? Look!' He pointed at the small bundle clutched tightly in the enormous creature's great curved talons.

Cowlquape gasped. 'Of course – it has to be! I should have known at once!' He laughed joyfully and clapped his hands. 'It is *the* caterbird. The one whose hatching Twig was present at when he was a lad. The one who has watched over him ever since!'

Rook stared, wide-eyed. 'I wonder where it's taking him.'

Cowlquape shook his head. 'That I couldn't tell you, young librarian.'

The caterbird, with its precious load swinging below its great body, had wheeled round in the sky and was heading towards the Deepwoods. Suddenly Twig's words came back to Rook – about his quest; his endless, futile quest to return to his waiting crew.

'There's only one place it could be taking him,' he said, his heart soaring. 'To Riverrise.'

374

The old nightmare was back. The baying whitecollar woodwolves, their eyes flashing, their teeth bared and fur bristling. His father shouting, his mother screaming. Running ... Running ... Got to escape the wolves ... Got to shake off the slave-takers ...

Now he was alone, lost and wandering through the dark, menacing forest. Eyes glinted at him from the shadows. Growls, grunts and bloodthirsty cries echoed in the darkness. All at once he heard something else. Something close by – and coming closer, closer.

He looked up. A massive creature was looming towards him ... But wait ... Shouldn't he wake up now, just as he always did?

This time, however, was different. This time the creature continued inexorably towards him. He could hear its footfall, feel its hot, moist breath in his face. Sobbing loudly, knowing there was no escape, Rook reached out with his hand – into the darkness, into the unknown.

His fingers brushed against thick, warm fur. His heart pounded; his legs went weak. The sound of low, lulling grunts whispered into his ear as he was swept up off the ground and enfolded in the creature's huge, but gentle arms.

They smelt mossy. They cuddled him warmly, tenderly. Cradling him. Protecting him. Rook had never felt so safe or known so much comfort . . .

'Rook, are you awake?'

Rook's eyes opened. He knew that voice. He looked round the small, cosy room. The ornate oil lamp on the writing desk was still burning, casting a soft amber glow into every corner of the room and spilling out across his treatise-journal which lay open on the desk beneath it – and beside his bed sat Varis Lodd.

'I heard of your brave deeds from the Professor of Darkness the moment I arrived from the Free Glades,' she said. 'All Undertown is talking of it!' She paused. 'But what is it? You look as if you've seen a ghost.'

'Not a ghost,' said Rook. 'A dream. I had a dream. A dream I've had many times before, only this time . . . Varis, when you rescued me as a child, do you remember where exactly you found me?'

'Found you?' said Varis.

'In the Deepwoods,' he said. 'What happened? You've never really said—'

'You mean you don't know?' said Varis. 'I had no idea. I thought they would have told you. Your parents, they were taken by slavers. You escaped. Earth and Sky know how. And then . . . Oh, Rook, it was miraculous! I found you, all healthy and plump, tucked up asleep in a nest of woven grass—'

Rook stared at her. 'A nest?'

'That's right,' said Varis, nodding. 'An abandoned banderbear nest, though how you got there, I've no idea.'

Rook trembled as the memories came flooding back; the huge, enfolding arms, the warm breath, the thick fur, the steady thud of a heart beating next to his. Safe, protected, watched over, in the vast depths of the endless Deepwoods.

'I know how I got there,' said Rook, with a smile. 'I know.'

THE
EDGE
CHRONICLES

THE SLAUGHTERER'S QUEST

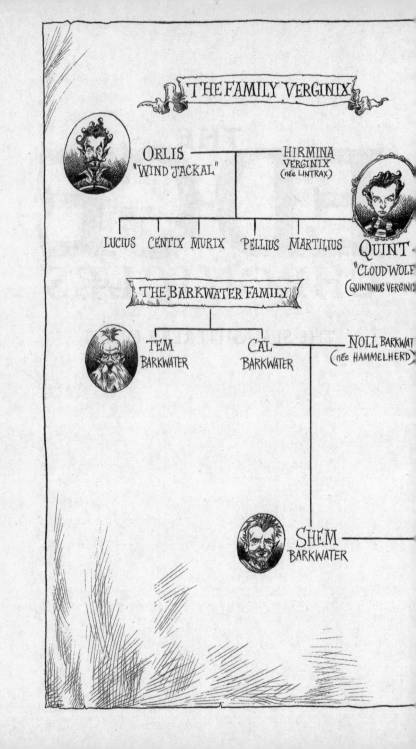

THE FAMILY VERGINIX

ORLIS ———————— HIRMINA
"WIND JACKAL."   VERGINIX
                       (née LINTRAX)

LUCIUS CENTIX MURIX PELLIUS MARTILIUS QUINT
                                           "CLOUD WOLF"
                                           (QUINTINIUS VERGINIX)

THE BARKWATER FAMILY

TEM   CAL ———————— NOLL BARKWAT
BARKWATER   BARKWATER   (née HAMMELHERD)

SHEM
BARKWATER

THE FAMILY PALLITAX

LINIUS
PALLITAX
(MOST HIGH ACADEME
OF SANCTAPHRAX)

YENA PALLITAX
(née VESPIUS)

MARIS
VERGINIX
(née PALLITAX)

TWIG
(ARBORINUS VERGINIX)

SINEW
VERGINIX
(née TATUM)

KERIS
BARKWATER
(née VERGINIX)

ROOK
BARKWATER

. CHAPTER ONE .

SUPPER AT DAWN

Keris pulled back the tilder leather door-hanging and stepped out of the hot, bustling kitchen cabin. It was a beautiful wintry night, with the full moon high above the treetops. It shone down, pure and white, casting the logwood cabins into slate-grey shadow and making the dusting of frost over the village clearing sparkle like phraxdust.

But Keris had no time to admire the moonlight. The wicker basket she was carrying on the crook of her arm gave off twists of sweet-scented steam, which mingled with the clouds coming from her own mouth as she hurried through the village. She needed to hurry, or the hot spicy drink would end up tepid and tasteless.

From the kitchen cabin behind her came the clatter of knives on chopping blocks, the sizzling of large copperwood frying pans and the low rhythmic song of the slaughterer sausage-makers. The cacophony of sound meant only one thing.

The village was expecting visitors.

Keris shivered as she strode past the churning huts, with their rows of drying cheeses; the tarping stalls, with their rollers and tanning vats, which billowed acrid crimson steam as the tilder leather inside them was slowly cured; and the rilking sheds, where great shaggy hammelhorn pelts hung in clusters. But it wasn't the cold that made her fingers tremble as she pulled her own hammel-hornskin waistcoat tightly closed at the neck, but rather a surge of excitement.

Tonight, there would be a feast.

Keris loved dawn suppers in her village when visitors came. And it wasn't just the traditional slaughterer hospitality that she loved – hospitality which meant that the huge communal table in the village clearing would be piled high with steaming tilder hams, spiced sausages, hammelhorn steaks and cauldrons of rich sweetmeat soup. No, it was what came afterwards that she looked forward to so much. With the great brazier's blazing heat warming the rows of family hammocks slung from the treetops above, and the pale light of dawn casting shadows across the table and its sleepy diners, the herdmaster would climb to his feet and propose a toast.

'We have eaten well and drunk deep,' he would boom, raising his tankard of woodale high above

his spiky red head. 'Now let us feast on the tales our guests have to tell of travels from places far beyond our pastures!'

And then the stories would begin. Gnokgoblin resin-traders would describe their homes in the branches of the mighty ironwood pines amidst the giant tree-fromps on whom they depended. Cloddertrog miners would retell bawdy stories recounted on cold nights in the deep caves to keep their spirits up. And solitary oakelves would talk wistfully of the lullabee groves of their childhood, and of their lonely quests for a place to hang their wonderful caterbird cocoons.

Keris loved all their stories and would memorize and repeat them to herself or to her many cousins at day in the hammock, when they couldn't sleep. But the tales she looked forward to most eagerly and treasured above all others were the tales told by sky pirates . . .

She smiled to herself, her dark eyes flashing and the tilder-greased points of her black hair, worn long and spiked in the slaughterer-style, glistening in the moonlight. She reached the edge of the village and headed down the broad droveway towards the lower pastures. Despite the high banks of protective thornbushes that formed an impenetrable barrier on either side of the path, Keris knew that the Deepwoods lay just beyond.

She could hear it all around her. The yowling and screeching of the night creatures seemed louder than ever this bright, moonlit night. From the shriek of gladehawks and squeal of hoglets to the distant yodelling of the solitary banderbears; razorflits, weezits, fromps and quarms, she knew their every cry . . .

'The Deepwoods . . .' she murmured.

The vast, brooding forest was full of unimaginable wonders and such terrible dangers. It was a place that every slaughterer was, from infanthood, taught to both fear and respect. Like their neighbours – the woodtrolls in the villages to the east and the gyle-goblins in their colonies to the west – the slaughterers knew only too well that survival meant sticking together and never straying from the droveways and pastures they knew so well. Those who did, as Keris had been told often enough, were taking their lives in their hands.

Perhaps that was why the village laid on such bountiful feasts for visitors who came to trade their goods for the slaughterers' finely worked tilder leather and expertly cured hammelhorn pelts. Knowing the perils well, the slaughterers admired their guests' bravery in venturing so far from the safety of their own homes. Moreover, they loved the travellers' tales of hardship and bloodshed told to them, safe in the knowledge that at the beginning of the day they could retire to the comfort of their warm hammocks above the brazier fire.

'Please let it be him, please let it be him . . .' Keris repeated to herself over and over as she reached the end of the droveway and stepped into the lush, knee-deep meadowgrass of the lower pasture.

In the distance, the hammelhorn herds – great mounds of shaggy grey and brown fur in a swaying sea of silver grass – grazed contentedly in groups of a dozen or more. They were watched over by thin, wiry herders with long crooks and spiky red hair.

Keris made her way quickly to the centre of the pasture where the herds were grouped, away from the dangerous fringe of the tree-line. A couple of the hammelhorns stepped aside, lowing as they did so.

'Uncle Gristle,' she greeted a tall herder in a tooled leather cape.

He turned a grizzled face towards hers; his skin stained a deep, dark red from the smoke of the curing sheds. Keris's own complexion seemed unnaturally pale by comparison, and her spiky hair even blacker.

'Goodnight, young Keris,' he smiled, his gaze falling on the wicker basket in her hands. 'Is that my midnight fodder? You are good to your old uncle.'

He took the basket from his niece and, spreading his leather cape on the meadowgrass, motioned for her to sit before unpacking the contents of the basket. There were three tilder sausages, hot from the pan, a wedge of rich hammelhorn cheese and a hunk of moist barleybread, together with a flask of spiced winesap – still steaming.

'To keep the cold out' – Gristle winked at Keris and took a long swig from the earthenware bottle – 'and warm an old herder's heart!'

Keris watched him wipe his mouth on the back of his hand. 'Have you seen them, Uncle?' she began excitedly. 'Our visitors? Where are they from? Are they . . . ?'

'Sky pirates?' said Gristle, with a smile and a shake of the head. 'I couldn't say for certain.'

Keris sighed. Once, the sky pirates had seemed to be regular visitors, filling the sky above the village with their great sky ships, which they would anchor to the tops of the largest trees. Recently, though, their visits had dwindled. The last time they had come must have been five, maybe six, years earlier.

'Whoever they are,' he said, 'according to the

village drums, they're on their way from the woodtrolls on foot. Should be with us before dawn by all accounts, but don't get your hopes up, Keris, my dear.'

'I can't help it,' Keris admitted, frowning and biting her lip. 'Every time the village has visitors I just can't help hoping it might be . . .'

'Your father,' said Gristle, laying a hand on her shoulder and stroking the hammelhorn fleece thoughtfully. 'You know, Keris, when your mother – my sister, Sinew, Sky rest her soul – died of the fever, your father Twig took it very hard . . .'

Keris stared down at the half-eaten barleybread in front of her and swallowed hard.

'He took to brooding, going over the past, blaming himself for all sorts of things – both real and imagined – until I began to fear he'd go the same way as your poor, dear mother. He got so thin and pale . . .'

Gristle picked up the bottle of hot winesap and took another swig.

'You see, he felt he'd abandoned his crew, and that your mother's death was some sort of punishment.' He shook his head. 'Convinced himself, he did, that the only way to protect you, his little daughter, was to go back out there into the Deepwoods and put things right. Three years old, you were, Keris, and scarcely bigger than a tilder fawn when he placed your little hand in mine and asked me to look after you as if you were my own. Then he left, promising to return once he'd been reunited with his crew . . .'

'That was ten years ago,' said Keris, unable to stop the bitterness creeping into her voice.

'That's as maybe,' said Gristle, turning his grizzled red face towards the tree-line. 'But wherever your father is, you can be sure that he won't let go of the memory of you, just like he couldn't let go of his crew. And believe

393

me, he'll do everything he can to come back . . .'

'But how can you be so sure, Uncle?' Keris interrupted angrily, her eyes glistening with scalding tears.

How many times had she lain awake in the middle of the day going over the few memories she had of her father, together with what she'd been told of him by her uncle? How many tears had she already wept?

Fourteen years earlier, a sky pirate ship had come to the village; the *Skyraider* its name. Its young sky pirate captain – a friend of her Uncle Gristle – was sick; his crew desperate. They had left him with the slaughterers, promising to return as soon as they could. Weak with fever, he'd been nursed by her mother, Sinew. It was a long, slow recovery, but gradually, he'd got better – by which time Sinew had fallen in love with the pale young sky pirate captain and he, unlike so many others in the Deepwoods who despised the lowly slaughterers, had returned her love. When the crew had returned, Twig had sent them away, promising to catch up with them later. But he'd stayed. And stayed – delaying his departure time and again.

A year to the day after his arrival, she – Keris – had been born . . .

What memories she had of him now were no

more than fleeting images. Sitting astride his broad, strong shoulders. Looking into twinkling green eyes – the same colour as her own. Snatches of a half-remembered lullaby sung in a soft lilting voice as she drifted off to sleep in a warm hammock . . .

Her mother had died when Keris was barely a year old. And, according to her Uncle Gristle, Twig had left the village two years later.

That was ten years ago. Ten years of sharing Uncle Gristle and his family's hammock, yet feeling apart – the black-haired, pale-faced child amidst flame-haired, crimson-faced cousins. Ten years of hope every time visitors were expected – and ten years of disappointment . . .

Of course she loved the stories at the dawn suppers, and on those occasions when sky pirates had arrived in the village she'd quizzed them eagerly for news of her father, Captain Twig – but without success. The stories, though! What stories the sky pirates could tell! They told of epic voyages across the muddy wilderness of the Mire; of raids through the Twilight Woods and thrilling intrigues in the great sprawling city of Undertown and the even more extraordinary floating palaces of Sanctaphrax.

For months after every sky pirate visit, Keris's days would be filled with vivid dreams.

Yet still, even after ten years, she couldn't help feeling that heady excitement – the blooming of a hope against hope that was so powerful it caused a pain in her chest – every time the village got news of visitors heading their way. The same old questions would spring up and go round and round in her head.

This time, would it be her father returning? If it wasn't, then where was he? What had happened to him? And would she ever see him again?

'How can you be so sure my father will come back to me?' Keris repeated, softly this time, wiping away a tear on her sleeve. 'How do you know he didn't just sail off with his crew and forget all about me?'

Gristle leaned forward and broke off a hunk of the barleybread, which he nibbled, his eyes glazing over.

'Because' – he said slowly, without looking up – 'a long, long time ago, before you were born and I was just a young strip of a lad, not half-cured and still pink about the ear-tips, who thought he knew better than his elders . . .' He paused and looked up once more towards the distant tree-line of the Deepwoods. 'Your father, Twig, saved my life.'

'He did?' said Keris, astonished.

This was one story about her father that her uncle had never told before.

'I'm not proud of myself, and don't like to speak of it,' said Gristle, 'because I was foolish beyond reason.' He shook his head. 'A terrible example for young'uns like yourself, Keris.' He coughed. 'You see, I left the droveway. I wandered off into the Deepwoods . . .'

Keris's jaw dropped. It was something she herself had often thought of doing. But then, as her grandmother had often pointed out, 'With all that sky pirate blood coursing through your veins, it's little wonder you've got the wanderlust.'

'I was curious,' he went on. 'And I thought I could scout out a new pasture, forge a new path – make a name for myself in the village. Instead, all I found was a great, fat, slimy hover worm with dripping yellow spots and a belly full of air . . .'

Keris gasped. All slaughterers knew about hover worms. They haunted the dells and glades at the pastures' edge, hovering just above the forest floor on powerful jets of air expelled through air-ducts that ran the length of their bodies. Unless an antidote of charlock and hempleaf was administered at once, a hover-worm bite was lethal.

'I blundered into a glade and the creature lunged at me,' Gristle told her. 'I'll never forget the sting of those tentacles embedding themselves in my ankle. The excruciating pain. Before I knew it, I was writhing in agony on the ground, calling out for help, and the hover worm was circling around me, waiting to strike again . . .'

397

Gristle paused and rubbed his ankle slowly, re-living the moment.

'And then Twig, your father, appeared from the depths of the Deepwoods, running full pelt in answer to my cries – only to trip head over heels over my poor swollen foot! Well, straight away, the hover worm turned its attention to him.'

Keris frowned.

'Your father was the same age as I – the same age that you are now – but tall and slim. And he was dressed in woodtroll clothes, with his hair twisted and knotted in that way that they have. But I could tell he was no woodtroll. I thought he'd turn and run – save himself. Especially as he'd dropped his knife when he fell. But not a bit of it. Twig jumped to his feet and then gave that slimy, hissing worm quite the run around, darting this way and that to avoid its lethal tentacles.

'"My knife . . . Find my knife . . ." he kept shout-ing as he did so, and luckily – despite the pain – I was able to lay a hand on it and throw it across to him. And just in time. The hover worm struck, but instead of ducking, Twig stood his ground. He raised his knife and sliced the creature from head to tail as it flew at him. The next thing, it exploded like a punctured bladder-balloon, scraps of it floating down to the forest floor all around us.

'Then it was *my* turn to feel like a bladder-balloon. You see, the hover worm's venom was in my veins by now, blowing my legs, my arms, my body and neck – even my tongue – to twice their normal size and making me float up into the air. I'll never forget the sensation, Keris – nor the look of horror on Twig's face. But he didn't panic. Instead, he seized a rope, tied one end around my foot and the other around his middle, and set off towards the village with me calling out directions as best I could as I bobbed along above his head.

'I was getting lighter and lighter, you see, and before long I was pulling us both off the ground and up towards the treetops – but he didn't let go . . .'

Gristle paused and when he resumed his story, his voice was raw with emotion.

'I'll never forget it, Keris, as long as I live,' he said, hoarsely. 'Twig was magnificent. He held onto that rope, even as we cleared the treetops and began to float off to certain death in Open Sky. He didn't let go. Just clung on tightly and hollered for help at the top of his lungs. That's how the patrol that the herdmaster had sent out to look for me found us. They lassoed his feet, dragged the pair of us down to earth and got me back to the village to give me some antidote before the hover-worm venom caused me to explode.'

He chuckled.

'There was quite a dawn supper that night, I can tell you. Singing, dancing, and Twig was the hero of the hour.' He frowned. 'Strange thing, though – following morning, he upped and left without saying a word to anyone . . . But I never forgot his bravery.

'Then, one fine night, years later, he returned as a sky pirate captain – and do you know what? Beneath his breast-plate and greatcoat, he was still wearing the hammelhornskin waistcoat my mother – your Gram-Tatum – had given him for saving my life . . .'

He paused for a moment. Then, leaning forwards, he gingerly stroked the corner of the fleece Keris was wearing.

'*This* hammelhornskin waistcoat,' he said softly.

'This belonged to my father?' whispered Keris.

She looked down at the beloved old waistcoat that she had worn for as far back as she could remember. She'd always thought the waistcoat was simply a hand-me-down, like the jackets and coats her cousins wore. She ran the tips of her fingers delicately over the soft fur. Tears welled up in the corners of her eyes. There was a painful lump in her throat.

'You see, Keris, your father doesn't let go of things,' said Gristle. 'That's why I am sure that, if he's still alive, Twig hasn't forgotten you. He didn't let go of me, he couldn't let go of his crew, and he won't let go of you . . . He'll do everything he can to come back to you.'

Keris wiped her eyes.

'Thank you for telling me the story,' she said at length, smoothing down the ruffled hammelhorn fur of her waistcoat. She climbed to her feet. 'I'd best be getting back – to help with the preparations for dawn supper.'

Gristle watched in silence as Keris turned and set off across the pasture towards the village. She looked so small and vulnerable in the silvery light of the moon. He couldn't see the tears streaming down her cheeks.

Sure enough, by the middle of the aftermidnight, the great table at the centre of the village clearing was groaning beneath the weight of heavily-laden platters. Great vats of pickled-tripweed sat next to oak barrels of woodale and large tilderskins of dark

401

winesap. Tall gyle-wax candles, as thick as a slaughterer's arm, cast a warm glow over the feast, while the branches of the trees overhead were decked out with twinkling glow-lamps.

Surely not even a lullabee grove could look quite so magical, thought Keris, as she carried a skillet of sizzling hammelhorn steaks to the table.

Just then, from the far end of the east droveway came the unmistakable sound of hammelhorn trumpets announcing that the visitors had been spotted approaching the village. With her heart in her mouth, Keris joined Aunt Chitling and her cousins as they found their places noisily on their bench. Soon the eight sides of the great table were bustling with expectant red faces, their spiky-haired heads quivering as they all peered across the village clearing.

'Here they come!' shouted one of the younger Totters, a cry taken up by the Welkins and the Scutshaw family next to them.

Keris strained to catch a glimpse of the visitors over the bobbing heads of her companions. When she did, her face instantly fell. One glimpse was enough to tell her that whoever they were, these visitors were certainly not sky pirates. As to what they were exactly, that was much harder to say. The small group walked past the glowing brazier and approached the crowded table.

They were slight in build, shorter than the average slaughterer, with long jaws and heavily lidded eyes. Their skin was green-tinged and covered with glistening scales, and each had a tall, scalloped crest on the top of their head – a crest which seemed to change colour subtly in the candlelight. But the oddest feature of these strange visitors, it seemed to Keris as she stared open-mouthed, was their feet.

They were huge in comparison to the rest of their bodies, webbed between the toes and with a long spike protruding from the back of each ankle, which seemed to click as they walked. They wore patched, leathery breeches, and belts bedecked with knives, barbed spears, hooks, flasks and – oddest of all – a heavy-looking pebble on the end of a long length of rope.

Their leader, who appeared older than the rest – with a larger crest, longer ankle spikes and a voluminous cloak of a dark grey leather that Keris couldn't identify – stepped forward and raised a scaly hand in greeting.

'Felfpht, chief of the north shore clan,' he announced in a soft, whispery voice, his large crest glowing a deep crimson. 'May your waters be unmuddied and your nets always full.'

He bowed, followed by his fifteen companions, whose crests all turned the same vivid colour as their leader's.

'Welcome to our humble village,' boomed the herdmaster, Rump Scutshaw, his red hair freshly greased and spiked and his broad shoulders glistening with a magnificent necklace of weezit fangs. 'Our neighbours, the woodtrolls, told us you were coming. Please do us the honour of joining us at our humble dawn supper.'

He swept his arm out in a broad gesture to indicate the magnificent feast piled high in front of him.

'We should be delighted,' whispered Felfpht, his

crest pulsating with ripples of orange and blue.

The crests of his companions did the same as they were shown to their places – eight to each side of the great table.

Keris couldn't take her eyes off these strange visitors. She shifted along the bench and tried not to stare too much as a small individual with a lower crest sat down beside her. At the head of the table – the side nearest to the brazier – Felfpht leaned over and whispered in the herdmaster's ear. Rump stood up and called for buckets of water to be brought from the troughs and given to the visitors.

When they appeared moments later in front of each of them, the slaughterers watched with astonishment – and not a little amusement – as their visitors tipped the cold, fresh water over their own heads. Keris was splashed by her strange companion, but she didn't mind, transfixed as she was by the look of contentment on his face as the water dripped from his glowing blue crest.

'Let supper commence,' announced Rump Scutshaw, and the feasting began.

According to custom, it was rude to press visitors with questions before they'd eaten their fill, so conversation was limited strictly to enquiries such as 'Can I pass you the tripweed?' or 'Another tilder sausage?' and 'More winesap, perhaps?'

Nevertheless, Keris's companion introduced

himself as Slifph and, in between mouthfuls of nibblick-cheese pie and spoonfuls of tilder stew, he told her that he was what was commonly known as a webfoot goblin – one of the webfoot clans that lived on the shores of the great lakes.

Keris was bursting to ask him more, such as where these great lakes were, how many clans were there and why that crest of his – and those of his companions – changed colour so often, and in such intricate patterns. But a stern look from her Aunt Chitling and an apologetic shrug from Uncle Gristle was enough for her to hold her tongue.

At last, just as Keris feared she was going to explode with curiosity, the herdmaster pushed back his chair and rose to his feet.

'We have eaten well and drunk deep,' he boomed, raising his tankard of woodale high above his spiky red head. 'Now let us feast on the tales our guests have to tell of travels from places far beyond our pastures!'

An expectant hush fell over the great table as Felfpht, the chief of the north shore clan of webfoot goblins, looked across at Keris's dining companion, Slifph. His crest rippled with red and orange stripes and, as if in answer, Slifph's crest did the same. Without a word being spoken, the young webfoot got to his feet and addressed the village.

'The four great lakes from whence we come lie

far from here, beyond the tree ridges of the west and the great ravines beyond that,' he began in a hushed, whispery voice. 'We are webfoot goblins of the north shore clan of the third great lake, whose waters we tend and from which come all the blessings and bounty we could wish for. Few venture to our remote lands and so, once in a spawning or so, some of us venture out into the great Deepwoods to learn something of the world beyond the lakes.

'We – my father, my brothers and I – have encountered many tribes: the white goblins of the depths, the trog hordes of the great ravines and the many tribes of the tree ridges; the flat-heads, the hammerheads, long-hairs, greys and tusked, to name but a few. We have traded for fish-hooks, fine rope twine and nets and come to you, red herders of the night, for your leather cloaks and fine pelts. We bring lake-pearls and silt-gems in return . . .'

The slaughterers nodded and raised jugs of woodale in response to this, and Felfpht, the webfoot chief smiled, then nodded to his son to continue.

'But that is for later,' Slifph said. 'Now, I wish to tell you of the strange sight that we witnessed in the valley of the ironwood stands, three weeks' journey from here. We had been trading for resin with the gnokgoblins of the high stands, and had pitched camp on one of the mighty branches of an ironwood pine. As dawn broke and the sun rose, a magnificent sky pirate ship appeared on the horizon . . .'

Keris gasped, and leaned forwards.

'As it sailed over the treetops towards us, a strange thing started to happen. The mighty vessel listed first to one side, then to the other, shuddering all the while like a speared lake-eel. It rose and fell, its flight-burners flaring until, low over the trees, it crashed down into the depths of the Deepwoods not far from our camp. That morning, as we continued our journey, we came across the fallen sky ship.

'Its timbers were remarkably sound and, though ragged and splintered from the crash, its tall mast and sails seemed in working order. But the strangest sight, and one that I must tell you of, was the massive flight-rock at the heart of the great ship. It had crumbled to dust and fallen through the bars of the rock cage, like sand escaping from a shattered hour-glass. We found the vessel's captain . . .'

Keris let out a small cry but, spellbound by the young webfoot's tale, the slaughterers didn't seem to notice.

'He was dying, that much was clear, but he gave his name as Captain Glade Harrier of the *Edgedemon*, last of the sky ships. He told us that a terrible sickness had overtaken all the great ships of the sky, attacking their precious flight-rocks and turning them to useless dust. Many sky pirates had already scuppered their ships in a distant encampment far out in the Mire, but he, Glade Harrier, had refused to give in. Now he was paying the cost for his reckless decision. With his dying breath he looked up at me and whispered, *"The age of flight has ended"*.'

Slifph sat down and, for a moment, everyone exchanged looks of shock and surprise. The sky pirates were the greatest traders in the Deepwoods, travelling further and more widely than anyone. Now, it seems, they were no more. Little wonder that their visits had become so few and far between. And without their sky ships, they'd just be common traders like everyone else.

'My father is a sky pirate captain,' said Keris quietly, turning to the webfoot goblin. 'Do you think his sky ship has crashed like all the others?'

'That, Keris, is something that only the great clam

could answer,' said Slifph, his crest turning bright crimson. 'It dwells in the depths of the third great lake and is the most ancient of all the mighty clams.'

Keris frowned. 'And this great clam of yours,' she said. 'You're telling me that it knows if my father is still alive?'

'And whether you'll ever see him again,' Slifph replied, nodding.

'So how do I find out?' Keris asked, her voice trembling.

'Simple,' said the webfoot goblin, his crest turning a soft green. 'Come with us, and ask it yourself.'

. CHAPTER TWO .

THE TILDERSKIN SATCHEL

A small scruffy satchel of dark red tilderskin containing ten sheets of barkpaper and a stubby leadwood pencil . . . I hope this will be enough. It was all that came to hand that frosty morning three weeks ago when I left the warm snugness of my family hammock and crept away like a stealthy thief-in-the-day.

Dear Uncle Gristle, by now you will have discovered that I am gone. I hope with all my heart that you'll understand that I couldn't bear to say goodbye to you and Aunt Chitling and my cousins. I know that if I had, you'd only have pleaded with me to stay, and I wouldn't have had the strength to refuse you.

I trust by now you've found my charms and amulets. I took them from around my neck and left them, one by one, by each of your sleeping spiky-haired heads. Now you should each be wearing them alongside your own, hanging round your dear necks and close to your beloved hearts.

411

Think of me while I'm gone. I know your loving thoughts will help to keep me safe.

As I write these words, the barkpaper is stained with my tears, but I knew I could not set out on such a journey without at least trying to get some of it down. How glad I am now, simple slaughterer that I am, that I studied the gift of markings on bark from old Taghair, the wise old oakelf in his caternest in that lullabee tree of his. He taught us slaughterer and woodtroll young'uns alike – and I daresay he never imagined we'd use this skill to keep anything more than tally-ledgers of timber and livestock lists. Yet here I am, putting down these marks that tell of the great journey I have set out upon.

Three weeks have passed already. I can hardly believe it – and only now has there been time to put leadwood to bark. But I'm so glad I can, Uncle, for what wonders I have seen out in these mighty Deepwoods – wonders that I am compelled to record.

My webfoot companions travel swiftly and quietly on those huge feet of theirs, following the trail they left on their outward journey. I cannot tell exactly what these markers are, but on different occasions they seem to take their bearings from sniffing closely at some spot on the forest floor or, more curious still, pressing an ear up close to a mighty tree-trunk and listening intently. They speak little, but make up for this lack of speech by a strange silent communication with those crests on their heads that change colour constantly.

We sleep by night, usually in the high branches of the trees, and travel by day, which I am slowly getting used to – although I do miss the moonlight. But in the bright, colourful daylight world, I have seen some extraordinary sights. Great bell-like flowers that hum and sing in the breeze according to the level of dew collected within their mottled bowls; spiky green creatures tall enough to walk beneath, with eyes on stalks and eight stick-like legs, which feed on the leaves on the lower branches of the trees; and vast flocks of black and white birds that sometimes take all morning or afternoon to pass overhead . . .

And there has been more. So much more. But I'm painfully aware that I have only ten precious sheets of barkpaper to last me I don't know how long, so I mustn't use them all up in one sitting.

But there is one thing that I must record, for it so reminded me of you, dear Uncle and Aunt, and my beloved slaughterers. We have set up camp with a colony of gnokgoblins, high in the huge branches of an ironwood pine. It is but one of over fifty in this ironwood stand, each with its own colony. And this afternoon, our gnokgoblin guests took us up into the highest branches where I saw the giant tree-fromps that live there feeding.

They are huge creatures with shaggy white coats, long trunks and great curved claws. They cling to the tree-trunk with their razor-sharp claws and probe deep into the crevices between the barkscales with their trunks, in search of the blackbark beetles on which they feed.

413

The gnokgoblins climb after them and collect the golden tree resin that oozes from the deep holes made in the trunks by the tree-fromps' claws. The gnokgoblins tend and nurture these huge creatures as tenderly as you, dear Uncle, and your herders tend the herds of hammel-horn. Tonight, as my old friend the full moon rises over the ironwood stands, from my resting place on this huge branch, I can hear the rumbling snores of the tree-fromps hanging upside down from the branches high above.

It has been three long months since that magical night in the ironwood stands. The journey has been long and hard and the webfoots have been relentless in their pace. But I have kept step with them every stride of the way through the endless tree ridges with their jagged peaks and misty, dew-soaked valleys. And as we've journeyed, I've gradually got to know my companions better though, like the mysterious Deepwoods themselves, I doubt I will ever discover all their secrets.

Slifph is my closest companion. Do you remember him? He sat next to me all those months ago at the dawn supper. He is one of a spawn of thirty or so hatched to one mother; the rest of our party are his brothers. We are seventeen in number, including myself. Our leader is their father, Felfpht. Back where they come from, he is the chief of the village, a cluster of huts on the north shore of one of their great lakes.

I've tried to probe Slifph and his brothers — Grulth,

Hiph and Spyve in particular – about the great clam that lives in their lake, but whenever I raise the subject their crests glow yellow and they evade my questions. Not that we have much time for fireside chats; just a few moments at the end of a long day spent climbing a tree ridge away from the gloomy, dank valleys below.

The tree ridges are home to goblin tribes too numerous to count. Most, like the fearsome flat-heads and their even more warlike cousins, the hammerheads – not to mention swarms of grey goblins and pink-eyes – move from ridge to ridge, never settling for more than a few days or weeks at a time, and engaged in constant feuding and petty warfare. Many's the night our small band has huddled together high in the branches of a copperwood or giant sallowdrop, trying to snatch much-needed sleep while below the terrible sounds of battle rang out amongst the trees.

Now, with supplies running low – tree-slugs and bark fungus our supper for the last two weeks – we have arrived in a clan village of long-haired goblins. The long-hairs are unusual amongst the warrior goblin tribes, for preferring to live in settled villages. Although vulnerable to attack, they make up for this by the size and grandeur of their defences.

The forest around this particular village has been chopped down and turned into a spike-topped barricade, surrounded by a great ditch. It is known as the Great Clearing of Threnody Battlerage, after their warrior chief who ordered the work be done. At the centre of the village is the clan-hut, around which circle upon circle of thatched long-huts have been built. I must admit I was both frightened and bewildered by the jostling crowds, the noise and the smoke as we made our way along the central path towards the clan-hut.

And the size of it all! Our entire village, Uncle, as well as half the lower pasture, could fit comfortably inside the great gathering place surrounding Threnody Battlerage's hut. Thousands of long-hairs – their hair spiked a little like we slaughterers wear it, yet altogether fiercer looking – had turned out to greet our little party. It seems that, on his outward journey, Felfpht had been able to warn the long-hair chief of a hammerhead raid on the village and Threnody now considers him a personal friend.

As we entered the open-sided clan-hut, I glanced up to see the grey-haired chief sitting on a throne of carved silveroak, raised high on a pile of long-hair goblin skulls, some with wisps of hair still attached. These, I was told by Slifph in a whisper, were the honoured heads of great long-hair warriors who had died in battle.

He then pointed to the roof-beams high above our heads. I looked up – and had to stifle a cry of horror. For there, hanging from the rafters, were row upon row of skeletons, the eyeless sockets in their skulls staring down at us as their bleached bones rattled against each other in the breeze. These, Slifph explained, were past chiefs of the clan, it being considered the highest honour to hang from the clan-hut's roof-beams after death.

The sight makes me shudder when I think about it, but it was a small price to pay for a delicious supper of roast snowbird and a soft bed of summer-grass in a long-hut. We shall rest here with the long-hairs for a week. Then, according to Felfpht, when we are fully refreshed, it will be time to embark on the most dangerous part of our long journey: the trog ravines.

As he whispered these words, Uncle, his crest turned a deep indigo ...

As I write this I am shaking so badly that I can scarcely hold the stump of leadwood pencil. Hunger is gnawing away in the pit of my stomach, and I'm not sure I have the strength for another day's journey – not that, in these dismal ravines, I can even distinguish day from night.

The past month has been the worst of my life, and I've lost count of the number of times I wished I was back with you, Uncle Gristle, Aunt Chitling, cousins Silver, Saddle, Brisket and little Scrag, in our hammock high above the brazier. The only thing that keeps me going is the thought that if I don't, my bleached bones will end up deep down in the abyss below.

I shudder to think of it. Felfpht had warned me that the journey through the trog ravines would be difficult, but as we set off that misty morning from the village of the long-hairs, I had no idea just how difficult. As we crested the last tree ridge and paused to look down at the landscape below, it slowly began to dawn on me.

The ravines – vast fissures in the barren and rocky land, like scratches carved out by giant claws – stood in our path. There was no short way round them. The only route, Slifph assured me, was down into the depths of each ravine and up the other side; several days of hard climbing through each.

The last and the deepest of the ravines made Slifph shiver and his crest turn a whitish grey as he spoke of it. Home to the mysterious white goblins of the depths, there was no avoiding it, he said, but would say no more about it, no matter how much I pressed him.

419

With heavy hearts, we entered the first ravine and clambered down over loose sheets of slate that shifted and slid beneath our feet, making the going slow and difficult. Finally, towards the end of the day, we reached the bottom of the ravine, a dank, gloomy place with a small stream running through it. We drank, and the webfoots splashed themselves in its icy water as is their custom.

From across the stream, several massive trogs wearing rough skins and bone earrings, and carrying crudely sharpened stone axes, watched us suspiciously. But thankfully, at our approach, they turned and lumbered off into the gloom.

It was the first of many encounters with the trog clans of the ravines – the most primitive tribes I have yet seen. Despite their great size and fearsome appearance, they were generally cautious and seemed content to keep their distance as we passed through their ravines. And what bleak, desolate, inhospitable places those ravines were, so different from our lush, moonlit pastures and warm, welcoming village . . .

The steep, stony sides were pock-marked with cave openings. Outside every cave was a pile of grey shells, mottled and ridged, each one about the size of a hammelhorn calf. Slifph told me that they came from the giant cave-lice that lived in the depths of the trog caverns and are the trogs' main source of food in that barren place. Judging by the number of shells scattered about outside their caves, there seems to be no shortage of these strange creatures – though what they might taste like, I shudder to think.

The good thing was, they seemed to keep the primitive giants well satisfied, and our small party – and our supplies – were all but ignored as we passed by. Except, that is, when we stopped for supper each night and lit a meagre fire from the dwindling supply of copperwood sticks we each carried.

Then, as we huddled round the glowing, flame-red sticks – a small bundle of which burned with an intense heat all through the night – we would all become aware of scores of pairs of watching eyes. Many was the time I'd peer up from the copper-red fire glow and glimpse a great shadowy crowd of ravine trogs standing in the darkness, transfixed.

As the days and nights passed, I slowly got used to this strange occurrence and, oddly, even began to look forward to it. You see, there was something about those great dark shapes and docile, watching eyes that reminded me of nights out in the silvery pastures, surrounded by grazing hammelhorns.

Six ravines we scaled in all, each one deeper than the one before. It took us twenty days – and twenty of those strange fireside nights. During the day, with the trogs keeping to their deep caverns, we saw few signs of life: the occasional rock-tilder, picking its way down the upper slopes; now and then a shaggy-winged vulpoon, circling the sky in search of carrion. Many was the time I yearned to be home.

As the dawn rose on the twenty-first day, our little party stood on the rocky lip of the last and deepest of the ravines, home to the mysterious white goblins, which the webfoots still refused to talk about. 'Better that you don't know, Mistress Keris,' Felfpht told me. 'Some things are best left cloaked in darkness.' But as I looked into the ravine, its sides falling away into an inky blackness far below, I couldn't help feeling that not knowing was far worse.

Felfpht whispered instructions for us to rope ourselves together and warned us to make as little noise as possible, though I swear my heart was beating louder than a village drum as I followed the others down the narrow, winding track, over the edge of the ravine and down the steep side below.

The further we descended, the darker it became and the more sheer the drop. Every so often, the path gave way to a mass of rocks and pebbles which, as we dislodged them, hurtled down into the abyss below. Finally it disappeared completely and we were reduced to clambering down a series of jutting ledges, one after the other.

We seemed to descend in this way for hours in the misty gloom until, at last, we reached a small stream at the very bottom of the ravine – at least, what appeared to me to be the bottom of the ravine. In fact, Slifph whispered, there were deep cracks in the ravine's floor – cracks that led further down into what were known as 'the depths', and from which, without any warning, the white goblins would soundlessly emerge in search of prey. It was, he impressed upon me, vital that we followed the path of the stream as quickly and quietly as we could through the ravine, until we reached a mound of jagged scree that marked the route of our upward climb.

What lay ahead, Slifph told me in an urgent whisper, was the most dangerous point of the entire journey. And from the sickly, mottled pallor of his crest, I didn't doubt the truth of his words. A tug on the rope interrupted our conversation and told us that the others had set off through the sluggish, brackish waters of the stream – and not wanting to be left behind in this terrible place, we hurried after them.

We walked for what seemed like several more hours and, although it must have been midday at least, the eerie darkness of the deep ravine was as impenetrable as ever. The damp and cold penetrated our clothing, even seeping through my hammelhornskin waistcoat and chilling me to the bone. Apart from our heavy gasps of exertion and the sound of our footfalls splashing through the icy stream, there was utter silence.

Then as we crept on, painfully aware of every breath and splash in the silent blackness, I felt something brush my cheek. It was faint, almost imperceptible, like brushing through a woodspider web, or against a tall blade of pasture grass. But I felt it again, and again. If they'd noticed the same thing, the others – ahead of me – made no sign of it. They pressed on through the stream, their webbed feet making surprisingly little sound considering *their size. I was about to reach forward, tap Slifph on the shoulder and ask him what these strange cobwebs might be, when something cold and clammy suddenly enveloped my face.*

I couldn't cry out. I couldn't even breathe. In the hideous darkness, I tried to kick out and flail my arms, but found that these too were gripped by something just as powerful. A brief twitch and snap told me that the rope binding me to my companions had been cut and – heart hammering in my chest – I found myself being half-lifted, half-dragged into the inky blackness, unable to scream or hit out.

I have never experienced anything like the blind terror of those moments in the depths of the ravine, in the grip of that terrible unseen monster . . .

Suddenly there was a blinding flash of light, and with it whatever was holding me released its grip. I fell heavily on the rocky shale and, moments later as my eyes adjusted, I saw what had snatched me.

Surrounding me was a seething, writhing mass of bony, hairless white bodies, as translucent as wood-beeswax and glistening like damp dew-slugs. The great mass retreated from the light and broke up into individuals, who stared at me with huge, black eyes, flared nostrils quivering and white tongues flicking the air. White goblins – a hundred of them, at least. Their huge hairless heads were covered in wispy tendrils that, as I watched in horror, darted out towards me, brushing my ankles and flicking at my wrists.

I took a step back and found Slifph at my side, two glowing fire-crystals in his outstretched hands. As we hastily retreated, more of the loathsome goblins clambered up out of the deep cracks in the ravine floor around us, the tendrils on their heads flicking out around them wildly like silvergrass in a storm-tossed pasture. It was at that moment I realized that the white goblins – despite their huge eyes – were all but blind, and that they were using their whiplash tendrils instead of sight in the inky blackness.

As we ran to join the others, their crests vivid purple with alarm, Slifph's crystals began to fade, and behind us we could hear the hissing sound of white goblin tendrils searching for us. A moment later, the light from the crystals was gone, and we were plunged again into absolute darkness. All at once, the previously silent ravine was full of hideous high-pitched shrieks and gibbering howls as the white goblins of the depths called for their kin to join in the hunt.

In this bleak and horrible place, our small band must have seemed like a rich feast for those emaciated goblins. Felfpht, though, had other thoughts. At his hushed command, we rummaged around in our back-packs for the remains of our supplies – strips of cured tilder and salted snowbird; wedges of dried hammel-horn-curd – and threw them back over our shoulders in a desperate bid to distract and slow down the terrible white goblins.

Soon, behind us, we heard snarling and squabbling as some of them fought over the paltry rations. We forged on, flailing wildly with the knives and small axes we carried, to sever the tendrils that whipped at our backs. Once I stumbled and fell to the ground, but Slifph – Earth love him – helped me to my feet and on we went. We arrived at the mound of scree not a moment too soon, and began a desperate scramble towards the light.

Of that appalling flight, I remember only the blind terror that drove us on, each of us determined not to get *left behind and fall into the clutches of our hideous pursuers. Only when those shrieks and bloodcurdling screams began to die away, and the air no longer hummed with the sound of searching tendrils, did we allow ourselves a moment to catch our breath.*

It was then that the dismal slog up the steep ravine face truly got underway; a journey that has continued, ever slower and increasingly arduous, the weaker and wearier we have become. Slifph tells me that this is the true test of our great journey, for the difficult climb out of this last ravine is the steepest and longest of all. Though it took us less than a day to descend into its appalling depths, footsore and hungry as we now are, it has so far taken us nearly a dozen to climb out of it.

As I write this on the last but one of my precious sheets of barkpaper, I can only hope against hope that these words will not be my last.

This is my final piece of barkpaper and, as I write on it, my thoughts are full of you, dear Uncle Gristle and Aunt Chitling and my darling cousins, so far away. I hope with all my heart that you are happy and well and that you think of me as you gaze into the glowing brazier fire last thing at day.

We climbed out of the terrible ravine of the white goblins into the bright sunshine and pleasant glades of a lush upland forest. I can tell by the renewed spring in my companions' steps and the happy reddish glow of their crests that we are in country they know well, and can't be too far from their distant watery home.

Now, round the campfire at night as we roast the log-grubs and barkshrooms we collect on our way, the air is full of laughter and talk of the loved ones they will soon be reunited with. I do my best to smile and share their happiness, but I find it hard — my heart as full as it is of thoughts of you, my dear slaughterers, and the little village I have left so very far behind . . .

But I must put such thoughts to the back of my mind, all tenderly wrapped and preserved, just like these barkscroll pages which I shall keep safe in this tilderskin satchel until the day comes when I can share these markings I have made with you. For now though, I must put down my leadwood pencil and face the future.

I have already glimpsed it!

Far beyond the grassy glades and treetops that spread out before our final camping place, like a vast green and blue quilt, lie the four great lakes of the webfoot goblins. There, I hope, I shall find the answer to the question with which I began this great journey. The hope of finding its answer has spurred me on through all the dangers and privations I have faced and will, I am sure, make them all worthwhile . . .

Is my father, Captain Twig the sky pirate, still alive?

. CHAPTER THREE .

MIRROR OF THE SKY

Grefphith's head, the crest glowing a bright yellow, broke the surface of the water. Ripples spread out in ever-growing concentric circles across the lake's glassy surface as he gulped in a lungful of air. A moment later, the same ripples turned to a ridged wake, as the webfoot goblin flexed his shoulders and, clutching his feeding-fork in one hand and his tether-line in the other, kicked out strongly for the shore.

There was no wind, not a breath. The third great lake was so still it more than justified the name given to it by the crested webfoot clan whose villages were clustered round its shores: Mirror of the Sky.

All four of the great lakes had been named by the different clans of webfoot goblins that lived beside them. The first lake – the smallest, yet with its great spire-clam in some ways the most unusual – was known as the Silent One. Lying at the bottom of a

bowl-shaped circle of forested hills, anyone whispering at one end of the lake could be heard by those standing at the other. It was a phenomenon of which the red-ringed webfoots who dwelt there were very proud. On long summer evenings, the clan of the first great lake could be found dancing on their stripy legs and singing to one another across its waters.

The second great lake was known as the Shimmerer by the tusked webfoot clan that lived beside it, for the lakes-skimmers and stormhornets that darted over its surface, both night and day, made the water itself seem to shimmer and glow. Although predominantly shellfish eaters, the tusked webfoots – smaller and more portly than their neighbours – were not averse to the odd stormhornet roasted over a slow fire. They carefully tended the great blackcap clam that had made its home beneath their lake's shimmering waters.

And then there was the fourth great lake – its milky waters leading it to be known by the resident white webfoot clan as the Lake of Cloud. These tall, warlike webfoots preferred to hunt in the forests around their lake, rather than fish its cloudy waters. But like the other webfoots, they carefully tended their lake's resident clams; the twins, Skeld and Skewa.

The Mirror of the Sky reflected everything around

it that bright afternoon – from the villages of stilt-raised cabins, made from woven lake-willow and roofed with meadow turf, which were grouped together on its north and south shores, to the distant ironwood stands, their jagged treetops silhouetted against the pale sky like mighty spear-tips. Even the eel-pool corrals – the great circular cork and rope enclosures which held the giant lake eels that the crested webfoot clans farmed – were absolutely motionless.

High up in the sky and honking loudly, a skein of migrating woodgeese flew overhead in a precise V-formation. Their passing was mirrored so perfectly in the placid lake, it was as though they were swimming underwater, far down in the turquoise and emerald depths.

Grefphith reached the north shore and picked up the anchor stone to which his tether-line was attached. No webfoot ever ventured into a great lake without first attaching a tether to an anchor stone and leaving it embedded in the lakeside mud. Grefphith rubbed his stone clean and secured it to his belt, before heading towards the village cluster. He'd spent the early hours at the bottom of the lake tending to the great blueshell clam, stirring up the nutrient-rich silt and laying traps for the giant lake snails.

It was hard work, but as a clam-tender, Grefphith

was proud to be one of the chosen few to care for the ancient mollusc. It certainly beat the other mundane village tasks – patching the fishing coracles, mending the nets; hook sharpening, spear grinding or feeding the lake-eels in the corrals. As a clam-tender, Grefphith had a special place round the cooking fire, and first choice from the stew-pot – after Milfphin, that is, who in Felfpht's absence was standing in as clan-chief.

That fat old excuse for a lake snail! Grefphith cursed silently.

Milfphin did nothing all day but sit on that eel-bone throne of his, being waited on hand and foot. If only his father Felfpht – the *real* clan-chief – were here, Grefphith thought, pulling on his snailskin cloak as he skirted round the reed beds on the north shore. But he had been gone this past year and more, together with Grefphith's spawn-brothers: Slifph, Spyve, Grulth, Hiph, Phlythiss and the rest . . .

Grefphith missed them. He missed their company and companionship – and their help with the great clam, for they too were all clam-tenders. Without them around to share the duties of looking after the ancient wise-one, there was only him and Milfphin's lazy, good-for-nothing sons – and *they* were usually too busy hanging round with their friends in the white webfoot clan by the Lake of

Cloud to be of much help. No, it was he, Grefphith, who ended up doing most of the work.

After what was now more than thirteen moons of toil, even though he had always tried his best, it was all getting too much for him. What was worse, Grefphith was sure the great blueshell clam itself was not happy. After all, throughout the entire time that he had been in charge of its welfare, the huge mollusc hadn't once spoken . . .

Grefphith hurried up the steep bank from the shore, past the beached coracles and fishing rafts, and onto the winding track at the top that ran between the tall, spiky bladegrass and the edge of the forest. Ahead of him, coils of brown-tinged smoke spiralled up from the cabin chimneys, where hunks of dried lake-peat burned steadily in the cooking-fires below.

As he reached the edge of the village, Grefphith found himself surrounded by webfoots of all shapes and sizes, their crests flashing and changing colour excitedly. After hours spent deep down at the bottom of the lake, the hubbub of the village cabin cluster always took a little getting used to – and today it seemed brighter and more excitable than ever.

Grefphith's crest glowed an enquiring green and blotchy orange. Everyone, it seemed, had come out to greet him.

There were his sisters, Mythwhull, Lyfph, Phlithym, Huwl and the rest; half a dozen massive spawn-nurses, each with two dozen or more young'uns tethered to the folds of their skirts, flashing their crests and pointing; there was a group of eel-farmers, their crests flecked deep purple with nervous expectation . . .

But what for? Grefphith wondered. His arrival back from the lake had never caused such excitement before.

'There. There they are.' a voice whispered, and all eyes turned towards the wooded slope behind the village cluster.

Grefphith found himself being jostled as the excited webfoots strained for a better view. Some even scampered up the sallowdrop trees or clambered onto the roofs of the cabins.

High up, just cresting the ridge of the tree-line, flickering torches could be seen. All round him, the crests of the webfoots glowed crimson and then yellow with black ripples as they speculated as to who the visitors might be. But Grefphith had no doubts. His crest glowed a deep red as he let out an uncharacteristically loud (for a webfoot) yelp of joy.

It was Felfpht, the clan-chief, together with Grefphith's brothers. It had to be! They were back, he was sure of it.

Grefphith fell into step with the great throng of

webfoot villagers heading for the edge of the village, where the north shore clan was soon joined by others. Word had spread that travellers had been spotted in the lake forests, and all sorts of web-foots – from neighbouring south-shorers to far-off fourth-lakers – had turned up to greet them.

There were webfoots from the first great lake, their brilliantly coloured red-ringed legs making up for their small, insignificant crests; lines of darts were attached to the front of their smocks for use in the long blow-pipes they carried. There were the small tusked webfoots from the second great lake,

whose heavily lidded eyes and pointed buck-teeth made them look – to Grefphith, at least – both docile and gormless. He had to stifle a snigger as a group trotted past. And then there were the tall warriors from the fourth great lake whom he would never, *ever* dream of laughing at.

Tall and rangy, with broad shoulders and low brows, the white webfoots were the fiercest of all the lake clans. They travelled everywhere with double-ended thornwood spears in their hands and coracle-shields strapped to their backs. They had obviously been the first to spot the travellers, for fifty or more had crossed the lake on their shields and now stood guard at the great waterwillow gates at the top end of the village, their thornwood spears at the ready.

'Here they come! Here they come! Here they come!' chirruped a gaggle of young'uns, tethered to a massive webfoot matron, the ones at the back straining to peek round the side of her voluminous bulk.

Grefphith – still far back on the other side of the cabin cluster – looked and, sure enough, the torches were getting nearer through the trees. He counted them. One, two, three . . . The light from the copperwood stick torches twinkled in the deepening afternoon light. Fifteen, sixteen . . .

Seventeen?

Grefphith's crest flickered with yellow ripples. If this was indeed Felfpht and Grefphith's brothers, then there was one extra. For a moment, doubt clouded Grefphith's thoughts, only to clear again as the unmistakable head and crest of Felfpht the clan-chief appeared through the trees, followed by his brothers, their crests all bright crimson in greeting.

Grefphith let out another yelp of joy. Behind him, several crested webfoot matrons tut-tutted at this

437

unseemly show of noise – especially from a clam-tender. But Grefphith was too excited to pay them any heed. Instead, he turned on his heels and ran, full pelt, back through the village cluster.

Avoiding the main track, Grefphith cut up the maze of narrow back-alleys that zigzagged between the clustered cabins. In his haste he almost skewered himself on a hanging boathook before turning a corner and nearly falling over a couple of young'uns – not yet old enough to understand what all the excitement was about – who were playing a game of crabclaws in the middle of the path. From above him came the steady munching and crunching of the tiny stack-tilder grazing on the grassy rooftops.

As he neared the end of the cluster, an old matron – her spawning days long since behind her – who was taking the opportunity to clean the empty clan-cabin, greeted him cheerily as he passed by her window.

'Have they arrived yet, Grefphith?' she asked.

'Not yet,' Grefphith replied breathlessly.

'Well, make sure to tell them Old Mafphwyllin sends her greetings when they do,' she called after him.

'I shall, I shall,' Grefphith panted as he hurried on.

As the pathway emerged onto the lakeside clearing, Grefphith's pace quickened. Past the curing racks he hurried, the horizontal bars of sallowdrop and waterwillow bowing under the weight of drying snailskin. Past the fish-bone mills and feed-stores; past the eel-smoking cabins, the air pungent with the odour of smouldering redpine chips – a little trick borrowed from the pink-eyed goblins.

Reaching the lake's edge, Grefphith grabbed a great hanging gourd with a long hose-like spout from a post embedded in the mud, and waded in. He sank the leathery sack into the water and waited impatiently as it filled, bubbles rising to the surface in a steady stream. When at last it was full, he heaved it up onto one shoulder, his hand clamping the spout shut, and set off back the way he'd come to the great arched gates at the entrance to the village.

He arrived just in time. The stout willwicker gates had been thrown open and a contingent of tall white lake goblins stood to attention on either side, their thornwood spears forming a triumphal arch overhead. A large crowd of webfoot goblins from all the four lakes had now gathered at the gates and, panting with exertion, Grefphith had to push and jostle his way through. Reaching the front of the crowd, he encountered Milfphin, the deputy clan-chief, his podgy hands clasped together over his pot-belly, standing just outside the boundary fence of the village, those indolent sons of his shuffling about impatiently beside him.

'Clam-tender,' Milfphin muttered gruffly as his eyes fell on Grefphith.

Grefphith snorted softly. Milfphin had never managed either to look him in the eye when speaking, or to utter his name.

'Clan-chief,' he replied, as he had done countless times since Felfpht and the others had set off – only this time adding softly, 'deputy.'

Milfphin's crest

shimmered with indignation, but he said nothing. Just ahead, emerging from the forest slope, came a small party of travellers.

'Spawn-brothers!' Grefphith shouted with joy and pushed past the indignant deputy clan-chief.

Pulling the water-filled gourd from his shoulder, Grefphith shoved it under one arm and pumped it vigorously like bellows, while with his free hand directing the nozzle of the spout towards the approaching webfoots. A jet of fresh cold lake water arched over the raised spears of the white lake goblins and fell on the crests of the travellers in a refreshing shower.

'Welcome, clan-chief,' wheezed Milfphin, his crest glowing an ambiguous pink. 'You must forgive the clam-tender's noisy outburst . . .'

Arriving at the gates, Felfpht raised a scaly hand to silence the deputy.

'There is nothing to forgive. Grefphith has greeted us with water from our lake, his anchor stone and apron still dripping from tending the great clam . . .' The clan-chief's eyes narrowed as he gazed past Milfphin to the deputy's fifteen sons, coracle shields strapped to their backs and thornwood lances in their hands. 'Whilst your sons, I see, seem to prefer the company of our white lake cousins to tending our own great clam.'

'Such headstrong boys.' Milfphin shrugged.

441

'Easily distracted. But your son, Grefphith, here' – he now patted Grefphith indulgently on the shoulder – 'has been looking after things in the Mirror of the Sky – and, of course, with my full support,' he added. 'Haven't you, Grefphith?'

'I have tended the wise one to the best of my ability, chief,' Grefphith whispered. 'No harm has come to it.'

'Very good, Grefphith. You have been a faithful clam-tender,' Felfpht replied, nodding stiffly. 'Clearly I chose wisely when I left you behind . . .' He turned to Milfphin's sons. 'You are free to return to the forests round the Lake of Cloud with your white lake friends,' he told them quietly. 'The sons of Felfpht have returned and shall tend the great blueshell clam from now on.'

Milfphin's bloated frame seemed to wilt at the clan-chief's words, his crest glowing a sickly green with shame and embarrassment as his sons shuffled off with their companions from the fourth lake, their thornwood spears lowered. The crowd watched them go, before breaking into quiet applause as their crests rippled with bright colours of greeting.

Felfpht's sons stepped forward and, while the crowd gathered round, embraced their brother Grefphith. Their faces were wet with a mixture of cold lake water and tears.

'It's so good to see you, brother,' Slifph whispered. 'My webs ache from walking.'

'Our lake mud will soothe them, brother,' laughed Grefphith delightedly. 'But first, what wonders from the lands beyond the lakes do you have to share with us?'

The crowd drew in their breath in anticipation as Slifph and his brothers removed their forage sacks from their belts and carefully opened them. As Milfphin and the rest of the crowd craned their necks for a better view, the clan-chief slipped away unnoticed and headed for the lakeside.

Slifph reached into his forage sack. He pulled out a dull orange block of a transparent substance and held it up for all to see.

'It looks like pinewood resin,' a tusked webfoot called out, to the tutted disapproval of the rest of the crowd.

'It *is* pinewood resin,' said Slifph, 'yet see how pure it is,' he added quickly, before disappointment could set in. After all, everyone there knew the uses of resin to waterproof their coracles and cleanse their nets. 'The resin we gather has dripped onto the forest floor, where it becomes mixed up with dirt and sand and pine-needles. This, in contrast,' he said, tilting the block so that the early evening sun shone through it, 'is perfectly clear.'

'But how?' bellowed a white lake goblin who had

remained behind, and whose own coracle looked as though it needed some work done on it.

'It was an art we learned from the gnokgoblins who dwell in the ironwood pines, far to the north,' Slifph replied. 'They share their home with giant tree-fromps, great placid creatures with huge curved claws. The goblins harvest the resin from the holes in the bark which the fromps make with their claws. When the resin begins to flow from the claw holes, they collect it in bowls – pure, clear, uncontaminated.' He waved the block of resin around. 'Like this.'

'And have you got one of these giant tree-fromps in your forage sacks, then?' a cheeky young red-ringed webfoot at the back shouted out.

A soft ripple of amusement went round the crested webfoots. Even Slifph permitted himself a smile.

'No,' he said, 'but we have one of their claws.'

Slifph's brother Grulth held up the long curved claw he'd found beneath one of the ironwood pines.

'We shall copy this design to make resin-tapping knives and then harvest our own resin . . .' Slifph gestured towards the ironwood stands behind the lake. 'After all, we have ironwood pines enough.'

The gathering of webfoots nodded and smiled, and the crests of those who had them glimmered with lilac and blue. As they watched, the other spawn-brothers reached into their forage sacks and produced small but extraordinary objects of their own.

Hiph brought out a smooth chunk of ironwood used by woodtrolls to hone their axes to a razor-sharp edge. His brother Phlythiss revealed a fistful of seeds from the woodflax plant, grown and harvested by lowbelly goblins to weave into strong cloth for their belly slings.

'Milfphin could do with one of those,' someone whispered, and a ripple of laughter went round the crowd as the deputy clan-chief glared furiously around him.

Spyve held up an ingenious harness-catch used by slaughterers; while three of his brothers revealed punnets of bright pigment – blue, yellow and crimson – easily manufactured from barks of trees according to the long-hair goblins of the tree ridges. Needles, fish-hooks, weaves for nets and shells for floats; the spawn-brothers held up each in turn and explained to the delighted onlookers how each could be copied, duplicated and put to good use by the webfoots of the four great lakes.

While the white, tusked and red-ringed webfoots in the crowd cheered enthusiastically, the crested webfoots contented themselves with beaming smiles and a dazzling display of iridescent green. Milfphin raised his head and sniffed at the air ostentatiously, then patted his flabby belly.

'My friends, it is time to celebrate this fine and

fruitful journey to the lands beyond the lakes. Everything is prepared. The cooking-fire is blazing brightly and the stew-pot is full. Let us feast and sup and give thanks for the safe return of clan-chief Felfpht and his sons.'

The crowd began to file away. But just then, as Slifph and his brothers were returning their forage sacks to their belts, one of the crested webfoots – little more than a young'un – stopped and pointed.

'You haven't told us what *she's* for?' he said.

The crowd turned and stared at the spot the young webfoot was pointing to. Grefphith gulped. There, standing by the willow-wicker gates – overlooked in all the excitement – was the bearer of the seventeenth copperwood stick torch, which still flickered with an orange flame. With her black, spiky hair and pale face, the stranger looked back at Grefphith with an intense dark-eyed stare.

'This is Keris,' whispered Slifph, 'from a village of the far-off night-herders known as slaughterers.'

She stepped forward, the crowd parting instinctively at her approach. Her dark eyes never left Grefphith's face. She stopped in front of him.

'Felfpht the clan-chief called you a faithful clam-tender,' she said softly.

As the others watched, Grefphith nodded, his crest rippling green and gold with a mixture of pride and shyness.

'The clam,' the slaughterer said, her eyes sparkling. 'It talks to you?'

Grefphith shook his head. 'Not for a long time . . .' He checked himself when he noticed the disappointment in Keris's eyes. 'Leastways, not since my father and brothers left these thirteen moons since.'

'Come!' Milfphin's voice cut their conversation short. 'The stew-pots await!'

The webfoots turned and streamed through the village towards the great cluster of lake-willow cabins, with their meadow-turf roofs. Keris, Grefphith, Slifph and

447

their spawn-brothers were swept along with them. By the time they had all crowded into the large oval hall at the centre of the cluster of cabins, the celebrations were in full swing.

A series of curved tables had been put up around the edge of the hall, each one looking towards the centre, where a vast bubbling cauldron dangled from a hook above the cooking-fire. The air was laced with pungent lake-peat smoke, overlaid with the mouth-watering smells of blatt-prawn and bloaterfish, lake-eel and rock-oyster, brieve and moonfin, and herbs from every corner of the Deepwoods, brought back and cultivated by generations of crested webfoots who had set out on foraging journeys of their own.

'Let's sit down here,' Grefphith said, ushering Slifph and Keris into a space at a table on the far side of the hall.

In front of them, on a raised platform, the village band was playing on reed-pipes, shell-horns and gut-string fiddles – strange, haunting music that made Keris suddenly so homesick, it was all she could do not to weep . . .

'Come on,' she heard Slifph saying, his voice breaking into her thoughts of her Uncle Gristle, Aunt Chitling and the cousins. 'Tuck in while it's still hot.'

She looked down to discover that her bowl had been filled with steaming fish-stew by one of the webfoot matrons, who were waddling back and forth between stew-pot and tables, ensuring that everyone had enough to eat. And it wasn't only the bowl that was now full. Her goblet, too, was full to the brim with a deep golden liquid that smelled curiously like the spiced winesap she would take to her uncle out in the hammelhorn pastures. How long ago that now seemed . . .

'To my spawn-brothers,' Grefphith said, his crest glowing crimson as he raised his goblet high. 'And our new friend, Keris.'

'To Keris,' chorused Slifph and his brothers in unison. Keris smiled bravely and sipped at her drink. She was about to thank her new friend and offer a toast of her own, but was interrupted by something going on at the other side of the hall.

The voice of Milfphin, deputy clan-chief, was sounding oddly high-pitched and querulous, and rose in volume as the band abruptly stopped playing. 'But I don't understand,' he blustered. 'It can't be true . . . No outlaker has ever . . . I mean, this must be some sort of misunderstanding . . .'

'There is no misunderstanding.' Clan-chief Felfpht's soft voice rose an octave as he strode to the centre of the hall, lake water dripping from his scaly chin and the tips of his lop-ears. 'I have come from the Mirror of the Sky and the great blueshell clam has heard of our new arrival . . .'

He turned to Keris.

'And it wishes to talk with you.'

. CHAPTER FOUR .

THE GREAT BLUESHELL CLAM

'The great blueshell clam has spoken!' Grefphith's voice was hushed with awe and his crest glowed an excited amber as he guided Keris out of the cluster of lake-willow cabins and towards the lakeside. Behind them, in the hall, Keris could hear the clan-chief and his sons in debate with the furious Milfphin.

'An outlaker being taken to the great clam,' he was protesting. 'This is an outrage!'

'She has journeyed far to see the wise one,' Slifph's voice rang out in reply.

'And the great clam wishes to speak with her,' clan-chief Felfpht repeated, to murmurs of approval.

Outside in the moonlight, Keris and Grefphith the clam-tender hurried along the lakeshore. Keris could hardly contain her excitement. At last, after all she had been through, she was to meet the great clam. Close by, a colony of reed-toads croaked, their

451

deep rumblings interrupted by the shrill cry of a blackheron flying low over the lake. Past the rest of the cabin cluster the pair of them went; past the beached fishing rafts and tarred coracles and beyond, picking their way between the rows of sallowdrops and weeping willoaks that lined the shore. Over their heads, the moon broke the horizon and rose in the sky, huge and golden, reflected in the mirror-like surface of the lake. They stopped at a place with no trees behind them, where a tussock of grass jutted out over a small curved beach.

Keris noticed footprints in the mud leading into the gently lapping waters of the lake.

'This is the place?' she said, her heart suddenly thumping in her chest.

Grefphith's crest glowed blue in assent. He padded on his great webbed feet over the soft lakeshore mud to a post from which hung a great leather gourd, similar to the one he'd filled with water to greet his brothers. Unhooking it, Grefphith reached into the forage sack that hung next to the anchor stone on his belt and drew out a handful of small, sponge-like mushrooms.

As Keris watched, intrigued, the clam-tender carefully poured the mushrooms down the long tubular spout of the gourd. Then he placed the gourd under one arm and pumped it like a pair of bellows. Almost at once, there was a loud hissing

sound, and the gourd's leathery folds stretched until it was twice its original size.

Grefphith motioned to Keris to join him at the water's edge, where he strapped the gourd securely to her back.

'We webfoots can breathe the waters of our lake, but you outlakers need a little help,' he told her, handing Keris the spout and indicating that she should place it in her mouth.

She clamped the end of the spout between her teeth, noting the taste of woodmint that filled her mouth as she did so. Carefully, Grefphith placed a small carved ivory clip over Keris's nose.

'Breathe through your mouth,' he told her. 'The silt-fungus will have absorbed enough air for your dive to the lake bed and back, but your time with the clam will be short . . .'

'But how will I be able to talk with this in my mouth?' Keris asked in confusion, taking the spout out of her mouth for a moment.

The clam-tender smiled and placed his anchor stone firmly in the lakeshore mud. 'You'll see,' he said. 'Now, when you're ready, place your hands on my shoulders and I'll swim for the both of us.'

Grefphith turned to face the lake with his back to her, and Keris did as she was told. The webfoot's scaly skin was cold to the touch and she felt the muscles in his shoulders give a sudden ripple.

Then, before Keris knew it, they had dived into the mirror-like surface of the lake and were plunging down into the clear depths suffused in bright moonlight. She breathed in cool, minty air. Behind her, on her back, she could feel the gourd expand and contract with each breath. With every kick of his powerful legs and great webbed feet, Grefphith propelled them both, faster and faster, through the crystal-clear water.

To Keris's left, a shoal of silver fish swam towards them, their fins flashing in the moonlight that sliced down through the water, before darting off to the left, a huge, brown fish with bulging eyes and a jutting lower jaw in hot pursuit. A nattertoad – all gaping mouth and kicking orange legs – swam past them at an angle, its target a great translucent stormhornet larvae, whose shapeless bodies writhed and wriggled in the shadows of the great plateleaf lilies up above.

Apart from the shallow streams that ran through the lower pastures of her home, Keris had seldom been in water before, and the sensations – coldness, wetness and the constant pressure coming in from all sides – unnerved her. Yet she felt safe with Grefphith. And as she relaxed and her grip on his shoulders loosened slightly, the webfoot began pointing things out to her – a frondy ball of pink weed that, as they came closer, revealed itself to be thousands of feeding watershrimps clustered together; a ten-legged creature with a body like a balloon, which sucked in and spat out water as it propelled itself across the lake; striped lakeworms and spotted waterscorpions. And far far below them, where the lakegrass swayed like barleyrice in a gale, she saw a long line of giant lake snails, their pearly shells gleaming as the moonbeams struck them, plodding sedately across the silty bottom of the lake.

All at once, Grefphith pointed

downwards. His crest throbbed deepest indigo with lines of silver as he kicked out even more strongly. Keris tightened her grip on his shoulders as they swooped down towards the lake bed far beneath them. The next moment, she felt the lake water bubble and swirl about them as, instead of being propelled by Grefphith's steady kicks, they were suddenly being shot forward by a far greater force.

With his crest bright orange, Grefphith clamped his arms to his side. Keris clung on tightly. Faster and faster the two of them went, hurtling through the water like . . . like . . .

Keris smiled to herself as the lake rushed past her in a blur of blue and silvery white.

Like flying!

Oh, Father, she wondered, was this what it was like on the bridge of a mighty sky pirate ship, speeding across the sky?

Down into the depths of the lake they raced, leaving the moonlit water behind. Ahead of them, yet getting closer with every passing second, the dark waters of the lake bed were illuminated by an eerie blue glow. And as they drew closer, Keris realized where the light was emanating from.

It was pouring out of a magnificent, ridged bicuspid shell.

The lower half was fused to the rocky lake bed,

while the upper half gaped open. A hundred or more strides high it was, and twice that in breadth. To Keris it looked like a vast grinning mouth – a mouth that was sucking them inexorably closer and closer on a great swirling current of water. And as they hurtled towards it, she was suddenly over-whelmed with a cramping fear that they were about to be swallowed up. Closer to the great gaping maw they came, closer and closer and . . .

With a great creaking groan, the two huge halves of the vast clam slammed shut. The swirling current instantly ceased, the blue light was extinguished, and Keris and Grefphith found themselves floating gently down to the lake bed, their eyes filled with the orange afterglow of the clam's dazzling light.

Grefphith motioned for Keris to let go of his shoulders and indicated a flat rock in front of the giant clam for her to perch on. Then, as she waited in the gloom, Grefphith swam off, feeding-fork at the ready, to deal with the line of giant lake snails they had spotted earlier. In the distance, the huge creatures seemed to sense his approach and began to scatter in clouds of muddy sediment. On her stone perch, Keris waited, the gourd on her back ris-ing and falling with each breath.

What now? she wondered. How long would she have to wait? Grefphith had said her time with the clam would have to be short. Should she do something? Tap on its shell perhaps?

In front of her, the clam remained resolutely shut, the join between the two shells now a zigzag line without even the hint of a crack. High above, the surface of the upper shell was like a vast garden, home to countless flowers, ferns, and towering tree-like plants that swayed in the ever-shifting currents of water, just as the massive trees of the Deepwoods forest did in the air far above. And as she sat there, Keris watched intrigued as dim shafts of moonlight from far above struck the striped fish and tusked eels which swam in and out of the fronds; at the rock lobsters scuttling along the ridges of the great blue shell – and on an ungainly crea- ture with twelve spindly legs and a disc-shaped head

which tottered imperturbably through the lush vegetation . . .

All at once there was a tremendous rumbling sound followed by an unearthly creaking. The fish all round darted for cover in the underwater vege- tation. The rumbling became louder and stronger, vibrating through the rocks beneath her feet and stirring up the mud once more. The water itself seemed to tremble.

At last! thought Keris, gripping the sides of the flat rock with a mixture of excitement and fear.

As the two shells of the giant clam slowly parted, the dazzling blue light shone out once more, flooding the lake bed all round with its intense radiance and pouring into Keris's wide, unblinking eyes. Slowly and sedately, the clam yawned open, to reveal a vast interior of mottled blue pleats and folds.

And there, nestling deep at the centre of the gaping clam, was a pearl. A huge, opalescent pearl. Flawless and spherical, it was the source of the light which was bathing Keris in its intense blue glow.

Keris was mesmerized and transfixed. Unable to stir herself and pull away, her senses were completely overwhelmed. Now there was nothing but the pulsating blue light, filling her eyes, her mouth and ears, seeping through her pores, banishing any thought of time or place.

It was as if she was dissolving. Her conscious thoughts faded; her sense of herself disappeared, like warm bubbles of breath rising up and being carried away on the lake currents.

She was no longer Keris the slaughterer girl, far from home and full of questions.

Instead she was now the great blueshell clam,

sharing its memories of the very start of its long existence . . .

A tiny insignificant speck, she was, being blown through the great empty void on strong currents, for ever. Back and forth, journeying restlessly through the endless tracts of Open Sky. On and on, gathering speed and power . . .

An intense and pulsating brightness. Tiny yet inexpressibly powerful until . . .

There was a blinding flash and great black storm-clouds swirled up overhead. There was a crash of thunder. And then came the sensation of falling, falling down towards the thirsty earth.

Then blackness. Everything quiet, muffled. Trickling slowly through rock, deep below the surface of the earth. Moving through cracks, over crevices, into pools – gathering speed, gaining momentum. Flowing faster and faster with the underground springs, this way and that. Becoming part of a mighty current blasting its way through the earth; powerful, surging, then . . .

Everything suddenly stopped.

Stuck fast to this very rock. Rooted, immovable, down here on the lake bed. After so long, finally at rest.

At last, all that pulsating power turned itself into growth. The speck got bigger – a wonderful feeling . . .

My shell formed, the currents flowed back and forth over my blue surface, the nourishing silt swirled beneath. The rock anchored my great blue shell.

And time passed ...

Now I am huge. Down here in the calm depths, I can sense the world above me. It seeps into the lake water, eddies up through the lake bed; it flavours the silt. I can taste it. I sift through it all as I lie, rooted to the rock; tasting, sensing, knowing ...

The coming of creatures, the slow growth of the forest, the storms passing overhead – I can sense them all.

Far off, the acrid taint of Undertown; the deathly must of the Mire that tinges the lake water; the flashing spark of stormphrax and the glow of the Twilight Woods; they ripple imperceptibly through the currents. Always changing. And I – the great blueshell clam – detect them. I can taste the migration of tilder and hammelhorn, feel the tramp of goblin tribes, sense the movement of clouds over the glassy surface of the lake overhead.

I am the first, the most ancient. I am the beginning of life. A speck from Open Sky that fell from the Mother Storm and took root here on this rock far down in the depths of this peaceful lake.

Now you, Keris – another tiny speck of life – have come to the great blueshell clam to find answers. You, Keris, are a speck that clings to life but has no place to root itself. Lost, far from the silver pastures and smoky brazier fires, you are seeking your roots. I can sense it . . .

You are seeking your father.

Yes, little one, the great blueshell clam can sense him. Out there, far beyond the four great lakes, is the trace of your father; one who has been touched by the Mother Storm. A tiny speck of life himself, but a strong one . . .

And there is someone else. Yet another speck of life. Connected to both of you. Faint, yet acrid, and glowing like the spark that starts a great forest fire, this speck of life has changed the forests all round her with her fierce intensity. This speck of life is changing the world.

The great blueshell clam can sense it.

It can sense something else, too. The time has come, as the clam always knew it would; the time to reach out into this world.

You, my little one, must reach out with me . . .

Keris's mind was filled with a cascade of dazzling images, one after the other, fleeting yet crystal clear.

'Yes,' she nodded, 'I understand.'

All at once the clam slammed abruptly shut and, like the blast of a hurricane or the thrust of a mighty waterfall sweeping a dam aside and gushing forwards, a powerful surge of water struck Keris full on, tearing her away from the blue light.

Ever faster she sped, twisting and turning in the dark water as she hurtled through the moonbeam-shot depths up towards the surface of the lake, before shooting out of the water like a leaping gladesalmon.

Gasping and spluttering, Keris came crashing back down into the lake. Great waves rippled out across the placid surface. On her back, the gourd deflated with a wheezing sigh as Keris pulled the breathing spout from her mouth and gulped in a lungful of fresh night air. A moment later, beside her, Grefphith's crest broke the surface of the water and his smiling face greeted her.

He reached out for Keris, who clutched gratefully to his arm, and together – following the long tether-rope – the two of them swam slowly back to shore where his anchor-rock nestled in the lakeshore mud. Crawling onto the grassy bank, Keris turned to Grefphith.

'The clam spoke to me,' she said softly. 'The answer I seek lies far from here in a place called the Free Glades. I must . . .' She frowned, for the web-foot was staring back at her, his mouth open and his crest pulsating with surprise. 'What?' she said. 'Grefphith, what *is* it?'

'It's incredible,' he said, looking her up and down. 'In all my time as a clam-tender, I've never seen anything like it . . .'

Keris looked down – and then she noticed. Her entire body – skin, hair, clothes – was covered in a fine layer of sparkling silt. It was powdery and pale in the moonlight, with slightly lighter streaks that had collected in the crook of her arm and the cracks of her knuckles. She licked a finger and ran it across her arm, and turned back to Grefphith.

'It won't come off,' she said.

CHAPTER FIVE

THE SILVER PASTURES

The ancient spindlebug turned his great angular head, lifted his lantern and peered down the new tunnel being dug to his left. Everything was coming along nicely, he noted with a satisfied clicking sound. The new contingent of spindle-bugs might be young, but what they lacked in size and strength, they more than made up for in enthusiasm.

Working in shifts, they had already excavated two large chambers and, following the detailed plans he'd drawn up, constructed a broad central tunnel. Now the transverse tunnels were being dug. These winding walkways would not only connect the completed chambers on this level, but would also link up with the existing cellars, caverns and galleries of the earlier excavations, transforming the old underground colony into a vast and thriving hive of industry where milchgrubs, nightspiders and chookbats would soon join the indigenous

slime-moles, and be farmed. Already, the new fungus beds had been seeded and the spongy toadstools that had sprouted were beginning to emit the glowing pink light that would soon make all lamps and lanterns unnecessary.

The spindlebug trilled with excitement. If this rate of progress continued – and there was nothing to suggest that it would not – then, by his calculations, the Gardens of Light should be completed in far less than the five years he'd originally planned for.

It was all most gratifying, Tweezel thought, as he made his way across one of the new viaducts, passed a group of young spindlebugs, newly-arrived and trilling with an excitement that matched his own. After all, this was what the Free Glades was all about – welcoming new arrivals and building a new life for them in peace and harmony.

Not that they'd had any idea of what they were starting when he, Tweezel, and the young mistress – Earth and Sky protect her – had first gathered up those urchins and alley-strays from the streets of Undertown and led them out into the Deepwoods in search of a better life. Almost four decades had passed since that small party, some three hundred strong, had stumbled upon the broad, grassy lakeside slopes of what was to become their new home.

At first they had all lived in the small burrows that, under Tweezel's supervision, they'd dug beneath the Ironwood Stands next to the central lake. Then, with the help of the small colony of oakelves they'd encountered on Lullabee Island on the North Lake, the older orphans had begun building simple log cabins. Ten years had passed in the blinking of a translucent spindlebug's eye, and that little settlement on the shores of the North Lake had turned into New Undertown.

Word had spread quickly, and by the time the Free Glades celebrated the dawn of its second decade, there had already been a great influx of new blood. Trappers, traders and fisherfolk came; gabtrolls with wagons laden with herbal remedies and cure-alls; mobgnome tinkers, red dwarves and black dwarves . . . In short, all those who found it difficult to fit in elsewhere found a welcome in the Free Glades and an offer to settle there permanently.

All, that is, apart from the slavers. Occasionally they would turn up, together with their terrifying packs of white-collar wolves, in search of victims for their foul trade. At these times, Tweezel remembered proudly, those urchins and alley-strays – now grown vigorous and strong in the pure Free Glades air – banded together and sent them packing with their tails between their legs.

Tweezel paused to watch a gang of young spindlebugs. They were moving a great mound of earth from one side of the excavated hall to the other, exposing the pillar-like roots of the ironwood pines on one side and shoring up the walls on the other.

'Very good,' he trilled, before moving on.

It was as the Free Glades moved into its third decade that the place really began to expand, he remembered. Word spread about this curious settlement at the heart of the Deepwoods, home to those who wanted to live in peace and harmony with their neighbours, no matter who they were, and increasing numbers decided to see the wonderful place for themselves.

Entire clans began to arrive. Cloddertrogs from various parts of the Deepwoods congregated at the cliff sides to the east of New Undertown. They set up home in the system of caves; some turned to mining, others to brewing. A while later an entire colony of gyle-goblins – grossmother and all – established a new home close by, together with a small band of waifs, who planted a thornwood enclosure on the eastern shores of the North Lake. At the same time, in the Ironwood Stands at the opposite side of the glades, two separate clans of gnokgoblins formed colonies in the ironwood pines; while beneath them – down among the roots

– spindlebugs came from far and wide to join Tweezel.

The population of the Free Glades was by now more than ten times its original number and bustling with trogs, trolls and goblins, fourthlings and waifs from all four corners of the Edge. They had little in common with one another, save one important thing – that all-embracing desire to live their new life in peace and harmony.

Tweezel sighed, causing the lantern light to flicker momentarily. Unfortunately, there were always others who hated peace and harmony, choosing instead to make war and enslave others. The Free Glades had reluctantly been forced to defend its freedoms, always trying to find peace if possible, but not at the cost of a Freeglader's liberty.

So it was that the Freeglade Lancers, the Cloddertrog Guards and the Librarian Knights had come into being – each full of brave Freegladers prepared to lay down their lives in defence of their home.

And just as well, thought Tweezel, for these were dark days in the Edgelands – dark days indeed, judging by the tales new arrivals to the Free Glades brought with them.

The floating city of Old Sanctaphrax, it seemed, was no more. In its place, a new Sanctaphrax was developing – but with a crazed tyrant, rather than professors, ruling over it. Shrykes had apparently been accorded special status for helping to construct a road across the Mire, while an army of goblins – under a bullying scoundrel by the name of General Tytugg – had reportedly enslaved the inhabitants of Undertown.

It sounded incredible. Yet the sudden influx of refugees from Sanctaphrax and Undertown spoke of little else.

In this latest wave of incomers, academics of every type turned up. Professors, alchemists, librarians – the latter carrying barkscrolls and treatises that they had rescued from the barbaric book-burning Guardians of Night who had taken over Sanctaphrax. They built the Academy of Lake Landing and brought their knowledge and love of learning to the Free Glades. Even in these dark times, the Free Glades had proved itself to be a shining beacon of hope – just as the young mistress, Earth and Sky protect her, had always intended it should.

Now, Tweezel noted with satisfaction, work on his beloved Gardens of Light was moving on apace. Soon the great caverns would match his dreams, with vaulted ceilings and swooping colonnades; arches, bridges and winding stairways, and everything bathed in the rose-coloured glow of the nourishing fungus – dreams he had had not just for decades, he realized with a chuckle, but for centuries . . .

As he turned a sharp corner, Tweezel could see bright daylight streaming in through the end of the tunnel ahead of him. After the subdued glow of the caves and tunnels, it seemed dazzlingly bright. He blew out the flame in the lantern he'd been clutching and proceeded briskly along the narrow corridor. Then, fifty strides or so along, he paused briefly at a small chamber to his left, where a solitary spindlebug was hunched over a leadwood desk, a pot bubbling on a small brass burner before him.

'Sisal,' the old spindlebug greeted him as he entered the small chamber. 'How's it coming along?'

'Pretty well,' Sisal replied. 'I've been stirring it for over an hour now, and it's just beginning to turn colour. The trick is not to let it catch on the bottom.'

'Excellent, excellent,' said Tweezel, clicking with excitement. He put down the lantern and leaned forwards for a closer look. 'When do you think you'll have some ready?'

Sisal paused in his stirring, lifted a spoonful up into the air and let the hot liquid pour back down into the pot. It was thick and viscous. He looked up.

'Any minute now,' he said. 'When it forms a long stringy line rather than a liquid trickle, it's done.'

He stirred the pot vigorously for a couple of minutes more, taking care that none of the liquid splashed over the side. Then, with another spoonful, he let the liquid run back down again. This time it did what he'd described. Instead of pouring, it formed a long rope-like twist that seemed to unravel rather than trickle.

'Done,' Sisal announced.

'Outstanding!' Tweezel exclaimed, reaching forward and picking up the pot by the handle. 'And if those librarians at Lake Landing aren't impressed, then . . . then' – he clicked, momentarily at a loss for words – 'then I'm a jack-stacking leafhopper!'

He crossed the chamber to a low shelf, where a series of logs of various woods were piled. He swept them all into a sack. Then, with the pot clamped in the claws of his left hand and the bulging sack slung over his shoulder, Tweezel left the chamber, headed down the corridor and emerged into the bright sunny afternoon outside. He paused for a moment, wisps of steam coming from the pot, and gazed across the lake.

It was so beautiful at this time of day, he thought; when the sun was past its highest and turning that rich yellow colour that changed everything beneath it to gold. He never tired of the view. The sun gleamed on the pointed minarets and jutting buttresses of the half-completed academy, already looking so self-assured at the end of Lake Landing in the centre of the shimmering golden lake. Beyond it, the circle of thorn-bushes the waifs had planted – fringed with gold – had grown almost as tall. And behind that, its rooftops and crenellated towers peeking over the top, was New Undertown.

'So much we have achieved,' he muttered to himself proudly. 'Yet we cannot afford to be complacent.'

He turned his head, eyeing the thick dark forest that surrounded them. To the north and east, the Free Glades had spread out into the woodland a little. The felled trees were used for buildings, while the newly cleared land was planted up with barleyrice, sour-cabbage and glimmer onions. But the forest was resilient. It took time and effort to keep it at bay if it wasn't simply to grow back and swallow up the new fields and pastureland.

No, thought Tweezel, the Deepwoods should

never be underestimated. And nor should those who dwell within it.

Far to the east, he saw that the blue sky was stained once again with brown. It was, he knew, smoke from the Foundry Glades – a terrible place by all accounts, where the worst type of leagues-men had established factories and forges which, if rumours were to be believed, were operated by slave labour. Moreover, according to a growing number of visitors to the Free Glades, others were also establishing more permanent settlements in the forest: goblins from various tribes and clans who had abandoned their nomadic ways and settled down in villages in loose alliances with each other.

Tweezel shook his head sadly. It wasn't peace these Goblin Nations sought, but merely a more effective way of waging war. Just like the leagues-men of the Foundry Glades, they would have to be closely watched.

The old spindlebug was a good watcher. He'd had plenty of practice . . .

Born more than two centuries ago, he had spent his earliest days in a gyle-goblin colony – until the slavers had come, that is. He'd lived in the Deepwoods, he'd lived in Undertown, and in Sanctaphrax – as servant to the Most High Academe, no less. Now he was back in the Deepwoods. Full circle.

But his long life was far from over. After all, there was so much still to do. Take this sticky liquid in the pot he was carrying, for example. If it lived up to his hopes and expectations, who knew what it could lead to . . . ?

Above his head a bevy of white ravens flapped across the darkening sky, cawing raucously.

With the pot swinging and his antennae trembling, Tweezel strode around the banks of the Great Lake. Once, he remembered, the entire shoreline had been fringed with long, waving speargrass that had grown down to the water's edge. Now there was a track which ran all the way round – narrow and muddy in places, paved with wooden boards in others. Tweezel was passing a small stand of woodsap trees when he first noticed the bunch of librarians ahead of him, their robes fluttering in the soft breeze.

'Nearly there,' Tweezel muttered under his breath and increased his pace.

As he approached, his feet clattering over the boardwalk of the academy at Lake Landing, the academics turned and looked at him. Parsimmon, the young yet ambitious Chief Librarian, glanced up at the sun. Tweezel looked at the gnokgoblin uncertainly.

'My dear sir,' said Tweezel a little breathlessly. 'Sirs,' he added, including the others. 'Humblest apologies for my late arrival.'

Parsimmon's leathery face broke into a smile. 'You're not late, old fellow,' he said. 'We were early. Early,' he added, 'because we are so keen to see what you have to show us.' He gestured towards the pot. 'Is that it?'

Tweezel nodded.

'Then let us go to the Long Hall and examine this varnish of yours,' said Parsimmon, and some of the librarians turned to go.

'Actually it might be better if we remained outside,' said Tweezel. 'Perhaps if we went out onto the jetty. If you have no objections . . .'

478

'None, whatsoever,' said Parsimmon, and he strode out onto the wooden landing.

On the great platform at the end of Lake Landing, the librarians sat down in a line on a long, rough-hewn bench, while Tweezel prepared a small demonstration. He pulled the logs from the sack and laid them out beside the pot.

'I'm sure I don't have to tell academics like your good selves that there are three orders of Deepwoods timber,' he began. 'In the third order are leadwood and copperwood – wood that is stable at every temperature. In the second order are lufwood and bloodoak among others. These woods fly when burned. Then,' he said, picking up a pale brown log, 'we have timbers from the first order.' He smiled. 'The most interesting order.'

The librarians frowned and glanced at one another. Had the old spindlebug really gathered them all together to talk about wood?

'This is sumpwood,' Tweezel continued, undeterred. 'Not only the most common wood of the first order, but also the most stable. A well-seasoned piece of sumpwood is twice as light as air. Of course, we have been using sumpwood for years – buoyant chairs, floating lecterns and the like. But, since the slightest change in humidity or temperature destabilizes the timber, this use has been limited to within buildings only.' He placed the log of wood down, and picked up the pot. 'My varnish will change all that.'

The librarians leaned forwards, their interest aroused. A couple of them sniffed the air as the curious spicy fragrances seemed to waft across from the pot.

'This varnish,' Tweezel announced, 'is the result of many months of patient experimentation. It will seal in the buoyant properties of sumpwood, while still allowing it to "breathe". This means that this first-order timber will remain stable in all but the most extreme temperatures, but can never overheat. For this reason, instead of being used solely for furniture in properly heated rooms, sumpwood can now be used out here in the open air.' He paused dramatically. 'For flight.'

As one, the librarians gasped. The significance of Tweezel's discovery was not lost on them. Reports of stone-sickness and the end of stone flight were everywhere. No sky ship had been seen for several years or more. Disconsolate sky pirates now packed the taverns of New Undertown with tales of doom and destruction. If Tweezel's varnish could make wood float, then a new age of flight might just be possible.

'Show us, Tweezel,' said Parsimmon, his voice both encouraging and excited. 'Show us what this varnish of yours can do.'

Tweezel held the sumpwood log in one claw and applied a coat of steaming varnish with a broad brush with the other. Then, waiting a few moments, he released it. The log rose a few feet on the gentle breeze, then hovered unsteadily above the spindle-bug's translucent head.

'Bravo!' the librarians shouted.

'Tweezel, you're a genius,' Parsimmon cried out.

But the spindlebug raised a hand to silence them. 'That was my first varnish,' he said. 'Produced from one hundred per cent slime-mole glue. Simmered for two hours. One coat applied.' He picked up the second small log. 'Whereas this varnish has been supplemented with oakpepper . . .'

'*That's* what I could smell,' one of the young librarians whispered to his neighbour.

'And I have applied three coats to the upper sur-faces, two to the lower . . .'

This time, the log rose swiftly and hung motion-less in the air before a gust of wind moved it smoothly and steadily towards Parsimmon's beam-ing face.

'Even better!' a librarian exclaimed.

'We're going to be able to produce skycraft to rival anything powered by flight-rocks,' another said excitedly.

'In theory,' Parsimmon broke in. 'But let's not get ahead of ourselves. Tweezel's varnish is indeed

481

remarkable, but there is a long way to go before we can claim to have solved the problem of wood flight.'

Tweezel nodded in agreement, and was about to explain some experiments he'd attempted using hanging-weights on the logs, when the unmistakable sound of a prowlgrin bark made everyone turn. Half a dozen Freeglade Lancers on prowlgrin-back approached, escorting a group of tired-looking individuals. The captain of the guard, Ferris – a tall, broad-faced individual with a tattered ear – pulled away from the others and trotted over to Parsimmon.

'Excuse the intrusion, sir,' he said gruffly. 'Wasn't sure where else to take them.'

'That's quite all right, captain,' said Parsimmon. As one of the more learned individuals in the Free Glades, he was used to new arrivals being brought to him. 'What have you got this time?'

'Group of webfoots,' said Captain Ferris. 'And a slaughterer girl.'

Parsimmon turned and watched them approaching. There were some webfoot goblins living in the Goblin Nations; small, frightened creatures, easily bullied and often enslaved. But these glowing-crested strangers looked nothing like them. As for slaughterers, so far as he knew, the Free Glades had none. He frowned.

'Is the slaughterer hurt, captain?' he asked, see-ing the figure slumped over the saddle of the nearest prowlgrin.

'I'm afraid she stepped on a poisonthorn in the Silver Pastures. Nasty wound on her heel,' the cap-tain reported. 'And the infection is spreading by the look of it . . .'

'I am Grefphith,' said the taller of the webfoots holding the prowlgrin's bridle. 'These are my brothers: Slifph, Hiph, Spyve and Grulth. We have travelled far from our home in the Great Lakes with this slaughterer, Keris, who has been told to journey here by our great clam. She is injured,' he said, his crest glowing a shimmering yellow. 'Can you help her?'

'Allow me,' said Tweezel, bending down and plucking Keris from the saddle. 'I shall tend to her in the Gardens of Light. She will have the best of care!'

With that, he set off at a galloping pace, back along the lake path towards the Ironwood Stands in the distance.

'Your friend is in safe hands,' Parsimmon said. He spread his arms wide open. 'In the name of the librarians of the Free Glades, I welcome you.'

Grefphith nodded briefly, then stared at the varnished log still hovering above the chief librarian's head.

'This wood's buoyancy is quite amazing,' the webfoot exclaimed, one hand instinctively going to his forage sack.

'Indeed,' nodded Parsimmon. 'It has been coated with a special varnish.'

'Varnish, you say,' said Grefphith, fascinated.

'Derived from the secretions of slime-moles,' Parsimmon explained. 'According to Tweezel the spindlebug.'

'Fascinating, fascinating,' Grefphith whispered.

'Of course,' Slifph observed, 'an expertly carved piece of wood could infinitely improve the properties of the varnish . . .'

Parsimmon nodded thoughtfully.

'Indeed,' said his brother Hiph. 'We recently visited some woodtroll villages whose inhabitants were masters of woodworking.' His crest glowed an inquisitive pale green. 'Do you have any woodtrolls living in these parts?'

Parsimmon shook his head. 'None,' he said, then added thoughtfully, 'though it might be an idea to invite some to settle here in the Free Glades . . .'

'And of course, after the varnish and the wordworking, you're going to need sails and ropes,' suggested Spyve, turning to his brother Grulth, who nodded. 'Slaughterers are the best ropemakers and sail-riggers I know of,' he added.

'Slaughterers,' Parsimmon repeated softly. 'Yes, we could do with some slaughterers . . .'

He stared out across the lake with a faraway look in his eyes, before shaking his head and gesturing to the webfoot goblins beside him.

'Come, friends,' Parsimmon said. 'While Tweezel the spindlebug tends to Keris's needs, you must join us in the academy for supper. You look as though you have journeyed a long way.' He smiled. 'Come and dine with us. And afterwards, I should like to discuss an idea I have just had that might very well interest you . . .'

As the librarians and the webfoots made their way to the refectory, the sun was already setting behind the Ironwood Stands, their jagged treetops glinting as though tipped with shards of gold and silver. High in the branches, the giant tree-fromps grunted and squeaked as they foraged for black-bark beetles and plump resin-grubs, while the gnokgoblins who now tended them lit communal fires and set their stew-pots and cauldrons to bubble.

'Almost there, little one,' Tweezel murmured as he proceeded down the tunnel into the Gardens of Light. 'You're going to be fine. Trust me. Old Tweezel will see to you.'

But Keris – her spiky hair limp and her face flushed with fever – did not respond. She could not.

Still unconscious, the only sound that came from her lips was a low and rasping breathing. Tweezel's heart tugged with pity, and he was taken back to a time, so so many years ago, when he had carried Linius Pallitax, Most High Academe of Sanctaphrax, from the blazing building of the Palace of Shadows. He, too, had been unconscious; his breathing low and rasping . . .

'Rest here, little one,' whispered Tweezel, pushing everything from the couch in his study-chamber and laying her gently down.

Then, taking care not to let her slip to the floor, he removed her hammelhornskin waistcoat and hung it over the back of the chair. With his arm at her shoulders, he laid her head back on the cushion, lit the lantern and inspected her leg.

It was a mess – swollen, purple-black where the infection had spread, and hot to the touch. What was more, it, like the rest of her skin, was covered with a fine layer of blue silt that shimmered in the light.

'Curious . . .' he murmured as he turned away and began sorting through the bottles and jars on the wall-shelves. 'Poultice to draw the poison. Hyleberry leaves, wood-juniper salve and a cold compress . . .'

With single-minded efficiency, Tweezel tended his patient. He delicately applied the thick cream

486

to the taut, shiny skin of her leg and wrapped the whole lot up in a length of bandage. He placed the cold compress against her forehead and, to ensure that her temperature dropped, smeared on her lips a little of the sweet-smelling wood-juniper salve – which, even in her unconscious state, Keris tasted with the tip of her tongue.

And when he had done everything he could, and there was nothing else to do but wait, Tweezel sat down beside the couch and watched the young slaughterer's face, willing her to get better.

Her fever ebbed

and flowed. One moment she was crimson and sweat-drenched, the next, leaden-cheeked and sunken-eyed, her teeth chattering so much Tweezel feared they might chip.

He lay a woven blanket over Keris and was about to place her hammelhornskin waistcoat on top of that when one of his claws became snagged in the lining. As the material ripped, there was a soft clatter as a small disc-shaped object that had been concealed inside the inner folds of the waistcoat tumbled to the floor.

'Oh, how dreadfully clumsy of me,' the spindlebug muttered as he bent down to inspect exactly what it was he had discovered.

He stared at the little disc for a moment, nonplussed. Then, with the lantern held close, he picked it up, flipped it over in his hand – and cried out with surprise.

'It can't be!' he cried, and his great glassy head shook from side to side in disbelief, his antennae trembling. 'It can't be,' he repeated. 'But it is . . .'

He turned back to Keris, searching her face for clues. Her breathing was coming a little more easily now.

'That's it, little one,' he whispered urgently. 'Rest, and recover your strength just as soon as you can, for there is someone very special I want you to meet.'

. CHAPTER SIX .

THE LULLABEE GROVE

The coracle lurched from side to side as Keris turned and looked back over her shoulder. Behind her, at the end of a small wooden jetty, stood the spindlebug. The light from the full moon shone through his transparent body, revealing the dark blood pumping through a latticework of arteries, the great bowed curve of his ribcage, the mighty buttress of his hip-bones, the arch of his spine and, deep within his great chest, his huge heart, rising and falling with a steady beat.

'Farewell, Mistress Keris,' the spindlebug's ancient voice boomed out across the dark waters of North Lake. 'And sweet dreams.'

Taking care not to make any more sudden movements, Keris slowly turned her back on Tweezel and gripped on tightly to the wooden bench-seat. Around her in the small boat, half a dozen cowled figures rowed in a silent, steady

rhythm. The coracle glided across the gently lapping water, leaving the lights of New Undertown
twinkling in the distance behind them.

Ahead, emerging from the mist that hung
above the surface of the water in languid swirls,
Lullabee Island – home to the Oakelf Brotherhood
– was just coming into view. Keris glimpsed the
shoreline. It was fringed with the great bulbous
lullabee trees, each one giving off a strange and
hypnotic turquoise light. She shivered with a
mixture of excitement and trepidation. The glowing lullabee groves looked even more wonderful
than she'd imagined . . .

That morning it had been all she could do to stifle a cry of horror when she'd opened her eyes.
There, staring down at her, was a great glass-
bodied insect, its huge angular head cocked to
one side.

'Feeling better, Mistress Keris?' it had trilled in
a quavery, yet kindly voice.

'W . . . who are you . . . ? And . . . h . . . how do
you know my name?' she had stuttered, bewildered.

'I am Tweezel the spindlebug,' said the insect,
holding out a great glass claw for Keris to shake.
'Your webfoot goblin friends sought my help,' he
explained gently. 'You stepped on a poisonthorn
in the Silver Pastures. You've been very sick.'

'I did?'

Keris tried to clear her thoughts. She remembered the great sea of silver grass they had come to, and the excitement she'd felt when she saw the crests of Grefphith and the others glow orange.

Not far now, she'd thought, running out into the glorious, sunlit grasslands, her spirits soaring at the sight of the great herds of tilder and hammelhorns grazing in the distance. Then she'd felt the pain – sharp, stabbing, and unbearably intense as it shot up from her ankle. She must have fainted . . .

'It was touch and go for a while,' the spindlebug was saying. 'The poison had made your leg swell and you were burning up with fever. I did what I could. A wood-juniper salve for the fever, a hyleberry and darkroot poultice for your leg – and then I sat with you through the night . . .' The spindlebug's eyes glistened. 'And you, Mistress Keris, did the rest.'

Curious, Keris leaned forwards. Her left leg was heavily bandaged from the ankle to the knee.

'I think it's time we took a look at that,' Tweezel told her. 'If you'll allow me.'

He bent down and gently unwrapped the bandage with his great claws. Keris watched curiously as the last strip of material pulled away, leaving a pale green paste on her skin. Tweezel delicately turned her ankle to the left, to the right, then up and down, before pronouncing himself satisfied.

'The poison is gone,' he said, and clicked with pleasure. He handed her a soft cloth and placed a bowl of warm water beside her. 'There,' he said. 'You can wash the poultice off now.'

As Keris wiped away the green paste, the fruity smell of hyleberry making her mouth water, Tweezel retired to the other side of the chamber. The poultice washed away easily in the warm water, but beneath it the tiny grains of sparkling silt still clung to the skin, as they did to the rest of her.

Ever since that extraordinary night when she'd emerged from the third great lake, Keris had sparkled with the gritty particles that no amount of washing seemed to shift. She placed the cloth in the bowl of water and looked up. Tweezel was standing over her, with the hammelhornskin waistcoat clasped in his claws.

'Is this yours?' he asked quietly.

'Yes,' she said, reaching out and taking the waistcoat from him. She held it to her cheek and felt the fur brush against her skin, soft and re-assuring. 'It was my father's. It's all I have of his to remember him by . . .' Keris's eyes suddenly filled with tears. 'He was a sky pirate captain, you know.'

Tweezel nodded, his enormous eyes staring into her own.

'Captain Twig,' Keris said, her voice thick with emotion. 'Captain Twig Verginix . . .'

She paused as she noticed the small rip in the green felt lining of the waistcoat. Tweezel followed her gaze.

'My fault,' he told her. 'Clumsy old creature that I am. My claw, you see . . .'

Keris smiled and wiped away a tear. 'I left my village to search for news of my father. So long ago it now seems. The great blueshell clam sent me here to the Free Glades . . .'

Tweezel's antennae quivered and his enormous eyes seemed to grow even bigger.

'I have heard tell of the great clams of the far-off lake country,' he trilled. 'Like the magnificent caterbird of the Lullabee Groves, they are ancient ones, their memories going back to the earliest of times . . .'

Keris nodded as she remembered the great blueshell clam's voice in her head.

'So the great clam sent you here, Mistress Keris, to the Free Glades,' Tweezel muttered, turning away and gathering a small teapot and two cups onto a tray. He turned back and looked her sparkling body up and down. 'Now it is all beginning to make sense . . .'

'It is?' said Keris, slipping on the familiar old waistcoat and sitting up in the sumpwood bed.

'I must take you to the Lullabee Grove,' said Tweezel, returning with the laden tray and setting it down between them. He poured two cups of hot, aromatic tea from the pot and handed one to Keris. 'But first I have to tell you a story . . .'

Keris took a sip of the tea. It was sweet and comforting, and filled her with a warm glow. Tweezel held up a small, round disc of lufwood between two curved claws.

'A story,' he continued, 'about a young lad I first met years ago in the floating city of Sanctaphrax, when I was the butler to the Most High Academe, Linius Pallitax, Sky rest his soul.'

Keris stared at the miniature painting on the lufwood disc. It was of a handsome dark-haired youth in glistening armour, tall towers rising in the distance behind him. As she gazed at those features – so strange and yet so familiar – the hairs on the back of her neck stood on end.

'Quintinius Verginix was his name, and this is his portrait,' Tweezel said quietly, his eyes fixed on Keris's face.

'Verginix,' Keris breathed, aware of a painful lump in her throat.

'He grew up and married my master's daughter, Maris. They voyaged the skies as sky pirates, and

495

had a baby son.' He shook his head solemnly. 'But then disaster struck and they were forced to leave him in the care of woodtrolls. Maris was unable to forgive herself – and never spoke again. I nursed her through a long illness and then, when she left Undertown for the Deepwoods in search of her son, I went with her. Quint set sail in his sky ship in an attempt to forget his own sorrow and I never saw him again. Until now.'

Tweezel turned the disc over several times, and peered closely at the painted image on its surface.

'This is a portrait miniature from a sword hilt.' The spindlebug paused. 'Passed down from father to son.'

Keris gasped.

'I found it last night,' he went on. 'It was sewn into the lining of your hammelhornskin waist-coat.' He looked up. 'It can mean only one thing, Mistress Keris. Quint found his son. He must have given him his sword when he knew – or thought he knew – he was dying . . .'

'And my father?' Keris asked, trembling.

'I would imagine he understood well enough that a pirate's sword would be of little use to his slaughterer daughter, so he took the portrait from the hilt and sewed it into the one thing she'd treasure always . . .'

'My hammelhornskin waistcoat,' Keris said,

finishing the spindlebug's thought for him. 'And my father?' she repeated, searching the spindlebug's glassy features for clues. 'Is he still alive?'

'The answer to that,' Tweezel said, holding out a claw and helping Keris to her feet, 'lies on Lullabee Island, in North Lake. Come.'

With the spindlebug showing the way, Keris left the chamber and stumbled through the series of underground tunnels and caverns, her eyes wide with amazement. The sheer scale of the lofty, pink-drenched halls took her breath away. And when Tweezel began to outline his plans for the place, explaining how the varnish he had invented would help to introduce the second age of flight, Keris shook her head in amazement.

'And here I am,' she murmured, 'at the very start of it all.'

As they emerged from the tunnel on the far side of the ironwood glade, the spindlebug took a narrow track that wound its way through the trees, between embedded boulders and clumps of tasselled yellow butterblooms. He walked purposefully, pushing low-hanging branches and thorny creepers out of the way, allowing Keris to follow unimpeded.

In front of them, the waters of the South Lake glittered in the mid-morning sun, cool, clear and inviting. Unlike the Great Lake and North Lake, South Lake had no settlements clustered round its shores. As they reached a low, rocky bluff jutting out over its waters, Keris suddenly paused.

She was aware of an extraordinary tingling sensation all over her body. And, as she gazed out over the still waters of South Lake, it seemed to become more intense. It was as if her skin was on fire. Behind her, Tweezel let out a trill of wonder.

'Why, Mistress Keris!' he exclaimed. 'It's as I thought. You're covered in clamdust. Go, the water is calling to you . . .'

Suddenly, Keris could bear it no longer. With a sudden surge of energy, she launched herself off the rocky bluff and high out over the shining lake water, before plunging down beneath the surface with a tremendous *splash*. Bubbles rose and burst, marking the spot where she had disappeared. Ripples rolled out in ever-widening concentric circles . . .

'That's right,' the spindlebug whispered, his heart thumping inside his glassy thorax. 'The lake will wash you clean.'

But Keris couldn't hear him. With powerful strokes of her arms and kicks of her legs, she was diving down deeper and deeper into the lake.

Below her, great underwater pastures of lake-grass swayed in the currents. Fish darted this way and that, their fins and underbellies flashing silver and gold. And all the while she swam, Keris herself gave off a stream of tiny sparkling specks. From her arms, her legs, her fingers, they came; from her cuffs and her hem. Sparks that twinkled like constellations of stars as they floated off into the indigo depths of the lake. Slowly the burning sensation was soothed, and then disappeared.

At last, with the glittering specks of lights all spent and her lungs aching, she soared back up to the light far above her. Her head burst through the surface of the lake and she gulped at the warm, fresh air.

'Mistress Keris!' she heard. 'Mistress Keris.'

Treading water, she twisted round. The great spindlebug was standing at the edge of the lake, beaming down at her benevolently.

'Does that feel better?' he asked.

'Oh, yes,' she called back. 'Wonderful.'

With that, she flipped over onto her front and began swimming towards him, her arms and legs pushing the water back behind her. Overhead, a pair of snow-white woodcranes flapped across the pale blue sky, while from the surrounding forest – wilder and less explored than the other lakes – the sounds of hunting woodwolves and the anxious whooping of quarms echoed through the trees.

Emerging from the water, Keris looked down at her arms and legs. For the first time since her meeting with the blueshell clam, they had been washed clean and were free of the sparkling silt. Beside her, Tweezel gave a knowing chuckle.

'Why, Mistress Keris, do you know what you've just done?' he asked.

Keris shook her still dripping head. 'All I know,' she said, 'was that when I saw the water, I just had to dive into it. My skin was on fire . . .'

Tweezel chuckled. 'You've brought a great gift

to the Free Glades. A gift that generations to come will thank you for.'

'I have?' said Keris, astonished.

'Yes,' said Tweezel, taking her hand and guiding her back to the path. 'You have seeded the South Lake with life. One day, it shall have clams growing in its depths. And who knows, maybe one day – generations from now – a giant clam of its very own!'

'You think so?' said Keris, amazed. 'That's why the blueshell clam sent me here?'

'I'm sure of it,' said the spindlebug thoughtfully, gazing across towards the Great Lake and the North Lake in the distance. He smiled. 'Amongst other things . . .'

They continued down the path, leaving the wild shores of the South Lake for the eastern side of the Great Lake, with its pastures and farmland. What with the breeze blowing and the sun beating down, by the time they approached the shores of the North Lake and New Undertown, Keris's hair and clothes were bone dry.

As they reached the bustling market stalls and timbered cabins on the northern lakeshore, Keris spotted a group of familiar and brightly glowing crests bobbing up through the crowds.

'Grefphith! Slifph!' she shouted, waving wildly. 'Over here!'

501

'Keris! You've recovered!' shouted Grefphith, hurrying towards her down the dusty street, followed by the other webfoots, their crests all flashing a joyful orange and blue.

'Thank you, kind sir,' cried the webfoots, each one bowing to the spindlebug in turn. 'Thank you for helping our friend.'

'It was my honour,' said Tweezel, proudly. 'And she has repaid the Free Glades a hundredfold already by seeding our South Lake with clamdust!'

'You mean . . . ?' exclaimed Grefphith and his brothers. 'There will be clams in the lake!' They did a delighted jig in the middle of the street, their great webbed feet kicking up a cloud of dust that made several passers-by sneeze, and many more stop and gawp.

'Well, that settles it,' said Slifph, slapping his brother Grefphith on the back. 'As soon as we've taken Parsimmon's invitation to come and settle in the Free Glades to the woodtroll and slaughterer villages, we're coming back here ourselves!'

'You're going back to my village?' Keris exclaimed excitedly.

Grefphith nodded. 'Do you wish to return with us?' he asked, taking her hands in his own as his crest switched from bright purples and reds to a soft, pale orange.

'I can't,' said Keris, her eyes glistening. 'At

502

least, not yet. There is someone Tweezel says I must meet first. But perhaps you could give my Uncle Gristle this . . .'

She unbuckled the dark red leather satchel containing ten slightly crumpled pieces of barkpaper, each one covered in tiny writing, and thrust it into Grefphith's hands.

'Here,' she said. 'And give him – and them all – my love.'

The crests of all the webfoots glowed a curious turquoise and yellow – a combination of colours Keris had never seen before.

She said goodbye to each of the webfoots in turn – then looked away before any of them noticed the tears welling up in her eyes. The five webfoot goblins – packs on their backs and knobbled sticks gripped in the hands – set off back the way they'd come, waving as they went. Tweezel waved back. And, when she was confident that they were far enough away not to see that she was crying, Keris turned and waved too.

'Fare you well,' she whispered, and though she knew they couldn't possibly have heard her, she noticed their crests change once more to the same rippling turquoise and yellow colour.

The webfoots passed the Parley Hall and disappeared round a corner at the far end of the street. Keris did not move. She stood rooted to the spot, staring ahead at the place she had last seen them – until Tweezel took her gently by the arm.

'Come along now, Mistress Keris,' he said. 'There is still much to do.'

They walked up from the lakeside and through the streets of New Undertown that bustled with life. Gabtrolls rubbed shoulders with cloddertrogs; mobgnomes, gnokgoblins and fourthlings of all descriptions filled the alleys and squares. As they approached a busy crossroads, Keris noticed a lop-ear and a gyle-goblin who would normally have had absolutely nothing to do with one another, standing at the far corner, deep in intimate conversation.

The Free Glades would be a fine place to settle, she thought, a place where everyone lived in peace and harmony.

She followed the spindlebug into a large tavern called the Lufwood Inn. Despite the lamps on the lufwood-stump tables and torches clamped to the walls, the tavern was far darker than outside, and it took a while for Keris's eyes to grow accustomed to it. As they slowly did so, she looked round to find herself in a huge, low-beamed hall, bedecked with sweet-smelling clusters of Deepwoods flowers. Great bunches of herbs and garlands of foliage hung from every beam. The air was rich and intoxicating and a large stove in the corner gave off a soft turquoise glow.

Tweezel, too, looked around for a moment, his own eyes growing used to the light. A young fourthling in a patched apron appeared and smiled good-naturedly.

'Master Tweezel, what can I do for you?' He smiled, his dark eyes flashing as they met Keris's.

Despite herself, Keris found herself blushing.

'Ah! Young Shem Barkwater, isn't it?' the spindlebug trilled. 'I'm looking for Brother Tredegar . . .'

'You'll find him in his usual spot by the stove, log watching, Master Tweezel. Can I get you or the young lady anything to drink?'

'Not just now, thank you, Shem,' said Tweezel, crossing the tavern to the stove, where a small group of oakelves sat warming their ears in front of the stove.

Keris followed behind, but not before the young tavern-keeper had winked at her and given her a dazzling smile.

At their approach, the seven oakelves turned and gazed past the spindlebug at Keris with their pitch-black eyes. Keris felt her knees give way, and she reached out to steady herself. Taghair – the kindly old oakelf hermit who lived in the clearing near her village – had eyes like theirs. Deep, dark and full of wisdom. His solitary gaze was unsettling enough, but seven pairs of oakelf eyes . . .

The oakelf nearest to her rose and took her by the arm, and Keris found herself looking back at her own reflection in his eyes. For what seemed to Keris an eternity, he said nothing. Then, with a trace of a smile, the oakelf said, 'Come, there is someone waiting to meet you.'

With that, the others rose, pulled their hoods over their heads and followed in a procession behind Tweezel, Keris and Brother Tredegar, out of the Lufwood Inn.

The coracle bucked and bobbed as it reached the shore of Lullabee Island. A moment later, there came a soft grinding sound from the bottom of the small boat as the hull scraped up over the gravel. Brother Tregedar jumped out, seized the rope and tethered it to a wooden stake sunk into the ground. Keris looked up and her eyes widened.

The pale turquoise glow she'd seen above the

island was much brighter here. The air was suffused with the pulsating blue-green light and, as
the breeze came wafting towards her, she heard a
faint music – slow and keening – which filled her
thoughts with longing.

The oakelves nimbly climbed out of the coracle,
the last one reaching out and helping Keris ashore.
Then, with Tredegar leading the way, a flickering
lantern in his raised hand, and the others following,
they set off through the trees. The path was winding and uneven and, despite the full moon, shot
with confusing shadows. Yet the further they went
into the island's interior, the brighter the turquoise
light became and the easier it was to see.

After a short walk, they emerged into a clearing fringed by the largest lullabee trees yet. Vast
knobbly trunks they had, and branches that
seemed to be reaching up towards the moon.
From the foliage that grew in dense clusters at the
end of every limb, there came the eerie turquoise
glow – a gleaming light that illuminated both the
tiny sparks hovering in the air around each leaf
and the long, sock-like cocoons that hung down
from the broadest branches.

They came to a halt and Keris craned her neck
back and marvelled at the great cocoons hanging
above them. Then, suddenly, the strange lilting
music of the trees grew louder and the turquoise

glow at the centre of the grove became more intense.

A cocoon – huge, intricately woven and twinkling with tiny sparks – slowly began to descend towards Keris, until it stopped in front of her, inches from the forest floor. Scarcely daring to breathe, Keris peered into the soft velvety darkness within the cocoon.

A hand emerged – old, frail and milky white, its palm upraised. From behind Keris, Tredegar reached forwards and placed the lufwood portrait in the outstretched palm.

The hand withdrew.

For a moment, nothing happened. Then the hand appeared again and cupped Keris's face in a soft, silken touch. It traced the line of her brow, the slope of her nose, her lips, her chin, as if comparing her features to those in the portrait.

'I am Keris Verginix,' whispered Keris. 'Daughter of Twig.'

She felt the hand tremble as she spoke the words and there was the sound of a half-stifled sob from within the cocoon. Then the hand beckoned to her.

Close beside her ear, Tredegar's gentle voice – little more than a whisper – sounded.

'Step forward, Keris, daughter of Twig; granddaughter of Maris, founder of the Free Glades. Those who sleep within a caterbird cocoon share the dreams of the caterbird . . . The answers you seek lie within.'

Keris looked at the dark shape in front of her. So this is what she had travelled so far for. Here on this strange island, in this mystical lullabee grove, was her grandmother, sitting in a great woven cocoon of glister-silk from which a mighty caterbird had hatched. The caterbird was, like the great blueshell clam, one of the ancient ones, and saw everything on its endless flights over the mighty Deepwoods. Now she was about to share its dreams.

509

Keris climbed into the velvety darkness and a warm embrace. She felt two arms envelop her, wet tears drip on her neck and gentle sobs tremble through the body holding her close. She reached out in the comforting darkness and returned the embrace.

'Grandmother,' she whispered, hot tears of her own coursing down her face. 'Will I see my father, Twig?'

She closed her eyes as a great wave of relief and tiredness washed over her, and her breathing slowed. In the darkness, as Keris drifted off to sleep, a voice whispered tenderly beside her ear.

'Yes.'

THE END

PAUL STEWART is a highly regarded author of books for young readers – everything from picture books to football stories, fantasy and horror. Together with Chris Riddell, he is co-creator of the *Far-Flung Adventures* series, which includes *Fergus Crane*, Gold Smarties Prize Winner, *Corby Flood* and *Hugo Pepper*, Silver Nestlé Prize Winners, and the *Barnaby Grimes* series. They are of course also co-creators of the bestselling *Edge Chronicles* series, which has sold over two million books and is now available in over thirty languages.

CHRIS RIDDELL is an accomplished graphic artist who has illustrated many acclaimed books for children, including *Pirate Diary* by Richard Platt, and *Gulliver*, which both won the Kate Greenaway Medal. His book *Ottoline and the Yellow Cat* was shortlisted for the Kate Greenaway Medal and won a Gold Nestlé Prize. Together with Paul Stewart, he is co-creator of the *Far-Flung Adventures* series, which includes *Fergus Crane*, Gold Smarties Prize Winner, *Corby Flood* and *Hugo Pepper*, Silver Nestlé Prize Winners, and the *Barnaby Grimes* series. They are of course also co-creators of the bestselling *Edge Chronicles* series, which has sold over two million books and is now available in over thirty languages.